E.A.P

The Untold Story

E.A.P

The Untold Story

Dutch Jones

Copyright © 2014 Dutch Jones

All rights reserved.

ISBN: 978-0-692-32950-4

DEDICATION

It's always easy to dedicate to a loved one, or a person or event that inspires. My dedication is to you, the reader. My goal is to have you take a trip with me, to feel and understand my characters. I truly hope you are entertained.

That said, none of my writings would be possible without the love, dedication and support of my wife, Ori. Thanks babe!

CONTENTS

Blue Hawaii … 1
August 16th 1977 … 4
Aaron … 8
Life Lessons … 12
The 17th Birthday … 16
Gone Fishing … 32
Big Fish Story … 50
Bad News … 64
First Adventure … 73
Here Comes Johnny! … 84
Elvis Expert … 95
Game Changer … 105
The Fair … 123
Elvis, The Younger Years … 141
The Diversion … 151
Graceland … 163
Turkey Hunt … 175
Home for the Holidays … 182
Nationals … 206
Fast Friends … 226
The Best Laid Plans … 243
The Wedding … 256
Best Kept Secret … 268

About the Author … 285

BLUE HAWAII

Elvis was the King, this night proved it. He owned every inch of the stage; his fans were completely absorbed, almost transfixed. As Elvis finished the final song on the final night of his Blue Hawaii tour he wiped his brow with a bright red silk scarf, then tossed it out to one last lucky fan. A memento that this fan would keep forever, a reminder of being in front of a legend. The concert was over; the tour was finally over. Elvis was dripping in sweat, he used every ounce of energy he had left to walk off the stage. The band continued playing in the background; some fans were screaming, others crying; no one wanted to leave, they didn't want it to be over. The entire concert hall broke out in a chant, "Elvis!... Elvis!... Elvis!"

After just a few minutes the arena lights came on, and you heard an announcer over the loudspeaker, "Ladies and Gentlemen." A second time only a lot louder and more forceful, "Ladies and gentlemen! I am sorry but I need to inform you... Elvis has left the building." There was a mixture of boos, some yelling and more screams. But the fans knew it was over... Elvis was not going to come back. No one, not the fans, not even Elvis's closest friends or maybe even Elvis himself could have ever imagined that this would be the last time those words were ever spoken. "Ladies and gentlemen... I am sorry, but Elvis has left the building... Good night and thank you!" the announcer said one last time. The fans began to file out of the arena, most with smiles of satisfaction, many still jumping up and down from the rush. You could still feel the energy.

Elvis was met just offstage by a couple of his long-time friends and personal bodyguards: some were both. Elvis was quickly wrapped in a large white robe that had a large gold 'E' embroidered on the left chest; he was escorted down to the parking garage to his waiting limo. As the limo pulled out from the arena tunnel the car was immediately engulfed by a mob of screaming fans. Some women were trying to throw themselves onto the hood of the car, only to be pulled aside by the police and security. Elvis didn't react and he said nothing; he just sat by himself staring out the car window.

One friend spoke up once they were out of the parking lot and safely on the road. "That was one of your best, E!" he said with a great deal of excitement in his voice. "It really felt like you were back!" All eyes quickly shifted to the friend who spoke up and then to Elvis to see what his reaction was going to be. Elvis didn't turn his head away from the window; he only smiled a little smile using one corner of his mouth. The friend who spoke up realized how bad his comment must have sounded and he feared he may have crossed a line. At first he thought to apologize but then decided it was best to just sit there quietly the rest of the way back to the hotel. No one else spoke.

As the limousine pulled up to the hotel, there were hundreds of fans waiting out front; many were holding up signs: 'I love you, Elvis' and 'Marry me!' were the two most common. The police were trying their best to control the fans; the fans were trying their best to get a glimpse of the King! The limousine drove around to the back of the hotel, through a security gate and into an underground garage where Elvis could not be seen or heard. Elvis spoke for the first time since leaving the concert.

"I think the time has come," he sang quietly to his friends with a face that, if you knew him, you only took seriously. As he stepped out of the limo Elvis turned his head back toward the guys. "I think I'm done," he added just loud enough for everyone in the car to hear.

The four guys in the limousine looked at each other but didn't say a word. One of the bodyguards tried to laugh but it didn't come out. No one else in the car saw this as a good time to laugh, and strangely no one was sure how seriously to take what had just been said. What they didn't know was that Elvis was in pain. He had been having chest pain since just before the tour started. Breathing was now a chore almost all the time, but especially when he was performing. Getting the air he needed into his lungs to be able to sing was laboring and painful. At one point the pain was so bad he thought he would have to stop, but he didn't. He told no one. Together the group moved toward the hotel elevator; Elvis stepped in first, then turned with his hand out. The others stopped at the elevator door. Elvis pulled down his sunglasses only low enough so you could see his eyes.

"I'm taking this ride alone," he told them. The elevator doors closed..

AUGUST 16ᵀᴴ 1977

A day of shock and mourning. Most people in the world couldn't believe it was true, it couldn't be possible... The King was dead? Aaron was nine at the time. He was as big an Elvis fan as there was. His mom and dad had always been huge fans but to Aaron Elvis was more, he was a role model, Elvis was his hero. Because of Elvis, Aaron taught himself to play the guitar at the early age of six. As he learned, he would also try to sing. As his mom told it, his singing got better than his guitar playing. Aaron practiced every day; he wanted to be just like the King. He watched Elvis movies whenever he could; his mom was pretty cool about it because she liked to watch them, too. He got so good after a while that his parents tried to convince Aaron to enter some local Elvis impersonation contests. These contests happened around Tennessee all the time. But Aaron always refused. He didn't think he was good enough and he didn't want to be embarrassed. His parents understood and respected his wishes, they didn't push him.

Aaron was an only child growing up on a farm in rural Tennessee. There wasn't much time for anything but school and chores, but Aaron would always manage to find time for his two favorite things, playing guitar and fishing; often he'd do both at the same time. Aaron's mom and dad loved his passion for music. Frequently after dinner they would ask Aaron to practice where they could watch and listen. They had so much fun with it. Sometimes Aaron's mom and dad would even get up and sing with him; his dad would try to do the Elvis pelvis moves, but Aaron's mom would laugh so hard he never lasted very long. Other than a few close friends no one outside of the family ever saw Aaron perform. He loved to play and sing but he was overly bashful about ever playing in front of strangers.

Aaron would always remember that August day. Early in the afternoon he rode his bike into town with his best friend Mike to meet up with some other friends and get something to eat. He and his buddies walked around town looking for something to do after they finished their burgers; Aaron always had his favorite, double meat with double cheese, extra pickles and a chili on top. Mike wanted to go to the sporting goods store to look at the new fishing rods that he had heard came in, so they jumped back on their bikes and headed off in that direction. They had a great time looking and playing around with all the new gear. None of the boys could afford to buy any of the 'awesome' equipment, but they had a good time pretending they were standing at a lakeside casting into the clear water.

"I got one! It's a biggie!" one of them would yell out every minute or so.

The store owner Warren was always good about letting the boys play around: he knew eventually they would all become good customers. As usual they swapped a few fishing stories with a couple of the old-timers who always hung out in front of the store. The old guys always had some entertaining fishing stories but sometimes they would part with some of their fishing secrets that the boys almost always trusted. It was starting to get late so the boys decided they had better start for home. Aaron and his friends thanked the old guys then jumped on their bikes and started peddling their way down Main Street. When they got toward the end of town Aaron noticed a group of people standing outside the front of the pharmacy. That's weird, he thought.

"Guys, check that out!" he yelled back at his friends, pointing in the direction of the pharmacy.

"What's going on?" Mike asked.

"I don't know... Let's go see!"

They parked their bikes in front of the hardware store that was right next door to Merrill's Fine Pharmacy and walked over to the group of people standing in front. People were talking loud and seemed really upset about something. They were all looking through the front window of the store, watching a television.

"It must be something pretty important," Aaron said to Mike.

"Do you think we've gone to war or something like that? My dad always says we're going to go to war with Russia someday," Mike told him.

Aaron worked his way to the front of the group to see what was going on. When he looked at the television it had a photo of Elvis Presley on it taking up the whole screen; it also had a ticker tape moving across the bottom that said: 'Elvis Presley dead at age 42'. Aaron stood there stunned. He read it over and over. He turned and looked at Mike, one of Aaron's only friends who knew how much Elvis meant to him.

"This can't be true... can it?" he asked Mike with despair and disbelief on his face. Mike lifted his hands up to his shoulders.

"I'm sorry, Aaron, I don't know. This is crazy." Unfortunately they couldn't hear what was being said on the television.

Aaron turned around to one of the ladies standing behind him: she was crying. "Excuse me, lady, can you tell me what's going on?" he pleaded.

The woman, obviously very upset, wiped the tears from her face; she leaned over slightly to be closer to Aaron. "Elvis died today." She started to cry again.

Aaron felt as if someone had just hit him in the stomach. He thought he was about to start crying, too, and he took a big swallow to clear his throat. "What happened?"

"Oh... They're not sure. Someone said they think it might be a heart attack."

Suddenly Aaron burst out, "Oh my God... my mom!" He turned to Mike. "I'll see you later, I've gotta go!"

Aaron ran, jumped on his bike and rode away as fast as he could. He peddled his bike as hard as he could without slowing down the entire way; he needed to get home before his mom found out. She's going to flip out! He skidded to a stop right in front of the house, dropped his bike and ran in. He could hear his mom whimpering in the family room by the television. Crap! Too late, he said to himself. He could hear a man on the television talking about Elvis. Aaron walked into the room visibly upset. His mom and dad were sitting on the couch watching the television; Marcos, one of the helpers on the farm and a close family friend, was standing right behind them. He noticed Aaron first.

"Oh hey, Aaron," he said loud enough to get everyone's attention. Both Aaron's mom and dad jumped up from the couch. Aaron's mom Alisha walked directly to Aaron; his dad John went and turned off the television. Marcos patted the top of Aaron's head and left the room. As soon as Aaron's mom began to hug Aaron she started to cry pretty hard; Aaron couldn't control himself anymore and started to cry, too.

He looked at his dad. "Is it true?" he asked, knowing it must be.

"Yes, son... I'm sorry. Elvis died today." Even his dad was a little teary-eyed. Aaron pulled back from his mom to look at her.

"Mom, what happened?" he asked, as the reality of it started to sink in.

"Dad and I have been watching the television for hours, the only thing they're saying is it might have been a heart attack. But really they don't know."

She started to get upset again. Aaron's dad suggested they all go outside to get some fresh air. The three of them walked around the farm for a couple of hours, talking, crying, trying to make sense of it. In their house Elvis was like part of the family. It was starting to get dark out when they finally calmed down enough and felt they could talk no more. Aaron and his dad headed to the barn to catch up on some chores, and Aaron's mom went into the house to start making dinner.

AARON

Aaron was unusually fidgety at his school desk while he waited for the school bell to ring. The teacher was saying something to the class, but he tuned her out a while ago. This would be the last time he heard the bell for this year; school was going to be out for summer, he couldn't wait. This was going to be an important summer for Aaron. His 17th birthday was fast approaching and he would finally be able to get his new truck - well, new to him. The truck was really a hand-me-down from Marcos, the manager of the farm and close friend to the family; but Aaron had always loved that truck, and tomorrow it would be his. Ever since his mom told him a few months earlier that he'd be getting the truck for his birthday Aaron had been counting down the days. Lately it was pretty much all he could think about. Suddenly the very loud school bell rang, breaking his daydream. "FREEDOM!" Aaron, who was normally pretty composed, yelled out.

"Finally," he whispered, only loud enough for him to hear. Aaron and the rest of the kids from his small high school ran for the school's main doors. The teacher was trying to say something to the class about having a good summer and being prepared for next year, but even the most studious students were only focused on one thing, the front door. The teacher dropped her well thought out parting speech and simply resorted to waving as her students very quickly filed past her desk.

Funny how excited Aaron was about getting out of school. He would spend most of his summer working, and it was not easy work. He helped run the family business, a small but busy farm. It was a type of work that Aaron mostly enjoyed and work he felt he was made for. As he and all the other kids poured out of the front of the school Aaron headed for his truck: an 'old family heirloom', Aaron called it. Along the way he said goodbye to a couple of friends and told them he would catch up with them later, knowing that he'd see most of them the very next day at his birthday party. Right now Aaron just wanted to get home.

Aaron was never a great student, not the worst either; he wasn't motivated but he still tried his best. He had just never been that interested in school; shop class was about the only class he ever did really well in - that and P.E. Aaron was pretty athletic but felt he never had time for sports. He had been born and raised on his family's farm in a very rural part of Tennessee, about two hours north-east of Memphis. He had worked on the farm ever since he could walk. He used to love helping his dad feed the chickens and the pigs, although when Aaron was very young he spent most of the time not feeding the animals, but trying to catch one. It was one of his favorite things to do, plus it always made for great family entertainment. Aaron, as hard as he tried, never came up with a pig or a chicken back then, but would always manage to be covered in so much mud from head to toe it seemed as though he should have.

His dad would always tell him, "You almost did it this time, remember it's the effort that counts." That would only make Aaron madder.

Aaron would smile at his mom and dad, always with this face of dissatisfied satisfaction: happy to be covered in mud, happy because it was so much fun, but mad because he just couldn't catch a pig. His mom never got upset about all the mud and dirt because she always felt that everyone getting a chance to laugh and have some fun was worth it, especially for Aaron's dad. He didn't get to laugh that often.

Aaron's dad died when Aaron was ten from cancer that Aaron's mom never fully explained and rarely ever talked about. Aaron watched as his dad deteriorated: every day he looked a little worse. From the day they confirmed it was cancer Aaron's dad never had what some might refer to as a good day. Aaron's dad had been sick for over a year but continued to work on the farm till his last day. That was a day Aaron would never forget. It was during the summer and it was especially hot and humid. Other than the heat it was like any other start to one of Aaron's busy summer days. It was just after sunup; he got up, got dressed, and went directly to the barn where he started to gather seed for the chickens. It was always the first thing Aaron did every morning, because after he fed the chickens he would gather up all of that day's eggs and take them up to the house for his mother. Aaron went into the chicken coop that was just behind the barn. The chickens were loud and hungry. After Aaron fed the chickens and gathered up all of the fresh eggs, he headed out of the coop back toward the house. Then he heard his dog Elvis barking incessantly: Aaron knew Elvis was upset about something. He called out to Elvis, and his head popped up from out in the field; Aaron could see his dad's tractor stopped in the same spot. Elvis was acting especially unusual, jumping around and barking, like he was excited or scared. Aaron set down the bucket of eggs and ran out to see what was going on.

When he got close to Elvis, he could see he was lying down next to Aaron's dad who was lying face-down on the ground, the tractor was still running. His dad was not moving. Aaron screamed out to his dad and ran as fast as he could to his side.

"Dad! Dad! What's wrong? Oh my God! Dad, are you okay?" he shouted as he turned him over.

Aaron screamed as loud as he could. "HELP!" Aaron was scared; he started to cry while shaking his dad feverishly. "Mom! Marcos!" he screamed and screamed. He was holding his dad's head in his lap, gently wiping the dirt from his face when he heard footsteps running up behind him.

"What's wrong?!" Marcos called out as he ran up to Aaron and his dad.

"Aaron, let me see him," he said as calmly as he could.

Marcos pulled Aaron back, away from his dad. Aaron didn't know what to do, he just stood there watching and sobbing. Marcos put John's head down on the ground. He leaned in closely, then set his ear right next to his mouth to see if he could feel or hear John breathing. He put his fingers on John's neck, feeling for a pulse, then he moved his ear down to his chest. Marcos was straining to find some sign of life. He slowly lifted his head and turned toward Aaron.

"Oh no! Please, Marcos, don't let this happen," he pleaded to Marcos.

Marcos got up from his knees; he turned and pulled Aaron to him. Aaron fell into Marcos's arms and began to scream. "No! No! Why?" He pulled away and looked at Marcos with hatred in his eyes, tears streaming down his face.

"I'm so sorry, Aaron, he's gone," Marcos somberly told him.

Aaron was generally a pretty calm kid but his emotions got the better of him and he started to become hysterical. Aaron knew for a long time that this day was coming; everyone knew this day was coming, but in the back of his mind Aaron hoped it never really would. Aaron's dad tried as best he could with a young son to prepare him; he told him many times to be strong, to understand that this was how life worked sometimes. As his dad got sicker and sicker, he would sit with Aaron to explain what he wanted Aaron to do, what he expected of him when he was gone. Aaron always sat there quietly and listened, but did his best in his own mind to pretend it wasn't real. Marcos grabbed Aaron's head and turned it away from his dad. He was trying his best to calm Aaron down as he started to walk him to the house. When they approached the front of the house Aaron's mom came running out the front door. She knew immediately what was wrong: she had a scared but stern look on her face. She ran down the front steps to Aaron and Marcos; Aaron collapsed into his mom's arms.

"He's dead, Mom... Dad is dead."

His mom tried to be strong but couldn't hold back the emotions. She and Aaron fell to their knees holding each other, as Marcos stood close by.

LIFE LESSONS

The next year was very hard for everyone, but none more than Aaron. The loss of his dad, a man he loved and respected, at Aaron's early age was having its effects. He cried himself to sleep almost every night; he would often lash out at his mom and even Marcos over nothing. Some days he would cut out on his chores and not come back for hours. He was failing at school; it seemed like every other day Aaron's mom or Marcos was picking him up from school for fighting or being disrespectful to a teacher. By the time Aaron was eleven he became so contemptuous his mom was considering putting him in a boarding school; she even considered getting Aaron some professional help. Then one day Aaron's mom caught Aaron and a friend out in back of the barn smoking cigarettes and drinking alcohol. Alisha completely lost it. She collapsed to her knees right there in front of Aaron crying, pounding her fists into the dirt and screaming to God for help. Aaron's friend took off running. Aaron's heart nearly burst out of his chest; he ran to his mom and held her like he was afraid he was losing her.

"I am so sorry, Mom!" he cried loudly. "Mom! I'm so sorry!"

It was like he just suddenly got it, he knew he was the reason for her pain, he was hurting the person he loved most. Aaron's mom pulled him to the ground and wrapped him in her arms. Together they cried for a long time, holding each other, not saying anything.

From that moment on Aaron changed. The fear of losing his mom was powerful. Almost immediately he transformed himself; he changed who he was, how he treated people and, more importantly even at that young age, he decided the type of person he wanted to be. He was determined to be the way his dad was, someone everyone loved and respected. From that day forward Aaron became a different kid. He was happy, his mom was happy; he even did better in school, although not much. It was like that year was a bad dream for everyone, especially Aaron and his mom.

Aaron had never been able to imagine leaving his mom or the farm, and had always questioned having to go to school. He figured for the most part school was a waste of his time. The farm needed him and his mom needed him. For Aaron the family farm was everything especially since his dad was no longer around. That's just how it was and he figured it would always be. Aaron was okay with that. Aaron jumped in his truck, pulled out of the school parking lot and started down the road toward home. Kids headed out away from school in every direction, ready to start their summer. Some of his friends honked as they raced ahead of him. Aaron honked back. One of his buddies came so close to Aaron it startled him and almost caused him to wipe out. His friends only laughed as they sped by. Aaron started to yell then realized it was a waste of time. A bit later he turned off the main road and onto a dirt road where he drove for quite a way, passing several small farms and farmhouses. He saw some of his neighbors working out in the fields; he waved to them as he went by. Finally Aaron reached the tall wood arch that marked the entrance to his farm. His dad and Marcos built it a long time ago, and carved a sign that adorned the top: 'Partly Ours'.

It was a small working farm, but home. They grew several different vegetables, and while not big, it was enough to get by and leave them with a little left over. They had one full-time worker, Marcos, who has been a part of the farm all of Aaron's life. They brought in seasonal workers during the harvest and planting seasons, which were Aaron's favorite times of the year. Aaron thought Marcos stayed mostly because he didn't want to leave all the work involved in running a farm up to Aaron's mom and Aaron alone. Plus Aaron thinks he's partly there out of a sense of loyalty to Aaron's father. Aaron's father and Marcos became good friends, and they worked together for many years on the farm and made it work. Even though Aaron's dad hired Marcos and was his boss, Marcos had always been treated like family, especially since he had no immediate family of his own. Marcos could easily make more money running larger farms, but he couldn't imagine being anywhere else. Marcos didn't ever try to be Aaron's father but taught him everything he knew about running a farm and then some, especially fishing, Marcos's true passion.

Marcos didn't talk about himself or his background very much. He had medium brown hair, brownish green eyes, and reddish, light brown skin. He wasn't tall, maybe five foot eight, but he was built like a bull. He wore a dark, well-tailored mustache and he always, always wore a cowboy hat and boots. He spoke Spanish and English fluently, and would often use Spanish to yell at someone even if they didn't understand him. The most anyone knew for sure was that he was fifty-five and he was, in his words, half-Spanish and half-Indian; but somehow he was born in Mexico. He came from a huge family, where he has six brothers and three sisters, all older. Marcos left Mexico when he was a teenager looking for a better life and ended up in Tennessee; he never explained why Tennessee but Aaron's dad always thought it was because of his passion for country music. He was always blasting country music from his house, truck or a radio when he was working. He didn't go often but he admitted he liked being close to Nashville. Marcos did tell some good stories, especially after a few beers. Marcos was generally a quite man, except when he and Aaron's dad would drink to celebrate the harvest, then he would get especially loud and a little boisterous. But he was always funny and mindful not to cuss or offend. He was always the perfect gentleman toward women, even Aaron's mom who would scold him for holding the door for her. He had stories that would make you believe he could be half-Spanish and half-Indian; but if you ever ate his tamales you'd know he could have only learned that from a true Mexican. Nearly his whole family from Mexico came to visit him every other year: it had become a tradition. It was like a Mexican festival when they were in town. Usually about thirty to forty family members show up: it was a very big deal at the farm and everyone gets involved. The Butlers were treated like extended family, no one was left out: food, music, dancing and a lot of drinking. Marcos and his brothers went fishing nearly every day they were around, and Marcos always made sure Aaron came along.

Aaron drove past the house to the barn. Marcos came walking out with one of the cows in tow.

Aaron yells out to Marcos as he pulls up, "Everything OK?"

"Oh yeah, I think Nanny here is ready to provide us with a new addition to the farm," he said, pointing to the cow's belly.

"It's about time! How much longer do you think?"

"Can't say for sure. The Doc is coming by tomorrow to check her out, but I'm guessing sometime by the end of summer."

Aaron jumped out of his truck and started walking back toward the house; as he approached the off-white and blue house, Aaron's mom stepped out onto the large covered porch.

"So… how was the last day of school?" she asked with an exceptionally big smile on her face. Aaron's mom knew Aaron did not want to be in school a minute longer than he had to.

"It was fine, we didn't really do anything but have a party. You know how it is."

"Well, I'm glad it's over, 'cause I have a lot of work for you here," she stated sternly.

Aaron's face went from a smile to a frown as he looked down, trying not to show his dissatisfaction. He was pretty upset.

His mom quickly spoke up. "Well, I guess you deserve at least the afternoon off: after all it's your birthday," she said, joking with her son.

Aaron smiled. "Not till tomorrow, Mom." He kissed her on the cheek as he walked past her into the house. As usual, Aaron was headed to the kitchen to eat.

THE 17ᵀᴴ BIRTHDAY

Birthdays were always special around the Butler house, especially when it was Aaron's birthday. This year, Aaron was especially excited because he was getting his own truck. Most guys were excited to turn sixteen, because that was when they could get their driver's license; but for Aaron getting his license was no big deal. He had been driving, like many boys in the area, since he was about ten, or as soon as he could reach the pedals and see out the windshield at the same time. Aaron normally didn't like the attention he got on his birthday, as his mom was always embarrassing him or throwing some crazy themed party; but this year Aaron knew his mom was going to go all out, so he decided to just accept it and go along, then maybe this year he wouldn't be too embarrassed.

Saturday started off just like any other Saturday. Aaron got up early, went in the barn and started raking up after the three horses they had; then he went out back to start feeding the chickens and cleaning up the chicken coop, some of his regular chores. Even though this day started out the same as every day, today felt a little different to him. Aaron didn't have to remind himself that today was the first day of summer, and today he was getting his truck. Two big reasons today didn't feel like just any day. Neither Aaron's mom nor Marcos understood why getting Marcos's truck was such a big deal to him. It was a nice truck, no doubt, but it had some serious miles on it. Aaron's mom, Alisha, thought that somehow it reminded Aaron of his dad, but Aaron would never say why he wanted that truck so much. Alisha even offered to buy him a much newer, 'cooler'-looking truck, one with far fewer miles on it. Aaron turned her down flat. But Alisha couldn't say no to the deal Marcos made her anyway: the price he sold her the truck for was ridiculous. Alisha actually felt guilty about it, but then that's who Marcos was.

Aaron fed the chickens, the pigs, the couple of goats they had, then the horses and lastly the cows. After all the animals were fed he started cleaning up, when Marcos walked in.

"Morning, Aaron, how's it going today?"

"Good. Glad to be done with school."

Marcos walked over to Aaron and handed him a little box with some kind of brown wrapping on it. "What's this?"

"It's your birthday gift. I wanted to give it to you now, you know how things will be at your party, so I thought this would be a better time."

That was Marcos's way; he didn't like the spotlight and really didn't care for crowds. Aaron started removing the wrapping; with a silly grin on his face he looked at Marcos. "Yeah, I'm sorry, I didn't have any birthday wrapping paper."

He opened the lid. "That's ok, you know that stuff is for kids anyway," Aaron joked.

He looked inside, there was some tissue paper crinkled up sitting on top. "Nice box," Aaron smiled. He wasn't sure what it was, but the box was so light, he had an idea, and he was hoping for something in particular. As he lifted off the tissue paper, he could see what was inside. "Wha Whoa!" he yelled out. Aaron was so happy. Inside the box was one of Marcos's famous handmade flies, like in fishing fly. This was exactly what Aaron was hoping for. Marcos's fishing flies were hard to come by and considered by fishermen from all over as the best there was. One of these handmade flies from Marcos all but guaranteed great fishing.

"Wow, thank you so much, Marcos, it's just exactly what I was hoping for. I can't wait to try it." Aaron reached out his arms and gave

Marcos a big hug. "You want to go fishing?" Aaron asked with a big smile and a great deal of enthusiasm.

"Let's put this new fly to the test," he suggested excitedly.

Marcos smiled. "That would be great except for two things." He held up two fingers. "One, I have a lot of work to do today, and two, your mom would KILL me if you were late to your own birthday party."

"Oh yeah, that," Aaron said with zero excitement. "I wouldn't mind skipping that," he admitted. "But I know it's a big deal to my mom and I know she's putting a lot of work into it."

"It's not every day you turn seventeen," Marcos reminded him.

"You say that every year," Aaron laughed.

"You need to relax and try to enjoy it this year. Besides you can't let your mother down, you know how she gets," Marcos said in a serious tone.

"I know, but my mom always goes so far overboard, it's always so darn embarrassing. It's not like I don't know how important this is to her, but she knows how much I hate it. It's so humiliating."

"Really? You can't suck it up for one year? You know this is likely to be the last birthday where she'll even try to throw you a party, you need to cut her a little slack."

Aaron grimaced. "Yea okay, I guess you're right. But if I have no friends after this party I'm blaming you!"

"I'm okay with that. Now let's get back to work," Marcos said as he pointed toward a bucket full of grain for the cows. Even though they were friends, in the end Marcos was the boss and Aaron understood that.

Well hidden from others, Aaron was actually pretty excited about his birthday, mostly because he was getting the truck - well, that and a particular girl was coming to his party. To Aaron, birthdays and especially birthday parties were way overrated. He didn't like having them and he didn't like going to them. Even as a young boy he always felt they were somehow degrading; the birthday boy or girl was made to do some awful things, embarrassing things. But Aaron was determined. This year it wasn't about him; this year he was doing it for his mom. Marcos was right, more than likely this would be the last year he would ever have a 'birthday party', and he knew his mom was going all out.

It was only a matter of time; Aaron couldn't stand it any longer, he had to go fishing, at least for a bit. He just had to try out the new fly he got from Marcos. He rushed to get all of his chores done early, and without saying a word to anyone, jumped in the truck with his rod and new fishing fly and headed out. He was in such a rush he forgot to bring his dog Elvis, who always went with him. As he started down the long dirt driveway to the road, both Marcos and Aaron's mom saw him leaving; both knew exactly where he was headed.

"He better be back in time for his own birthday party!" his mom announced. Aaron had several favorite fishing spots, but they were all too far away; he knew he would never make it back in time for his party. He decided this time he better stay close to home so he pulled off the main road onto one of the first dirt roads he came to. At first he thought it might be a service road. This road looks like it might head in the direction of the river. So he decided it was worth a try. The Watson River had always been a great source for fishing for everyone in the area, and fishing this river had a lot of history with Aaron. His dad, Marcos and most of his friends all had 'their' favorite spot along this river somewhere. It was from the Watson that Aaron caught his very first fish; that was all it took, he was hooked after that. As a younger kid, Aaron had ridden his bike past this small dirt road many times but he wasn't sure if he'd ever actually been down the road before. He was keeping his fingers crossed that it would lead him to the river. The road got narrow almost right away: it became more like a trail than a road, but drivable. The further he drove, the narrower the road got; then it started to get really rough with big holes, rocks and trees. The truck was bouncing around like it was in a tornado. Aaron began to think he wasn't on any kind of road at all; it started to feel more like a goat trail. The thing was, now the road was so narrow there was nowhere to turn around, too thick with trees and bushes, so he had no choice but to keep going. His truck had been on a lot of tough roads and in many tight spots before, but the truck was old, it wouldn't take much for it to break down. I guess I know why I haven't gone down this road before, he said to himself. It crossed Aaron's mind more than once: it's going to be a seriously long walk back if I get stuck… Mom will kill me.

Aaron was starting to get really worried. He stopped a couple of times, got out of the truck to see if he could see anything; maybe a place to turn around or maybe even the river: that would be good, he thought. The road was no wider than a large foot trail and rougher than most dirt bike trails. He tried his best to steer the truck away from the trees and rocks, but he didn't have much room to work with. He was actually considering backing all the way out if he didn't come across a clearing soon. Almost before that thought left his head the road came to an abrupt end, right in front of a small beach… Right on the river! Whew, Aaron was sure he was about to miss his own birthday party. He stopped the truck and got out. This is beautiful, he said out loud. Looks like a great fishing spot to me. He started pulling his gear out of the back of the truck. Wonder how come we never came here before?

Aaron cast out his first line: as he did he started thinking about his dad and how he wished he could be here with him, it would have been great. Suddenly Aaron felt a slight jerk on his line, the unmistakable nibble of a fish. Holy smoke, Marcos's flies really work! Then all at once a hard tug and his reel started whizzing as the fish took the bait. Aaron let the fish run a bit but he didn't want it to get itself under some rocks or branches so he started to slowly reel in his line. This had to be a good-size fish, it was putting up quite a fight. Aaron was having a great time, he loved it when a fish would give him a good fight. It took a while but Aaron won the day and brought in an 18" rainbow trout. What a beauty, Aaron said excitedly. This is a keeper for sure. It seemed like mere moments and Aaron was already out of time and had to start making his way home. As he got the truck turned around and pointed himself in the right direction, he was already thinking about when he could come back. Maybe tomorrow… Maybe this time I can get Marcos to come; of course first I have to get home. Come on, truck! he said out loud as he patted the truck's dashboard.

As Aaron pulled down the dirt drive for home he could see that out in the back of the house his mom was already deep into decorating for his birthday party. Wow, Mom went all out this year, he observed as he drove closer. He could see all kinds of streamers and balloons, then he saw a big banner attached to the back of the house facing the backyard: 'Happy 17th, Aaron!' As much as Aaron wasn't into the attention, he was kind of looking forward to this party. He couldn't care less about getting any presents: he was already getting the gift he really wanted. But he was excited to see and hang out with all of his friends, no matter what the reason. Something he didn't get to do much anymore.

Aaron pulled up to the front of the house and jumped out of the truck. Marcos was there to meet him.

"How was the fishing?" Marcos asked with a grin.

"Great." He handed Marcos the fish he caught.

"Not bad," Marcos said with a little gleam in his eye.

Aaron knew what he was looking for. "Yes," Aaron said with a big smile, "I used the new fly you gave me."

Then he looked excitedly at Marcos. "I swear, Marcos, I barely had the pole in the water, maybe for five minutes before I caught the fish. It was awesome!" Marcos laughed and smiled with satisfaction. "Oh, and I found this new fishing spot; it was hard to get to but it was great, we have to go." Aaron was already making the pitch for the next day.

"OK, we'll go sometime but right now you better hit the shower: your guests are going to start arriving soon, and you know your mom."

"Right!" Aaron yelped as he ran for the front door.

Aaron flew through the front door like a strong summer wind and in a matter of seconds he was at the top of the stairs barely touching any of the stairs on his way up. Aaron was getting more excited than he was willing to admit. Aaron didn't normally make a fuss about his looks or what he wore, but he took a little extra care to pick out some clean jeans and one of his nicer shirts. He knew that would make his mom happy; besides, there were going to be some girls at the party. He was trying to decide between two shirts when he heard the unmistakable whistle his mom did when she wanted him. Aaron had heard this very loud and distinct whistle all of his life. Aaron was pretty sure one time he heard his mom's whistle when he was out on his bike from over a mile away! Aaron threw one shirt on, left the other on the bed and started down the stairs.

His mom met him at the bottom of the stairs. "It's about time," she said as she tapped her left hand nervously on the stair railing.

"Your guests are starting to arrive." She paused. "Look at you, so handsome!"

"Cut it out, Mom, I just cleaned up a little." Aaron smiled. As he got to the bottom step he reached out to hug her.

"Well, you should clean up a little more often. You look great." She kissed him hard on the cheek, holding his face in her hands.

Aaron looked up. Standing right in front of him was Maria, one of the prettiest girls in his school; really… One of the prettiest girls in the county! Aaron immediately turned beet-red. Aaron's mom saw his red face and his eyes change; she turned and saw Maria behind her.

"Oh, hi, Maria, I didn't see you there. How are you, sweetie?"

"I'm great, Mrs. B. It's great to see parents and kids who can still show affection," she said with a big grin on her face.

Aaron grabbed Maria's arm. "Let's go before I turn any redder."

Maria was one of the first to show up for the party, and Aaron was particularly pleased she did; this might give him a minute to talk to her before everyone else started to arrive. But that thought didn't last long: minutes after Aaron got Maria a drink and they sat down, his friends started to pour in by the truckload… pickup truck, that is. Soon the backyard was full of teenagers, Aaron's mom, and a few family friends. Aaron's mom had truly gone overboard this year. The backyard was covered from one end to the other with streamers, and balloons attached to wires stretched above the grass and back deck; there were two large colorful banners with 'Happy 17th Birthday, Aaron!' attached to the back fence. Plus all around the back deck and in the large oak tree were hundreds of white Christmas lights strung everywhere.

"Mom must have gotten Marcos to help," he told Maria.

Maria smiled. "It's beautiful." It was a bit overwhelming, but amazing, Aaron had to admit. Aaron felt a sense of pride that his mom would do this for him. He knew it meant a great deal to her: this year he was going to let himself just enjoy it. Aaron stood on the back deck next to Maria talking with some of his guests as they arrived. His best friend Mike walked through the kitchen door onto the deck.

"Aaron!" he yelled loudly, throwing his hands into the air. "Happy Birthday, bro!" he shouted again as he walked up to Aaron and gave him a hug. "I can't believe you're seventeen, and I can't believe we are going to be Seniors!" Many of their high school friends who were close enough to hear started to cheer.

"Finally... Senior year," Aaron gasped.

Mike was older by one year and he never let Aaron forget it. His parents held him back a year on purpose before they sent Mike to school. He had been Aaron's best friend since Aaron was two, when they could almost talk to each other. Both families were very close and often got together for holidays and family events. They relied on each other during tough times to get through things like a bad harvest season. When Aaron's dad passed away, Mike and his family were at the house nearly every day for weeks, bringing food, helping out or just being there. Mike's dad was the best tractor mechanic in three counties: he saved their behinds many times. Their farm was about a mile further down the road, about twice the size of the Butlers'. Mike and Aaron learned, shared and experienced almost everything together. Mike was a big, stocky, dark-haired kid. He was loud about everything but a good guy. If you didn't know him, he was a little intimidating just because of his size; Aaron liked that and sometimes used it to his advantage. He was smart, but like Aaron hated school. He kept up his grades, though, because he'd already been threatened more than once of getting cut from the football team if he didn't. Mike had played football for as long as Aaron could remember. As Mike got older and bigger the coaches used him mainly as a tackle because he was fast, strong and smart. Aaron never missed a game: usually the whole family would go. It was always fun, and besides there wasn't much of anything else to do on a Friday night. Mike tried many times to talk Aaron into trying out for the football team, but Aaron didn't get the calling: playing football was just not a priority to him. The farm was. Unlike Mike's farm where they had several full-time workers, Aaron was needed. It never bothered Aaron that he didn't have time for sports; he was content to watch and cheer on his friends. Everyone knew, or thought they knew, that Mike was headed for a big college some day to play football. Nearly every year since being a freshman Mike had had scouts watching every one of his games. Aaron was not looking forward to the day Mike would have to leave. But... that was not something he had to worry about for another year.

"What do we have to eat around here? I'm starving!" Mike yelled out for everyone to hear.

Alisha snuck up behind Mike and gave him a big hug. "Who's this big handsome lug?" she laughed.

Mike turned around. "Why if it isn't the Royal Queen herself, Mizz Butler!" he said as he took her hand and did a little bow.

"Grand Master Fields," she responded with a little curtsy.

This was something Mike and Alisha had been doing for years: no one knew when or why it started, but now it was expected. Everyone always got a chuckle out of it, especially Aaron's mom.

"There are tons of snacks and drinks over there," she pointed at a table set up on one end of the deck. "The food will be ready in a bit."

"Fantastic. It already smells great, and I see we have the Master Q Man himself hard at work!" he yelled as he waved to Marcos.

Marcos waved his spatula in response. Aaron looked over to the barbecue; Marcos was in his favorite barbecue apron working the grill, smoke billowing everywhere. Marcos stepped up to handle the grill ever since Aaron's dad had passed, and had actually become a better grill man than his dad. Although no one would ever say it.

The party was underway, the sun had set, the music was getting a little louder, the stars and party lights were burning brightly. It was a beautiful June night. Aaron was really enjoying himself; all of his friends were there. There was dancing and laughing in a collaboration of celebration. Everyone was out of school and it was the first day of summer. What a great day to have a birthday, Aaron thought. Suddenly and loudly the dinner bell rang out. The dinner bell has been in the same spot at the back of the house since the day his parents moved in; it has been one of those things that Aaron has never underappreciated. All his life from wherever he was on the farm when a meal was ready his mom would ring that bell. It was a great sound to Aaron. Sometimes the bell would be backed up by Alisha's whistle but not often; the sound of the bell was able to resonate to all corners of their farm. No matter how far away or what piece of equipment was running Aaron's ears would tingle: the bell!

Everyone started to line up for food. Aaron got in line with a few of his friends when Maria came up to him. "Can I cut?" she asked with a smile.

"Are you kidding? Of course," Aaron said as he gestured her to get in front of him. His friends didn't say a word, only smiled. Soon they had plates full of barbecue ribs, pulled pork, beans and corn on the cob. All of Aaron's favorites. His mom set up tables all around the back, not enough for everyone to sit at once so Aaron, Maria, Mike and a couple of his other closer friends sat down on the stairs of the deck. They were all digging in pretty hard - not much talking going on - when Marcos came over to the group. "So… How is it?" All he got in response was a bunch of jumbled-up words because they all had mouths full of food. But lots of smiles! "That's good enough!" Everyone started to laugh.

Maria is special, not just to Aaron. She and Aaron have only known each other for about two years, since late in their freshmen year when

Maria moved into the area to live with her grandmother. Her parents were killed earlier that year in a car crash in Memphis. Maria luckily was not in the car at the time, otherwise she would likely not have made it either. Maria's grandmother was the only close family she had in the US. She did have two uncles with young families; one in California and one right in Memphis, but neither family volunteered to take her in. All of her other family, which she has never really known, were in Italy; where her grandfather and grandmother migrated from with her father when he was a baby. When Maria first moved into the area she pretty much kept to herself, but she needed to forget her pain; so she decided with some coaching from her grandmother to get more involved. She was an excellent student and often helped out other struggling students. She volunteered at a children's shelter several days a week that is over an hour away; but the drive was worth it, she loved it there. She was petite, maybe 5' 1", thin, and had long curly black hair. She had a very soft face with big dark eyes. She was strong and self-motivated, mature for her age. She had a fun, outgoing personality, and she was always smiling. Her grandmother said it was the work at the shelter that snapped her out of it. She hadn't gotten the farming dress code down so most of the time she wore dresses; Aaron said she was always the best-dressed girl in school.

Aaron actually didn't meet Maria until the summer between freshman and sophomore years. They saw each other in school and at school events, but they never had any classes together and they didn't have any mutual friends. Clover High was the only school around. It went from 6th to 12th grade, so there were a fair amount of students - not that that kept Aaron from spotting Maria early on. When it comes to girls he was pretty shy. He wanted to talk to her, but never worked up the courage. Plus Maria always seemed to be surrounded by people, mostly guys. Then one day last summer Aaron was out on his bike riding to Mike's house when he saw that Maria and her grandmother had stopped along the road with a flat tire. Aaron stopped and helped them replace the tire with the spare. Maria's grandmother was so thankful she insisted on making Aaron dinner. It didn't take much convincing, especially when Maria smiled at him. So Aaron put his bike in the back of their truck and rode with Maria and her grandmother to their house. Mike will understand, he thought. They had an amazing meal, and for Aaron it was a surprisingly entertaining conversation. Aaron learned a great deal about what it was like growing up in Italy and what it was like for Maria's grandmother, grandfather and her father when they first moved to the United States. Aaron was actually fascinated. He also for the first time got to really speak with Maria and get to know her a little. He was immediately smitten: she has such a great smile, he thought.

After that night Maria and Aaron became friends but they weren't able to see each other very much. Between Aaron's work (and fishing outings) and Maria's summer school and her volunteer work they were only able to get together a handful of times. Even then it was generally only when someone was having a barbecue or some other type of get together. Once they were back in school Aaron tried to hang out with Maria whenever he could, but she was way too popular for him. Aaron had many friends, most of whom were now friends with Maria, but never having the opportunity to be by himself with her made him uncomfortable. Aaron liked Maria, but like many other young teens he was afraid to tell her - actually he was afraid to tell anyone. So they went most of the school year seeing each every day but not getting much time to hang out or talk. While at school when they did see each other, they sort of made a game out of it: they'd pretend they were only meeting each other for the first time and joke around, introducing themselves to each other. Their friends thought it was corny but Aaron and Maria had fun with it; for the time being, that was as good as it was going to get.

While they sat on the deck stairs finishing their dinner, talking and laughing, and Mike was on his way back with thirds, Aaron's mom came up to them.

"How's it going, guys?"

Mike spoke up first. "Are you kidding, Mrs. B? The food is great, the place looks great, and the company... Well, that's okay, too!" Everyone laughed.

"Aaron, I need to ask you for a favor?" she said, looking right at him with a silly but stern smile.

Mike looked at Aaron, then looked back at Alisha. "I know what this is," he stated proudly.

Aaron did, too, and was a little upset that his mom would put him in this position, especially in front of his friends… Especially in front of Maria. But then, knowing his mom, that's probably why she did it.

"Mom… Really?" he pleaded.

"Come on, dude. You have to, it's your birthday," Mike goaded.

"What's going on?" Maria asked Aaron.

A couple of Aaron's other friends started speaking up, which eventually turned into a chant: "Aaron! Aaron! Aaron!" Even Maria, still not understanding what was going on, chimed in. Then everyone at the party began to chant: "Aaron! Aaron!" Aaron stood up and they all cheered. Alisha started clapping and giggling. Maria thought maybe this was some birthday ritual she didn't know about.

Aaron walked over to his mom and got very close. "This is not fair, you know that, right?" Aaron was not happy.

"Of course I do. I'm your mother and I love you, please do this for me?" she pleaded.

"Mom, you can't do this anymore, it's not cool!"

Aaron knew he had no choice, he was hoping this wouldn't happen, but then we are talking about Aaron's mom, so it was inevitable. As he got up Aaron smiled at Maria who looked confused; Alisha was beaming. He walked up the steps to the deck where conveniently Marcos was standing holding Aaron's guitar.

Aaron smiled at Marcos. "Traitor." Marcos laughed and stepped away.

Everyone gathered in close to the deck in front of Aaron.

Maria leaned into Mike. "What's this? What's going on?"

"You've never seen this?"

Another friend turned around toward Mike and Maria. "You're in for a big surprise!"

Mike just smiled: "Watch."

Marcos turned off the music that was playing in the background; Aaron put the guitar strap over his shoulder and turned his back to the party-goers.

He turned back around to face the group. "Do I really have to do this?" he pleaded. Everyone started clapping and cheering: Aaron's mom whistled. Aaron smirked and turned back around putting his back to the group. He bent forward slightly and with his right hand he shook his fingers through his hair making it loose and fall in front of his face. He slowly turned around to face everyone. He looked at his mom, then Maria; Maria still had a puzzled look on her face. Aaron loosened his jaw and made sort of a pout, trying to look mysterious or cool. His mom began to clap jumping up and down, Mike was cracking up. Aaron strummed the guitar one time, and all the girls, including Mom, swooned. And then Aaron let it go: he played, sang and performed like his idol Elvis Presley. He was performing his favorite song 'Teddy Bear'. Even Aaron's not sure why that's his favorite Elvis song, all he knows is when he sings it, it makes his mom laugh and cry, a good cry. Aaron's been a fan since before he was born. His mom would play Elvis every day in the house and would often stand in front a small speaker and push her pregnant tummy right up to it so her unborn son Aaron could hear the music. Some moms play Bach or Beethoven: Aaron's mom played Elvis.

Maria's mouth was literally hanging open. She was in shock, not so much because Aaron was standing in front of all of his friends singing, dancing and playing, but because he was so good.

Mike saw Maria's face. "What do you think?"

"I'm completely blown away!" she said excitedly. "I had no idea!"

"Oh, just wait, it gets better."

"What? Really?"

In full Elvis mode Aaron began to do some Elvis signature moves, lifting one knee and gyrating his hips slightly.

Alisha was screaming in support and excitement. It was never that easy to get Aaron to do this but when he did he gave it one hundred percent.

The song ended, and Aaron lifted his head. "Thank you, thank you very much," he said in his best Elvis voice. Everyone clapped, laughed and the girls all screamed, even Maria. Aaron started laughing. But he was in his groove now... Bam went the guitar: "One for the money, two for the show, three to get ready..." He was into the next song, rocking it hard. If you had closed your eyes, you'd have sworn you were listening to a young Elvis Presley. He was that good. Now Aaron was all over the deck, jumping and singing, laying it all out there. It was a small backyard personal show from Elvis himself. And Aaron's friends didn't let him down, the more he got into it the more they clapped and screamed.

Aaron performed three songs: he was tired and sweaty. When he set down his guitar on the table everyone let out an "Awe..." in disappointment. Aaron smiled, grabbed a paper towel to wipe his face, and headed back to his friends.

At the bottom of the stairs he was cut off by his mom. "That was amazing. Thank you so much for doing that for me," she whispered in his ear.

"No problem, Mom, it was fun. Besides I think it may have effected a few other people," he said, looking over at Maria.

"I think it did, too," she smiled.

As Aaron walked through his friends to get to Maria, everyone was slapping him on the back telling him how great he was. Aaron takes it all in his stride. He had never really performed in front of any kind of crowd, mostly small groups of friends and family. Aaron's mom had pictures of him playing a toy guitar and singing Elvis songs when he was only two. He loved to play for his mom and dad, and did so often; it always brought his parents back to the Elvis concert they went to on their first date, when they both realized their relationship was going to be something more.

Maria's face was almost comical. She had this look of total disbelief, with an added pinch of pride. "Truly blown away!" she started as Aaron approached. Aaron smiled. "Wow, I didn't see that coming," she said gleaming at Aaron. She stepped right up to him and gave him a big hug, even though he was pretty sweaty.

"That was so amazing! Beyond impressive... I'm not sure what else to say." She was a little in shock.

Mike laughed and put his arm around Aaron. "You rocked it pal, that was great!"

"Thanks, man, I appreciate it. It was fun," he told them.

One of Aaron's other good friends, Bobby, came up to Aaron with his girlfriend April, also a friend of Aaron's, and they both gave him a hug.

"Fantastic, dude. Oh and the performance... That was pretty good, too." April slapped Bobby on the shoulder while everyone laughed.

"No seriously, Aaron, every time I hear you, you get better and better; you really ought to do one of those Elvis impersonation contest things, I bet you could win." Aaron laughed, trying to play it down while everyone around him who heard the comment started chiming in.

Maria was looking at Aaron and could tell this attention was bothering him. She walked up to Aaron and grabbed him by the arm. "Don't you think it's time for birthday cake?" she said very loudly as she pulled Aaron away and up to the deck.

Aaron looked at her and mouthed: "Thank you." She smiled. Perfect timing, too: out came Aaron's mom with the cake, lit with eighteen candles (one to grow), and Marcos in tow with plates and forks. Everyone spontaneously broke out in song: "Happy Birthday to you..." Aaron stood there watching and listening - he was having the best birthday ever.

"Cake for everyone!" Aaron's mom yelled out. Cake was being cut and passed around at a frantic rate.

GONE FISHING

The next day Aaron was up early but not before his mom and definitely not before Marcos. The smell of bacon was in the air; Aaron was in a great mood.

"Morning, Mom," he said to her as he walked into the kitchen.

"Well, good morning, birthday boy. How are you feeling today?"

"I feel great. Yesterday was so much fun. Thank you again, Mom, for everything," he said sincerely as he snatched a piece of bacon.

"What, no hug?"

"Oops, sorry." He turned right back around and gave his mom a big hug.

"Okay, sit down, breakfast is almost ready," she commanded with a smile. Aaron sat down at the small kitchen table and poured himself a glass of orange juice.

"So what's up?" Aaron asked his mom. "Did you have fun last night?"

"You know I did," she said with a huge smile. "I love all of your friends and I'm really liking this Maria," she smiled coyly.

"Ah, come on, Mom, she's just a friend."

"Yea, right," she laughed. "I know all of your friends and I promise you none of them look at you like Maria looks at you," she laughed.

Aaron laughed, too. "I hope not!"

"So… your birthday continues," his mom told him.

"Why? What do you mean?" he asked, a little surprised.

"Marcos and I have decided that you should get the whole day off today... Take your new truck and go fishing, visit some friends or maybe hang out with Maria... I'm just saying," she joked as she put down Aaron's plate of breakfast.

He hesitated before he answered. He would love to go see Maria or go fishing. "That's really cool, Mom, but I can't do that, it wouldn't be fair to you or Marcos. I have a lot of work today."

"Well, it's too late. Most of your morning chores are already done and we are kicking you off the property," she stated as if she was the sheriff that rolled in to kick off some squatters.

Aaron smiled. "Really? That's amazing, Mom; I guess I'll have to find something to do then."

"Really? Why?"

"Naw, Mom, I'm just kidding, but I can't see Maria, she does her volunteer work today, and I already know most of my friends are busy. So you know what that means?" he said joyfully.

"Yes... fishing," his mom said, half-disappointed.

"FISHING!" Aaron made up for her disappointment with his over-the-top excitement. "Wow, this is great, Mom." He jumped up from his chair and started for the door.

"Wait one minute, I didn't make this breakfast for myself, sit down and finish so I can make you some food to take with you."

Aaron knew when he needed to just do what his mom said, and this was one of those times. So Aaron finished his breakfast and got up. His mom handed him a bag with sandwiches and snacks, he kissed her on the cheek, thanked her again, and was out the door. "Man, that kid."

Aaron ran for the barn, calling out for Elvis the whole way. Elvis came running from behind the barn at full speed: even Elvis knew what was about to happen. Aaron opened the barn door, ran in, grabbed his favorite fishing poles and fishing box, then ran for the truck. Elvis jumped in first and within minutes they were 'off the land'. "Elvis, do you know where we're going today?" Elvis looked at him. "We're going to my new fishing spot. You're going to love it!" Elvis barked with approval. They only had to go a few miles before they got to Aaron's newly discovered road. I wonder if this was ever a road at all? he was thinking as he turned off onto the small dirt road and started slowly making his way to the river. Elvis was being thrown all over the cab of the truck when the road started to get really rough, so Aaron made Elvis sit on the floor. It was a rough ride for Aaron, too, but he took it nice and slow; he was a little nervous, but his new truck was handling the road much better.

Once they got to the river, Elvis jumped from the truck and ran for the water, barking and racing up and down the small beach. Elvis was just as excited to be there as Aaron was. Aaron opened the tailgate of the truck and jumped into the back of the truck to start getting his pole set up. He sat down on the tailgate with his feet dangling below him, his rod stretched across his lap. He was setting up the fly Marcos gave him for his birthday when he saw Elvis coming down the beach with something pretty big in his mouth. Aaron called out to Elvis: "Elvis! Come here!" he commanded. "What do you have in your mouth? Come over here, boy, let me see what you've got!" Elvis came running up to Aaron. "What the heck is that?" Aaron asked out loud as Elvis set it on the ground in front of him. Aaron reached down and picked up what looked like a badly chewed-up rubber duck, the kind a hunter would use to train a dog to retrieve. "Huh. I wonder if someone was hunting around here or maybe this floated down the river? Oh well, it's yours now, Elvis," he said as he tossed it back toward the water. Elvis took off after it.

Aaron had finished setting up his pole and looked up to see what direction he might like to go. The last time he was here he dropped his pole in the water right in front of him, but this time Aaron wanted to venture out a little. As he looked north and then south he couldn't help but notice how beautiful it was: so many trees, grass growing all around, total privacy. Wow, what a great spot, he thought to himself. I might be having second thoughts on who I tell about this place. He decided on south, grabbed his pole and backpack (with all the food his mom made him) and started out. Elvis quickly came up to be alongside.

As they began their quest south they ran out of beach almost right away. The trees, bushes and grass came right up to the water's edge, making it nearly impossible to move forward. The bushes were only getting thicker and thicker. "Wow, this is really thick!" he yelled to Elvis. Elvis was out in front of Aaron: he'd already given up and jumped into the river to swim along. Aaron wasn't willing to jump in the water yet. He couldn't see very far downriver if there might be a good spot to stop, so he decided to move inland to try to work his way around all of the foliage. It was slow-going but Aaron was determined; Elvis didn't seem to mind, every other bush had something interesting in it.

They walked for about an hour when they finally came to another small clearing with a beach and several large boulders right at the waters edge. This is perfect. "Let's go, Elvis!" When they got to the water Aaron realized just how perfect this spot was; the small beach was crescent-shaped, making the water right in front of him much calmer than that of the river. The big boulders all around him blocked the wind, and the trees blocked the sun almost all the way to the edge of the water. Perfect! Aaron set down his gear on the grass and headed to one of the smaller boulders to throw out his first cast. Elvis lay down on the grass behind Aaron to chew on his new toy. Aaron cast out several times, then after a particularly good cast he proceeded to sit down on the rock.

Within minutes he could feel some nibbles: they were hard and often. He waited till the right moment and then jerked the pole back as hard and as quickly as he could. He got one, a nice one, too. That was easy, he thought. Marcos is not going to believe this, he laughed, giving Marcos and his new fly all the credit. Aaron carefully took the hook out of the trout's mouth, jumped off the rock, showed Elvis his prize, then released the fish back into the water.

That was awesome. He climbed back onto the rock to try for another one.

As Aaron sat there with his line in the water he started to think about Maria. He thought about how they became friends and how he wished they could be more. *I wonder if she feels the same?* But before he could answer he had another fish on the line. *Wow! This is amazing.* He started pulling the hook out of the fish's mouth, *I think I'm going to try to talk Maria into coming out here… But what if she doesn't like to fish? That would be a bummer.* This fish was a beauty, at least 20" and maybe five or six pounds. "This is a keeper," Aaron told Elvis, holding up the fish to show him. Elvis barely looked up, he was too involved with his duck. Aaron took the fish to the waters edge and hooked it to a chain so the fish could stay alive in the water until Aaron was ready to go.

Over the next couple of hours Aaron caught nine fish! Two he kept. "Time for lunch!" he announced. He grabbed his backpack and bottle of water and sat down next to Elvis on the grass. He ate nearly all of the food his mom had given him. *That was good.* He was so comfortable there on the grass under the trees he decided to put his head down for a minute to take it all in. He looked up at the powder-blue sky: there was a nice cool breeze quietly flowing through the tress, and it was so peaceful. Minutes later Aaron was fast asleep.

Aaron woke up abruptly when he heard Elvis bark several times. He turned to look, but Elvis wasn't there. "ELVIS!" Aaron called out as he jumped to his feet. "Where are you?" he called out again. Then he heard Elvis bark again and again. "ELVIS!" Aaron yelled as he started to run in the direction of the barking. He whistled for Elvis as he usually did, but his dog wasn't responding. *Man, I hope he's not hurt!* He worked his way through the thick forest. "ELVIS!" he yelled again. Elvis's bark got louder. *I must be getting closer.*

Suddenly Aaron found himself standing on a small dirt road in the middle of the woods. He didn't stop to think about it, but started running up the road in the direction of the barks. A minute later he came to a clearing: there was a small house with a big front porch, and there was Elvis standing in front of the house barking incessantly at something he had cornered. "Elvis! What the hell are you doing?" As Aaron got closer he could see it was a large bobcat! "Get away from him!" The large bobcat was hissing and growling, backed up against the steps of the front porch, coiled as if it was ready to spring. Aaron called Elvis several times but he wasn't listening, and the more Aaron called out for Elvis the more the bobcat seemed to get upset.

Aaron was freaking out: he didn't know what to do. If Elvis moved in any direction was likely the bobcat will attack; if Aaron moved any closer to Elvis the bobcat would likely attack. Aaron spotted a good-sized rock on the ground just in front of him. Maybe if I hit it with a rock, it will run off? he was thinking. Even if I miss it, I might scare it into moving, at least that's what he was hoping. Aaron slowly moved forward, small baby steps. Then he very slowly bent down to retrieve the rock, always keeping an eye on the bobcat. The cat was getting more anxious, growling louder and louder, striking his paw out at Elvis; Elvis would not stop barking. Aaron knew he had to do this now!

He got the rock in his hand and started to stand back up: that second, the bobcat leapt for Elvis! Aaron wasn't even back to his feet but he cocked his arm to throw the rock… BLAM! A shotgun went off from just behind Aaron. Aaron fell to the ground. Aaron's ears were ringing badly; he got part way up and scrambled toward Elvis. "Elvis! Are you alright?" he yelled out as he approached his dog and the dead bobcat. Aaron looked in amazement. "Oh my God, you're okay!" he said to his dog as he grabbed his face and kissed his forehead; Elvis licked him on his face. With his ears still badly ringing he looked back to see who had fired the shot. It was an older man, tall with a medium build and long gray hair down to his shoulders; he had a goatee and mustache, and he was wearing a baseball cap down to his eyebrows. The man lowered the gun. Then Elvis casually walked toward the man as if nothing had happened. Aaron stood quickly and tried to call out for Elvis to stop. Suddenly he got dizzy and his eyes got blurry: he put his hand to his head, but before he could say anything he passed out - thud! - right to the ground.

Aaron's eyes opened slowly. Without lifting his head, which now had a thumping headache, he looked around. He was in a house, but not his house. He didn't recognize anything: where am I? He was having trouble remembering what happened. "Elvis?" he said quietly. As he turned to sit up he saw Elvis lying on the floor next to the couch he was on. Elvis sat up and put his face on Aaron's lap. "Are you okay, boy?" All of a sudden everything came back to him. I must be in that guy's house, he realized. He looked around the room, considering the little bit he saw on the outside and the way it looked: the inside looked pretty nice, really nice, actually. It looked much bigger than he thought it was. Aaron felt a sharp pain on his left cheek and reached up to touch it.

"Yeah, man, you took a pretty hard fall," came a man's voice from the other side of the room. Aaron jumped back so hard he nearly hit his head on the wall. That scared the crap out of him! The guy laughed loudly, a deep powerful laugh.

"It probably wouldn't be a good idea to hit your head again," the man said sarcastically. Aaron tried his best to gather his wits.

"Sorry, mister, I didn't see you there." Elvis barked then walked over to the stranger. "Elvis, come back here. Sorry, mister." Aaron moved a little to one side of the couch so he could see the man. He was sitting in a cow-skinned, oversized chair next to this huge boulder fireplace. The man appeared to be eating something. Aaron spoke up again. "What happened?" he asked as he tried to stand. "Listen, kid, I'd give yourself a few minutes before you try to stand up, you don't want to pass out again," the man suggested, chuckling.

"Yea, good idea." Aaron took his advice and sat back down.

"I'd get you some ice for that welt on your face but I'm clean out: not many Piggly Wigglys around here," the man joked.

"That's okay, thank you, though."

"Boy, that was a close one, but it was the bobcat or your dog," the man started to explain. "By the way, who names their dog Elvis? I love it," he laughed. Aaron couldn't tell if the man was serious or not, so he answered the question.

"Oh, thanks," Aaron began as he tried to get his mind together. "Actually I named him that for my mom, she's like the biggest Elvis Presley fan ever." There was a strangely long pause.

"You don't say? And you? How did you get your name?" The man seemed intrigued. Strange question, Aaron thought. "Actually I'm not totally sure. My mom says she and my dad had decided on my name long before I was even around. But they both loved Elvis Presley so I can only assume..." "Assume what?" the man interrupted.

"Oh sorry, I thought everyone around here knew Aaron was Elvis Presley's middle name. That's where I think my name may have come from."

"Your mom and dad are both Elvis fans, then?"

"Well... yes. My dad was. He passed away several years ago. My dad always told me he fell in love with my mom when they went to an Elvis concert together; maybe that's why they decided on my name - does that makes sense?" Aaron smiled just at the thought of it.

"Sure, kid, it makes sense."

Aaron realized he was having this rather unusual conversation with a complete stranger in the middle of nowhere, and started to get a little uncomfortable. And what the heck was going on with Elvis? He wouldn't leave the man's side.

Aaron stood up, feeling a little more stable.

"Mister, I can't thank you enough for saving my dog and helping me out, but I better get going; it looks like it's starting to get dark out."

"You're right. How are you going to get home?"

"Oh, my truck is just a few miles away parked on this abandoned road: it's no big deal."

Maybe I shouldn't have said that, he thought to himself. Getting more anxious, Aaron started to walk toward the door and called Elvis to follow. As he walked past the man he spotted a beautiful acoustic guitar leaning against the wall next to the fireplace.

"Nice guitar," Aaron couldn't resist saying. The man stood up and walked toward the front door. Aaron could see him better now. He wasn't as old as Aaron had first thought: maybe in his fifties?

"Oh. Thanks, kid. Yeah, she's pretty special to me; that was a gift from an old friend."

"That must be a really good friend," Aaron suggested. "Yes," was the one-word response.

Aaron walked closer to the guitar. "That really is a beaut. I'd love to try it sometime." He was surprised at his outburst and kept on for the front door. The man looked upset.

"It's gonna be dark soon; right now you need to get going," the man said, a little defensively. "I don't want to be responsible for you out there in the dark."

"Yes, sir, you're right. Again, thank you for saving my dog, really for everything."

Aaron reached out to shake the man's hand. The man hesitated but just before Aaron pulled his hand back the man reached out and shook it. Aaron noticed he was wearing a ring on his index finger. It was very big, gold, with a big black stone in the middle. Aaron thought that was kind of strange.

"You're welcome. You be safe, kid, that was a pretty hard knock on the head," the man said, holding back a chuckle. "Hey! Take good care of Elvis!" he laughed as Aaron and Elvis disappeared into the trees.

"I will!" Aaron shouted back. The man turned back toward the door, shaking his head. Well that just sucks, he said to himself.

Aaron felt he didn't have time to go back for his fishing gear: it was getting dark fast. Last thing he wanted was to get lost or try to drive out on that road in the dark. So he and Elvis humped it back directly to the truck. Aaron wasn't too worried about his gear anyway.

It was hard enough for him to find the place; besides, it gave him an excuse to come back. Aaron and Elvis got in the truck: Aaron's head was thumping hard in pain. They started down the rough road to get back to the highway. As the sun began to set, Aaron turned on his headlights.

"Just in time, Elvis."

They bumped around for what seemed like forever until they finally made it back to the main road.

"Whew!" Aaron let out a sigh of relief.

It was dark by the time he actually pulled up in front of the house, but then that was not unusual when Aaron was out fishing. His mom knew too well that Aaron would milk the day to the last minute and the last fish. His mom came out of the house as the truck came to a stop. Aaron got out and then Elvis jumped out and ran straight to Aaron's mom.

"Hey, Elvis," she smiled. "How'd you boys do?" Elvis barked and ran into the house.

Alisha was thirty-six. Born not far from where she lives now. Like a lot of kids at that time, she was born at home. Due to complications during birth her mom died when she was born; Alisha nearly died as well. Her dad often referred to Alisha as his miracle baby. She was the youngest of four and the only girl. It was a crazy and colorful life being the only female in a house with four males. Alisha was born and raised as a farmer, but what she really was, was a cowboy's dream; she cooked, rode and could arm wrestle the best of most men.

She was strong and soft all at once. She lived in her jeans and boots, and didn't mind getting dirty. A grown-up tomboy was what Aaron's dad always said. But every time she put on a dress, men would stop in their tracks. Especially Aaron's dad. She was not much for fishing, but every once in a while Aaron's dad would talk her into going out. She loved being with 'her guys'. But when they brought home the fish… no one could cook it up better. Alisha was very pretty, but you had better not say that to her, she would sock you. She had medium-length blonde hair that was always flying around, of medium height, and she stayed pretty fit: all that physical work would do it. She was full of life and outgoing; always laughing, always smiling, always joking around; especially with Aaron and his dad. Although Marcos was not immune, she constantly messed with him, too. He always acted like she was pestering him, but really, he loved it. She was the spirit of the farm. She always said that the sole purpose in her life was to keep all of the important men in her life happy.

Alisha and John, Aaron's dad, met in high school: they were high school sweethearts. They fell madly in love when Alisha was only seventeen, and John was eighteen. Aaron was pretty sure it 'happened' when his dad took her to their first and only Elvis concert in Memphis for a graduation present for his mom. First came family, then came Elvis! Elvis was 'the other man' in her life; Alisha was a through and through Elvis fan. Always had been, always would be. When she was in school Alisha was the head cheerleader, and Aaron's dad was the all-round 'every sport guy'. Captain of this and that, good at all of it. He may have actually gone on to college because of sports, but his dad's failing health meant he had to be home to manage the farm. Alisha and John were married one year after Alisha graduated high school. They moved onto the farm and that became their life, a life Alisha and John loved. Aaron is Alisha's only child, not by choice.

Aaron walked over to his mom to give her a hug when she grabbed his shoulders and stopped him in his tracks. "What's this?" she asked as she reached up toward his face. "It's nothing, Mom, just a bruise."

"A bruise my behind, get in the house so I can see it in the light."

"Honestly, Mom, it's nothing." He did as she said anyway.

As he walked into the kitchen he thought about what he was going to say; he knew he would tell his mom the truth, he always told his mom the truth; but how to tell her to keep her from getting too upset? Nothing came to mind, the story was hard enough for Aaron to believe; to try to find a way to make it more believable would only make things worse.

"Sit down at the table and let me take a look." She grabbed a washcloth and some ice from the freezer. "Man! You are swollen up like a squirrel who has his whole winter supply in his mouth." She gently put the washcloth full of ice on Aaron's face. He wrenched. "Bruise?" his mom joked. "So are you going to tell me what happened?"

"Mom, like I said, it's no big deal, but it is a little unusual," Aaron kind of laughed, then smiled, even though it hurt.

"Unusual? Well... this would be a first," she teased.

Alisha loved a good story, especially when it was from her son. She looked at him and smiled back. "Uh huh. I can tell this is going to be a doozy."

She tried to reposition the cloth on Aaron's face. "Ouch!"

"Oh yea, it's nothing. Hold it here. Get going with your story," she said as she sat in the chair right next to him.

"Well, I didn't have time to tell you yesterday with everything that was going on, but when I went out fishing I came across a new spot that I'd never been to before." Aaron got interrupted right there.

"Really? How's that possible? Between you, your dad, Marcos and all your buddies, how could you not know about this spot?"

"I know. I can't answer that. Honestly I think we all had 'our' spots for so long, we never ventured too far from them. But really, Mom, that's not the story."

"Right! Sorry," she laughed.

"Okay. So I took Elvis back to that same spot today, I wanted to check it out again. It's so beautiful, you'd love it. But you know, it was the fishing: the fishing was amazing. Anyway, when we got there I decided to move downriver a bit where Elvis and I found this other really awesome spot. By far the best fishing spot I've ever been to. Mom... in three hours I caught nine fish! All big and all with a lot of fight," he told her excitedly.

"That's really cool. Are the fish in the truck?"

"I only kept two, the rest I released," he explained. Holy crap! I forgot about the fish!

"Perfect, I'll go get them," she said as she got up from her chair.

"No, Mom!"

"What... why?" she snapped at him.

"Come on, Mom, sit down and I'll tell you: that's part of the story."

So Aaron spent the next hour telling his mom about his day, and reluctantly he included the bobcat and the shotgun. Alisha sat there stunned, but she managed not to say anything the whole time, except every couple of minutes she would put her hand to her mouth - "Oh my God!" - followed by a few loud gasps. But she never interrupted. Aaron finished his story; he told her every detail he could remember. His mom sat back in her chair and looked up at the ceiling, both hands on her face. She looked at Aaron. Aaron couldn't tell if she was going to get mad and yell at him or what.

"Okay, here's the deal," she started out cautiously. "I am so thankful that you are alright; I'm thankful that Elvis is alright, this could have gone really, really bad. And I'm not mad at you, although I feel like I should be," she said, looking sincerely at her son. "I am, however, going to have to put my foot down and not allow you to go back to that spot again," she stated emphatically.

"Mom! You've got to be kidding! This is like the best spot ever. It's my spot, no one else even knows it's there!"

Even though he was pissed, Aaron was actually surprised how his mom was dealing with his story. He expected her to be a lot more upset, but he didn't think she would ban him from going back.

"This just sucks!"

"Aaron Butler! I'm sorry but I'm not going to flexible on this one. We know nothing about this 'guy' and let's be honest, some guy living in the middle of nowhere... by himself... is just plain creepy. I don't care if he helped you out or not, I don't like it. How the heck do we know what he's doing out there? Maybe he's hiding something or worse, hiding from someone. Oh my God, what if he's... you know, one of those sickos." She shook from giving herself the chills.

"That's a little much, isn't it, Mom?" Aaron laughed.

"You just never know, Aaron, and I'm not anxious to find out."

Aaron's mom might have been overreacting a little but Aaron reluctantly understood. Their family consisted of the two of them; they needed each other, they relied on each other, and he knew she was right. She was still Aaron's mom, and her word was law, even when his dad was alive. If Aaron's dad ever heard Aaron speak back to his mom… the leather belt would come out faster than a gunslinger could pull his pistol. Aaron learned a long time ago, and ever since has had complete respect for his mom and her decisions; he may not always have agreed, but he tried his best to respect her wishes. Aaron was bummed out in a big way. Not only did he lose the fish he caught and his gear, most importantly he lost the brand new fly Marcos had given him.

How am I going to tell Marcos? Man, this will be tough. He's going to hate me. Aaron's mom invited Marcos to dinner that night so he, too, could hear the story. Marcos never really needed to be invited, as he ate with the two of them nearly every night; but by inviting him, Alisha felt it made things a little more formal. Maybe at dinner with Marcos there it would soften the situation for her. As the three of them sat down to eat Aaron jumped right into his story. He didn't leave out a single detail, but he did take a long pause when he fessed up to not bringing back his gear, including the fishing fly. Aaron finished his story, and took a deep breath.

"That's it. That was my crazy day."

Marcos sat there with a small grin on his face. He looked at Alisha then back at Aaron.

"I can't decide which part I think is more interesting to me, the fact that you found a never before known fishing spot, or that Elvis's life was saved by a guy with a shotgun that happened to be there in the middle of the woods in a house no one knew existed. I am very grateful to this man that you and Elvis are okay: this is a fact. But this is one of the strangest situations you've ever gotten yourself into," he tried to say with a serious face.

"That's the truth," Aaron's mom added.

"The question is where do we go from here?" Marcos questioned the both of them. "Well, Mom already told me I can't go back, so I guess that's that. I'm really sorry, Marcos, for losing the fly you just gave me. I know you worked hard on it."

"Can't go back?" Marcos questioned, looking at Alisha.

"Yes," she said sternly. "This whole story is a little too bizarre for me and I don't want Aaron anywhere near this guy or his house."

"Oh, I get that, but what if Aaron and I went together? We wouldn't have any reason to go to this man's house but we could go together and get Aaron's stuff and maybe fish a little while we are there!" he said with a really big smile on his face.

Alisha laughed. "I knew it! You guys… a one-track mind. I don't know, Marcos, let me think about it, OK?"

"Of course, I completely understand. Aaron, don't worry about the fly. I knew this would eventually happen so I made two."

"Awe, man! That's awesome. Thank you, Marcos."

For the rest of the dinner and into the evening Aaron's adventure was all they talked about. Thankfully for Aaron it was mostly laughing and making jokes.

A little over a week had gone by. Aaron's mother never mentioned the incident one time; Aaron was afraid to bring it up, so he didn't. Marcos talked about it with Aaron but he, too, was afraid to ask Alisha about going out there. Aaron was trying to move on, working hard every day getting ready to plant for the next season. He only had a chance to go fishing once since, but not back to 'the spot'. There's no way I'm not going back there again. I'll just have to wait this out a while. It is pretty hard for him, every time he drives past that abandoned road he is tempted to turn onto it. Man I'd love to just get my fishing fly back, he thought. Then one day a strange thing happened. Aaron had just gotten back from the feed store; he pulled the truck past the house to the barn and started to unload supplies. Marcos came over to help out.

As they were pulling goods out of the back of the truck Marcos spoke up. "Did you see the special delivery you got today?"

"Special delivery? What the heck are you talking about?" Aaron asked, thinking Marcos was joking around about something.

"You didn't stop by the house?"

"No, why?"

"When your mom came out of the house a couple of hours ago to go to the horse barn, she practically tripped over your fishing poles and tackle box."

"What? Are you kidding with me?"

"Go check it out for yourself, I'll finish up here."

"Awesome. Thanks!" Aaron ran for the house.

Elvis was sitting on the porch as Aaron got there. "You don't seem too excited to see me: are you okay?" he asked the dog. Elvis sat up so he could be petted. "That's better. So what's with this 'special delivery' I got today?" he joked with Elvis. Elvis barked and ran into the house.

"Mom!" Aaron yelled as he walked into the house. "Mom!"

She came into the front room from the kitchen. "What?" she responded in kind. "Marcos just told me that all of my fishing gear was here. Is it?"

"It is… Kinda strange, a bit of a mystery."

"Why? What are you talking about?"

"Earlier, I came outside and right there on the front porch were your fishing poles and all your gear." She pointed out the front door to the center of the porch. "Everything was there, that is except for one thing."

"Okay, I give in, what one thing?"

"The only thing that appears to be missing is the fishing fly Marcos made you. Like I said… strange."

"Are you messing with me, Mom?" Aaron smiled. "Marcos went and got my gear, didn't he?"

"No, nothing like that. Marcos swears he didn't."

"Where's my gear now?"

"Just over there by the side of the house."

Aaron ran outside and across the porch. Sure enough there were his fishing poles, his tackle box, his backpack and a small styrofoam cooler sitting next to his gear. What's this? Aaron asked himself, knowing he didn't take a cooler with him. Aaron opened up the cooler: it was packed with ice and it had four really good-sized trout packed inside.

"What the heck?" Aaron said out loud.

His mom came from around the corner, "I did say strange, didn't I?"

Aaron went through all his stuff, his mom was right: the only thing missing was his fishing fly from Marcos.

"Wow, this is strange," he told his mom, but he was really excited to have his stuff back. "And you're telling me this wasn't Marcos?"

"I promise you it wasn't Marcos."

"Okay then, who was it?"

"No idea. I came in and out of the house twenty times today. All day there was nothing, then like magic your stuff was there. Honestly, I didn't hear or see a thing."

"I'll be right back!" Aaron yelled to his mom as he ran off toward the barn.

Aaron ran right up to Marcos who was fixing the brakes on the small tractor just outside the barn. "Marcos... tell me the truth... You did this, right?" he asked completely out of breath.

Marcos stood up to address Aaron, he put his boot on the step of the tractor, leaned back into the fender, and took off his hat. "I know that's what you'd think, but honestly I didn't. Trust me, I thought about it more than once but I've just been too busy. Had I, I would have told you anyway."

"Well, who then?" Aaron began to settle down.

"No idea. I am as surprised as you are to see your gear back. No note, nothing."

"Four nice fish, though. That's pretty cool," he smiled.

"I'm telling you neither your mom nor I heard or saw anyone come or go - even Elvis didn't bark. You know it's impossible for a stranger to come onto the property without Elvis sounding the alarm." Aaron shook his head in agreement. "What do you make of the fly missing?" Marcos asked Aaron.

"Yea, that is weird, I mean the whole thing is just crazy. You don't think it was that guy from the woods, do you? I mean how could it be? He doesn't know me or where I live?"

"You know that was your mom's and my first thought: we asked ourselves the same thing. You did give him your name, didn't you?"

"Well… I know I told him my first name: remember how he asked about it?"

"Yea I do. I don't think you mentioned telling him any more than that? But you know what, it's not like there are other Aarons around here: he could have asked anybody about you and where you lived and they would have known."

"Should I be creeped-out right now?" Aaron asked, a little concerned.

"I don't know but I don't think so," Marcos laughed.

"So why do you think he didn't come to the door or look for someone to give my stuff to?"

"I can't answer that except to say… Look, where he lives, how he lives. I don't think he's too interested in being around people but when he came across your gear, he must have decided to try to get it to you. Kind of nice, actually. Besides, we don't even know if it's him, for all we know it might have been someone else, someone that knows you who came across your gear while they were out fishing. Maybe they brought it back when we weren't paying attention and dropped it off. Who knows."

"I guess… Still weird if you ask me." Marcos just smiled and went back to repairing the tractor.

BIG FISH STORY

Over the next few days it was all Aaron could think about or talk about. It bugged the heck out of him. He asked every friend he could think of, but no one knew a thing. Aaron decided not to tell anyone too many details about why his stuff was missing in the first place; he didn't want to lie, so he exaggerated a little and told them he thought he loaded up the gear and didn't realize till he got home that he didn't.

"Dumb, I know," he would admit.

He wasn't so much afraid to tell them about the incident, but more worried about having to tell anyone about his new fishing spot!

One late Saturday afternoon Aaron was coming back from his friend Mike's house when he saw his mom standing out in front of the house.

"What's wrong, Mom?" he asked as he pulled up to her.

She stepped up to the driver's window. "Nothing's wrong, I'm just glad you're home. I thought you were going to be home hours ago."

"I'm sorry, Mike and I got busy…" She cut him off.

"No, honey, it's okay, but you need to hustle up."

"Hustle up for what?"

"Maria and her grandmother are going to be here in like… five minutes," she smiled.

"What?!" he yelped.

"What's going on, Mom?" he asked sternly.

"Nothing's going on. I ran into them today at the market and after we talked a bit I invited them over for dinner, that's all. I thought it would be nice, don't you? I really like Maria," she insisted.

"Awe, Mom, you're crazy... you know that," he jested. "All right, let me go park." The truth is Aaron hadn't seen Maria in weeks and was really happy that she was coming over. After parking the truck he ran upstairs and jumped into the shower. It took him a while to decide on what shirt to wear but he finally had one picked out: suddenly looking good was important to him when he knew Maria was going to be around. When he got downstairs his mom was busy in the kitchen. Through the back window he could see Marcos behind the grill.

"What are we having tonight?" Aaron asked as he sat down at the counter to help cut up some veggies.

"Trout, of course," his mom told him with a big smile on her face.

"Oh yea, laugh it up, Mom, it's not funny."

"Have you told Maria your story yet?"

"No... I haven't. Why?"

"Good. It will give us something to talk about tonight." She laughed harder as she walked toward the back door with the tray of vegetables in her hands.

Maria and her grandmother arrived at the house right on time. Aaron opened the door for them and invited them in. He shook Maria's grandmother's hand, but as Maria walked through the door Aaron was uncertain what to do. He awkwardly started to lean in like he was going to hug her, then stuck out his hand. Maria laughed. She stepped up to him and kissed him on the cheek.

"Hi, Aaron," she smiled.

Aaron, a little embarrassed and red, couldn't come up with more than "Hi". Alisha covered for him right away.

"Thank you so much for coming. It's such a delight to have you in our home."

"Oh Alisha, the pleasure is all ours. We are honored to be here, thank you," Maria's grandmother responded sincerely. "Here, we brought you a little something," she said as she held up a home-made apple pie.

"Wow!" Aaron let out. "I love apple pie."

"We know," Maria coyly grinned.

Aaron looked at her, puzzled. "Your mom told us when we ran into her at the market," she laughed.

Embarrassed again. "Ohhh," Aaron moaned.

"Why don't we go out back? It's such a beautiful night," Alisha suggested.

"I'll put the pie in the kitchen."

"I'll go with him just to be safe," Maria offered.

The adults went out back where Marcos was still hard at work: the food smelled fantastic.

"Are you alright?" Maria questioned Aaron as they got into the kitchen.

"Yea, I mean yes, I'm good. Why?"

"I don't know… You seem a bit off."

"No, I'm okay. At least I think I'm okay," he joked. Maria smiled.

While Aaron and Maria were making small talk in the kitchen, which Aaron got better at as time went on, the others were outside having ice tea and making conversation. "Marcos, it's so good to see you," Maria's grandmother told him. "I can't even remember the last time I saw you."

"It is a pleasure to see you, too, Mrs. Muccino. It has been a long time… too long," he admitted. "How have you been feeling?" Marcos asked her, knowing she had had some health issues recently.

"I'm fine. I thank God every new day that I can be here for my Maria," she said somberly.

"Yes, I understand."

"You know, if you ever need some help, whatever it might be, you know you can call on us?" Alisha told her.

Mrs. Muccino reached out and put her hand over Alisha's. "I know, dear: knowing that gives me some peace."

Aaron and Maria walked out to join the group.

"Any pie left?" Aaron's mom asked. Everyone laughed.

Dinner was fabulous. Everyone really enjoyed it; Marcos knows how to work some magic on the grill. After the food and dishes were all picked up, Alisha came out with the pie; Maria was right behind her carrying some plates and forks.

"Now we're talking," Aaron replied.

As they sat down to enjoy Mrs. Muccino's pie Alisha spoke up.

"So Aaron, why don't you tell Maria and her grandmother about your recent adventure that nearly got you killed," she lovingly threw out there.

"What?" Maria reacted.

"No no, Maria, I'm sorry, I was just exaggerating," Alisha explained. "But not by too much."

"Excellent. Thanks, Mom," Aaron said to her with a stern look. So with great hesitation he began to tell the fishing story. At first he started telling the story just like he would any other story, but at one point when he saw Maria's face and how focused she was on what Aaron was telling, he moved it up a notch. He started to tell the story more like it was a camp story, adding emphasis to key parts and clapping his hands really loud to mimic the shotgun sound, scaring everyone at the table - even Marcos jumped. He was having fun with it. When he was done, his mom looked at him with a certain satisfaction, but Maria looked at him terrified.

"Is everything okay, Maria?" Aaron asked.

"Oh my God, Aaron… You're lucky to be alive!" Maria looked at Alisha. "Did you find out who this man was? Is he a criminal?"

"No, we know nothing really, we actually don't even know his name. No one ever went back, and Aaron hasn't seen him since."

"Well, thank goodness for that," Mrs. Muccino added.

"But wait!" Alisha told the group. "That's not the end of the story."

"There's more?" Maria asked.

"Go ahead, Aaron, finish the story," she egged him on.

"It's nothing, Maria, really."

He proceeded to tell Maria and her grandmother the rest of the story, about the strange return of all of Aaron's gear, minus the fishing fly.

"Oh, and the fish we had for dinner tonight… That was courtesy of the mystery man who left the fish in a cooler with my gear. Strange, right?"

"This is just like one of those mystery stories you hear about," Mrs. Muccino told the group.

"This is the scariest story I've ever heard," Maria admitted nervously. You could see on her face she was frightened by the whole thing.

"Honestly, Maria, it's been weeks, everything is okay. Come on, you want to go for a walk?"

She jumped up with a big smile. "Sure!" she said like she'd been waiting for Aaron to ask her for hours. Aaron confidently took her hand and they walked toward the front of the house and the fields.

"They'll be okay?" Mrs. Muccino asked with some concern in her voice.

"Don't worry about them, they'll be fine," Marcos told her. "Besides, look, Elvis is going with them," he said as they saw Elvis running in the direction of the kids.

"That was a seriously scary story," Maria told Aaron as they started their walk. "I mean… it could have been so bad," she added with a lot of concern.

"I know it sounds scary, and it was kind of scary at the time, but really other than the bobcat almost attacking Elvis, the rest of it was not that big a deal."

"Really? It all sounds pretty scary to me. Do you think you'll ever go back?"

"Back to the fishing spot or back to that house?" Aaron questioned.

"Well, I don't know: both, I guess."

"Truth is," Aaron started, "I think about going back to that fishing spot almost every day. It was as close to the perfect fishing spot as I've ever been," he said enthusiastically. "It was so beautiful and peaceful there; actually, I think you would love it. I'd go back in a minute if my mom would let me," he said as he thought about it.

"What about the guy and the house?"

"I don't know. I don't think so, but then sometimes I think about it, and I think I would like to go back there," he admitted.

"But why?" Maria asked a little surprised at the answer.

"I guess I'd like to know if it was this guy who brought back my gear and brought us the fish. I know it's nuts, really I do. I guess I'm just curious."

"You know what they say about curiosity?" Maria smiled.

"I knew the second I said that, that's what you were going to say," he laughed. "That totally sounds like something my mom would say."

"My grandma, too," Maria laughed. "That's sad, isn't it?" Maria begrudgingly admitted. "I think if you ever decide to go back I would like to go with you," she told Aaron.

He stopped in his tracks and turned to look at her. "You're kidding, right?" he asked, very surprised. Her face didn't give Aaron the sense that she was kidding.

"Sure. If it's as nice as you say, I'd love to go there with you… It'd be fun."

Shocked, Aaron asked, "But didn't you just tell me five minutes ago how scary it all sounded?"

"It still sounds a bit scary, but if you are there I don't have anything to be scared of, right?" she teased.

Aaron laughed. "Right."

They started to walk again. Elvis came running past them at full speed after a rabbit he'd never catch. He tried but he had never actually caught one as far as Aaron knew.

"It doesn't matter anyway, there's no way my mom would ever let me go back."

"I'm not so sure… I bet I could talk her into it," Maria said assuredly.

"Really? I know my mom likes you, but I'm pretty sure she won't flex on this one."

"I guess you'll just have to wait and see," Maria teased. "You do want to go, don't you?"

"Yes… of course. That would be awesome," Aaron reluctantly admitted. "But I'm not holding my breath, okay?"

"Just wait," she smiled coyly.

Not even a day went by. Aaron was headed for the kitchen to get something cold to drink when he heard his mom on the phone. "Okay, sweetie, I'll talk to you later," she said as she hung up the phone.

"Who was that, Mom?"

"That was Maria."

"Maria? Why would you be talking to Maria?"

"Settle down there, big boy. I didn't call her, she called me."

"She called you? About what? Did she ask for me?"

"No, she didn't. She is such a good girl, I really like her."

"Yes, Mom, I know but why did she call?" he asked again.

"Well, at first she called to thank me for having her and her grandmother over for dinner last night. She was telling me what a great time they had. But then we got to talking about a bunch of stuff. She's really smart, you know," his mom was taunting him. "Did she at least ask about me?"

"No, not really. Although we did talk a bit more about your fishing spot."

"Really? What about it?" Aaron's demeanor quickly changed.

"Apparently she really wants to go there with you; she thinks it would be a great way for you two to spend a day together."

"Uh huh." Aaron was waiting for the other shoe to drop.

"I told her I think it's a wonderful idea."

Aaron took a big drink of his lemonade. He was completely unsure of what he wanted to say. If she was joking, Aaron would hear it all day; but if she wasn't, I can't question her decision, it might cause her to rethink about it.

"Yea, Mom, that sounds fun," he said calmly. "I'll talk to her and we'll plan a day. Does that sound okay with you?"

"Sure, but I want you guys back well before dark, and I want to know a day or two in advance so I can make sure I have food to pack for you," she requested.

"Of course, Mom, no big deal. I'll let you know for sure." He finished his lemonade and quickly rushed out of the kitchen. How did she do that?

Three days later the fishing trip was on. Aaron was very excited, excited to finally go back to his fishing spot, but even more excited to spend the day with Maria. His mom packed so much food they could have stayed for a week.

"You're nuts, Mom, you know that, right?" he said, using his favorite tease.

Alisha was surprisingly calm about them going back out there. The only thing she said was to be careful and to be polite to Maria, like she had to tell him. Marcos, on the other hand, acted all fatherly and explained what to do if they had any unexpected visitors. He showed Aaron how a fishing pole could be used as a weapon if needed.

"Thanks, Marcos... Really, I'm sure we will be fine."

"I know, but you have to be prepared."

Aaron got to Maria's house early, around eight am, not nearly as early as if he was going by himself, but he didn't want to push it. Maria was ready; she and her grandmother were sitting in rocking chairs waiting on the front porch. Maria looked so pretty in the morning light: not exactly fishing clothes but that's okay with me, he thought. As Aaron pulled up, Elvis started barking with excitement. Aaron jumped out of the truck, and Maria walked up to the driver's side window to pet Elvis.

"You look ready," Aaron told Maria.

"All ready!" she said excitedly.

"Aaron, my grandmother would like to speak to you for a second before we go, is that okay?"

"Of course," he trotted up the steps of the porch.

"Good morning, Mrs. Muccino, how are you today?"

"I'm fine, son." She waved him closer to her.

Aaron stepped up and she gave him a big unexpected hug. Aaron turned his head and saw Maria smiling at him. He couldn't help but smile: it was a good hug.

Mrs. Muccino stepped back, then reached up and grabbed his face with both of her hands. "Aaron, I know you will take the best care of my granddaughter, of this I have no doubt." Aaron nodded. "Please have fun and catch me a couple of fish," she requested as she pinched his cheeks.

Aaron laughed, not expecting that was what she was going to say. "No problem, Mrs. Muccino, you'll have plenty of fish for dinner tonight!"

Aaron walked back to the truck and opened the door for Maria. "That was nice," he told her.

"She loves you," Maria explained.

Aaron closed the door and looked back at Mrs. Muccino. "We'll see you a little later," he told her as he got into the truck.

Mrs. Muccino stepped off the front porch, close to the truck just as it started pulling away. She took what looked like a cup of water and tossed the water from the cup toward the truck.

"Did you see that?" Aaron asked Maria. She shook her head as she looked into the side mirror of the truck.

"Did she throw water?"

"Yea, she did."

"It's a good thing," she explained. "Very old school, but she was blessing us."

"Oh...really? That works for me." Maria smiled at him. They turned onto the main road and headed for Aaron's fishing spot.

When they got to the little road that led them to the river, Aaron pulled the truck over.

"What's wrong?" Maria asked.

"Oh, nothing, but this road is really bad, so I just want to make sure everything is secure. Can you do me a favor?" he asked Maria as he checked on the gear in the back.

"Sure... what?"

"Would you mind putting Elvis down on the floorboards in front of you? I don't want either one of you to get hurt."

"Get hurt? Uh... sure. This sounds a little scary," she sort of asked as she helped Elvis get down on the floor.

"It's not that bad, but we will get tossed around a lot and Elvis is so light; I just don't want to take any chances," he explained.

"No problem, Elvis and I are good to go," Maria said cheerfully.

Aaron got back into the truck, smiled at Maria, reached out and petted Elvis, then proceeded down the narrow road.

Five minutes later. "Boy, you weren't kidding, were you?!" Maria yelled out as the truck bounced from one side of the road to the other.

"You did call this a road, didn't you?" Maria joked.

"I know it's bad, but it'll be worth it, you'll see. We're getting close now, it's not that much further."

Even though Aaron had slowed down even more than usual to make the ride as smooth as possible, they really did get there pretty quickly. Aaron pulled right up onto the small beach.

"Wow!" was Maria's first word. She opened the door and let out Elvis who went running right for the water. Both Maria and Aaron got out of the truck. "This is fantastic," she said excitedly.

"I'm so glad you think so. I was a tiny bit worried about it," he confessed.

"Are you kidding? It's everything you said."

"The thing is, this isn't even the spot I was talking about," he told her.

"What? I don't understand, what do you mean?" she asked inquisitively.

"This spot is great," she admitted.

"Yea it is. This is the first spot I found when I came out here on my birthday, but then the next day when Elvis and I came out we took a little hike downriver and found 'my spot'," he explained.

"Oh wow."

"But we'll stay around here today," Aaron suggested. "You're not exactly dressed for a hike," he joked.

"Oh, that's nice, make fun of the city girl," Maria joked back.

"I'm just kidding. You look awesome," he said, then turned beet-red.

Maria laughed. "Excuse me, kind sir, but after all that bumping around I'm afraid I must excuse myself to find the ladies´ room," she laughed, then turned to walk away. "Maria, don't go too far... Please take Elvis with you," he strongly suggested. "Elvis! Come on, boy!" Maria called out.

Elvis happily ran to her side to be her escort. Minutes later they were back. Aaron hadn't even gotten a chance to get the poles out and hooked.

"What can I do to help?" Maria asked.

"Well if you don't mind grabbing the food, I'm going to get the rest of our stuff to the beach. I thought we could set up over there," he pointed to a tree that looked like it was about to fall over, it was leaning so bad. But it produced the perfect shade right on the water's edge.

"Perfect," Maria said excitedly. She grabbed the food and started working her way over to the water. "Come on, Elvis," she called out. Aaron picked up the fishing gear, the cooler and the two chairs they had brought and quickly followed.

Together Aaron and Maria spent the day, talking, laughing, eating - oh and fishing. They caught many fish; even Maria managed to haul in a few... with Aaron's help. Elvis spent most of his day swimming, chasing squirrels or sleeping. Aaron and Maria talked and talked. Really for the first time since they'd met it was a chance for them to get to know each other. They both knew they liked each other, something that was now hard to hide, but they both got a great deal out of the time they spent together that day.

Aaron learned so much more about Maria and her family; especially the hard truth about what it was like for Maria when she lost both of her parents at the same time. Maria thought she already knew a lot about Aaron but she, too, learned much more than she expected. She had even more respect for him and an understanding of his commitment to his mom and their farm. She also was moved by the story about how Aaron lost his dad and how close they were. At one point Maria even started to cry: she couldn't help herself.

"It's so sad," she told Aaron.

"Yes… it is. But we've both moved on, right?"

"Yes, at least trying. Thank God for your mother and my grandmother."

Aaron moved across the blanket to be closer to Maria. Maria leaned into Aaron. He held her under his arm for quite a while, at one point Aaron thought about kissing Maria, but he was too afraid. Just as he began to build up the courage to kiss her, Elvis showed up soaking wet and shook the water from his fur all over them, completely changing the mood. They both laughed and chased Elvis all over the beach. It was kind of the perfect way to end what was a perfect day. They packed up all their stuff; Aaron cleaned the fish - this part Maria wanted no part of - and they were soon headed back down the rough road, on to home.

When they got to Maria's house her grandmother was sitting on the front porch. "Have you been here all day, Nana?" Maria asked her.

"No no, I just came out a few minutes ago to enjoy the beautiful day. How was your day? Did you catch any fish?" she asked with a big smile on her face.

"Of course we did!" came a young man's voice from the other side of the truck. Aaron stepped from around the truck, reached into the back, opened the ice chest and pulled out a string with five nice-sized fish on it.

"Here you go, Mrs. Muccino. There are some nice ones on here."

Mrs. Muccino stood up and started clapping. "These are beautiful! Oh but Aaron, we cannot keep all of these," she demanded. "You must take some home to your mother."

Maria spoke up, "Not to worry, Nana, I invited Aaron and his family to come over here for dinner this weekend. I thought maybe you could show them how you prepare fish the Italian way."

"Awe... yes that is a very good idea," she said as she winked at Maria.

"Nana!" Maria turned toward Aaron but thankfully he was not looking.

"Okay, I have to get going, I'm sure my mom will be worrying soon," Aaron told them.

"Oh, Aaron, can't you stay for a bit? You just got here," Mrs. Muccino asked.

"I really shouldn't, Mrs. Muccino, I should go... but I'll see you this weekend, right?"

"Yes," Maria spoke up.

"Okay okay. Well, let me get you something for your drive home," Mrs. Muccino insisted.

"Oh, that's okay, Mrs. Muccino." But before he could finish, Mrs. Muccino was already in the house.

"I think she does love me," Aaron half-joked to Maria.

"Yes she does, I told you. But that's not why she went into the house, you know?"

"Why? What do you mean?"

As he stood there towering over Maria, he suddenly got it. Maria stepped a little closer, looking almost straight up to see Aaron's eyes. Aaron looked down at Maria, he felt a little sick, but before he could think about it a second longer, Maria reached out with her right hand and put it into Aaron's. With her other hand she gently pulled Aaron's face down to her. They kissed. All of a sudden there was this tiny scream coming from the kitchen window.

Aaron jumped back. "Nana!" Maria yelled out.

"What? I didn't see anything... especially that kiss!" You could hear her giggling as she moved away from the window.

"I really do have to go," Aaron explained.

"Tell your grandmother thank you anyway."

"Of course," Maria smiled. Now she felt a little sick. Aaron leaned down and quickly kissed Maria one more time and then headed for his truck.

"Let's go, Elvis!" he yelled out.

Elvis ran from inside the house and jumped in the passenger side of the truck. Maria closed the door and Aaron and Elvis drove off. After they were off the property, Maria turned toward the house. "NANA!" she yelled as she ran through the front door.

BAD NEWS

Aaron, his mom and Marcos did go over to Maria's that weekend for dinner: it was fantastic. Not just because of the food, but also because of the time the two families got to spend together. They all got along so well. It wasn't as if it was official or anything but Aaron and Maria were together, to the delight of both Maria's grandmother and Aaron's mom.

The evening was going great but Alisha was starting to have some concerns. She was watching Mrs. Muccino as the evening progressed and she got the sense that something was wrong. Mrs. Muccino was not herself; she was not as energetic as she usually was and she seemed to be having a hard time moving around. This was a seventy-three-year-old woman who had the strength and energy of a woman half her age. At one point Marcos even had to jump up from his chair to help stabilize her.

"Oh, thank you, Marcos. Just a little light-headed," she explained. Everyone in the room was quiet: they were all looking at Mrs. Muccino.

"Knock it off, you guys, I'm okay!" she insisted, waving her hand in disgust at everyone's reaction.

Alisha was the first one to break the awkward silence. "Isn't it about time for some dessert?" she asked the group.

"That is a great idea, Mrs. B," Maria told her.

"Maria, why don't we let your grandmother relax and you and I can get it?" she hinted.

"Absolutely," Maria replied as she stood up and walked with Alisha into the kitchen. Mrs. Muccino didn't argue like she normally would have: she didn't have the strength.

"Is everything okay?" Alisha asked Maria as they got into the kitchen. "Your grandmother doesn't seem quite right."

"I don't know what's going on, she's been acting this way for the last couple of days. I'm very worried," Maria admitted.

"Have you taken her to see the doctor?"

"That's just it, I've tried several times but she won't let me."

"Why?"

"I'm not sure. Yesterday she was even worse and I begged her, but she just wouldn't," Maria told her. "Then today she was fine all day till just before you guys got here. I thought maybe she was better. Do you think I should have taken her to the hospital?" Maria started to cry.

"Awe, Maria, I'm sure your grandmother will be fine. I'll tell you what, I'm going to stay the night here tonight, if that's okay with you and your grandmother, and tomorrow you and I will make sure she sees the doctor, okay?" she suggested to Maria. Maria practically jumped into Alisha's arms and started to cry some more. "Thank you, thank you. That would be great," Maria told her with her face buried in Alisha's chest.

"Maria, it's no problem: this is what we do for each other, right?"

"Yes, thank you. I'm just so scared for her," Maria whispered.

"I know, honey, but I'll be here and we will get to the bottom of this, okay?"

"Okay," Maria answered.

"So wipe your eyes and let's get back out there before Aaron thinks I'm in here filling your head with a bunch of stuff he would kill me over." Maria laughed.

Mrs. Agnese Maria Muccino was born in 1912 on the family vineyard and winery in Northern Italy where she lived and worked all of her young life, with her mom, dad and two older brothers. It was a very hard life, but a good life. Over the years their vineyard became moderately successful and was actually able to expand even during the war because of the quality of the wine they produced. Agnese was too young to remember when her dad went off in 1915 to fight in World War 1. She remembers when he came back, though: the war had changed him. In 1931 Agnese met Alberto: he was a young ranch hand on a large cattle farm on the other side of the valley.

They met when Agnese was nineteen at a local wine festival where she had won a prize that year for her famous Florentine dessert cookies, a recipe that was passed down to her from her grandmother. Agnese and Alberto had only met one time before when they were barely teens; however, even back then Alberto made a strong impression on Agnese. It wasn't until the festival that they had the chance to get reacquainted. Once they found each other, they proudly held hands the rest of the night. Three months later they were married.

Albert and Agnese moved about an hour away from the family vineyard to a small cattle and vegetable farm they bought with dowry money and some money Alberto had saved. They had their first child, a daughter, a little over a year later. Eighteen months following, they had a son, and then two years later Maria's mother was born. Within months, World War 2 started and everyone knew Italy was going to be caught in the middle of it. Alberto decided it was the time to get out and head to America. He was not going to put his young family through what everyone said was going to be a long and hard war.

Agnese was very upset about leaving Italy and her family, but she was, if nothing else, loyal. Loyal to her husband and to her young family. She loved and trusted her husband more than anything. He sold their farm very quickly, and just days before Italy formally announced its involvement in the war, Alberto and his family were well across the Atlantic with their feet firmly on United States ground. No one knows why, but Alberto moved the family to Tennessee and that's where they stayed. They bought a nice-sized farm and began their new life.

As each of their children graduated from high school they went on to college and ended up living in different cities to advance their careers; Alberto was always a little upset his son never came back home to take over the family business and was often pretty vocal about it. Fortunately, their youngest daughter Gemma and her family lived in Memphis, which was only about two hours away. Agnese and Alberto loved living in Tennessee, and they loved all the people in their community.

When Alberto passed away, Agnese thought there was no way her son or even one of her daughters' families wouldn't come to be with her on the farm, but none did. For Alberto's funeral nearly all of her closest family, including many from Italy, came to Tennessee. Even though it was meant to be a somber occasion it turned out to be a festival, a celebration of Alberto's life. It was great for the family to be together again after so many years. Most stayed for about a week, each trying to talk Mrs. Muccino into coming back to Italy with them. Most of her family from Italy thought that, after Alberto died, Agnese would likely move back, but she never even thought about it.

"That's not what Alberto would want and that's not what I want," she would explain emphatically. "My life is here." She politely declined the offers; she wasn't ready to give up the farm just yet. Plus it was important for her to stay should one of her children or grandchildren need or want her; she didn't want to be on the other side of the world. Agnese was always thankful that Gemma and her family lived close enough to visit once in a while, otherwise Agnese would have seen very little of her family. She loved, loved, loved her grandchildren, and because she rarely got to see them she would write and send gifts to all of them often.

Mrs. Muccino was very grateful that Alisha was staying over, so was Maria. Maria set up the extra bedroom for her and offered her one of her nightgowns to wear to bed. "That's very sweet, Maria, but I think I might have fit into this when I was ten," she said, laughing. Maria embarrassedly laughed along.

"How about this? This is the only other thing I have that might fit you," she said as she handed Alisha a man's tee shirt.

"Yes this will be fine…" Alisha paused. "Why does this look familiar to me?"

"Oh," Maria said shyly. "I got it last summer. I got soaking wet at a party at the lake. Aaron was there, too; he was such a gentleman, he took his shirt off and gave it to me. I never gave it back," she admitted bashfully.

"This is more than perfect. Thank you, Maria."

Maria smiled and walked out of the room. A little later Alisha went into the kitchen to get herself a glass of water before turning in for the night. As she headed back to her room she noticed that Mrs. Muccino's bedroom light was still on.

Alisha lightly knocked on the door, "Yes?" came the response. Alisha slowly opened the door. Mrs. Muccino was not in bed; she was sitting in an armchair on the other side of the room, next to the window.

"Mrs. Muccino, is everything okay? Can I get you something?" she asked in a concerned voice.

"No, honey, I don't need anything; but would it be too much to ask if you wouldn't mind sitting with me a while?"

"Of course." Alisha went over to her room and picked up a small make-up chair, brought it into the room, and placed it right next to Mrs. Muccino.

"Is everything okay?" she asked again.

"Alisha, I have to ask you something that I have no right to ask." Alisha knew this was serious. This is not going to be good.

"Whatever I can do, anything, you know that." Mrs. Muccino smiled and reached out and picked up Alisha's hand.

"I don't need to go to the doctor tomorrow."

"Why? I think it's a good idea. Maria is very worried about you… and frankly so am I," Alisha said, trying to convince her it was the right thing to do.

"No, I'm afraid it doesn't matter."

"Doesn't matter?" she strongly questioned, thinking Mrs. Muccino was just being stubborn.

"Alisha, I have cancer," she blurted out.

"You what?" Alisha gasped, immediately in tears. She reached out and grabbed Mrs. Muccino's other hand, holding them both close to her.

"I've known for quite some time."

"Oh my God, Mrs. Muccino… I am so sorry. I had no idea. There must be something that can be done to help you?" she insisted.

"No dear, I'm afraid not, the doctor's told me there was nothing to be done, that I should live out my life around those I love and create as many memories as possible. That is exactly what I've been trying to do," she said in a strong voice.

"Well…" Alisha started to ask but couldn't.

"How long till I die?" Mrs. Muccino asked the question for her. Alisha nodded. "They can't say for sure, it could be tonight and it could be a year from now, but I can tell… it's getting worse quickly." Alisha collapsed forward into Mrs. Muccino's hands. She started to cry.

"Listen, Alisha," she said as she stroked Alisha's head. "I need your help." Alisha looked up. "Maria doesn't know: she thinks I'm going through something, something that can be fixed. The fact is I've kept it from her for so long, I never had the heart to tell her, especially after everything the poor child has already been through."

"I understand. How can I help?" she asked wiping the tears from her face.

"I have to tell Maria. I'm getting so much worse, I need her to know. I can't have her just find me one day: I would ruin her life forever."

Tears rolled down Mrs. Muccino's face. Alisha was trying not to cry but she couldn't hold it back.

"I can be there, I am happy to be there if you want me," Alisha told her between sobs.

"I wouldn't ask but I know how upset my Maria will be. I need someone strong, someone she cares about to hold her up. This is going to be really hard on her."

"Don't you worry, I'm here. And I'll be here for as long as you need me or whenever you need me," Alisha said strongly.

"You and your family have been such a blessing to us, I will never forget this," Mrs. Muccino said as she slowly got up from her chair. "Now we both need to get some sleep," she insisted. "Will I see you in the morning?"

"Yes, of course. And I'm right across the hall if you need anything."

"Thank you dear, good night."

Alisha went back to her room and sat on the bed. She didn't move for a long time, she just stared at the shadows on the wall. Then it was like the reality hit her all at once and she started to sob. She had to bury her head in a pillow to muffle the sounds.

The next morning before Alisha even got to the kitchen she could smell bacon. I was planning on making breakfast this morning. Maria must have beaten me to it, she thought. As she came around the corner and entered the kitchen she saw Mrs. Muccino standing in front of the stove.

"Mrs. Muccino? What are you doing, let me do that," she insisted.

"Alisha, I'm fine. I feel better today than I have in a while. You can get the plates if you like."

Just then Maria walked in. "You guys are up early. Nana, how are you feeling today?" she asked in an upbeat tone.

"Quite well, dear, thank you. I don't think I'll be needing to go to the doctor's today, but I would like to talk to you about something after breakfast."

"Sure, Nana. Is everything okay?" she asked as she turned to look at Alisha.

"Maria, grab some utensils and let's eat, I'm starving," Alisha said, quickly changing the subject.

After they were all done and the dishes were clean Mrs. Muccino invited Alisha and Maria to sit in the family room to have some coffee.

Maria was starting to get worried: this had never happened before. Usually it was straight off to start the chores. Maybe because Alisha is here? she wondered. They all sat down, Maria next to her grandmother on the couch, and Alisha in a chair nearest Maria. Before Maria could take the first sip of her coffee her grandmother spoke up.

"Maria, there is something very important I need to speak with you about," she started. Maria's nervousness was now justified. "I've asked Alisha to be here to help me explain." Alisha nodded her head in support.

"What is it, Nana?' she asked calmly, but her mind was racing.

"I have to explain to you why I've been sick lately and why I don't need to go to the doctor's. Maria…" She hesitated long enough for Maria to take a deep breath. "I have cancer," she said to her calmly.

"What?!" Maria cried out.

Alisha got up and went to sit down next to her. Maria looked stunned. Her eyes began to tear up and then in a matter of seconds she started crying hysterically. She fell into her grandmother's lap.

"I am so sorry, my angel," Mrs. Muccino said, trying to comfort her. Alisha put her hand on Maria's back and started to stroke it.

Maria sat up: she was panic-stricken. "But we can get you treatment or something like that, right?" she pleaded. "Many people survive after getting sick, don't they?" she turned and looked to Alisha for support.

"Maria, it's just not possible," her grandmother explained.

"What's not possible? Getting treatment or medicine?" Mrs. Muccino looked at Alisha for help.

"Maria, I know this is bad… terrible, I only just learned last night when your grandmother explained the whole thing to me. I'm sorry but your nana and her doctors have done everything possible; there is nothing else that can be done."

Maria was crying so hard she couldn't see. Alisha reached for her hand. "Listen… right now your grandmother needs you and me and those around her to be strong, we need to focus on her. We need to be here for her," she tried to explain.

Maria was literally holding her breath. "This just can't be true!" she screamed. She got up and walked to the window.

Alisha got up and walked over to her. "I know that it doesn't seem possible right now, but you need to understand, you are truly blessed." Maria made a face that no one had ever seen before: she was angry - no, she was pissed!

"How is that possible?" she snapped.

"Maria!" her grandmother snapped back.

"It's okay. Maria, you have every right to be angry, you do, but I want to remind you how lucky you've been, too; having your nana around has made you the person you are today, and you are a great person," she said, trying her best to calm her down.

"Oh my God, Nana! How long?" She ran back to the couch and forced her way into her grandmother's arms, laying her head on her chest.

"I don't know, Maria. I'm afraid it's not long."

Maria was going into shock; she started to hiccup uncontrollably from all the crying. Her grandmother was patting her back, trying to calm her down. Maria was so pale she was sheet-white. At one point Alisha was concerned she was going to pass out, so she ran to the kitchen to get her some ice.

"I have my good days and my not so good days: today I feel good," her grandmother told her with a big smile.

The three of them continued to talk for several hours, during which Maria would randomly break down and start hysterically crying. Alisha felt so bad for both of them. She couldn't always find words, so she would just sit there in support of both of them. The least Alisha could do was make food, hand out drinks, tissues and hold Maria's hand whenever possible. Late that afternoon Alisha drove home, completely exhausted, and went straight upstairs to bed.

FIRST ADVENTURE

Life seemed like it went back to normal for a while, except that Aaron spent much more time at Maria's. The families would get together often. Alisha made sure of it just so she could keep an eye on Mrs. Muccino. Aaron and Maria would go fishing together as often as possible; Maria was becoming quite the fisherwomen. One day while they were at the river, Maria asked Aaron if he ever thought about the guy he ran into earlier that summer.

"Not really, but sometimes I think about my other spot downriver, though," he smiled.

"Why don't we go there sometime?" Maria asked excitedly.

"What... really? Why?" He was very surprised at her question.

"I just think it would be fun. You've talked about it so much, I want to see it."

"Oh man! My mom is rubbing off on you. A month ago you would have never considered it, let alone asked to go," Aaron joked.

"Please? I think we should: can we?" she pleaded. "Let's do it before summer runs out."

"Sure. I guess so. When do you want to go?"

"Tomorrow!" she demanded.

"Tomorrow? Okay... who's going to tell my mom and your grandmother?"

"Actually, I don't think we need to tell them," she said as a matter of fact.

"What? Okay, now you're starting to scare me. What did you do with my Maria?" he smiled.

"I'm serious."

"Really? Okay… I guess I'm game if you are. Elvis, what do you think?" Aaron yelled out to his dog. Elvis barked and ran back into the river. "I guess we're on."

"Great," Maria said excitedly, then she leaned over and kissed Aaron. "Come on, let's go."

"Go? Why go? There's still a ton of daylight," Aaron asked but didn't get an answer.

Back at home eating dinner with his mom, Aaron thought about asking her. What if she says no, he thought. Maria would be so mad at me, and what a chicken I would look like. He convinced himself not to say anything.

"I thought you should know, I had to go over to Maria's house today," Alisha told Aaron.

"Oh really, why?"

"Mrs. Muccino had a bit of a spell and with Maria not being there she got scared."

"Oh man, is she alright?"

"Yes, she is much better now. I think she was more scared than anything."

"This means Maria's not going to be able to go tomorrow," Aaron said, all bummed out.

"Go where?"

"Oh, well we had so much fun today we thought we'd go back again tomorrow. Summer's running out fast, Mom."

"Yes it is," she said supportively. "There's no reason why you and Maria can't hang out tomorrow; Mrs. Muccino was feeling much better when I left and I assure you she's not going to say anything about today to Maria. If she did Maria would never leave the house, and I promise you Mrs. Muccino would not let that happen. So don't worry about tomorrow or Mrs. Muccino, everything will be fine, go and have fun," she insisted.

"That's excellent. Thanks, Mom," Aaron said excitedly.

"Do me a favor right now, though, will you?"

"Sure, Mom, what?"

"Call Maria and check in. I just want to make sure everything is okay with her grandmother."

"No problem, Mom, I'll go do it right now."

Aaron showed up earlier than usual the next morning at Maria's. He wanted to make sure they had extra time because of the hike they would have to take to get to his spot. Maria was waiting out by the road with all of her things.

"Why are you out here?"

"Nana's still asleep, I didn't want to wake her."

"Is she okay?"

"Yes, she's doing really well," Maria said as she jumped into the truck.

"Hi, Elvis," Maria said as she pushed him to the middle of the seat. "I'm excited."

"Yea me, too. I hope you're going to like it. I see you're dressed for the occasion this time," he laughed.

"I am." Maria was wearing some overalls, likely her grandfathers, with the legs rolled up what looked like twenty times. She had on tennis shoes, a tight tee shirt and a baseball cap. To Aaron she looked fantastic, as cute as she could be. They pulled up to the river where they had always gone, and jumped out of the truck. It was very cool out, so Maria put on her sweatshirt.

"Are you ready?" Aaron asked.

"I'm ready," she said gleefully. "Which way?"

"This way," Aaron pointed as he started to walk south along the shore of the river. They hiked for a bit: Maria showed no signs of needing to stop but Aaron asked anyway.

"Do you want to take a break?"

"I'm doing great. How much further do you think?"

"Maybe thirty minutes or so… I think we should stop."

"No really, I'm fine. I'm excited to get there!"

"Okay then, let's keep going." Aaron was very excited that Maria was being such a good sport. He was especially excited to show her his 'spot'.

It actually only took about twenty minutes when they finally came to the clearing with the small crescent beach Aaron had spoken of. Maria knew immediately this was the spot. She stopped on the grass in front of the beach and put down her things.

"Aaron, this is so beautiful. You were right, this is a special place." She ran up to Aaron, and hugged and kissed him.

"Thank you. I knew you'd like it." Aaron was so happy to be back, and with Maria, it couldn't have been any better for him. Aaron started putting together the fishing poles and getting them ready, while Maria spread out the blanket they brought and unpacked the food and things from her backpack.

"I could live here," Maria declared.

Aaron laughed. "I've actually had dreams about this place. It's so peaceful and relaxing."

"I can see that," Maria said as she sat down on the blanket to take off her shoes. She ran up to Elvis who was swimming in the water. "Oooh, the water is pretty cold!" Elvis of course loved it. Maria threw a stick a few times for Elvis to chase into the water but then was called by Aaron.

"You want to give it a go?" he said, holding up the fishing poles.

"That's why we're here, isn't it?" she jested. Aaron handed her one of the poles and together they climbed up on one of the boulders at the water's edge. Aaron got Maria positioned on the boulder, then she cast out like an old pro.

"Impressive… very impressive."

"Yes yes, thank you. I've been taught by masters; if you'd like a lesson just contact my people and I'm sure they can set something up for you." She tilted her head coyly and smiled. Aaron burst out laughing.

This was one of the things Aaron liked most about Maria: she was always so fun and she could make Aaron laugh with very little effort.

"I think you're all set," he chuckled. "I'm going to move just over there on the beach and stay out of the master's way!" He barely got his first cast off when Maria screamed.

"I've got one!" Aaron put down his pole and ran to Maria.

"Remember what I taught you, let him have a little line first," he coached. She was laughing and screaming, especially when the fish really started to pull.

"This is a strong fish," she told Aaron. "Wow, he's strong!" Her face was beaming with excitement.

Aaron was mesmerized; he couldn't take his eyes off of her. She asked Aaron a question but he didn't answer: she turned to look at him, and he was just staring.

"Aaron!" He snapped out of it. "Are you going to help me?" she laughed. The fish was at the surface of the water splashing and fighting.

"Wow that is a big one!" He reached down to the water s edge with the hand net. "Keep it steady, Maria." He scooped in the fish. He handed the net to Maria: she held it up high to look at the fish but it was so heavy. "Here, let me get that for you." Aaron reached into the net and grabbed the fish by its gills. "This is a nice one."

"It's beautiful!" she said excitedly. "How big do you think it is?"

"Just a guess but I'd say twenty-four inches, and I don't know… at least seven or maybe eight pounds."

"Is that good?"

"Good? I'll say. You won't believe me, but I think in all my fishing I've maybe caught two or three fish this big."

"Really?" Nah… you're just messing with me."

"No really, if you want to keep it, we can measure it at home, then I'll know for sure."

"Keep it? Of course I'm keeping it," she said proudly. "I didn't do all that work to throw it back!" *The city girl has left the building!* Aaron thought to himself.

"I get it, no problem. Come on, let's get you set up again, maybe you do the fishing and I'll just relax and watch," he joked.

They had a very successful morning. It got to the point where they could be very picky about the fish they decided to keep; the rest they released. Aaron put the fish they were keeping on a line in the water; Elvis was fascinated by all the splashing, but knew not to touch. As the day went on it warmed up quite a bit, to the point of being hot, even near the river. Maria would step into the water every now and again to cool down. Elvis helped out by clearing his coat of water whenever he was near Maria. She didn't mind. They decided to take a break and sit down to eat something.

"Aaron, I am having such a great time!"

"You sound surprised."

"No, not at all. You and I always have a good time together, no matter what we're doing, but today is special, really special," she said with a big smile.

They ate, talked and relaxed, even Elvis finally took a break and fell asleep next to them.

"This food is awesome, did your grandmother make it?" Aaron asked.

"No, not really. I made most of it."

Aaron was a little surprised and was about to step in it when he caught himself. It was a pasta dish of some kind, full of vegetables and chicken, and a lot of things Aaron didn't recognize.

"Fantastic, really," he told her.

"Thank you. It's a very old family recipe. My grandmother makes it all the time when we go on picnics like this one." Aaron lay down and put his arms behind his head.

"This is the best part."

"What is?" she asked.

"Lie down, you'll see." Maria lay down right next to Aaron and put her arms behind her head, too.

"Oh, wow. I see what you mean, this is so beautiful. It's like looking through a scope."

"It relaxes me like nothing else," Aaron admitted. "Watching the clouds blow by... the sound of the wind as it goes throughout he trees." He paused. "A little corny, huh?" He turned and smiled at her.

"Corny? No, not at all, it's fantastic."

"What do you think: should we take a little walk, go and adventure some?" Aaron asked. Just as he asked the question he suddenly remembered the incident. Something he'd done a pretty good job of putting out of his head.

"Ahh, never mind, let's just stay here and relax."

"Did you forget about the last time you ventured out from here?" Maria asked.

"Yea, I kind of did."

"I'm up for it," she said excitedly as she sat up.

"Up for what?" he asked, afraid of the answer.

"Let's go check it out, I want to see this guy's house!" Maria stood up and grabbed her backpack.

"You're kidding, right? You do remember what happened the last time, don't you?"

"Of course. But we have Elvis our protector, he'll watch out for us," she joked. "Are you okay?" Aaron asked her in a serious tone.

"Okay. Why, what do you mean?" she snapped back.

This was a first: Aaron had never heard Maria snap at anyone or anything before. Maybe something is wrong?

"Maria, I'm not so sure this is a good idea."

"You love me, don't you?" Aaron jumped straight to his feet. "Well? Do you?" she insisted on an answer.

"Yes. Yes, I do, but..." Aaron was at a loss.

"No buts, I love you, too, and I am sure you would not let anything happen to me," she announced.

"Of course not, but I don't see..." Maria held up her hand to interrupt him. Then she walked up and stood right in front of Aaron, stretching her neck to look up at him. "What?" he asked.

She reached up around his head and pulled him to her, then she kissed him - a long, hard, passionate kiss.

"I know you think every now and then that I've been acting differently, maybe even crazy... at least for me. The truth is, my nana is dying and there's nothing I can do about it." Her eyes welled up. "But what I can do is live my life. That's what Nana would want and that's what I'm going to do!"

"Okay then." There was no way Aaron was going to argue with that logic. He reached down for his own backpack. "Let's go!"

Elvis quickly took the lead. "Elvis! Don't wander off too far... Remember what happened last time!" he yelled out, more for Maria's sake than Elvis's. They hiked for a bit, stopping to look around and take in the beauty.

"Boy it's really thick in here, isn't it?" Maria asked.

"Yea, and it will get even thicker in a minute: you sure you want to keep going?"

"Yes, this is great," she said, although that was not the look on her face. It did get thicker and Aaron was about to force them to turn around when they came to a dirt road cut right through the trees.

"I remember this! This is the road that led to the house," he said excitedly.

"This is unexpected," she told him.

"I know, it doesn't make sense," he agreed.

"I guess I forgot about this detail when I was telling my story. But this will lead us to the house, I remember that now."

"Great, let's go." Maria started marching down the road in the direction Elvis was already headed in. Aaron quickly followed. They didn't have to go far when the forest around them started to clear. There was a small meadow, then an opening in the trees at the edge of the meadow. There sat this little house. From the front, the house looked small and worn: it reminded Aaron of a fishing cabin.

"Wow, this is really amazing," Maria said as they approached the house.

"It's not too impressive from the outside but it's something on the inside. At least that's what I think I remember," he smiled.

Elvis didn't wait, he ran right to the front door. "Elvis!" Aaron called out, trying not to yell. "Elvis! Get back here!" he demanded.

"Why don't we see if anyone is at home?" Maria suggested.

"What? I thought you just wanted to see it?"

"Well, we're here, let's see." Maria started to walk toward the front of the house.

"Maria!" Aaron called out. "I don't think this is a good idea." Awe, man, he thought to himself, now I have to go. Aaron was making his way to the house when Maria went briskly up the front steps, walked right to the front door and began to knock. "Maria!" Aaron whispered as loud as he could.

"Whaaaat?" she asked, whispering back, with a big smile on her face.

"This is not exactly what we talked about. Why are we bothering this man?"

"I thought we should thank him: it is the right thing to do," she stated as a matter of fact.

"What are you talking about now?" Aaron was getting a little frustrated, and frankly nervous. It seemed no one was home: no one came to the door and there were no sounds. Aaron was relived.

"Oh well, I guess no one is home," Maria deduced.

"Thank goodness." They turned and started to walk down the front steps. Aaron turned back toward the house to call Elvis but he wasn't there.

"Maria, where's Elvis?"

"I don't know... Wasn't he on the front porch with us?"

"That's what I thought, too... Elvis!" Aaron called out: no response.

"Elvis!" Maria called out: no response.

"We need to look around," Aaron suggested.

"Okay," Maria agreed.

They walked to one side of the house, called out and looked as far as they could, but there was no sign of Elvis. They went to the other side of the house: it faced the meadow and it had only a handful of trees. The dirt road ran past this side of the house and continued for some distance. They walked toward the back of the house, quietly calling out Elvis. As they almost reached the back of the house they finally heard Elvis bark.

"Oh thank God," Aaron said to Maria. "Man, I don't know what happens to Elvis when we get out here. He goes a little nuts... Oh, but then so do..." Aaron received a slap on his back.

As they came around the back they could tell the house was much larger than it looked from the front. It was an odd shape, something like a backwards 'L'. The back, or what they now determined was really the side of the house, was really nice, much nicer than it looked from the front. And certainly nicer than anything you'd expect to see out here. It had a small grassy area, a big patio which was almost completely shaded in by perfectly placed trees, and it had a big barbecue and bar. There was fire-pit, a few chairs, a lounger and a hammock hanging between two of the trees closest to the house.

"Wow! Check this out!" Aaron exclaimed.

"This is amazing," Maria agreed. Elvis came running up to them, chewing on something.

"What have you got this time, Elvis?" he laughed. Aaron bent down to open Elvis's mouth. "It's a rib bone," Aaron told Maria.

"Huh. Must be a leftover from a recent barbeque," she suggested.

"Here, boy, you can keep it." He put the bone back in Elvis's mouth. Elvis ran over to the patio, sat in the shade and continued gnawing on the bone.

"What's that over there?" Maria asked, pointing to the other end of the patio opposite the bar and grill.

"I think it's one of those hot tubs," he said.

"Really?" Maria said excitedly. "Let's check it out." Before Aaron could say a word, they were on the back patio walking to the hot tub.

Maria lifted one corner of the cover that was on it. "Holy smoke! It's really hot!"

"Hot?" Aaron put his hand into the water. "Wow, it is hot. This guy must use it quite a bit to keep it hot all the time." Aaron started to get nervous again. "Don't you think we should get going? It's starting to get late and we have a fair hike to get back to the truck."

"Unless you want to jump into the hot tub?" Maria smiled. Aaron knew this time she was teasing him. "That sounds fun: I've never been in one, but maybe next time," he teased back. They both laughed.

HERE COMES JOHNNY!

Just as they turned to start the hike back to the truck, a loud voice came from inside the house, startling both of them.

"Whoever is out there, you need to leave now!" the man's voice bellowed, followed by three or four bad coughs.

Aaron stepped in front of Maria. "We're sorry, mister, we…"

"I said, get off my property, you are trespassing!" he yelled and then came the sound of a shotgun being ratcheted and two more hard coughs.

"Oh crap! Let's go, Maria!" Aaron reached for her hand.

Maria stepped closer to the house. "Maria!"

"Excuse me, mister," she started, "we only came by to thank you," she said in a firm but polite voice.

"Thank me? Thank me for what?" the man questioned her through the back door.

"I'm here with Aaron."

"Hi," Aaron said with a ripple in his voice.

"I don't know any Aaron!" the man yelled loudly and again was followed by several deep coughs.

"He was here a while back and you saved his dog," she explained.

"Boy, didn't I tell you not to come back here?" he said loudly and sternly.

"I'm sorry, sir, I don't remember much from that day."

The man started to cough and cough and cough. At one point you could tell he was struggling to catch his breath.

Maria stepped right up to the door. "Mister, are you alright?"

No answer.

"Mister?" she asked again.

Aaron stood right next to Maria. "Mister, are you okay?" he asked loudly with his face as close to the door as possible.

"Aaron, I think something is wrong with him," she said, very concerned. Aaron reached for the doorknob. He turned it slowly, and started to open the door.

"Maria, step back," he commanded.

Aaron wanted to make sure if this guy took a shot, Maria would be well out of the way. He was surprised the door was unlocked; he pushed it open a little more. Now he could see in: there sitting on the floor of the kitchen was this man resting his shotgun in his lap leaning up against a refrigerator.

"Mister?" Aaron spoke softly. "Are you okay?"

Maria pushed the door all the way open and stepped in. The man looked at Aaron, then Maria, but didn't say anything. When he opened his mouth to speak, he started to cough again, violently.

Maria stepped past Aaron. "Mister, let me help you," she insisted. The man looked at her but still didn't say anything. "First, let's get rid of that," she gently demanded as she signaled to Aaron to pick up the shotgun. "And now let's try to get you up."

Aaron set the shotgun down on the counter and stepped to one side of the man, Maria the other. Together they got him to his feet and helped him to one of the chairs at the kitchen table. The man was very weak, and he practically fell into the chair; Aaron had to hold him for a few seconds to keep him from falling off. The man lifted his head, looked at Maria and smiled.

He looked at Aaron and held up one finger pointing at him and in a very low scratchy voice he said, "I remember you… Where's Elvis?" What an odd question, Aaron thought to himself.

"He's just outside, mister."

The cough wasn't the only thing that was bad, this guy looked like he was really sick. He had no color in his face, his clothes and hair were all disheveled, and it looked like he hadn't slept in a while.

"Don't you have someone here to help you, mister?" Maria asked. "Or maybe there is someone we can contact for you?"

"I think maybe we should take you to the hospital, don't you, Maria?" Aaron suggested. Maria was agreeing but before she could respond a loud "NO!" came from the man as he pounded his fist on the table, startling both of them.

"Okay... No problem," Aaron held up his hands as he was responding to the man.

"Mister, at least let me make you something to eat, it looks like you haven't had a decent meal in a while," Maria told him as she observed all the empty boxes of macaroni and cheese and cereal lying around. Surprisingly he nodded his head yes.

Maria took over from there. "Aaron, please get him some water and set the table for him; then go to his bathroom and bring me all of his medications."

"NO!" the man demanded again.

Maria looked at the man, expressing her frustration. "Okay then..." Maria looked at Aaron, Aaron threw up his arms in a I don't get it kind of way, and Maria smiled. "Aaron, then maybe you could just straighten up in here a bit, and take out this trash, would you?" she sort of asked.

While Aaron was gathering up all the trash, Maria started poking around the refrigerator and the cupboards to figure out what she was going to make. She was very surprised to see how well the shelves were stocked, better than at her home, that was for sure. In the refrigerator she found so much meat; there were steaks, ribs, ground beef, chicken, and a lot of fish. There was a ton of vegetables and fruit. She wanted to ask but she resisted saying anything.

"This will definitely work," she announced happily. She started to go to work. Aaron came back in the house with Elvis behind him and asked Maria if he could help. "Of course you can. Grab those carrots and celery and start cutting," she smiled.

"No problem," Aaron laughed as he looked over at the man. Elvis was sitting right next to him with his head on the man's lap. The guy seemed to enjoy the attention from Elvis as he stroked the dog's head.

"I'm sorry, mister, I can take him out if you'd like?" The guy didn't acknowledge Aaron's question and kept petting the dog. "Why don't you have a dog of your own? Especially being out here, a dog would probably be helpful."

After taking a sip of the hot tea Maria prepared for him, the man answered slowly, "I had two dogs, actually."

"Oh. Where are they now?"

"You remember that big bobcat…?"

Maria stopped what she was doing and turned to face the man. "Oh my gosh… that's terrible."

Aaron was just as shocked. "I'm so sorry, I had no idea. I'm even more grateful now for what you did for Elvis." The man was starting to get a little color back in his face and the coughing settled down some.

"Okay, I think that's enough with the mister thing," he half-smiled. "My name is…" He paused for a few seconds. "Johnny," he proclaimed. "Yes, please call me Johnny."

"Okay, Johnny, here's some more tea and some hot broth. This should help with your cough." She smiled at him.

"Thank you."

While Maria was working her magic in the kitchen - it already started to smell really good - Aaron sat down at the table across from Johnny and poured himself a glass of water. "I know it's not my place to ask, but why are you way out here, all by yourself?"

Aaron could really see Johnny now, compared to the first time they met. It was very hard to tell how old he might be: in some ways he looked like he might be in his seventies, but he could have just as easily been in his fifties. His skin was pretty smooth, and he had surprisingly few wrinkles. His eyes looked tired, brown with dark brown eyebrows. His hair, though, was so gray it was nearly white, and long, down to his shoulders. He wore a thick gray mustache and goatee. He had a pretty good-sized scar across one of his cheeks. Aaron wanted to ask but didn't. He was as tall as Aaron had originally thought, but he didn't look as heavy.

"You're right," Johnny replied. "It's not your place," he told him, looking Aaron straight in the eyes.

Maria stepped over. "How's the broth, Johnny?" she asked in an attempt to deflect. "It's excellent. I wouldn't mind some more," he asked, half-smiling.

"Of course, your food is almost ready, too." She nudged Aaron on her way back to the stove.

"I apologize, Johnny, I was just curious."

"That's alright, kid, no harm. So… this is Elvis, and you're Aaron," he remembered. Aaron and Maria both were surprised. "Where's Presley?" he chuckled, almost spitting up some broth.

Maria was walking back to the table. "What's so funny?" she asked as she put a plate of food down in front of Johnny.

"Man, this looks really good," Johnny told her. "This one's a keeper." He pointed at Maria as he spoke to Aaron.

Aaron swallowed and smiled. Maria put together a plate of fried chicken, some steamed vegetables and some rice. It looked so good Aaron was going to ask for some but didn't want to get smacked by Maria again. Johnny started to eat, slowly at first then he really began to dig in.

"Funny story, Johnny…" Aaron started to answer Johnny's question. "There were actually two Presleys."

"You're kidding. What were they, cats or something?" he chuckled again.

"No… actually they were goldfish I won at the fair when I was a kid, but they only lived for a couple of weeks."

Johnny laughed so hard he almost fell out of his chair. "Wow, that's pretty bad," he chuckled after he got his composure back.

"Okay, I'm completely lost," Maria jumped in. "What the heck are you guys talking about?" she demanded with a smile.

She was surprised at how quickly Aaron and Johnny made this strange connection. Maybe it's a guy thing, she thought. "Well, the last time I was here as I was kind of coming out of it, Johnny and I were talking. He asked what Elvis's name was and when I told him, he put that together with my name," Aaron explained.

Johnny put his fist over his mouth and chuckled with a mouth full of food. "That's right," he tried to say.

"What's right? I still don't understand," Maria said, a little frustrated.

"How long have you lived in Tennessee again?" Aaron jokingly asked Maria. "Why?" Maria didn't think it was funny.

"I'm just kidding with you. This is Elvis country, you know… Elvis Presley," he told her a little too sarcastically.

"I know who Elvis Presley is," she said, feeling insulted.

"That's who we're talking about. You know how big a fan my mom is, so when she first gave me the puppy I named him Elvis for her."

"Oh, I didn't know that, that's very sweet." Aaron could tell she was still confused.

"I'm also named after Elvis Presley… well sort of," he further explained. "His middle name was Aaron." Johnny smiled.

"Your kiddin', right?" she looked at Johnny.

"I'm afraid it's true," Johnny told her, trying hard not to laugh.

"Wow, I knew your mom was a big fan…"

"And my dad," Aaron added.

"Yes, and your dad, but wow. I'm not exactly sure what to say." She paused to think about it. "But you know what? I love your mom and Aaron is a great name. I think it suits you perfectly."

"See… I told you she's a keeper," Johnny smiled at Aaron while pointing at Maria.

Johnny was doing much better: he was sitting all the way up, his eyes were clear, and he could talk without coughing every other word. "Have you ever seen Elvis in concert, kid?" Johnny asked Aaron.

"No… I wish. He died before I had a chance. I've been to Graceland, though."

"He's a bit of a fanatic, too," Maria told Johnny.

"Really, how do you mean?" Johnny asked.

"Awe, I've always been a fan, you know, a little hard not to when Elvis is in my house every day, all day." Aaron was trying his best to play it down.

"He's not giving you the whole story, Johnny," Maria smiled sheepishly.

"Maria… knock it off… Besides, shouldn't we get going?"

Maria didn't miss a beat. "Aaron is like one of the best Elvis impersonators around," she gleamed.

"Really," Johnny chuckled again. He turned to Aaron. Aaron was immediately embarrassed.

"She's just messing around. I play a little and sing a little… mostly for family and a few friends now and then. Just for fun," he overemphasized.

Johnny was intrigued. "I don't normally admit this, but I've been an Elvis fan most of my life, too."

"Really?" Aaron was surprised. "No disrespect, but I wouldn't have taken you for an Elvis fan."

"Why... what does an Elvis fan look like?" Maria asked Aaron sharply.

"It's okay, I get it," Johnny said to Maria. "So how about one song before you get going there, Aaron?"

Elvis barked. They all laughed.

Johnny directed Maria to go into the family room and get his guitar. "I play a little, too," Johnny explained. Maria jumped up to go retrieve it.

"This should be interesting," Johnny said to Aaron.

"Yea, interesting."

"Here you go!" Maria said excitedly as she handed Aaron the guitar.

"Oh wow, I remember this… what a beautiful guitar. Are you sure you don't mind me playing it?"

"I barely touch the thing anymore: someone should get some use out of it. Play away," he directed Aaron.

At first Aaron didn't think he wanted to do it, but after getting this beautiful guitar in his hands you'd have had a hard time taking it away.

"Any favorites?" Aaron asked.

"Play whatever you want," Johnny suggested. "Unless the lady has a favorite?"

"No Aaron, please play whatever you like."

"Okay... one song."

He pushed himself back away from the table and lowered the guitar to his lap; he held his fingers across the neck of the guitar and strummed it one time, it made a beautiful rich sound. He looked at Johnny and smiled. Aaron picked a song he thought Maria might like, and it was one of his all-time favorites. The second he played the first chord Aaron was fully committed: he was disengaged from his world into the world of his music.

"Oh won't you let me be your teddy bear..."

Johnny sat there silent, no distinguishable look on his face: he just listened. Maria, on the other hand, was a girl filled with emotion and disbelief. She could not believe how good Aaron really was: to have him play for her, five feet away, she was mesmerized. "Oh won't you let me be, your teddy bearrrr..." He lowered his head, he was done.

Maria sat up straight and started clapping frantically; Johnny also sat up straight, smiled then leaned into Aaron.

"Aaron," he started to say, "now that was something special."

"Oh, thanks, Johnny, I appreciate it. I don't know about 'special' but I do love to sing his songs."

"That was amazing, Aaron, really," Maria said excitedly. "I've never heard you sing that song before... It was just great." Aaron laughed, too shy to say anything but he loved how excited Maria got. I guess I should have broken out the guitar a long time ago, he told himself.

"Listen, kid, I'm not messing with you, you've got some talent," Johnny told him. "I'm surprised you don't perform or a least do some of these Elvis impersonation contests." He looked at the both of them, Maria nodding her head in agreement the whole time.

"Awe, you guys. I truly appreciate it, but that's just not me. It's just for fun." Aaron started to blush. "We really need to go, Johnny."

"You're right, Aaron," Maria agreed and stood up.

"Well, okay," Johnny said as he slapped his hand down on the table. "It has been a pleasure having you guys here, unexpected and… well, nice." He looked at Maria. "I believe you may have saved my life today," he told her solemnly.

Maria smiled and put her hand on his shoulder. "Just being neighborly… you know. My chicken broth does work wonders, though," she laughed.

"She's a keeper!" he told Aaron again, shaking his finger at him. "Don't let her go."

"Okay, Johnny," Aaron politely agreed.

Maria was all smiles. They slowly walked together to the front door. "Come on, Elvis!" Aaron called out. Johnny laughed. "What?" Aaron asked.

"I'll never get used to that," he told them as he opened the front door. "Hey, listen, you guys… I really did enjoy your surprise visit, and you can come back any time you like. I just need you to do me one favor." They both nodded. "If you see a red truck parked out front here - it's usually only here on Mondays and Thursdays - please don't stop in," he requested with no further explanation.

"Uh… Sure, Johnny, whatever you like," Aaron told him. "Maybe next week I'll come by and we can go fishing, if you'd like?"

"Like? Oh man, that would be really cool," he answered with his first real smile. "I'll look forward to that then," he told the two of them as they got to the bottom of the porch. Aaron, Maria and Elvis waved goodbye and then disappeared into the woods.

"That was so fun!" Maria said excitedly to Aaron after they were a fair distance away from the house.

"I'm glad you had fun… I'm a little confused and surprised, but I enjoyed it, too," he admitted. "It was a little strange, though, right?"

"Well, I guess so. If you mean in there's a guy living in the middle of the woods, by himself, with no phone, no family and no car, well yea, then I'd say it was a little strange." They both began to laugh.

All the way back to the truck they talked about their strange encounter with Johnny. At one point Aaron asked Maria, "Did he look familiar to you at all?"

"No... not even a little, why?"

"I dunno, I just felt like I've seen him before."

"Maybe around town or something like that?" she suggested.

"That's probably it," Aaron agreed.

"Although it doesn't look like he gets around much," Maria added.

"Yea, you're right. I don't know, it's probably just me."

"What do you suppose the red truck thing is all about?" Maria asked.

"Yea, I've been thinking about that, too. I figured it must be someone that brings him food and things... I guess. Why, what do you think it is?"

"I think you're probably right."

"Strange that he doesn't want us to come on those days; he must not want us to meet whoever it is," Aaron thought.

"Or the opposite," Maria suggested.

"Why do you think he never leaves his house?" Aaron questioned.

"Maybe he's too sick or something like that... I mean when we first saw him he didn't look good at all; at first I thought we were going to have to figure out a way to get him to the hospital!"

"I know! Me, too!" Aaron agreed. "He snapped back pretty fast, though."

"Well yea, it's my broth," she laughed.

"Oh that's right... the broth. Maybe you should bottle that stuff and we can sell it for a lot of money!"

They got to the truck, put their gear in the back and got in. Maria leaned over and gave Aaron a long kiss. "Thank you."

"Thank you for what?"

"The song... That was for me, wasn't it?"

Aaron got as red as anything instantly. "What'd you think I'd sing a song like that for Johnny?" They both laughed and Elvis barked. Then they headed down the now very familiar dirt road toward home.

ELVIS EXPERT

It was funny: neither Aaron nor Maria said anything about Johnny or their visit to their respective families. They both talked about the great day they had, though.

That first night Aaron could barely sleep. He couldn't stop thinking about Maria, the way she could take control and make everything easy. She really stepped up today, Aaron thought. Johnny's right, she is a keeper. Aaron also couldn't get his mind off of Johnny. What's up with this guy? he would keep asking himself. So strange. I know he's weird, or at the very least different... but there's something about him... He fell asleep without getting any answers. The next morning he called Maria right away after his morning chores.

"What did you tell your grandmother?"

"I told her what a great day I had, you and I hanging out and fishing. She's surprised how much I like fishing now."

"But what about Johnny, what did you say about him?" he asked.

"I... well... Actually I didn't bring Johnny up," she confessed.

"Really? Me neither. How funny is that?"

"I don't know about funny, I guess I didn't feel it was necessary. I didn't want to take a chance of upsetting Nana."

"Right, that makes sense. Me, too. I don't think my mom would have understood anyway."

"Are you going to go back out there like you said?" she asked.

"Yea, I think so. Why?"

"I'd like to go, too, but you know I can't this week."

"Right... the kids. That's way more important, I can wait to go back when you can, if you want?"

"Nah, I mean, it's up to you."

"School's just around the corner, you know... It's really more about the fishing," he joked.

She laughed. "I know. You should go. You and I can go another time, maybe next week?"

"That would be perfect," Aaron admitted. "Only this time, could you pack some of your chicken broth?"

"Funny. Really funny."

"You know that's the last week of summer... we should do something special... don't you think?" he asked coyly.

"I do. What did you have in mind?"

"Well... I've been thinking about it. I want to do something really special, something we'll remember..."

"Trust me, this summer has already been something amazing, a summer I'll never forget."

"Yeah... me, too. But I think you'll like this idea," he said sounding a little mysterious.

"Okay... sounds fun!"

"Great. A week from Saturday, okay?"

"Perfect," she replied. "What do I need to bring?"

"Not a thing, just you."

With Maria's blessing Aaron planned to go out fishing as early as possible the next day. This time he planned to go to Johnny's first to see if he wanted to come.

"You've really been milking the last of your summer, haven't you?" his mom asked as Aaron sat in the kitchen eating some breakfast.

"Yes, I have... But I've been getting all of my chores done, Mom, I haven't skipped anything," he said defensively.

"No no, you misunderstand. I'm not worried about your chores, I'm happy for you. This has been one of the busiest summers I can ever remember you having, I think it's great."

"Oh, sorry, Mom, I'm just a little jumpy."

"Jumpy? Why? Is everything okay between you and Maria?"

"Oh yea, everything's great. Actually can't be better," he told her. "You know... I've never had a girlfriend before, so this is going to be really strange when we get back to school," he admitted.

"Heck no. You'll be fine. Just go with the flow and be yourself. Trust me, Maria will know what to do if needed."

"Yea, I think you're right," he laughed. "By the way, Mom, how is Mrs. Muccino? Maria never really says much."

"Uh, well, truthfully she has good days, bad days, and then really bad days. Unfortunately there have been many more bad days and really bad days lately."

"That's so sad," Aaron said.

"It's scary is what it is. I'm not sure how much longer she's going to be with us and I'm very worried about Maria."

"I wonder why Maria hasn't said anything?"

"She might be uncomfortable or doesn't want to upset you. Who knows, but you know Maria she has her reasons. I do know that someone from the hospital comes and visits Mrs. Muccino twice a week or so, just to make sure everything's alright," she explained.

"Really? I didn't know that."

"Maybe that's why she hasn't said anything, maybe she doesn't want you to know?" his mom suggested.

"I guess." Aaron felt strange about the whole thing. "Mom... what will happen to Maria if her grandmother dies?" he asked in a very concerned voice.

"That's what I'm talking about... I don't know. Her closest family is in Memphis, otherwise I don't really know. I feel like I need to talk to Mrs. Muccino and find out what arrangements she might have. This way I'll know, and then I can help if necessary," she explained.

"That's a good idea, Mom," he agreed. "I can't even imagine if Maria had to ever move: man, that would suck." For Aaron this was the first time he thought about how real that possibility was.

"I understand, we'll get through this, all of us," his mom said confidently. "So… listen," she held her hand up to her ear, "aren't those fish I hear calling you?" she joked, trying to lighten things up.

Aaron smiled. "I believe you're right," he laughed.

Aaron felt strangely guilty about going fishing; he felt that maybe he should be with Maria, to help somehow. As he and Elvis bumped down the narrow dirt road he almost turned around a couple of times.

"Elvis, are we doing the right thing here?" he asked his dog. Elvis barked. "Yea, I don't know either," he said out loud. "I know… let's catch plenty of fish, we'll make it a short day and then take the fish to Maria's to surprise her and her grandmother. That's a good way to help," he told Elvis, and Elvis barked again.

After he parked the truck and got his gear together, he stood at the river's edge wondering if he should go to Johnny's to see if he wanted to tag along; or would that take too much time? After thinking about it for many seconds, he decided to try Johnny's first. It'll be fun, he thought. Besides I think it might be good to get him out of his house. "See that, now I'm helping two people today just by doing what I love the most," he explained to Elvis. Aaron and Elvis worked their way through the woods: after so many trips Aaron had pretty good bearings on the best and easiest way to get to Johnny's house. It wasn't long till Aaron could see the meadow, then the house. Elvis was just about to take off when Aaron grabbed him.

"Hold on, boy… I don't think we can see Johnny today." Aaron was looking toward the house when he saw a red truck sticking out from the far side. "I believe it must be one of those days," he explained to Elvis. What the heck day is it today? Elvis was getting impatient and barked a couple of times. "Shhh!" Aaron looked carefully at the house: it didn't seem like anyone heard Elvis. "Come on. Let's get going."

They were having a pretty good morning: they had already caught plenty of nice fish to take home, and as much as Aaron didn't want to stop fishing he decided it was time. He started packing up when Elvis started to growl, a low deep growl, something he only did when he sensed danger.

Aaron turned to look behind him into the woods. "Hey, man, don't shoot me or nothing!" came a familiar voice. Elvis ran to Johnny when he stepped into the clear. "That's quite a guard dog you have there," Johnny laughed.

"Yea, not too consistent but better than nothing, I guess. How'd you know I was here?"

"Wasn't that Elvis I heard bark back at the house?" Johnny asked.

"Oh, you heard that? Sorry."

"It's alright, man, don't worry about it. But I do appreciate you not coming to the house. I know it's weird…"

Aaron interrupted. "It's okay, Johnny, no biggie really. It's my fault, I completely forgot what day it is, I didn't realize it until I saw the red truck," he tried to explain. "I guess that's when you heard Elvis."

"We're good, kid."

"That's excellent. How did you know I'd be here… in this spot?" he questioned Johnny politely.

"Awe… well, I come to this spot every chance I can, I love it here. Plus you can't beat the fishing," he smiled. "A while back I was here and someone had left their fishing gear, and some nice fish too, by the way," he smiled.

Aaron slapped his own forehead like he suddenly got it. "You found my gear and brought it to my house, right?"

"Well no, not exactly. I did figure it was your stuff, but I actually had a friend find you and take it to your house. He didn't want to freak anybody out so he just slipped in and left the gear. Did you get the fish, by the way, those ones I caught myself?!"

"Yes, I did, they were great, thank you."

"That was an awesome fly you had," Johnny told him.

"My fly! So you have it then?" Aaron asked. "I mean you can keep it, that's fine, I just couldn't understand why you brought all my other stuff but not the fly."

Johnny smiled. "I wouldn't have minded keeping it, but that's not what happened."

"What do you mean?"

"Well... one of these fish out here has it," he smiled, pointing to the river. "He put up one hell of a fight but in the end he snapped my line and took off with your fly. Sorry about that, kid. I tried to get you a new one, but no one had anything like it. That must have been custom-made, right?"

"Yea, my friend Marcos who works on our farm gave it to me for my birthday,"

"Awe, man, now I really feel bad," Johnny told him.

"Nah, it's part of the sport, it happens."

"So... how's the fishing today?" Johnny asked.

"Really good actually... Really good!" He picked up his string of fish out of the water to show Johnny the catch so far.

"Nice."

"You want to give it a go?" Aaron asked.

"Sure. Maybe for a little bit." Aaron set him up and Johnny cast off like a pro. "Impressive," Aaron smiled.

"Lots of practice, kid, lots," Johnny laughed. "By the way, where's that life-saver Maria today?"

Aaron laughed. "Oh, she's out saving more lives." He went on to tell Johnny about how Maria volunteers.

"I'm telling you, kid, she's a keeper." Aaron smiled and nodded in agreement.

"Yea, I think I'm getting that."

Both guys were sitting on their own rock, relaxing and talking while the fishing lines were out in the water doing their jobs. Johnny pulled his baseball cap down tight and looked at Aaron.

"Hey, man... that was one heck of a performance last time you were here, I mean like... it was real," Johnny said with a small cadence in his voice.

Aaron started laughing hysterically. "What's so funny?" Johnny asked.

"That was the worst Elvis impersonation I've ever heard!" he told him.

Johnny started to laugh, too. "Really? I thought it was pretty good."

"But I'm glad you liked my singing. Actually, about that: can I ask you a question?"

"What?"

"Well, remember when you told me you thought I should enter an Elvis impersonation contest?" he reminded him.

"Sure, kid, why?"

"Well, agh... I personally think I'm nuts, but, well, I was thinking about doing it... just one time," he announced. Johnny smiled really big and kind of chuckled.

"Maria, right?" he asked coyly. "You're doing this for Maria... I get it."

"Well yea, I guess so, she likes it when I perform."

"Of course she does. Not only do I think it's cool but I'm telling you, you're good. Who knows, worth a try, right?" he suggested.

"Besides, I know one judge who, above all others, no matter how well you do, will be over-the-top excited for you," Johnny told him.

"Maria?"

"Yea, dummy... Of course Maria. You can be kinda thick sometimes, kid. Let me tell you something; I know a little about this... being able to sing... especially like you do, and then being good-looking, too, well... it's a game-changer," he explained. "I'm surprised you haven't tried this before."

"Yea, people say that all the time to me. My mom's been bugging me for years. I don't know, I just never wanted to do it. Especially after my dad died, since then the only times I play are when my mom asks or when I need to I'll use it to cheer her up... works every time."

Johnny smiled. "I used to sing to my mom all the time, too," he admitted somberly.

"You sing?" Aaron asked.

"A little. But you know, like you, when I sang for my mom it always made her happy."

"That's pretty cool," Aaron told him.

Johnny had a fish on his hook. "Finally!" he yelled. "I thought maybe you caught them all." Aaron laughed. "Excellent fish!" Johnny said excitedly.

"It's a beaut, that's for sure," Aaron told him, then paused. "Johnny, this is a blast and everything but I've got to get back soon. Maria's grandmother isn't doing too well; I need to try to help out somehow so I thought I'd bring them back some fish."

"Maria's grandmother... she's worse?"

"Yes, really bad. My mom is concerned she's not going to last much longer."

"Poor Maria." Johnny's face changed. "Man, that sucks! I think taking them some fish is a really good idea. Maria will know what to do with these babies," Johnny smiled, holding up the line of fish. "I'll tell you what... walk me home and I will give you some of my special fish seasoning to take to Maria. Trust me, it'll be worth it."

"Sure, that'd be great."

As they worked their way back to Johnny's house, Johnny asked Aaron, "So when is this contest anyway?"

"Oh, well... if I do it, it's a week from Saturday."

"Are you backing out already? You're going to do it, right?" Johnny strongly suggested. "I mean, I think you should do it."

"Yes, I'm going to do it. Honestly, I want to, I just don't want to make an idiot out of myself," he explained. "I'm not telling anyone, not even my mom," Aaron admitted.

"Why not? I mean you're going to all this trouble, and you already know your mom lives to hear you sing. That's just silly, why shouldn't you tell her?" he insisted.

Aaron lowered his head. "Seems dumb now that you put it that way."

"It is dumb!" Johnny snapped. "Here's the thing, kid... I'm going to tell you something you cannot say to anyone, I mean anyone," Johnny said sternly. Aaron stopped walking and turned to face Johnny.

"What is it?"

"Aaron... I need your word, this is important to me, you understand?" He emphasized by pointing his finger. "Not Maria, not your mom, no one."

"Sure, Johnny, I get it. But why are you telling me this big secret?"

"Because I want to help you," he said, looking surprised at Aaron.

Aaron stood there not sure what to make of all this fuss but he agreed. "Okay, Johnny, you have my word," he promised.

"Good." Johnny paused. "I worked for Elvis for many years," Aaron immediately interrupted.

"What? Come on!" Aaron knew he had to be joking. Johnny smiled.

"I know, it doesn't seem possible or maybe even make sense, but I did. And I can help you." Judging by Johnny's face and tone he was being serious.

Aaron was curious. "Okay, let's say that's true... first of all, is it true?" Aaron asked a little more excited, realizing the possibility of what Johnny just told him.

Johnny laughed. "Yea, kid, it's true, for a really long time, actually." For some reason Aaron instantly believed him.

"Wow! I mean WOW! That is seriously cool!" Aaron was so excited. "But how can you help me?"

"Well, for starters, I know every nuance to every song; I know every move he ever did. Trust me, I can help you," Johnny said with confidence as they started to walk again. Aaron was bursting with excitement.

"This is just crazy," he said out loud.

"You'll see. It'll be fun," Johnny laughed.

"So what should we do, meet somewhere or what?"

"No, that's not possible for me, you'll have to come here," Johnny told Aaron.

"Okay, that's no problem."

Johnny looked at Aaron. "And you can't bring Maria."

"Oh... sure, I guess that makes sense. Okay... so when can we get started?" Aaron had a total change of heart and was now completely motivated.

They got back to Johnny's house and went into the kitchen; Johnny grabbed the bottle of seasoning and handed it to Aaron. "Take the fish to Maria and be there for her and her grandmother tonight, then, if you'd like, come back tomorrow."

"Great! I'll be here tomorrow, just me and Elvis."

"That's right, just you and Elvis," Johnny agreed.

Aaron and Elvis nearly ran all the way back to the truck. He was excited, nervous and anxious to get started. Maybe with Johnny's help I might do alright, he thought. Wow, this is going to be a hard secret to keep.

GAME CHANGER

Aaron drove straight to Maria's house. He was so excited he didn't know how he was going to keep anything in. When he pulled up to the front gate he was surprised to see so many cars out in front of Maria's house, including Marcos's truck. Aaron suddenly had a bad feeling in his stomach. He pulled up behind Marcos and let out Elvis.

Aaron's mom came out the front door, crying. Aaron ran up to her. "What's is it, Mom, what's wrong?"

"It's Mrs. Muccino," she answered quietly. "They're saying she's not going to make it through the night." Aaron took a deep breath and let it out slowly.

"Oh my God, and Maria? How is she?"

"You know, as well as can be expected, I guess. Their family from Memphis just got here, they're not taking it very well." Alisha paused and then started to cry. "I just saw her yesterday, she seemed like she was doing so much better. This just sucks!" she said angrily.

"It does, Mom, it does." Aaron hugged her.

He knew she was also thinking of his dad. Just then Maria came out the front door, she looked at Aaron, sat down on the top step of the porch, put her hands in her lap and started to cry. Alisha pulled back from Aaron and nudged him toward Maria. Aaron sat so close to her he practically sat on top of her. He pulled her in tight, put her

105

head on his shoulder and just let her cry. Alisha walked back into the house passing her hand over Aaron's head as she did.

"I wish there was something I could say," Aaron told her softly. "I feel so bad."

Maria sat up so she could look at Aaron: her eyes were red and puffy, full of tears. "I just can't believe this is real," she said, shaking her head.

"I know."

"She means everything to me... everything."

Her whole body was tight, her teeth were clenched. She was starting to get angry. "I am so sorry, Maria. I know this sucks," he said gently to her. "Is there anything I can do? Anything at all?"

Maria took in several deep breaths. "No. I'm so glad you're here, though." She began to cry again.

"Don't worry, I'm not going anywhere. I'll be right here as long as you need me," he told her as he comforted her.

They sat there alone for some time. Every once in a while someone would come out front, in most cases just to get out of the house. Not a clear eye among them. Aaron finally met Maria's aunt and uncle, but it was difficult to make much conversation due to the circumstances. After a bit, Maria started to calm down and it seemed like she was doing better.

Alisha came out and brought them both a glass of water. "Oh thank you, Mrs. B, I really needed this," Maria told her.

Marcos opened the front door and looked out. "Hey, Aaron." He greeted him for the first time since Aaron had gotten there.

"Hey, Marcos."

Marcos waved his hand, gesturing to Alisha to come to the door. Alisha walked over to Marcos. "Mrs. Muccino asked to see Aaron."

"She's awake?" She was surprised.

"Yes, well, drifting in and out."

"Hey, Aaron..." Aaron stood up with Maria. "Mrs. Muccino would like to see you," his mom told him.

Maria looked at Alisha in a look of surprise. Alisha held her arms up. "I have no answer, that's what Marcos just told me... Come on, let's go."

Aaron, Maria and Alisha walked upstairs to Mrs. Muccino's bedroom. Inside were Maria's aunt and uncle and one of their three kids. The two younger ones were out back playing. The room smelled funny to Aaron; it was dark inside, darker than he expected. There were many burning candles all over the room. When he first walked in he couldn't really see Mrs. Muccino, she was blocked by the people who were standing or sitting at her bedside.

Alisha stepped up to Mrs. Muccino on the far side of the bed. "Mrs. Muccino, you're awake, I'm so glad," she smiled. Mrs. Muccino nodded her head and gestured her to come closer.

Alisha stepped right to the top of the bed and leaned in to be closer to Mrs. Muccino; in a very low, soft voice Mrs. Muccino said to her, "Remember what we spoke about," she reminded her as she squeezed her hand.

"Yes of course," Alisha smiled.

"Is Aaron here?" Mrs. Muccino asked before Alisha could say anything else.

"Yes, he's right here," gesturing to her son to step closer. Alisha stepped back and out of the way.

As he did, Mrs. Muccino lifted her hand and Aaron took it. She pulled him closer; she was surprisingly strong, Aaron thought. "Yes, Mrs. Muccino, I'm here," he said softly.

She pulled Aaron even closer, right up to her face. Aaron turned his head, knowing she wanted to say something to him. Aaron got as close as he could. Everyone in the room watched: they couldn't hear the exchange at all no matter how hard anyone strained to do so. Even Alisha, who was right next to them, couldn't hear what was being said. They talked for several minutes; Aaron kept nodding yes as they spoke. Then Mrs. Muccino grabbed Aaron's head with both of her hands, turned his head and gave him a kiss on his forehead, then everyone could hear her give Aaron a blessing. He smiled at her, she smiled back. Aaron turned and walked out of the room. Alisha stayed in the room with Mrs. Muccino, but Maria followed Aaron out. Aaron walked downstairs and into the kitchen. Marcos was there and so were the two younger cousins.

Marcos strained to smile as they walked in. "How'd it go?" he asked Aaron.

"Fine. It was fine," Aaron said, a little shaken.

"What did she say?" Maria asked.

"Uh, well… I can't really tell you," he answered. "I promised."

"What?" Maria asked sharply. "What does that mean?" - even more sarcastically. Aaron shrugged his shoulders, "I'm not trying to be mean or funny, but your grandmother wanted to tell me some stuff and asked that I not talk about it. I'm sorry, Maria, but I can't disrespect your grandmother's wishes."

"This is a dying woman's wishes," Marcos spoke up.

Aaron nodded his head in agreement. Maria had already cried so much, been angry so much and been in so much pain, she didn't have the energy to push back.

"Okay, Aaron, whatever."

Aaron walked to her, kissed her and held her close. He could feel Maria's body loosen up. "Reality sucks! Doesn't it, Marcos?"

"It does sometimes," Marcos suggested, "but then there are the other times. Times like this summer you and Maria had together, that's a reality, too, isn't it?" he asked them both.

They both nodded in agreement. "Still sucks," Maria tried her best to joke. Marcos and Aaron both laughed. Maria smiled for the first time that day.

Marcos and Aaron drove home together later that night in Aaron's truck, with the promise to Maria that they would be back first thing in the morning. "Rough day," Marcos said to Aaron as he walked toward his house.

"Rough is right," Aaron responded, completely forgetting about the first half of his day hanging out with Johnny. "I'll see you in the morning!" Aaron yelled.

Marcos waved. Aaron threw some ice in the ice chest with the fish in it, went to his room, dropped on his bed fully dressed, and fell right asleep. He was abruptly woken, what seemed like minutes later, by a loud ringing. He sat up and looked around his room trying to get his bearings. It took him a second but he quickly realized he was at home and it was the phone: he ran to get it, and it was his mom.

"She's gone," she said between sniffles. For the first time since this all started Aaron felt like he was going to cry.

"Awe, man. I'm sorry, Mom... Are you okay?"

"Yes, I'm fine. Can you come right away?"

"Sure, Mom, no problem."

"Please do me a favor: when you come would you bring me some fresh clothes?"

"Yea, Mom, I'll do it right now then I'll get Marcos and we'll head right over," he told her.

"Thank you, Aaron," she said in a quite somber voice. "Oh... Aaron," she paused, "be prepared, Maria's not doing so well."

"It's okay, Mom, I understand."

Aaron called Marcos at his house to wake him up, then he took a quick shower. Marcos was already in the kitchen before Aaron finished getting together some clothes for his mom.

"I made some coffee," Marcos said as he handed a cup to Aaron.

"Oh thank goodness, you're a life-saver."

"We better get going," Marcos suggested.

By the time they got to Maria's the sun was up and it was getting hot. When Aaron pulled up to the house there were all kinds of cars out front, including a police car and an ambulance. Aaron's stomach suddenly started hurting: poor Maria.

"Aaron, this is going to be hard and awkward; you and I need to be strong, okay?" Marcos explained.

"Okay..." Aaron agreed. "That's pretty real," Aaron said when he realized that the car right in front of the house was a hearse.

Marcos didn't reply. They got out of the truck and walked toward the house. Alisha saw them coming and met them on the front porch.

"Oh thank you, Aaron," she said as he handed her some clothes. "I'm going to jump in the shower real quick." Alisha looked like she hadn't slept all night. You could see the exhaustion and pain on her face.

"Mom!" Aaron called out to her.

She turned back. "What is it?"

"Well, how is it in there?" He was unsure of exactly what he wanted to ask.

"Weird, if you really want to know. You need to go in, I'm sure Maria is expecting you."

He and Marcos followed Alisha into the house. Most of the family were sitting in the front room: some with their faces covered, some crying and the two young ones were playing on the floor. The aunt appeared as if she'd had enough. "You two need to take it outside, you understand me!" she snapped. The uncle looked at the kids and nodded in support of his wife. The kids quickly retreated to the backyard.

Aaron looked around downstairs but didn't see Maria. He started upstairs when he was confronted with two paramedics who were trying to manage a gurney down the stairs. Aaron turned around and receded to the landing area at the bottom of the stairs. The men got to the bottom step and then they adjusted the gurney to a level position. Mrs. Muccino's face was not covered, Aaron was surprised. He looked at her as if he expected her to say something to him. Maria was following behind, sobbing, carrying her grandmother's cross that she kept above her bed. Maria was wearing a black veil over her face. Everyone in the front room stood up and came to the gurney: most reached out to touch Mrs. Muccino, others set flowers from her garden on her. They all said what Aaron could only guess was some kind of prayer in Italian. Aaron stood where he was and didn't move. They all proceeded outside, the paramedics put Mrs. Muccino into the hearse while everyone gathered around. Alisha came out and ran up to the car, she put her hand on the back door and said a small prayer. Maria looked at Aaron but didn't acknowledge him or approach him. Aaron understood.

Alisha walked over to be next to Aaron and hugged him. "Did Maria see you?"

"Yeah, but I didn't talk to her yet."

"That doesn't matter, she needed to see you, she needs to know you're here."

Marcos came over a few minutes later just as the car with Mrs. Muccino was driving away. You could tell he had been crying. In all his life Aaron has never seen Marcos cry. He truly cared about Mrs. Muccino and Maria: he was in pain, too. Everyone slowly went back into the house, Maria first. Once inside it was as if no one wanted to confront Maria, maybe as a way to not remind her of her new reality, but Aaron felt he had to at least give his condolences and offer his support. Maria was in the kitchen putting together platters of food for everyone. His mom was in there as well to help. Aaron walked right up to Maria: when she lifted her head to look at him she nearly collapsed into his arms. She started to cry frantically. Aaron was holding her tight but had no idea what to say to her. Alisha came over, and family from the front room came in; everyone stepped as close to Maria and Aaron as possible to do what ended up being a group hug. You could feel the emotion running through all of them: the sadness, the pain and the love.

It lasted for a number of minutes before Alisha announced, "Okay everyone, that's enough! Mrs. Muccino would not want us to stand here and feel sorry for ourselves, you all know that! Instead, let's do what she would do and eat something and celebrate her life!" Alisha demanded.

"Yes," said Maria as she wiped away her tears. "Everyone move to the front and let's eat together," she said, agreeing with Alisha. "That's what Nana would have wanted." As instructed, everyone left the kitchen and moved into the front room.

Aaron was supposed to visit Johnny today but knew there was no way that was going to happen. He needed to be available for Maria. I wish I had a way to let him know I wasn't coming, he thought to himself. Aaron pondered and wrestled with what to do for some time. It's still early, I can quickly drive out there and let him know, then I can be back before anyone realizes. After Maria retired to her room, without saying anything to his mom he jumped in his truck and headed for the river. He quickly made it through the woods, got past the clearing, and entered the meadow. He could see Johnny's house: Johnny was sitting on the porch.

"I didn't think you were coming," he said to Aaron as he approached.

"Yea, I almost didn't. I need to tell you something."

"Sure, kid, what's up?" Johnny asked.

"It's Maria's grandmother, she passed away last night. It's been a really rough day, especially for Maria."

"Awe, man," Johnny said, shaking his head. "I didn't know the woman at all, but I didn't have to… Knowing Maria tells me what a great woman she must have been."

"That's very cool, thank you, Johnny. I'm sure Maria will appreciate that."

"You told me how she was sick, but the next day?"

"Yea, it happened kinda quick," Aaron told him, shaking his head. "Maria's a mess right now, I'm not sure how to help her."

"Well, first of all what in hell are you doing here? You should be with Maria and your mom!" Johnny strongly scolded Aaron. "You know, you have to be there for her, I mean one hundred percent," Johnny told him, bouncing his finger off Aaron's chest. "It's not an option."

"Yes, I know."

There was an uncomfortable pause. "You know she loves you," Johnny stated. "Loves me?" Aaron laughed, "I don't know, man, I mean we've only been going out for a little while…" he said, trying to play it down. "And besides we're only seventeen."

Aaron knew he loved Maria, but he wasn't ready to admit it. "I know that, you don't think I know that you're seventeen?" Johnny pressed. "What does that have to do with anything anyway? I fell in love at eighteen and had things been a little different, we'd still be together now," he said in an unusual admission. "Look… this is a serious, life-changing event. Trust me, I've had my share. The one thing I know is you need to be strong for the ones who need you most, there is no you right now... You get me, man?" he questioned Aaron strongly.

"Yes, Johnny, I get it. Honestly I wasn't going to come: the only reason I did is because I didn't want you to think I blew you off. I'm going to head back right now." Aaron paused. "Plus... I wanted to let you know I decided not to enter the competition next week; I don't think I can do it right now, it's bad timing," Aaron explained. "Right now I need to be there for Maria and my mom."

Johnny shook his head in frustration. "That's just wrong, man," Johnny started in on him. "First of all, to not do this is an insult to Maria, your mom, and even Maria's grandmother."

"What do you mean? I don't get the connection."

"Aaron, seriously... think about it. How bad is Maria feeling right now? How down is your mom?"

Aaron tried to answer. "Well, you know... it's bad. But what..."

Johnny interrupted him. "Hold on." Johnny raised up his hand. "If you do this contest, no matter how it comes out, what do you think would be your mom's reaction?"

Aaron just stood there.

"I can tell you for sure: at least for a bit she would be so happy, she would forget about everything else. And Maria? If she came to watch you... how would she react?" Johnny asked rather sharply.

Aaron started to shake his head in acknowledgment. "Ahhh. I'm getting you now. You think this would be a way to give them some distraction and maybe even some happiness now, right?" Aaron smiled.

"Uh... yea... you think?" he snapped. "Can you even imagine? Your mom and Maria would not just be happy, they would be so excited for you. Aaron, you have no choice... You need to do this, now more than ever. This is not about you anymore, this is for everyone you care about," Johnny expressed strongly.

"I get it. I understand. Okay... you're right, I'm going to do it, I need to do it, for my mom and especially Maria. I think this will be good - well, if I don't blow it. There is that, you know," Aaron tried to smile.

"Not going to happen, not if I'm around. What say you get going today but try and come tomorrow, bring Maria if she's up for it and I'll give you some good stuff. Trust me... you're going to love it," Johnny explained.

"Yea, I think I can do that. I'll try. Thanks, Johnny. I'll try my best to be here tomorrow," Aaron said as he left the porch and started the walk back to his truck.

"Bring Elvis next time!" Johnny yelled out.

"Okay!" Man he loves that dog, he laughed.

Aaron was back home by noon. Everything seemed unusually normal: he could see Marcos out in the field talking to one of the workers, and he could see his mom was just outside the barn tending to the young calf that was born a few days earlier; the calf was mooing up a storm. Aaron headed toward the barn to finish his chores from that morning. "You're back," his mom remarked.

"Yea, Mom, sorry."

"No that's fine, I just didn't know where you were... Is everything okay?"

"Yeah, Mom, everything's fine. I just wanted to get away for a bit. And you... how are you?"

"Numb," she responded. "Just numb."

"Yea, I guess I'm still having a hard time believing it's true, you know what I mean?"

"Yes, sadly I do."

Aaron realized that was a pretty stupid question. "Sorry, Mom, I..."

"Aaron, it's fine." His mom walked over and gave him a hard, long hug. "Look, you finish up here. I want to clean up, then I'd like to go to Maria's as soon as possible. I think you should come."

"Sure, Mom, of course. I'd need to see Maria and make sure she's okay."

Aaron finished up his chores and walked out to the field to meet up with Marcos. "Hey, Marcos," Aaron said as he got closer to him.

"Hey, Aaron. How you doing?"

"I'm okay, I guess. I'm just worried about Maria, you know."

"That's good, that's the right thing," Marcos told him. "You need to be there for her, you need to be her rock right now," he said clenching his fist. "You can do that, right?" Marcos asked him.

"Yes, Marcos I can," he answered confidently.

"Good. That's really good, Aaron," Marcos paused. "I haven't said anything in a really long time, and I'm thinking now's that time," Marcos said in a very serious tone. "I want you to know... your dad would be proud of you. I mean, you know, he would have been so proud of how you turned out and who you are as a man," Marcos was trying to explain. Aaron smiled at him; it was a valorous attempt for a guy who didn't express his emotions well.

"Thank you, Marcos, that means a lot."

"I wanted you to know," he told him as he reached out to shake Aaron's hand. Aaron explained to Marcos that he and his mom were going to go and check on Maria and that they weren't sure how long they would be. Marcos understood. Aaron headed back to the house where he met his mom out front.

"You ready to go?" Aaron asked.

"Let's go," she said with a nice smile. In her hands she had a basket of food and flowers.

"I smell chili," Aaron smiled.

"You stay away from it, it's for Maria and her family," Alisha laughed.

On the way to Maria's, Alisha told Aaron that Maria's family, her aunt, uncle and cousins, were going to be headed back to Memphis soon, likely in the next couple of days. "I know, Maria told me. It sounds like Maria's not going to have a choice, she's going to have to go with them," he said, overtly upset. "I don't like it, and I know Maria is pretty upset about it."

"There's something you need to know," Alisha started to explain. "Her family in California wants her to come and be with them. The family in Memphis would like to take her, but they really don't have the room."

"Oh my God! Mom, are you kidding me? California? Why didn't Maria tell me?"

"She only just found out this morning. Apparently the whole family talked about it and decided that would be best," his mother told him.

"And Maria?"

"Oh yea, she was part of the discussion, she had to be," Alisha told her son.

Aaron was getting really upset. "I can't believe this... California... That really sucks!" he said angrily, then he hit the dash of his truck with his fist as hard as he could, making a dent and small tear in the leather.

"Aaron! Get a hold of yourself! What's wrong with you? This is not the time or place. You don't think Maria's not upset about this? Do you think she wants to go to California? I had to talk her out of running away last night! You... you need to take it easy. Don't you dare let Maria see this anger, you understand me? It's already hard enough for that child. Get it?"

Aaron looked at his mom, tears were building up in her eyes. Alisha reached out and grabbed Aaron's hand. "We'll get through this, all of us, I promise."

Aaron took a deep breath and let it out slowly. "Sorry, Mom. What about the farm, what's going to happen to that?"

"I don't know if you remember the night when Mrs. Muccino wasn't doing so well, when we were all there for dinner and I stayed over?"

"Sure, I remember."

"That night Mrs. Muccino and I had a long talk, she explained to me she did not want the farm to be sold under any circumstances. She wants it for Maria." Alisha went on in great detail about the talk and how Mrs. Muccino made Alisha executor of her estate. "I have control of what happens to the farm, and, to some extent, Maria," Alisha explained. "So Mrs. Muccino and I agreed that we, you, me and Marcos would take over the farm, and keep it running until Maria is eighteen and comes home. Then she will have total control," Alisha told Aaron. "That's what her grandmother wants."

"Wow. Does Maria know all of this?"

"She does now, and let me tell you her family wasn't too happy about it when they found out."

"I bet," Aaron responded.

They pulled up to the front of the house. Elvis jumped out first, he ran to the door and barked. Maria answered the door right away, "Elvis!" She knelt down, grabbed him around the neck and hugged him. Elvis licked her face feverishly; he was so excited to see her.

Aaron and Alisha walked up. "Hi, Maria," Aaron said. Maria stood up and gave Aaron a kiss and a hug.

Alisha stepped up for her turn. "How you holding up, honey?" she whispered into Maria's ear.

"Better today."

"That's good. Hey, I brought you a few things."

"Trust me, I already smelled your chili. Thank you very much," Maria told her as she accepted the basket.

"Yea... I was sworn off the basket," Aaron added. They all laughed.

"Come on inside," Maria said, waving to them as she held the door.

There was quite a bit of activity in the house when they got all of the way in.

Alisha first noticed Maria's uncle. "Hey, Thomas," she said.

"Hey, Alisha," he replied emotionlessly.

"Everything alright?"

"Yes... well sort of," he answered.

"Is there a problem... Can I help?" In a far from friendly voice he replied, "Well... actually yes. We have to go home, I have a bit of a thing I have to take care of, and we have to go today."

"Today?" Alisha questioned, not happy with the news.

"Yes, today!" he snapped.

"But what about Maria?" Maria and Aaron were out back so they heard none of this exchange.

"That's how you can help," he snapped again. "We're leaving, and Maria is not scheduled to fly to California for two more weeks."

"Two weeks?" Alisha questioned. "I thought she was going to go to Memphis with you in a couple of days and then fly out from there in a week or so?" She was getting visibly upset. Alisha knew there was no 'thing'; they were just pissed. Wow, I guess in times like this you really know who your friends are: poor Maria, she thought. What a jerk! she nearly said out loud.

"Have you told this to Maria?"

"Me? No. You need to figure this out," he said sharply.

"You want me to figure this out?" She paused. "Not to worry, Thomas, I think I've already figured this out. Have a safe drive home," she said gritting her teeth.

Truth is, Alisha would love the chance to be with Maria a little longer: it would be good for Maria, and Aaron certainly wouldn't mind.

"Great, it's settled then," Thomas retreated up the stairs.

And this guy's supposed to be family? Alisha went to the back to be with the kids.

"Hi guys," she announced as she came out the back door.

"Hey, Mom."

"Hi, Mrs. B."

"You guys... can we sit down for a minute and talk?"

"Of course," Maria responded, and Aaron nodded.

"Everything okay, Mom?" They all sat at the patio table.

"Yes."

It was important to Alisha to somehow make this as positive as possible, but she had to start with the truth.

"Maria, are you aware your uncle and aunt are leaving, like in the next couple of hours, and they don't plan to take you with them?"

Maria's face changed from happy to genuinely shocked in a split second and then she started to tear up. "No, I didn't know that, but I'm not entirely surprised either; ever since they found out Nana left me the farm they've been so different. Almost like I didn't matter anymore."

Aaron was as surprised as Maria. He scooted his chair closer to her and picked up her hand. "That completely sucks, Maria."

"No, actually, it's a good thing," Alisha said confidently.

"Why?" Aaron asked. Maria was also surprised.

"Because this means for the next two weeks Maria is staying with us. We get to hang out and finish the summer with Maria before she has to leave… How great is that?" she said jubilantly.

"Really?" Maria asked, lifting her head with a smile.

"Yes, Maria, really. We would be honored to have you and we will make sure you catch your flight in two weeks to California. No problem, right, Aaron?"

"Right. This is great news, Maria, we'll have so much fun!"

Maria started to cry. "I don't know what to say. I am so happy. I don't want to leave. This is my home, this is where I belong."

Aaron spoke up. "Maria, you don't need to worry about anything. Mom explained everything to me, we are going to take care of your place and when you're ready to come back it will be here for you. Everything will be exactly as you remember."

"And you?" Maria asked shyly.

"Me?"

"Will you still be here for me?" she said as quietly as one could and still have it be heard.

Alisha stood up, she knew this was her exit. "Maria, pack a bag for tonight and after your family leaves we'll go back to our place and have a barbecue, okay?"

"Yes, Mrs. B., that sounds great," she smiled. Alisha walked back into the house. "Maria…" Aaron took a breath. "Of course I will be here for you, you know how I feel about you," he leaned in and gave her a kiss. "It sucks that you have to leave, but you'll be back next summer after you graduate and then you can stay forever… If that's what you want."

"That's what I want," Maria said with strong emotions. "That's the only thing I want."

"Good," Aaron smiled.

Then teens did what teens do, especially when they know they're not going to see each other for a while. "You should go pack up your stuff," Aaron suggested.

As Maria's family was packing the car getting ready to leave, they were as cold and short as they could be. Maria was upset and confused. Her aunt at one point made an effort to offer support should Maria ever need them, but was quickly cut off by her uncle. "Maria, we know you'll be fine. We'll touch base with you when we can," he told her. Alisha was as close as she had ever been to hitting someone. Aaron could see it in her eyes. He went and stood next to her and held her hand. Maria was on her knees hugging and kissing her cousins, trying not to cry.

"Goodbye, you guys, I'm really going to miss you," she told them.

The youngest one, Caitlyn, cried a little. "I wish you could stay with us."

"I know, but I'll see you when I get back from California; we'll spend a lot of time together then, okay?"

She nodded then turned and got into the car. As they drove off Aaron walked over to Maria. "Are you okay?"

"Yes," she said strongly, "I believe I am," she said, looking at Aaron's mom.

"Good," Alisha smiled. "Go get your things. Aaron, you make sure everything is locked up," she commanded.

"No problem, Mom." They both ran into the house.

Maria kept herself together through most of dinner. It was a warm night but no one seemed to care as they finished up the fantastic barbecue meal prepared by Marcos. It was light conversation and some much-needed laughs through the dinner; mostly headed by Marcos. He told several stories about his memories of Maria's grandmother, but even more about her grandfather, Alberto. "The man just never knew when to say give," Marcos was saying as he finished up a funny story about him. They all laughed. Then there was a difficult silence. Maria put her head down and started to whimper. Alisha was first to break the ice.

"Maria, I know things are… well… things are a little crazy for you right now. But I promise, it's going to be alright, you're going to be alright." Aaron squeezed Maria's hand.

Maria first looked at Aaron and then at Alisha. "Thank you," she smiled, "thank you for being my friends, thank you for being there for me and Nana; I don't know what I would have done without you guys." Marcos got up and started clearing the table.

"That's okay, Marcos, I'll get that," Alisha insisted.

"I've got it. You guys just relax out here and enjoy the stars. I'll grab some drinks and be right back."

"Thank you," Alisha gave him an understanding smile. "What would we ever do without Marcos in our lives?" she asked Aaron and Maria.

"He's been a godsend for us," Maria said.

"Yeah, us, too. You know… I have a thought," Alisha smiled coyly.

"What's that, Mom?" Aaron asked, relieved that they moved off the current topic.

"Maria's going to be with us for two weeks, just enough time for us to plan a surprise party for Marcos," she said excitedly. Aaron and Maria looked a little puzzled. "You know… a 'thanks for being a great friend' party! What do you think?"

"That's an excellent idea," Maria said equally excited.

"Brilliant, Mom. But you know how Marcos is," Aaron reminded her.

"All the more reason to do this. He so deserves it. This will be perfect." Two birds with one stone! Alisha thought to herself. She knew planning a party for Marcos would help keep Maria distracted and at the same time properly express how everyone felt about Marcos being in their lives.

"When can we get started?" Maria asked.

"Right away, let's start tomorrow."

"Started on what?" Marcos asked as he stepped back out with a pitcher of lemonade in his hand.

"Maria's trip to California" was the only thing that came to Alisha.

"Why? I thought everything was all set?"

Alisha panicked.

"It is, but Maria was telling us how much she wants to see Graceland, so Mom thought we'd go up a day early and make a trip of it," Aaron quickly responded.

"Oh man, I love Graceland," Marcos told them. "You're going to enjoy it," he said to Maria.

"I'm really looking forward to it, I can't wait," she said with a big smile on her face.

Alisha was relieved. "It's all set then." Alisha, Aaron and Maria were doing everything they could not to laugh.

THE FAIR

At first it was strange for Aaron having Maria stay at his house. He didn't mind it, he liked it. Aaron, like his mom, was a bit of a free spirit when he was at home. He loved sitting around the house in his underwear, especially to watch TV, so he knew he had to change his habits. The rest of it was easy because his mom set down some pretty strict (and embarrassing) ground rules.

While Maria and his mom where busy during the day packing up all of Maria's things to ship to California and working on the plans for the party, Aaron easily had time to head back out to Johnny's.

"I'd almost given up on you," Johnny said to Aaron as he opened the front door. Elvis ran in.

"This whole thing with Maria's grandmother has been nuts," Aaron told him. Then he went on to tell Johnny about how her relatives just left Maria hanging and how weird they all acted once they knew Maria was getting the farm.

"That's a real shame," Johnny started. "Gold-diggers!" he said angrily. "That's just pathetic, Maria doesn't deserve that. Sadly I can relate, I know what she's going through," Johnny confided.

"Yea, it was a bad scene, for sure."

They talked for a while about Maria and what was going on and what was now going to happen, until Johnny changed the subject.

"So, are you all signed up for this weekend?" he asked, a little concerned at what the answer was going to be.

"Yes... I decided to do it, you were right."

"Really..." Johnny laughed.

"I'm going to do it for my mom and Maria, like we talked about. I just hope I don't choke," he grinned.

"Well, I understand. That wouldn't be good. So grab the guitar and let's get to work," Johnny said in a serious tone.

Aaron picked up the guitar and sat back down. "What are you doing?" Johnny asked.

"Why? What do you mean?" Aaron was confused by the question.

"How many times have you seen Elvis in concert sitting down?"

"Oh..." Aaron stood up and pushed his chair back out of the way.

"Better," Johnny said. "Have you given any thought to the song you're going to sing?"

"Sure," Aaron answered confidently. "Heartbreak Hotel, one of my all-time favorites."

"Yea, me, too," Johnny told him as he shook his head no.

"Why? What's the matter?" He could tell Johnny wasn't happy with his choice.

"You and every other Elvis in this thing will start with that or Jail House Rock," he explained. "We need a song that no one else would do, or would want to do, or a song that no one does well," he suggested.

"Okay, like what?" Aaron sort of laughed. "What Elvis song hasn't been covered a million times by a million people?"

"This is the question, isn't it?" Johnny sat there thinking a while; Aaron began to strum the strings of the guitar while he thought about it, too.

Aaron and Johnny went back and forth. "What about Teddy Bear?" Aaron threw out.

"Nah," Johnny answered. "How about All Shook Up?" Johnny suggested.

"I could do that. I like that one, or how about Love Me Tender?"

"Yea, but that one's really overused, too," Johnny said.

Aaron thought about it for a minute, then he started to strum the guitar to 'Can't Help Falling in Love'. "Can't help falling in love... humm," Johnny was thinking out loud. "That's pretty popular, too, but it's a hard song for sure: most guys who I've ever heard try it bomb it bad."

"Which might make it the perfect song, right?" Aaron suggested.

"This song doesn't have any of the quote unquote Elvis moves so it's all about the song," Johnny explained. "Let me hear it, kid, give it a go."

Aaron smiled, paused for a second, cleared his throat and started to play. This song was hard enough, but without the support of a band it was really tough. Aaron got to the chorus. "Like a river flows, surely to the sea…" Johnny stopped him almost right away.

"Are you feeling it, kid? I can tell… you're not feeling it."

"Why? What am I doing wrong?" Aaron asked.

"Well, nothing really, your voice is almost right on… really good, actually."

"Then what is it?"

"You may not know this: everyone had differing opinions on the subject, but I know for sure this song is, well… it was one of Elvis's favorites," he confided. "Trust me, it was a hard song for him to sing, too. But every time, just before he would perform it, he would close his eyes, take a deep breath and try to imagine he was singing it to one person," Johnny explained as he gestured the motions.

"Wow, that's crazy. How do you know that?" Aaron asked as he got goose bumps all over.

"You're gonna just have to trust me, kid," Johnny smiled. "Now close your eyes, take a deep breath and imagine you're singing this to your mom or maybe Maria."

Aaron nodded his head in agreement. He closed his eyes, took a deep breath and started the song over. This time Johnny let Aaron get all the way through. "That's good kid, really good."

"Thanks. Any holes? What do you think I should work on to make it better?" Aaron asked inquisitively.

"Right now, nothing. This event is in three days so what you've got you'll have to go with: trust me, this song will get you to the finals," Johnny told him confidently. "Really?" Aaron reacted sarcastically.

"I think so, yea. So what about a second song… you know, just in case you make it to the final round?" Johnny joked.

"I should pick it up a bit, don't you think?" Aaron suggested.

"I agree. I think this is when you should do Heartbreak Hotel."

"Really?" Aaron was surprised. "I thought you told me…"

He was interrupted. "Yes, for the first round, but I promise you no one is going to the finals with Heartbreak Hotel being the second song out of the bag. If you deliver it right, you'll surprise everyone."

"Cool," Aaron smiled.

Aaron was home before dark; he went straight into the house to see what Maria and his mom were doing. "Well… look what the bird dog dragged in." It was one of his mom's favorite sayings.

"Hey, Mom," Aaron smiled. "How was the fishing?" she asked, noticing Aaron didn't bring in any fish.

"Ahh, I decided not to go fishing today, Mom, I just played around at the river with Elvis. I needed some time to relax and not think."

"Oh… that's good, I guess."

"Where's Maria?"

"She's in her room resting, it was kind of a hard day for her today, what with the packing and all."

"Yea… I bet. How'd it go with all of her grandmother's things, was that hard for her?"

"Yeah it was. It was torture watching her face with every item she picked up. You could see the memories rushing back to her. I finally had to put a stop to it. I told her I will get all of her grandmother's things together for her after she leaves for California."

"That's cool, Mom. That makes a lot more sense."

"You should go and bug her, besides I'll need her to help with dinner soon," Alisha told him.

"Sure, Mom."

Aaron ran upstairs to Maria's room and gently tapped on the bedroom door. "Yes," came the response.

"Can I come in?" The door opened about halfway with Maria blocking the opening.

"Are you okay?"

Maria opened the door the rest of the way and stepped out into the hall and into Aaron's arms. Aaron held her tight. "Aaron..." she started, "I've been thinking about this a lot."

"Uh oh," Aaron joked as he stepped back.

"It's not funny..." she said seriously. "I think we should break up."

"What? What are you talking about?" he asked, caught completely off guard. "Why would we break up?... Just because you're moving?" He tried to smile.

"Yes. It's too far for too long. I don't want you to feel you have to stay with me, it's not fair to you." Maria was very emotional, it looked like she had been crying for hours.

Aaron stood there looking at her; his smile faded. "I'm not sure what to say," he told her. "Do you want to break up?" he asked in a gentle voice.

Maria reached out and picked up Aaron's right hand. She put it to her face. "No... I don't want to break up," she admitted as a single tear rolled down her cheek.

"Good. Me neither. So I'll tell you what... Let's not," he said confidently with a big smile. "Maria, I know things have been, you know, hard. But there's no reason for you and me to break up... I don't want to, you don't want to, so that's all that matters, right?"

"Right," she smiled.

"Let's just see what happens. We talked about this, we'll write, we'll call, and you're going to be back here over your holiday break," he reminded her. "After you're done with school you'll be back home to stay."

"Yes, good, oh wow... I really didn't want to break up," Maria was coming out of it. "I wanted to do the right thing."

"We are the right thing." Aaron gave her a long, hard hug, then he kissed her. "So we're good?"

"Yes, we're good," she answered with a sweet smile and in a more positive tone.

"Come on, Mom needs us in the kitchen," he told her as he took her hand.

"Where's Marcos, Mom?" Aaron asked. It was very unusual for Marcos not to have dinner with the family: to Aaron and Alisha he was family and they included him in everything as such.

"Well, believe it or not, I think he's on a date," she smiled, and then burst out laughing.

"A date!" Aaron and Maria almost said in unison.

"I know, right?" she chuckled.

"What makes you think he's on a date?" Maria asked.

"Well, a couple of hours ago he told me he wasn't going to be here for dinner. When I asked him if everything was okay, he told me he was going out with a friend. I said great, no problem, and I wouldn't have thought anything more about it except about an hour ago, just before you got home, Aaron, he came in the house to ask me if he looked alright!" She chuckled harder.

"You're kidding!" Maria was all ears.

"I don't get it, what does that have to do with anything?" Aaron asked.

"Come on, really?" his mom asked sarcastically. "This is Marcos we're talking about; when was the last time he ever cared about how he looked?"

"Oh yea, I guess you're right," Aaron admitted. "That would be a little unusual."

"And if that wasn't enough he smelled like he poured a whole bottle of cologne on his head," she said, trying not to laugh any harder.

"Is that what that smell is?" Aaron asked.

His mom started to laugh so hard she couldn't answer, so she just nodded. Aaron and Maria couldn't hold back either: Alisha's laugh was too contagious. The three of them had a great laugh at Marcos's expense. It was so not Marcos, Alisha didn't know how to process it. The fact is they all loved Marcos and only wanted the best for him. They would never do anything to hurt him, and naturally they would support him no matter what he was doing. It was time for Aaron to make his move. "So, Mom?" he asked as she was starting to calm down. "Technically this will be Maria's last weekend with us - I mean because of the party the following Saturday," he started. She nodded, trying to calm herself down. "So… I was wondering, this Saturday is the last day of the fair."

"The fair!" Maria interrupted. "Ohhh, I love the fair."

"You know things have been so nuts around here, I completely forgot about the fair," Alisha admitted.

"Well…" Aaron started again. "If I promise to get all of my Saturday chores done on Friday, do you think we could all go? You, Maria, me and Marcos?"

Maria was bouncing in her chair with excitement, waiting for the answer from Alisha. Alisha smiled at Maria. "What do you think? You think I'm going to say no?" she laughed. "Maybe we can get Marcos to bring his new girlfriend," Alisha joked. They all started to laugh again.

"This will be great," Maria said excitedly as she leaned over to kiss Aaron.

Both Thursday and Friday Aaron went out of his way to make excuses to his mom and Maria so he could get out to see Johnny. The two of them were busy anyway planning the surprise party for Marcos, something Aaron had no interest in. He had his chores done well before the sun was up, then he'd head straight to the river to fish so he could always bring some home, plus he wanted to bring some fish to Johnny.

"How you feeling, Aaron?" Johnny asked. "Tomorrow's the big day."

"I'm not sure." Aaron admitted. "When I'm here, everything feels totally natural. When I think about being in front of a big crowd my stomach starts to turn and my head starts to swirl. I've never really performed in front of a crowd before, you know, just my family and a few friends." Johnny nodded his head like he understood. "I really don't want to look like an idiot," he admitted.

"Yea I get it, kid, I do. Every performer, especially those who perform live almost always get some kind of stage fright, even Elvis."

"Really? Elvis?"

"Are you kidding, it was the worst. Elvis used to have pretty serious stage fright, although most people never knew it. In fact over the years he developed all kinds of rituals he would do before he went onstage just to try to calm himself down. Folks around him thought he was just being eccentric but it really helped him. So you see, he was just like you."

"I'm not too sure if this is helping," Aaron let out a loud burp. "I'm starting to feel a little sick right now just thinking about it." He quickly sat down.

"Look kid, we've done all we can do for now, you're going to be great. Let's eat something… I'm starving," Johnny suggested as he got up and headed to the kitchen.

"Good idea," Aaron said as he followed Johnny.

"Johnny… I haven't asked you…"

"If I'm going?" Johnny finished his question for him.

"Yes," Aaron nodded.

"I would - really, kid. I'd love to see you out there shaking it all up, but I can't."

Aaron looked totally dejected. "Awe come on, man. I told you from the beginning I wasn't going to go, why are you bumming me out about it now?" Johnny raised his voice.

"I know… I just thought maybe you might have changed your mind, that's all."

"Even if I wanted to I can't, I've got other obligations that day."

"Okay, Johnny. Don't worry about it. I'll give you the play by play next week, and I'll bring you some of the tomatoes that get thrown at me," he joked.

You could see Johnny's face relax. He smiled. "That'd be good, I'm running low on tomatoes. The fair has the best tomatoes."

They went on for some time talking about the show and what Aaron was going to wear; they were having a great time hanging out, talking about music, Elvis, love and stage fright. Aaron completely forgot about his anxiety. Johnny even told Aaron some inside, 'no one knows' stories about Elvis, which Aaron completely ate up.

"Johnny... I've got to get going. I wanted to thank you for all of your help," Aaron said sincerely. "I don't think I'd even think about doing this if you hadn't have helped me," he admitted.

"No big deal, kid. You already have the talent, I just polished it up a little. You're going to be fine," Johnny reassured him. "And look, kid, even if you blow it, I mean, you somehow lose in the first round or choke or whatever; it doesn't matter. Trust me... it just doesn't matter. You're doing this for Maria and your mom, and hopefully you're doing it for fun. I mean that's it, you know?"

"Fun?" Aaron smiled. "I'm hoping I won't puke onstage," he said laughing.

After having a bite to eat they both got up and walked to the door. "Alright, kid, you break a leg. I'll see ya next week... We'll go fishing."

"Perfect," Aaron told him as he headed off the porch back into the woods. "Come on, Elvis!" he yelled as he turned back toward the house. Elvis ran off the porch barking.

To say Friday night was a rough one for Aaron would be a serious understatement. He barely ate dinner, which his mom noticed.

"Aaron, what's wrong with you? You barely ate a thing, are you feeling alright?"

"Yea, Mom I'm okay, I'm just not hungry, I guess."

"You're not hungry? Well, that's a first," she laughed.

"It's really delicious," Maria chimed in.

"No, I know. It's very good, Mom... I just have an upset stomach."

Marcos could see that Aaron was getting uncomfortable. "So, Aaron, I think you and I should get an early start tomorrow so we can head out to the fair by early afternoon. What do you think?"

"Yes, sir, good idea."

"Oh, I'm so excited about going to the fair," Maria told them as she clapped her hands. "I can't wait!"

"I'm really looking forward to it, too. It will be a nice break," Alisha said.

"Say, guys… how would y'all feel about me bringing a friend along tomorrow? To the fair, you know?" Marcos was turning red as he was asking.

"A friend?" Alisha asked with a big smile. Aaron and Maria were trying not to laugh.

"Yes, a friend," he smirked.

"Well, I think it's just great." Maria spoke first.

"Absolutely," Aaron added.

"Great with me," Alisha said. "Do we know this friend?" Alisha asked.

Marcos paused. "Yes… you know her," Marcos answered reluctantly. "It's Patty," he said with a little more bravado.

"Patty?" Aaron repeated.

"Yea, you know… the woman who moved into the old Peterson place a few months ago. She started working down at the feed store… Patty!"

There was a collective "Ahh".

"I think that's great," Alisha told him. "She's more than welcome. Any friend of yours is a friend of ours," she said slapping the back of his hand as she got up from the table. "I've talked to her a few times… she's very nice. It will be fun to have her along," Alisha added. "Tomorrow's going to be a great day," she announced. Aaron grabbed his stomach and ran out of the room.

As planned, Aaron and Marcos got an early start on their work so they could be done in time to get cleaned up and head out to the fair well before dark. Marcos actually cut out a little earlier because he wanted some extra time to pick up Patty.

"I'll see you over there," Marcos said to Aaron as he headed to his place.

"Okay!" Aaron yelled. Aaron was excited and nervous.

He was trying to calm himself down: you know I actually don't have to do this, he told himself. No one except me knows, well... Johnny, but he won't be there, so I don't really have to decide if I'm going to do this or not until I get there. I mean it's the fair, everyone will be happy just to be at the fair, he convinced himself. He found a way out for himself, it was working; most of the stress and the sick stomach went away.

The women spent entirely too much time primping and prancing; Aaron was about to lose it.

"Come on, guys! We've gotta get going!" he yelled up the stairs. You would have thought they were headed to the Derby itself.

"Okay, Aaron!" Maria yelled back.

"I just need one more minute!" Alisha yelled.

One more minute from his mom usually meant ten: some things never change, Aaron laughed. He decided to run out front and make sure Elvis was good and to recheck on the clothes he had stashed behind the back seat of his truck. Within a few minutes both Maria and his mom came out front. They stood on the front porch,; posing like they were modeling the clothes they were wearing. At first Aaron laughed, but then he really noticed Maria, she looked so beautiful. She was wearing a colorful summer dress with thin shoulder straps. She had on white tennis shoes, her hair was super-curly, and her smile was huge.

"You look fantastic, Maria," Aaron spouted out.

"Why, thank you, sir." Maria smiled and started down the front steps. Aaron ran up to greet her and grabbed her hand to escort her to the truck.

"Uh um!" came the sound from Aaron's mom.

"Oh, Mom... so sorry. You look fantastic, too!"

"Uh huh, great," she smiled. "Well maybe someone at the fair will notice," she laughed. They all waved bye to Elvis as they headed out. Elvis barked.

Aaron was starting to feel sick again as he pulled the truck up to the front gate area of the fair to drop off the ladies. Marcos and Patty were waiting near the ticket booths. "Hey, guys!" Alisha yelled out to Marcos. Maria and Alisha got out of the truck, and Maria turned back toward Aaron.

"I'll be right there, I'm just going to park the truck," he told her.

Then he thought about it and jumped out of the truck. "Hey, Mom!" Alisha turned toward him. "Would you buy Maria's ticket and I'll just meet you at the fountain in a few minutes, okay?" he asked, knowing he needed to get his clothes inside without anyone noticing.

"The fountain? Sure, we'll see you there."

Aaron smiled at Maria. "I'll meet you there, it will be easier." Maria didn't understand but agreed. Aaron parked the truck some distance from the front gate and waited for a number of minutes. He didn't want to take any chances he'd run into them until he had a chance to drop off his things at the main stage area. His plan, if you could call it that, worked: he got in, ran to the main stage, met up with the promoters, checked in and put his clothes in a locker backstage. A few minutes later, a bundle of nerves, he showed up at the fountain.

"Hey everybody," he said a little too enthusiastically announcing his arrival. Maria walked straight up to him to give him a kiss.

"Where were you?" his mom asked.

"Oh sorry, I got sidetracked by a friend... Marcos!" Aaron called out, quickly changing the subject.

"Aaron, I'd like to officially introduce you to my friend Patty," he said proudly.

"Patty, it is a pleasure and an honor. Any friend of Marcos's is my friend, too." Marcos nodded with pleasure. Patty smiled: she was a very sweet genuine salt of the earth type of woman, exactly the type Marcos would be attracted to.

"The pleasure is all mine," she said in a beautiful Southern accent. Then they all burst into laughter; Patty wasn't sure what was so funny so she just laughed along.

"Aaron, did you know there is an Elvis impersonation contest here tonight!" Alisha announced to the group excitedly.

"Oh, well we're not missing that," Aaron stated.

"That should be fun," Maria laughed in a supporting way.

"But what about tickets?" Patty asked.

"I bet this thing has been sold out for some time?" Alisha added.

Aaron started to panic.

"Not to worry… I got it covered," Marcos told the group. Everyone looked at him a little surprised. "I found out about the contest and got us tickets, no big deal."

Aaron took a deep breath: how could I have forgotten to get tickets! he scolded himself. Everyone thanked Marcos.

"Okay, where should we go first?" Marcos asked the group.

"Food!" Aaron said, laughing.

"Good idea," Alisha agreed. "I'm dying for some barbecue, not that it compares to yours, Marcos." Everyone laughed as they headed in the direction of all the food vendors.

They sat down at a shaded bench eating the wide selection of food they bought. When they were at the fair they liked to put out the food 'family'-style so everyone could taste a little of everything. That's how they always did it, kind of a 'going to the fair' tradition. Aaron really enjoyed talking with Patty, she was fun and had many good stories. It was easy to tell Marcos had a thing for her, and because of that everyone treated Patty as if she was already part of the family.

"Maria, you're so beautiful," Patty told her.

Maria was caught a little off guard. "Wow. That's so nice. Thank you," Maria responded. "You're beautiful, too," Maria replied.

"Oh you're sweet, honey, but I think I may have had a few too many trips around the barn, if you get my meaning."

"That's ridiculous," Marcos said in support. "You are very beautiful." Then he remembered they weren't alone and quickly got embarrassed.

"Thank you, Marcos, that may be the sweetest thing anyone's said to me in a long time."

Everyone wanted to laugh, especially Aaron and Alisha but they kept it in. Last thing they would ever want to do was hurt or embarrass Marcos. So after they ate they all decided to walk through some of the buildings, especially the ones with the livestock. It was always amazing to everyone the level of quality in some of the animals being judged.

"They almost seem too perfect," Maria observed as she was looking into one of the pens.

"They do, don't they?" Alisha agreed.

Aaron was petting the nose of a huge prize bull when he spoke up. "Hey, guys, I saw a couple of friends a little earlier: would you mind if I went and caught up with them for a bit?"

"What about Maria?" Alisha snapped at Aaron.

"No that's okay, I'm fine."

"Well then, what about the Elvis contest?" Alisha demanded.

"I'll meet you there, before it starts, I promise," Aaron told them.

"Okay, whatever," Alisha said to Aaron, a little upset. "We'll see you over at the main stage then. You know this thing starts in, like, thirty minutes?" she reminded him. "Yeah, I know... You guys might want to start heading over there to get some good seats," Aaron suggested.

"That's a good idea," Marcos agreed.

"Good, I'll see you then. Save me a seat," Aaron asked as he walked away.

Alisha looked curiously at Maria, and Maria held her hands up to her shoulders. "Don't ask me," she laughed.

So the group slowly worked their way to the main stage area and took in as many things as they could on the way. Once there, Marcos used his influence to get them second-row seats, right in the middle aisle. Actually his influence consisted of two of his best farmhands that worked for him in season every year and worked at the fair every summer for extra money.

"This is perfect," Alisha said to Marcos, "thank you." Everyone agreed.

Marcos sat next to Patty, who sat next to Alisha; she and Maria left an empty chair between them for Aaron. It was starting to get dark out, the main lights for the fair were starting to come on. After what seemed like only a few minutes every seat in the arena was full. The main stage was dark except for a few low lights pointed at the huge black curtains which were closed. There was country music playing in the background, everyone was talking and having a good time. There was always a high level of anticipation for this annual event. The lights for the whole arena came on all at once, the music stopped, then all of the stage lights went off except for a single spotlight that lit the center stage. Everyone in the audience started to clap and cheer. Marcos, Patty and Alisha were all clapping; Alisha started whistling loudly, as she always did at these kinds of things. Maria leaned over and put her hand on Alisha's shoulder to get her attention.

Alisha leaned toward Maria. "Where's Aaron?" Maria asked, a little concerned.

"Oh, don't worry, he's fine. Screwing around with his friends, I'm sure. But I know Aaron, he won't miss this," Alisha said confidently. "He'll be here shortly." Maria nodded.

"Ladies and gentlemen!" a man who appeared center stage in the spotlight announced. The main arena lights dimmed. "Ladies and gentlemen! If I could have your attention, please!" The capacity crowd stopped clapping and quieted down quickly. "Thank you and welcome," he started. Maria was getting upset that Aaron wasn't there yet: she kept looking around for him. *What if can't see us?* she wondered. Alisha noticed Maria being fidgety, she could tell she was getting upset. Alisha reached over and grabbed Maria's hand and pulled her into the chair next to her.

"Maria, Aaron will find us. In the meantime, relax. Let's enjoy the show," she suggested. Maria smiled and turned her attention to the man on the stage.

The announcer continued. "Welcome to the second largest Elvis impersonation contest east of the Mississippi!" Everyone started to clap and cheer; Alisha whistled. "This is going to be great," she said excitedly to Maria, squeezing her hand. Hardcore fan for sure, Maria thought. Alisha was already on the edge of her seat. "Are you an Elvis fan?" Alisha asked Patty.

Marcos leaned in front of Patty. "We wouldn't be dating if she wasn't!" he laughed.

"I'm a huge fan," Patty told Alisha. "I've seen him in concert twice."

"Wow, that's fantastic," Alisha responded. "I've only been to one concert: in fact it was here."

"That's very cool," Patty replied.

"My husband proposed to me after that concert," Alisha explained.

"Really?"

"Oh yes… it was very romantic," Alisha told her proudly.

"Wow, that's a serious memory!"

"This is a very special night!" the announcer continued. "We have Elvises here from all over, even Japan!" The audience laughed and clapped. "What you might not know is that, in order to compete tonight, these gentlemen had to win at least one regional contest this year. The only exception to that rule is we allow up to three local impersonators to compete who don't necessarily have any previous experience. Some local color, if you will. It always makes the whole thing that much more fun," he winked, knowing these three guys could be just awful, but it was always entertaining. The audience also knew and started to laugh. "Okay… each Elvis will perform one song and our judges will then vote. Only the top three will move on to the final round where each Elvis will have a chance to sing one more time. For the finals, each Elvis will have to choose a different song than the one they sang in the first round. Then… after the votes are in we will have our winner!" The audience cheered, and Alisha whistled. "And... the winner from tonight qualifies to go to the 'Big Show', the National Championship in Memphis this December! So sit back... if you can, and have fun." Everyone clapped excitedly. "Here we go... first up is Elvis number one, Mike, who hails from Calgary, Vancouver!" Everyone was very excited, no one more than Alisha; the audience clapped hard and loud. When Mike walked onto the stage, the audience roared. He was wearing the infamous white jumpsuit with all the rhinestones, and Mike looked exactly like Elvis in his later years. Mike waved and bowed as he took center stage. He jumped into character, pointed his finger at the audience, and twisted his right foot, bending the knee slightly. Alisha was going nuts, whistling and screaming before Mike sang one word. The music started: just as Johnny said, it was 'Jail House Rock'; everyone started to cheer. Mike pulled the whole thing off nicely, great moves, very good voice and an excellent costume. The group agreed that he was excellent and likely to be in the top three. For a couple of moments Alisha felt like she was hearing the real Elvis, but then there was always something that brought her back. After Mike came several more Elvises all playing the role of 'Elvis the later years'. They all sang pretty well and most of them had great costumes; 'Jail House Rock' and 'Teddy Bear' up to this point seemed to be the songs of choice.

"What do you think happened to Aaron?" Maria was asking Alisha between acts.

"I don't know, it's hard for me to imagine he's not here."

"He's probably here, but couldn't find us so he sat down wherever he could," Marcos spoke up.

"You're right," Alisha agreed. "I'm sure that's what happened. He'll catch up with us when the show is over." Maria wasn't happy but agreed that's probably what happened.

"Up next our first local Elvis... Everyone please give a warm welcome to Monty!" the announcer said as he stepped out of the light. Monty was already a total departure from what they had heard and seen so far. Many in the audience started laughing even before he got all the way onstage. Alisha and Maria put their heads down to try to smother their laughs. Monty looked pretty bad. He was at least six foot five inches tall, and he looked like he maybe weighed a hundred and fifty or sixty pounds. He appeared to be in his fifties but he could have been much younger: he was weather-worn. He had bright red hair that he wore very short. His Elvis costume consisted of overalls and no shirt.

"You'd think he'd at least have dyed his hair!" Patty said to the group.

"I have a feeling he didn't volunteer for this," Marcos chimed in, betting his wife or someone like that put him up to it.

The music started. Monty just stood there holding the microphone down next to his thigh. He slowly lifted the microphone to his mouth. "Love me tender, love me true..." he started sing, nowhere close to being in tune and definitely not sounding like Elvis. The entire audience burst into laughter, even Alisha and Maria couldn't resist. He was bad, really bad. About halfway through the torturous song the announcer came back onstage. "Monty! Monty!" the announcer interrupted. Everyone started cheering. Monty looked surprised but relieved. "Monty, that was one heck of a try!" the announcer continued. "Don't you think, folks? Let's hear it for Monty, everyone!" he said with the straightest face he could muster. The audience clapped and cheered as best they could. Monty finally smiled and waved as he walked off the stage.

"I need a drink!" Patty announced.

"Me, too," Alisha chimed in.

"I got it," Marcos said as he jumped up from his seat. "Usual for everyone?" he asked, "Maria, a lemonade right?"

"Yes please. Marcos, will you see if you can find Aaron while you're out?" she pleaded.

"No problem." The next act was just coming onto the stage. Marcos hustled out of the arena.

ELVIS, THE YOUNGER YEARS

Marcos was quickly back: he only missed one Elvis. "That was fast!" Alisha commented as Marcos handed her her beer. "There was no one there, everyone must be in here," he explained. The next several Elvises were alright, no standouts in anyone's mind, but then a guy from Memphis took center stage. This guy John came out wearing black leather pants and a black leather jacket that had a very high collar, and it was covered in silver rivets. He wore a white silk scarf around his neck and he had on dark sunglasses. He wasn't heavy or thin, kind of in-between. Alisha immediately thought of the Elvis television special 'Elvis Up Close'. The jacket was unzipped about halfway, exposing a full chest of hair, totally Elvis. Before he had a chance to open his mouth all the ladies (and a few men!) were screaming their heads off. Not only did he look cool with his long black hair, but he could also deliver. Johnny? Maria questioned herself. He was unbelievably good. Everyone in the audience was completely blown away. Most stood up right away and started dancing and waving their hands. John was older, maybe in his late-fifties but he had some moves; every time he shook his hips the women would all scream. Alisha was transfixed. He was so natural; many in the audience were transformed back to the time when they first became Elvis fans. He was singing 'Hard-Headed Women' and he brought it: every nuance was Elvis.

When he was done, he finished in true Elvis style: at first he froze in his final position, then stood up straight and slowly bowed. Then he took off his white scarf, wiped his forehead and chest and then threw the scarf into the audience of screaming fans: you would have thought it was money! Alisha, Maria, Marcos and Patty were all jumping up and down, and Alisha was whistling louder than she ever had before. John walked off the stage. "Wow!" the announcer said, clapping his hands as he walked to center stage. "How was that?" he asked excitedly. The audience responded loudly. "I'm not a judge, so I can't say anything, but man… I'd hate to be the guy who has to follow that!" he exclaimed. Marcos looked over at Alisha; she was shaking her head in agreement. She was no longer part of the group, she was somewhere else.

"Okay, we need to move on." The audience got quiet: "we've got three to go, and now I'd like to bring to the stage our last local Elvis who is also the youngest of the Elvises. Let's give Aaron a big home town round of applause! Come on out here, Aaron!" the announcer shouted. Maria looked at Alisha and then Marcos. Nah! She thought to herself. "Hello? Aaron, are you back there?" the announcer asked jokingly. The audience laughed. "What are you waiting for, kid!" came a voice from behind Aaron who was standing just offstage.

Aaron quickly turned around. "Johnny!" he yelped. "Holy crap… that was you!"

"Shhhh!" Johnny demanded. "Of course it was me." Aaron was in shock as he looked Johnny up and down.

"Man, you look so much like the real Elvis! I didn't recognize you with that jet black hair," he laughed.

"Yeah, if you're gonna do it, do it, you know what I mean?" Johnny said.

"Seriously, Johnny, you were amazing," Aaron said excitedly. "You're nuts if you think I'm going out there now! I can still just walk away and no one will be the wiser." Aaron could see how upset Johnny was getting. He stopped smiling.

"Really? You're going to quit now… because of me?" Johnny asked sharply.

The announcer was still calling out Aaron. "Aaron were going to give you like fifteen more seconds and then we'll have to move on!" he threatened.

"Why didn't you tell me?" Aaron asked, starting to get kind of upset at the realization.

"Listen, kid, right now it's not about me… it's about you, your mom and Maria. You can use me as an excuse if you want, but remember our talks? No matter what happens, no matter how well or not you do, your mom and Maria will never forget tonight for the rest of their lives," Johnny blasted Aaron as he shook his shoulder.

Aaron's face changed. He was confused. Then suddenly he heard the audience, "Aaron! Aaron! Aaron!"

"See, they want you, Aaron! Get on out here!" The announcer said, trying to coax him out. "Go on, kid, get out there!" Johnny gave Aaron a shove. Aaron got just past the curtain, he turned back to look at Johnny. "You'll be fine, we'll talk later."

Aaron slowly walked out onto the stage. "Ah, there he is!" The announcer was relieved. "So happy you decided to join us," he added. The audience was clapping, trying to offer up support for one of their own. It wasn't until Aaron made it into the spotlight that his mom, Maria, Marcos and even Patty realized it was their Aaron.

"Holy shit!" Alisha said a little too loudly.

Maria couldn't do anything; she froze with her hands over her mouth. Marcos stood up and started yelling like a proud father at his kid's soccer game, "Alright, Aaron! You bring it!" he yelled loud enough for Aaron to hear. Aaron smiled.

He strained to try to see anyone he knew but because of the bright lights he couldn't make out anyone's face. He adjusted his guitar to get ready to play. He stepped up to the microphone, leaned in close, and cleared his throat. "This is for my mom, Marcos and Maria," he said softly.

Alisha screamed and then started whistling like crazy; you could see the people in front of her were getting upset, they had to cover their ears because Alisha's whistle was so loud. Alisha saw this and reacted by patting them on their shoulders and pronouncing "That's my son!" Maria still sat frozen, but the smile on her face was so big it was poking through her hands.

Aaron strummed his guitar, then cleared his throat again. He started the song that he and Johnny had practiced dozens of times together, but he was having a hard time focusing: he couldn't get Johnny out of his head. Then he heard his mom's whistle again: he would recognize her whistle anywhere. Aaron stopped and smiled. In an instant he was transformed, he blocked everything else out and fully committed himself to the song. He even lost track of the audience; he was the only one there, he only cared about doing his best, doing it right. The audience was at first stunned by this young man who not only sounded like Elvis 'the younger years', but had down all the moves and attitudes. The audience was completely focused on Aaron; every time he would move close to the edge of the stage and bend down to touch a lady's hand, every woman in the audience would scream. One lady even pretended to faint after Aaron touched her, it was pretty funny. Aaron dressed old-school Elvis, jeans rolled up at the ankle with a white tee shirt and black hard shoes, he could have come right out of the fifties. He pulled it off... completely. When he finished the last words of the song and took the last strum of his guitar, the audience jumped to their feet with applause and cheers. The announcer came onstage and walked right up to Aaron. Together they stood in front of the microphone.

"Son... that was simply amazing," he told the audience while looking at Aaron.

"Thank you," Aaron said meekly.

"I said I felt sorry for the guy who had to follow John from Memphis, but boy, was I wrong!" the announcer yelled out loudly, looking for support from the audience, which they provided. Aaron backed away out of the light and started for backstage.

Alisha sat down. "Oh my God! That was that amazing! Did you know he was going to do this?" she turned to ask Maria.

"Maria, what's the matter, are you okay?"

Maria had her head hanging down low, her hands over her face. When she lifted her head and pulled her hands away, she had streams of tears coming down her face. Alisha quickly grabbed a napkin and handed it to her.

"Maria, what's wrong?" Alisha asked again.

"I don't want to leave," Maria confessed, now crying hard.

Alisha grabbed Maria and pulled her in tight for a motherly hug. "Aaron was fantastic," she muttered with her face buried in Alisha's shoulder and neck. "I felt like he was singing to me."

"Honey, trust me, he was," Alisha admitted. "That was for you."

The next singer was about to come on. Marcos leaned over to Alisha. "Should we stay?"

"Yes!" Patty jumped in, "we have to see who makes it to the finals."

"Oh, right... okay," Marcos replied. "That was so exciting I just wanted to get to Aaron right away and congratulate him," he admitted.

Alisha got up. "Maria and I are going to go to the restrooms and get a drink: what do you guys want?"

As they exited the arena area into the main fairgrounds, Maria put her arm around Alisha. "Thank you. I needed to get out of there for a minute."

"It's okay. Me, too."

"Okay... So your son, holy smoke! He was amazing!" Maria said excitedly as she hopped up and down. "I must have gotten the shivers five times!"

"Me, too!" Alisha said excitedly.

"Did you know this was going to happen?" Maria asked.

"Me? No clue," she told her. "I thought maybe you knew!"

"No... no idea. Wow, that makes it even more impressive," Maria said full of smiles and excitement. This meant it really was for her.

"That was quite a surprise he pulled off," Alisha admitted. Maria couldn't stop smiling and just nodded.

After cleaning up a bit, they got some drinks and headed back to their seats. "What did we miss?" Alisha asked as she passed out the drinks.

"The last three guys were all really good, but none of them even came close to Aaron... or that John guy," Patty told them. Marcos agreed.

The announcer stepped up to the microphone. "How was that, ladies and gentlemen?" The audience clapped excitedly, and Alisha whistled. "Come on out here, guys!" the announcer said, calling all of the contestants onto the stage. There were fifteen guys in total, all different; young, old, tall, short, fat and thin. But they all, except for the one local guy, did really well. Most of them impersonated the older Elvis, a couple were somewhere in-between, and then there was Aaron, who looked and played a much younger Elvis. "I'm pretty sure this is one of the best groups of Elvises we've ever had!" the announcer admitted. Again the audience showed their support. "So many of them deserve to go to the next round but we can only take three. So the three that are going to move on to the final round are John from Memphis, Bobby from Atlanta and Aaron from... well, here!" he announced excitedly. The audience went nuts but Alisha, Maria, Marcos and Patty went berserk. The other Elvises slowly walked offstage. "Come on over here, guys," he called out to the three finalists. "Are you ready for a final round?" They all nodded yes. "Okay, in this round, Bobby, you'll be first followed by Aaron and then you, John," he explained. "You ready to go?" he asked, looking at Bobby.

"I am."

Aaron and Johnny walked off the stage. Johnny excused himself and told Aaron he'd be right back. "Okay," Aaron said, then ran back up the steps to the stage and stood behind the curtains to watch Bobby. He's good, Aaron thought. As Bobby walked offstage after his performance, Aaron walked on. Aaron wasn't as nervous this time; he had sung this song a thousand times, and 'Heartbreak Hotel' was one of his and his mom's favorite. Aaron didn't hesitate for a second, he started right in: "Well since my baby left me... Well I found a new place to dwell..." Within seconds he owned the audience: it was powerful, it was special. Maria started to cry again, and this time Alisha was right there with her. Alisha, Maria and Patty put their arms around each other and swayed to the music. When Aaron was done, the audience gave him a standing ovation: it was amazing. Aaron left the stage feeling pretty good about his performance: he was pumped.

As he passed the curtain Johnny was coming onto the stage. "That was really good," he told him. "Well done."

"Thanks, Johnny!"

Aaron stopped and stood just behind the curtain so he could be as close as possible when Johnny started. Johnny sang 'Blue Suede Shoes', also a favorite of Aaron's. This time it was Aaron who was blown away. Wow! Johnny is the real deal for sure. He's got this thing so down, he was thinking as Johnny was finishing his song. Johnny also received a standing ovation, only it lasted for several minutes. Johnny took one bow and walked offstage. Aaron barely had a chance to congratulate Johnny when the announcer called the three finalists back onto the stage.

Aaron, Johnny and Bobby stood center stage right next to the announcer; the other competitors stood back a few feet. "Again, I just want to say what a terrific job by all of our competitors, they were fantastic; let's give them all a round of applause?" he challenged the audience. "Also, before I announce the winner I want to say thank you to our judges: tough job, but they did a great job this year," the audience applauded.

"We'll see if they did a great job," Alisha whispered to Marcos.

"Okay, this is it, only one of these Elvises will go on to the nationals; but I want to remind the guys who don't win today that each one of you still has the opportunity to go to the nationals by winning other sanctioned regional events. But... I'm sorry to say there can only be one winner here today." A young pretty woman dressed like a cowgirl with white boots and a white cowboy hat walked onstage and handed the announcer an envelope.

Aaron was very nervous: he knew he hadn't won but the excitement was overwhelming. He and Johnny were lined up on opposite sides so they couldn't talk to each other; Aaron tried to find Johnny after his first performance, he was really anxious to talk to him. He looked everywhere but couldn't find him. "Okay, in my hand I have the winner of this year's 'All County Fair, Elvis Presley Impersonation Contest'! Are you ready?" he asked the audience, and they all cheered and clapped loudly. "I am proud to announce this year's winner is..." He opened the envelope and pulled out the card. You could see the announcer already had a name on his lips just as he looked at the card. Then you could hear him stumble. "Hmm," he murmured, then glanced over at the judges. He quickly regrouped and held the card up high over his head. "This year's champion is Aaron Butler!"

Everyone in the audience was shocked: not upset, but shocked. It took a second for some to catch their breath - well, except for Aaron's friends and family; then everyone gave Aaron the recognition he deserved. Maria and Alisha were holding hands, jumping up and down wildly. Even Marcos got into it and was throwing his fist into the air. It was a pretty funny sight. It was obvious that most thought John would be the winner; Aaron was fantastic but John was the whole package, and many people reacted to John because he so accurately portrayed the Elvis they remembered. All of the other Elvises onstage were naturally disappointed, except one, but still they went out of their way to congratulate Aaron and shake his hand, even Johnny.

Aaron leaned into Johnny. "What happened?"

"What do you mean, what happened? You won, kid, you were awesome... really," Johnny said proudly.

"Yeah, I think I did alright, but you... you were amazing."

He wanted to say more but the announcer put the microphone right in Aaron's face; Johnny and the others walked off the stage. "Aaron, so tell everyone out there how you're feeling right now?" he asked abruptly. Aaron liked to perform but this kind of thing made him very uncomfortable.

"I feel good," he said into the mike.

"Good?" the announcer questioned.

"Oh, well great!" he said with more confidence.

"That's what I'm talking about! Let's hear it again for our winner, Aaron Butler!" Aaron waved to the crowd, then quickly walked offstage.

Before he could even get to the bottom step backstage, his mom, Maria, Marcos and Patty were standing there right in front of him.

Alisha was practically giddy. "Aaron!" She ran up to him. "Oh my God, that was fantastic! You were fantastic!" she was acting like she was a fifteen-year-old girl who was meeting her first rockstar. She must have kissed him twenty times all over his face. Aaron was cool with it, completely.

"Un Um!" Maria spoke up. "You think I could get a turn?" she laughed.

Alisha proudly but reluctantly passed Aaron to Maria. "I have no words," she said to him. She gave him a long, bold kiss then a big hug. As she did she leaned in close to whisper in his ear. "You're going to pay for this," she threatened.

"Really?" Aaron was all smiles, only this time it was too dark to see him blush.

"Come on, ladies! Make some room for his other fans!" Marcos demanded with a big smile. Maria stepped back so Marcos could get closer. "Aaron... that was..." Marcos started to get a little emotional when Patty stepped up.

"Fantastic!" she announced.

"Yes! Fantastic! I am completely bowled over." Marcos reached out and picked up Aaron's hand to shake it. He shook it hard and squeezed Aaron's arm with his other hand.

"Your dad would have been so proud," he told Aaron as he started to get emotional again.

"Okay, that's enough of that," Patty announced strongly. "Let's go celebrate!" she suggested.

"Great idea, Patty," Alisha told the group. They all agreed.

"Oh wait!" Aaron burst out. "Can you guys wait here for a second, there's someone I want you guys to meet." Aaron ran off behind a wall deeper into the backstage area. Four or five minutes later he was back by himself.

"Well, where is this person you want us to meet?" his mom asked.

"Sorry, guys, he's already gone," Aaron said a little dejected.

"That's okay, maybe next time?" Maria offered.

"Right, next time," Marcos agreed. "Come on. Let's go do some celebrating!" Marcos commanded. "I'm buying!" he announced happily.

Aaron and Alisha looked at each other and smiled. A rare day that Marcos 'buys'. He will take the shirt off his back for you, but to 'buy' - that means everything.

THE DIVERSION

Aaron barely slept that night; he was so excited to go to Johnny's. Well before the sun came up Aaron did some serious damage to his chores. He passed on breakfast without saying anything to his mom and was on the road before anyone knew he was gone.

"Marcos, have you seen Aaron?" Alisha asked with a great deal of difficulty: her voice was nearly gone.

Marcos chuckled. "I did, yes. About two hours ago, he was hustling like a madman, he acted like he had someplace else he needed to be."

"Does Maria know he's gone?" Marcos asked.

"No I don't think so," Alisha squeaked, "but I haven't seen her yet either this morning."

"Seen who?" Maria asked as she walked into the kitchen.

"That's funny," Marcos laughed.

Maria looked at him with a sleepy smile. "You," Alisha said in a low, raspy voice.

"We were just mentioning we hadn't seen you yet and we were wondering if you knew that Aaron already left," Marcos explained.

"Left?"

"Yeah, he was in a big hurry this morning. He had all of his chores done very early, next thing I knew he was driving off with Elvis."

151

"Huh. That's strange?" Maria sort of asked.

"Ever since last night he's been acting a little crazy," Alisha said.

"Where do you think he went?" Maria asked the both of them.

"Fishing would be my guess," Marcos chimed in.

"I bet you're right," Alisha said in a very low, weak voice. "That only makes sense, it's his way of calming down."

A light bulb went off for Maria. "Ah huh," she blurted out.

"What?" Alisha asked.

"Oh nothing, I think you guys are probably right. I'm sure he needs to come down after last night's craziness, that's for sure."

But Maria knew exactly where Aaron was: he's over at Johnny's. Maria sat down at the kitchen table next to Alisha and poured herself a cup of coffee. "That was quite a night last night," she remarked. Alisha sort of laughed then grabbed her throat.

"What's so funny?" Maria inquired.

"She can barely talk," Marcos laughed, too. Alisha's voice was so hoarse from the contest that when she opened her mouth to speak barely anything came out, and then it was nearly impossible to understand her.

"Amazing," she tried to say, in a mouse of a voice.

Maria started to laugh with Marcos. "I'm sorry, I don't mean to laugh, but that is pretty funny." Maria got up from the table and went to the cupboard. "I'm making you some hot tea, that's what you need."

Marcos was still chuckling. "This is the quietest I've ever heard Alisha." Alisha gave him a death stare but then smiled.

"So what's the plan for today?" Maria asked.

Alisha tried to answer but couldn't speak a word. "Right now we just need to finish up at your house which we should be able to do today, and we're good, you'll be all set," Marcos said, speaking for Alisha.

Maria smiled and thanked him. "I'm not too worried that Aaron has 'gone fishing' but I am a little worried about how he's going to react when I leave; he has barely spoken about it the last couple of days." Marcos and Alisha both nodded. "Every time I bring it up he changes the subject."

Alisha took another big gulp of the hot tea. "To be honest, I'm a little worried about it, too," she admitted in a low but clearer voice. "I know he's been strong and supportive, but trust me, once you leave... Man, he's going to be a basket case. I'm not looking forward to that," she admitted. The tea was working: Alisha was getting her voice back.

Marcos got up to leave. "Where are you going?" Alisha scolded. "Not my department," he smiled, "but Alisha is right," he said, looking at Maria. "Aaron's going to be a handful when you leave."

Maria didn't know what to say, so she smiled. She was clearly already hurting, but she didn't want to say anything. She was dreading the day she had to leave. "I know, it's going to be a long year for both of us," she admitted, holding back her emotions. "Maybe between school, and now the responsibility of two farms - hopefully that will keep his mind preoccupied," she tried to joke.

"Oh trust me, I'm going to have that kid hopping," Marcos told them as he walked out.

Aaron arrived at Johnny's front door pretty early the next morning. He decided it was too early so he took Elvis down to the river to play around and kill some time. Aaron relaxed at the water's edge skipping stones while Elvis ran around chasing birds. After about an hour or so he decided that it had probably been long enough, so he and Elvis headed back to Johnny's. As he cleared the trees and could see the house he abruptly stopped. The red truck was there! Awe, man, he thought to himself. Today's not Thursday. I wonder why the truck is here today?

Aaron knelt down to pet Elvis. "What do you think, boy? Should we go say hi anyway?" Elvis barked. Aaron argued with himself for a minute or two. I did promise, he reminded himself. He really wanted to see Johnny and talk about the contest; he really wanted to ask Johnny why he didn't tell him that he was going to enter... But he was conflicted. "What the heck, Elvis?" Aaron knew the rules, but he decided to go to visit Johnny anyway. "Come on, Elvis, Johnny will be happy to see us." Elvis barked. As Aaron approached the house the front door opened. A stout, medium-height older man with short dark red and gray hair came out onto the front porch. He closed the door behind him.

"You must be Aaron?" the man asked as he knelt down to pet the dog. "And this must be Elvis, right?" he laughed.

"Yes."

The man stood and walked closer to Aaron. "I'm Red." He put out his hand to shake.

Aaron shook the man's hand. "Hi."

Must be the driver of the red truck, he thought. Aaron felt like he recognized the man. "Do I know you?"

"Oh I doubt that. You did pretty well yesterday, I thought you were spot on," he told Aaron.

"Oh thanks. Nothing compared to Johnny, though. I'm actually very excited to talk to him about the contest. Is he around?"

Red didn't answer.

Aaron was confused. "So you were there?"

"Sure, I was with Johnny. I saw the whole thing, very impressive. Are you excited to go to nationals?" he asked.

"Nationals... Oh, I don't know, honestly I haven't given it a minute. So... Where's Johnny?" Aaron asked abruptly. "Is he here?"

Red's face changed, it became stern and serious. "He is, but he's not going to be able to see you today, he's not feeling well," he explained.

"Oh. That sucks. Can I just say hi then?"

"No!" Red snapped, then cleared his throat. "Listen... Johnny is not doing well, he's sick and yesterday's little event pushed him over the edge. He needs to rest... okay?" Red explained sternly.

"Sure... of course... I understand," Aaron told Red, even though he wasn't sure he did. "Is he going to be okay?"

"He just needs rest," Red emphasized.

Aaron remembered the first time he met Johnny, and how he collapsed on the kitchen floor, maybe that has something to do with it. "Is there anything I can do?"

"No, but thank you, Johnny just needs some quiet time. I'll tell him you came by, though, okay?" Red assured him.

"Sure, that'd be great, thank you," Aaron answered reluctantly. "Oh... would you tell him I thought he was amazing yesterday? He totally stunned me. I never got to see the real Elvis live before, but it sure felt like I did yesterday."

"I will, that will make his day," Red grinned. Aaron started to walk away, "Aaron!" Red called out.

Aaron stopped and turned around. "Yeah?"

Red walked down the steps of the front porch to Aaron. "Listen… Johnny was meant to be out of here over a week ago. He decided to stay on a bit longer to help you out and see you perform. It was a big deal to him," he told Aaron. Aaron was really confused. "Now summer is over and I have to get him home," Red explained.

"Home? I thought this was his home?"

Red knelt down again to pet Elvis. He looked up at Aaron. "Johnny didn't tell you?"

"Tell me what?"

"This house is where Johnny summers. He loves it here and he loves to come here to be alone; he says it's the best way for him to rest and think." Red smiled. "You kind of changed that this year."

"He never mentioned anything about that. I just assumed this was his home. So is he leaving today?"

"No, first thing in the morning, though," Red responded.

"To where? Where does he live? Maybe I can come visit him there?" he insisted.

"I'm afraid that's not possible," Red told him calmly.

"Why's that?" Aaron was starting to get really frustrated. Red stood up.

"Aaron, Johnny is your friend. He thinks you're a great kid, he trusts you. I think you need to leave it at that."

"Man, I don't get it," Aaron was getting pissed.

"I know, I know. Johnny is a complicated guy, but you're lucky like I'm lucky to have him as our friend," Red said sincerely. "This I can tell you, he'll be coming back again next summer, I'm sure he's hoping you'll still be friends."

"Yeah, I guess so... I mean... of course." Aaron was shaking his head out of frustration and confusion. "So that's it? Johnny's taking off tomorrow till next summer?"

"Yes, that's the plan anyway. Look, I'm sorry, I've got to run. It was a pleasure meeting you and I'm sure we'll see each other again... soon." Red reached out and shook his hand.

"Okay..." Aaron turned to walk away then turned back. "Please tell Johnny I hope he gets better quickly."

"No problem." Red smiled then walked back up the steps to the front porch.

When Aaron got to the tree line he turned and yelled at Elvis to catch up. "Let's go, Elvis!" he called out. Then he noticed a curtain on one side of the house slowly close. "Man, I hope he's going to be okay," he said to Elvis. "Summer home? Next summer? A little nuts, right, Elvis?" Elvis barked. "Come on, let's go!" Aaron started to run with Elvis right behind him.

The reality that Maria was leaving on Sunday was starting to sink in for everyone. The tension around the farm all week was palpable. Everyone was on edge. If it wasn't for the last-minute planning and preparation for Marcos's surprise party, someone was sure to explode. It was nice because Patty jumped right in when she heard about the party and really helped out. She was especially helpful in planning a diversion while everyone else got the house ready.

That Saturday morning was frantic around the farm. Aaron woke up mad and frustrated. Not just because Johnny took off without so much as a goodbye, but also because Maria was leaving the next day and Aaron was already starting to feel the hole in his stomach. Aaron was pissed about it. Who has a house in the middle of nowhere to summer in and then takes off to some mystery place and he won't tell me about it? Maybe I'm better off! he tried to convince himself. Truth was, with Maria leaving and now Johnny gone, Aaron was starting to feel sorry for himself; he was already feeling lonely.

When Aaron told Maria the Johnny story, at first she laughed. "Come on, really?"

"Yea, I'm not making this up, it was so weird," Aaron explained.

"That is weird. I'm sorry, Aaron. I know how much you like Johnny and enjoy hanging out with him, but you have to admit things were a little 'different'."

"They were. But then that's what I think I liked about him most, I don't know, whatever. He's gone now."

"Look, I thought he was cool, too. Maybe he's some eccentric millionaire and doesn't want anyone to know it? Who knows?" She smiled. "Besides, you still have me for one more day. Doesn't that count for something?"

"That counts for everything!"

Maria hugged Aaron. "Are you going to be all lonely?" she teased, mussing up his hair.

Aaron laughed. "Well... yeah."

They both laughed. Aaron shrugged it off.

"We need to get back to work, there's still a lot to do," Maria commanded.

"Yes, ma'am," Aaron complied. What Aaron did not tell Maria, or anyone, was how much Johnny helped him get ready for the contest or even that Johnny was the 'John from Memphis' at the contest. He was surprised Maria didn't make the connection, but he decided he was going to keep it to himself... for now.

As soon as Marcos was done with his regular rounds he headed out early for a special day with Patty. It worked like a charm. Everyone else got to work setting up decorations out back and getting the food ready.

"Marcos is going to be so mad at us!" Aaron said to his mom.

"I know... isn't it great!"

Maria came into the kitchen where Aaron and his mom were talking. "Almost everything outside is done," she announced. "Aaron, the guys just need your help getting the big banner hung right."

"No problem," he immediately headed out back.

"Alisha," Maria started.

"Yes, honey?" She knew the instant she looked at Maria's face something was wrong or Maria needed to tell her something.

"While we have a minute I wanted to talk to you," she said, starting to tear up.

"Of course, honey. Sit down." Alisha gestured toward the kitchen table. They sat down and Alisha poured them both a glass of lemonade.

"I don't know where to start," Maria confessed.

"That's okay. Just tell me what's on your mind." Alisha reached over and picked up Maria's hand.

"I know I've thanked you a million times for helping me with my grandmother and her affairs, but you guys went so far beyond, I cannot put into words…" Maria started to shed some tears. Alisha got up, grabbed a tissue from the counter, and then moved her chair as close to Maria as possible.

"Here" She handed the tissue to Maria.

"You took me in when my own family wouldn't. You're helping me with my farm… Alisha, I just wanted you to know…" She took a deep breath. "I love you like I would my mother," she said softly. Alisha instantly started to tear up. "I hope that's okay?"

"Oh my God, Maria." She reached for Maria's other hand. "You are and will always be the daughter I never had. We will, all of us, always be here for you whenever you need. It's not even a question… To us you are family," Alisha said strongly and convincingly. They cried together as they hugged.

Just then Aaron walked back into the room. "That's all… Oops."

Alisha lifted her head and gave Aaron a very strong signal that he needed to leave. He got the hint and quickly left the room. "Maria," Alisha started, "you don't ever thank me or Aaron or Marcos again, you understand," she told her sternly, holding Maria by the shoulders. Maria nodded. "This chapter of your life is done, we will never forget but we will move onto the next chapter… all of us… together."

Maria stopped crying; she sat close looking into Alisha's eyes, listening intently. "You are not moving away, you are going away for school, that's all," Alisha explained. "I expect you here over the holiday break and then when you graduate, this is your home... If you want it to be." Maria started to cry again and leaned into hug Alisha, then Alisha started to weep. They quickly ran out of tissues.

"Surprise!" everyone yelled out as Aaron turned on all the lights when Marcos and Patty came through the back door of the house. Marcos was truly surprised: it fact, it scared the heck out of him! Not only could you could see the shock on his face, but he nearly fell down. Aaron and Alisha loved it, but Maria felt bad. She ran up to Marcos and gave him a kiss on the cheek.

"Happy Marcos Day, Marcos!" she said with a big smile. Marcos almost immediately calmed down. Since it wasn't his birthday the group decided to call the celebration 'Marcos Day'.

He grudgingly smiled back at her. "Thank you. What the heck is Marcos Day?"

Then Aaron came up to wish Marcos a happy Marcos Day followed by Alisha: "Happy Marcos Day, Marcos!" she said, only the way Alisha can: fun, coy and with sincerity. Marcos couldn't resist and smiled back at her.

"What the heck is Marcos Day?" he asked again.

"We all decided that you are so special to us that we needed to have a special day just for you: Marcos Day!" Alisha excitedly exclaimed.

"You know I'm going to be mad at you tomorrow!"

"I'm okay with that," Alisha laughed.

They hugged and then everyone started to sing 'Happy Marcos Day' to the tune of 'Happy Birthday': it was really funny. The night was turning out to be a big success: everyone, even Marcos, was having a great time. "Speech!" Aaron yelled out at one point, which was quickly picked up by the rest of the party-goers. "Speech!" they all cried out. Marcos shook his head no and tried to resist, but he wasn't going to get away with it. So he reluctantly walked to the top step of the porch, and the group started to cheer and clap. Marcos cleared his throat.

"I have no idea what to say!" he started. Everyone laughed. "Thank you so much to all of you for being here and celebrating this strange day with me: this was truly a miraculous surprise," he told them as he looked first at Alisha and then at Patty. Everyone laughed. "I am blessed to have you as my friends and my family," he said sincerely. Marcos had to clear his throat again: he was having a hard time getting out the words as he became more emotional. He took an extra long breath and let it out slowly. "You, this family and this farm mean everything to me... Thank you." Then he walked back down the steps to Patty and Alisha. "Whew!" he let out. "Don't you ever do this to me again!" he joked to Alisha pointing his finger at her. "Do we have any cake at this party?"

Everyone was having such a good time; Alisha was so happy, every time she looked at Marcos he was laughing or smiling. There were probably about fifty people at the party, all friends and family, his Tennessee family. No one was supposed to bring gifts, but they did. Marcos was surprised and embarrassed about the whole thing, but he was never too good at receiving gifts. Some of the gifts were cool; others were very funny gag gifts, like the box of adult diapers he got from Patty. Marcos took it all in his stride. He only made one request during his party, and that was for Aaron to sing.

Aaron thought this might be coming so he was ready for it. He ran into the house and grabbed his guitar. When he came back out he put the guitar down and went and grabbed two patio chairs and set them next to each other at the top of the steps. Everyone looked at him a little confused, including Marcos. The group gathered in close to the patio, they knew what was coming. Aaron stood in front of the chairs. "Marcos has asked me to do a song for him for his special day." Everyone cheered. "I am excited to do this for you, Marcos..." Aaron started, "But... only if you sing with me," he smiled.

Everyone in the group started to laugh and cheer. Of course Marcos was completely caught off guard; so, too, were Alisha and Maria. Marcos naturally refused and laughed with the rest of the party-goers; Aaron was completely prepared for that reaction. Patty grabbed Marcos's hand, and he turned to look at her. "Here you go," Patty told him as she handed him a glass of his favorite whisky. Marcos looked at Patty as if she was a traitor, then he took a big gulp.

"Everyone help me get Marcos up here!" Aaron yelled out.

Patty pushed, Alisha and Maria pulled, eventually they got him to the top step. Aaron grabbed his hand. "Come on, this will be fun," he whispered in his ear.

"You're going to pay for this… oh man, big!" Marcos said but couldn't help it, and started laughing. They both sat down in the chairs, everyone started to clap and cheer. "Go Marcos!" someone in the group yelled out.

Maria looked at Alisha. "I didn't know Marcos could sing?"

Alisha laughed. "I don't think anyone else knows either!" Maria laughed.

"Okay, guys, settle down. I'm not sure how this is going to go so we need to bring it down a little," Aaron suggested. Everyone quickly quietened down. Aaron strummed his guitar. "This is one of Marcos's favorite songs, I know he loves it and, more importantly, I know he knows the words." Everyone laughed, Marcos, too. Aaron turned to Marcos. "This is for you, so don't be shy," he asked of Marcos. Aaron started to play a country song that Marcos loved.

Aaron heard this song coming from Marcos's house or truck nearly every day. Marcos had the biggest smile on his face, Patty started to tear: she knew. Aaron started singing first. Marcos was in awe how well he sang his favorite song. When he got to the chorus Aaron whacked Marcos on the knee with his knee. "Jump in," he said so only Marcos could hear. He looked terrified. He closed his eyes and started to sing with Aaron, at first very quietly. Aaron whacked him again. Marcos jumped. He opened his eyes and smiled, then suddenly out came this deep bellow of a voice, deeper than anything Aaron had ever heard. Everyone was surprised how perfect his pitch was. Aaron and Marcos did the rest of the song together; Alisha, Maria, Patty and the rest of the group were laughing with excitement and cheering through the entire song. When the song ended, Aaron stood up and raised his hands with his guitar in one of them over his head.

"How amazing was that?" he asked the group.

Marcos sat there smiling. Aaron leaned over, grabbed his arm, and pulled him to his feet. Then Aaron put his arm around his shoulder and forced him to take a bow with him. Marcos just kept laughing, maybe the whisky was finally kicking in, or he was just having a blast. Patty ran up and kissed him, something that surprised everyone. Marcos looked at her, then the group, then turned beet-red and promptly hustled off the patio. Pats on the back, hugs and kisses: it was a great moment for Marcos. Aaron was about to set his guitar down and join the party when Marcos yelled out, "Not so fast, mister!" Aaron turned back around. "Okay, now it's time for my request!" he demanded. The group cheered. Aaron smiled and picked his guitar back up. He walked to the edge of the patio and jumped right into 'Hard-Headed Woman', Marcos's favorite Elvis song.

GRACELAND

The next morning everyone was up early. Marcos brought in some fresh eggs. Alisha was making Maria's favorite breakfast, pancakes. They were all laughing and talking about the night before, sharing stories and teasing Marcos. They ate a huge breakfast and started to clean up, but then the conversation suddenly came to a stop and the mood became very somber.

Marcos went to Maria who was doing the dishes. "Maria, I have to get going. I wish I was going with you today, but I wanted to tell you if you need me for anything, or if you have any questions about your farm..." Maria leaned in and gave Marcos a big hug.

"Marcos... I'll be fine. The farm will be fine, but thank you."

Marcos started to tear up. "What's with these damn allergies all of a sudden!" he proclaimed as he quickly walked out the front door. "I'll see you soon!" he shouted. Alisha looked at Aaron: she could see he was starting to feel it.

"Alright, guys... we need to get going, especially if we are going to keep our promise to Maria and see Graceland," Alisha announced.

"Right!" Aaron shouted. Maria was excited to see Graceland, mostly because she knew how important it was to Aaron.

"Aaron, help Maria with her things then get the truck, please?" He and Maria went off to gather up Maria's bags and brought them to the front porch.

"I'll be right back," Aaron told Maria.

As he went to bring the truck around, Alisha came out front. "What a beautiful day."

"It is," Maria agreed.

Aaron pulled up and turned off the truck. After her bags were loaded and she said goodbye to Elvis, they were off for Memphis. A two and a half-hour, very long and uncomfortable drive for all of them. To keep things light, Alisha did her best to only discuss Maria's return.

When they pulled into the city, there were signs everywhere reflecting Elvis this and Elvis that. 'See where Elvis played', 'See where Elvis ate': it was kind of disgusting, actually. Thankfully no one had to figure out how to get to Graceland: there were signs on every corner. Alisha had been to Graceland many times; amazingly Aaron has only been once, but it was when he was very young. He was starting to get really excited.

"Wow, look how busy it is!" he announced as they drove around looking for a parking place.

"Mom, we're never going to get in, look at all the people waiting."

"Not to worry, Marcos has got us covered," she told him, holding up three prepaid tour tickets.

"Fantastic," Maria said.

"That Marcos… he has friends everywhere," Aaron laughed.

"Come on! Let's go!" Alisha was starting to get excited as well.

After they finally found a parking spot they walked to a small building just outside the front gate of Graceland to check in. It wasn't long at all and they were on their way inside. "This is exciting!" Maria told them. She was surprised how excited she was getting. They were in a group of about twenty people; the tour guide was an older man who looked like he could have been Elvis's grandfather. With his slicked-back, gray hair on his half-bald head and deep Southern accent, he was masterful in his details of every aspect of not just Graceland, but also Elvis and his family. Before they even got into the house the guide made many stops as they went up the tree-lined drive. He explained how Graceland came about, what life would have been like if Elvis was at home. It was fascinating. He told the stories so well he made you feel as if Elvis was about to walk out of his own front door right that second.

"This is great, Mom," Aaron said excitedly.

You could tell by her face she was having a great time, too. The group entered the house through a side door that led directly into the kitchen. "Wow, this is so not impressive, it looks like anyone's kitchen," Maria told Alisha.

"Yes that is true, young lady," the guide responded. "Elvis wanted his mom to feel like she was at home when she stayed at Graceland so it was important to Elvis to make the kitchen as close as possible to what his mother was used to, with some notable exceptions, like the oversized double oven. This kitchen was really her kitchen. Notice the carpet on the floor," the guide pointed out.

"Yuck!" was Alisha's response.

"One thing many people didn't know is that Elvis also loved to cook, especially for his friends. So it was not unusual to find Elvis in here doing some of his own cooking. Everyone has heard of Elvis's special peanut butter and banana sandwiches?" Everyone nodded. "Some of you may not know it was Elvis himself who came up with the concoction and he was the one who first tried frying it." Everyone had different reactions but Maria's cringe was the funniest. They moved on into the living room.

The group continued to move from room to room, which were for the most part all roped off; they were set up for viewing only. Each area they passed garnered different reactions from different people. Truthfully, Aaron didn't like any of the rooms, not even the den. The den was famous for its ornate decorations and unusual furniture. But there was one room that you could freely move around in: the guide referred to it as the trophy room. In this room were all of Elvis's gold records and album covers, which consumed one entire wall. The coolest thing was the outfits. In glass displays were many of Elvis's most famous jumpsuits and capes worn by Elvis mannequins.

"I saw him in this one!" Alisha said, all giddy. She read the plaque: 'Circa 1975'. "Yup that's the one," she was pointing out to everyone around her.

Aaron and Maria were standing together looking at the hundreds of photographs on the walls. Elvis was in all of them, posing with everyone from the hot Hollywood stars at the time to Richard Nixon, the President of the United States.

"Pretty impressive," Maria said to Aaron.

"Yeah." Aaron was completely engrossed.

Aaron was studying each photograph very closely. Maria enjoyed it, but felt like they were in some sort of strange temple and she had gotten her fill. She wrapped her arm inside Aaron's. "Don't you think we should get going now?" she asked softly. Aaron was straining to look at a picture that was high on the wall. "Aaron?"

"Oh my God!" Aaron burst out, startling Maria and everyone around them.

Aaron strained even harder to look at this one photo. A security guard and the tour guide quickly approached Aaron. "Are you okay?" the guard asked.

Aaron came down off his toes and looked at the guide. Aaron's face was one of shock. "Mister, can you tell me who that man is in that picture with Elvis?" Maria was a little concerned, as were many in the room.

Alisha walked up to see what was going on. "What's wrong, you guys?"

"Mister, please... who is that man?"

The guide looked up at the photo. "Which one? You mean the one with his friend Red?"

"Oh my GOD!" Aaron burst out again.

The security guard grabbed Aaron's arm. "I'm sorry, sir, you're going to have to come with me," he demanded.

The guide, Alisha and Maria followed Aaron as he was being escorted out of the house and off the property. "Aaron! What the heck was that!" his mom demanded. "How completely embarrassing! What's wrong with you?"

Aaron sat on a bench that was just outside the gate. Maria sat down next to him. "Are you okay? That was a little weird."

"Yeah... I'm sorry." He looked up at his mom and then the tour guide. "I'm really sorry. I don't know what came over me."

"Are you okay?" the guide asked Aaron. "I've had people cry, even faint, but I've never had a reaction quite like that."

"I am so sorry," he told the guide. Aaron couldn't help but smile.

"No, that's okay, it's over now... but I am curious why you were asking about Red?"

"Ah, weird, right? I'm sorry. I don't know, I felt like I'd maybe met him before or something. Like I said, weird."

"Well yes, that is unlikely. No one has seen Red in, oh I don't know, eight years or more." Aaron looked surprised. "He disappeared about a year after Elvis died. He told his family that he couldn't handle all the pressure and the questions anymore," the guide explained. "No one has seen him or heard from him since. He just disappeared."

"Wow," Aaron chuckled.

"What's so funny, Aaron?" his mom questioned, still really upset.

The guide looked concerned and puzzled. "You're sure you're alright?" he asked again.

"Yes. I'm sorry... actually I couldn't be better. Thank you so much for your excellent tour. I enjoyed it more than you could ever know."

Aaron stood up from the bench, reached out and shook the guide's hand. "Come on, guys, we've got to get to the airport," he announced as he started to walk away. Alisha and Maria stood there looking at each other.

"Do you know what's going on?" Alisha asked Maria.

"Not a clue, I was hoping you'd be able to explain." They both thanked the guide and hurried after Aaron who was nearly back to the truck.

Aaron helped them get in the truck and closed the door. Maria sat in the middle, Alisha on the passenger side; Aaron started the truck and pulled out of the parking lot. "Nothing?" Alisha asked sharply.

"Just a little bizarre back there, don't you think?" Maria sat quietly, shaking her head in agreement.

"I know, Mom, I'm sorry. I… I saw that picture and something came over me. I'm not sure I can explain."

Aaron's back was now against the wall. He never told his mom about going back to Johnny's and how they became friends. He tried to tell her several times but with Maria's grandmother dying and Maria leaving, plus the party, Aaron just couldn't find the right time or truthfully tried to avoid it. He knew he was going to have to say something. He had never lied to his mom, and now he was afraid that, however he explained this one, she would be upset and hurt.

"I met him!" Aaron blurted out. He couldn't hold it in or keep it a secret a second longer; he felt that if he was going to come clean he'd have to come completely clean.

"Met who?" Alisha asked.

"The man in the photo… Red."

"What are you talking about? You heard the tour guide: no one has seen this guy Red in a really long time. How do you figure you 'met' him?" She was still mad but she was asking in a joking type of way, teasing almost.

"Okay, Mom, this is a bit of a story."

"Perfect. We have an hour's drive to the airport and then we have what, maybe an hour before Maria has to go in?" Maria sat quietly and shook her head in agreement.

"What are you smiling at?" Aaron asked Maria.

"Me? Oh well, nothing really. But this is kinda fun," she smiled harder. Alisha tried not to smile but ended up laughing.

"Okay but you're not going to be happy with me," Aaron explained to his mom.

"Happy? I'll be the judge of that… So get going… spill."

Aaron smiled. "You remember the man I ran into down at the river, Johnny." He was quickly interrupted.

"Oh, it's Johnny now? So you know his name? How'd you find that out?" His mom wanted to know.

"Mom, if you let me tell you the whole story you'll understand, otherwise this will take a week!"

"Okay, you're right. Go ahead." Maria sat up a little straighter and stopped smiling. She knew Aaron only went back to see Johnny because of her.

"Okay, well I went back to see this guy a few weeks after you told me not to. I can't explain why, I don't know, I just wanted to." Maria squeezed Aaron's hand.

Aaron's story went on all the way to the airport without a single interruption. He told his mom about when he first went to Johnny's house and how sick he was and how he tried to help him out. Aaron shared some of the things he and Johnny talked about while they sat in Johnny's kitchen. He even told her about the red truck. Then he told her about how Johnny worked with Elvis, and Alisha suddenly lit up.

"What do you mean worked with? Is this the Red guy you saw in the photo?" she asked, getting all excited. Maria was shaking her head no: thankfully Alisha was too excited to notice.

"No, Mom, Johnny's Johnny. Let me finish," he pleaded. They parked the truck, grabbed Maria's luggage and went to the ticket counter in the airport to check her in. "Okay, we have a little over an hour. What do you say we get Maria some food from the coffee shop before she has to head in?"

"That sounds great, Mrs. B.," Maria told her. She was hungry but equally excited to hear the rest of the story.

After they sat down and ordered food Aaron was asked to continue. Aaron didn't leave out anything. He told them how it was Johnny who talked him into doing the contest and how much he helped him prepare for it.

"Yeah, I feel pretty bad about lying to you, Mom, but all those times I went fishing, I also was visiting with Johnny," he admitted.

"Hmm... okay, go on." Alisha was more intrigued than mad.

Maria smiled; Aaron couldn't help but laugh.

"What?" Alisha asked.

"Come on, we don't have a lot of time," Maria said urgently. "You have to finish the story, Aaron, there's no way I'm getting on that plane without knowing the rest!"

"Okay," Aaron smiled.

He knew he was likely out of the woods with his mom, so he felt much better about telling the story. "This you're not going to believe," Aaron started in again. "John from Memphis... at the fair? Well, that was Johnny."

"I knew it!" Maria said excitedly. Aaron looked at Maria.

"You did? Why didn't you say anything?"

"Well, I wasn't sure and I thought if it was Johnny you'd tell me."

"Holy crap... that was your friend Johnny?" Alisha interrupted.

"Yeah it was, is that crazy?"

"Your friend Johnny was the John from Memphis?" Alisha asked again. Alisha was a little shocked. "Well I can tell you for sure that guy was amazing," she admitted.

"I know!?" Aaron admitted, too.

"How come you didn't introduce us?" Alisha asked.

"I tried, but when I went to find him he had already gone."

"Oh that's what that was," Maria said, remembering the incident. "Did you know your friend Johnny was going to be in the contest?" Maria asked.

"I had no idea. Red told me he only did it because I inspired him, if you can believe that," Aaron laughed.

"Red!" Alisha burst out. "What do you mean, Red?"

Aaron laughed. "That's the next part of the story, if you let me get to it." Both Alisha and Maria were completely engulfed at this point.

"This is where things get a little strange. The day after the contest I went over to Johnny's. I was so excited to talk to him about the contest, plus I was a little... I don't know, surprised he didn't tell that he was going to be in the contest. I didn't think that was too cool. But before I even got to his door this man came out and met me on the front porch. He introduced himself as Red." Aaron smiled. "You know, I thought I recognized the guy but I wasn't sure and I didn't know from where."

"Well what was 'Red' doing at Johnny's?" Maria asked.

"Yeah, what was he doing there?" Alisha chimed in.

"You remember the red truck?"

They both nodded. "That was his truck," Aaron explained. "Can you believe it?"

"Okay... let's say that was the Red you saw in the photo. I still don't understand why he was at Johnny's?" Maria questioned.

"Honestly, that part is a little complicated."

"Why?" Alisha asked.

"I'm pretty positive it was Red in the photo back at Graceland, and Johnny told me he worked for Elvis... so if you put those things together... I guess Red is friends with Johnny because they know each other through Elvis, and now Red is helping Johnny out... I guess. Why... I don't know. I do know it was Red who was bringing Johnny supplies every week, you know the Thursday thing?" They both nodded. "I think he was there yesterday to take him home or... somewhere."

"What do you mean?" Maria asked.

Aaron told them the conversation he had with Red. "I never got to see or talk with Johnny at all; Red said he was too sick." Aaron went on to tell the rest of the story, as best he could remember it. He told them how Red explained that the house was only a summer home for Johnny, and that he stayed longer than he planned to and that he was leaving the next morning.

"Where's he going?" Alisha asked.

"I don't know, Red wouldn't tell me. All he would say was he was taking him home."

"That's strange," Maria responded.

"I wonder why he wouldn't tell you?" Alisha asked.

"I'm not sure. I asked a couple of times but I could tell if I asked again Red was going to get really upset, so I let it go." Aaron paused. "Now you know the whole story."

"What... that's it?" Alisha proclaimed. "This mystery guy Johnny lives, at least in the summer, in the middle of nowhere in the middle of Tennessee; he worked for Elvis and is friends with the long-lost Red; also a friend of Elvis's. Is that right?" she asked in a frustrated voice.

"That's pretty much it, Mom."

"Wow," Maria exclaimed. "I'm blown away. That was an amazing story, Aaron, amazing. Do you think Johnny is really coming back next summer?"

"Honestly I don't know. Red said that's what he does, I don't know why but I didn't get a strong sense he was coming back," Aaron told them.

"Oh my God, Maria! Look at the time, honey, you've got to go!" Alisha announced.

"Oh crap!" Aaron said as he picked up Maria's carry-on bag.

They ran to security. Maria gave Alisha a hug and thanked her, then she kissed and hugged Aaron.

"I'll talk to you tonight, okay?" Aaron asked.

"Yes, I'll call you as soon as I can."

Thankfully there was almost no line at security so Maria was through quickly. From the other side of security she waved feverishly; Alisha blew Maria kisses. Then she disappeared deeper into the airport.

Aaron and his mom sat in the hot truck in the parking lot for a minute or two not saying a word. Aaron spoke up. "Thanks, Mom." She looked at him, the reality of what just happened was starting to sink in.

"I think I know now what it's going to feel like if you ever leave me," she said as she started to cry.

Aaron leaned over and put his arm around her. "Mom... where would I go? I love it here, this is my home, I'm not going anywhere," he explained to her, gently rubbing her back. "Maria will be back before we know it."

Alisha smiled. "I thought I'd have been the one comforting you," she smiled, as she wiped the tears away. She got herself back together. "Come on, let's go home."

"You got it." Aaron started the truck and pointed it toward the highway.

"By the way, what are you thanking me for?" Alisha suddenly remembered.

"Oh, I know what you did… for Maria; keeping her occupied and busy to make everything going on in her life a little easier to deal with. That was very cool, Mom. You're the best."

Alisha smiled, she reached over and squeezed Aaron's hand. "Okay… Now I have some questions for you, young man," Alisha smirked. Aaron smiled: he knew this was just in fun. "For starters…" she started in and went on asking questions all the way home. She wanted as many details as possible about Johnny, Red and the whole bizarre story. The two-and-a-half-hour ride home flew by. Elvis came up running as soon as he saw the truck. Aaron stopped and opened his door, Elvis jumped in to ride the rest of the way to the house.

They stopped just in front of the house and got out of the truck. "I'm exhausted," Alisha announced. "How about some lemonade and leftover chicken?"

"Perfect, Mom."

Alisha paused. "It's going to be different around here," she said in a somber voice.

"Yes it will, really different."

Alisha stopped at the front door and held it open as Aaron walked in. "Hey, I have one more question," she told him.

"Sure, Mom, what?"

"Do you think Johnny was like a professional stand-in for Elvis, like maybe for his movies or something like that? I mean when he was onstage he looked and definitely sounded like Elvis, the best I've ever heard, actually."

"Really? The best?" Aaron laughed.

It took her a second but then Alisha laughed when she got it. "Well, you know?"

Aaron walked in behind his mom. "I guess that's possible, Mom, I don't know. It's funny, though, when you see him as just himself... You know, not dressed like Elvis, he only looks a little bit like him."

"Good make-up, I guess?" Alisha suggested.

"I guess so. Still I'm going to miss him, he was a good guy."

TURKEY HUNT

The first day of school was torture for Aaron. His friends tried their best to keep his mind off of Maria, but hardly a minute would go by that he didn't think about her. They had only been able to talk twice since Maria left for California just over a week ago. They agreed to talk every Sunday each week at the same time, except in the case of an emergency. Sunday couldn't come soon enough for Aaron.

He placed the call. "Hello?" Maria answered the phone.

"Maria!" Aaron said excitedly.

"Aaron... I'm so happy to speak with you," she confided. "This week has been terrible."

"Why? What's wrong?"

"I don't want to sound like a whiner but I just don't like it here."

"But you've only been there a little over a week, don't you think you need to give it a chance? How's it going at school?"

Maria chuckled. "School? You would love it out here. No one seems to take school very seriously, but they definitely take what they wear to school seriously." Aaron laughed. These people are way different," she added.

"Yeah I've heard all the stories but I'm sure you'll eventually make some friends, then it will get easier." Aaron was trying his best to be supportive.

"I know, I just miss you…"

"Yeah, I miss you, too. School sucked before but now it seriously sucks without you here. How are your uncle and his family treating you?"

"Okay… It's still pretty uncomfortable, though. I can tell they have some kind of resentment toward me. I'm sure it's because of Nana."

"That's crappy. They'll get over it. Just be yourself, they won't be able to help but love you." Aaron could feel Maria smiling through the phone.

"Aaron… I love you," she said quietly.

"I know… You know I love you, too," he admitted, clearing his throat.

"Is that Maria?" came this loud voice. "Me! Me!" Aaron's mom ran up and grabbed the phone from him. "Maria!" she blurted out excitedly. "Oh, we miss you so bad! How are you doing? Do you need anything?" She was blasting Maria with questions like she hadn't talked to her in a month.

"No, Mrs. B. I'm all good here," Maria was laughing. "I miss you too, though: can't wait to see you in three months, two weeks and one day, but I'm not counting or anything like that." Alisha laughed but it was hard for her to hold back the tears.

"Come on, Mom," Aaron cried out.

"Maria I've got to go, you call me any time if you need anything, okay?"

"Yes, ma'am, I will, thank you."

"Hey, Maria… sorry about that."

"Are you kidding? Your mom just made my day! I love that woman."

"Yeah, she loves you, too… that's for sure."

"Aaron I've got to get off the phone, I don't want these guys to get upset at me or anything. Next Sunday? Same time?"

"Yeah, I guess so. That sucks, you know…"

"For me, too. Okay, I have to go… I'll talk to you next week… I love you." Then she abruptly hung up the phone.

"How'd that go?" Alisha asked Aaron as he somberly walked into the kitchen. Aaron first made some kind of grunting noise. "Okay, I guess," he replied as he sat down at the table. "I can't wait till this year is over."

"Trust me, Aaron, I know it's hard right now, but it will go by fast, especially once planting season comes, then you won't have time to think about anything else."

"I know... I can't wait. Has Marcos hired all the help yet?"

"Yup, we're all set. He's got a crew for here and I believe he's got the crew for Maria's place all set, too."

"Great," Aaron paused. "Hey, Mom... when did you first know Dad was the one?"

Alisha held one hand to her heart; the other she put over her mouth. "The one? You mean in like... the one?"

"Yes, Mom. The one," he looked at her funny.

"Why do you ask?" she gently responded.

"I was just wondering."

Alisha needed to sit down. "Well the truth is, the first time he took me out... I knew then. Believe it or not, that was the first time I told him that I loved him. You know, it was after the Elvis concert we always talk about."

"How old were you and Dad then?" Alisha was stunned at this line of questioning; Aaron never much cared for this kind of conversation before.

Oh crap! He's growing up, Alisha thought to herself. "Ah-um, well, let me think..." She knew she'd have to tell him the truth, even though she'd rather not. "Well, I guess I was..." She paused. "Oh I don't know, I must have been around eighteen and your dad was older, I think he was nineteen."

"Yeah, that's what I thought."

"Why do you ask?" Alisha asked again cautiously.

"No reason. Just curious."

"Oh, okay," she responded nervously.

"Hey, guys," Marcos said as he walked into the kitchen with a handful of steaks.

"I just wanted to get these babies in the fridge... Barbecue night! Oh, by the way, I invited Patty, is that okay?" he asked a little too excitedly.

"Marcos, really?" Alisha whipped her head around and smiled at him. "Do you really need to ask us?" Marcos smiled; Aaron thought it was pretty funny. "Hey, we just talked to Maria, she said to say hi," Alisha told him.

"Awe, man, I missed it?"

Aaron smiled. "Next Sunday, same time. I can remind you if you want?" he told him.

"Yes please, that would be great. So how is she? Does she miss me yet?"

"Oh yea, she misses you." Alisha smiled. "She's doing okay. She really misses all of us and I think she's already feeling a little homesick."

"Awe, that's a shame. She'll be fine, though, I'm sure of it. Okay, I'm off to get Patty, then I will get the grill going, okay, Aaron?"

"Yes, sir. I'll be here."

Alisha was right, once the planting season was in full swing it was hard to think about anything else. Aaron loved the planting season, second only to harvest season, just like his dad, just like any farmer. Even though it was hard work and long hours, he loved it. It always made him think of his dad and how excited he would get. Back then, Aaron didn't understand the financial side of operating a farm, but his dad's energy and positive attitude were contagious. Everyone got into it; not only did Alisha help out in the fields but she always had tons of food and drinks available for anyone who wanted it any time of the day. As busy as he was, Aaron was fixed on only one thing; as soon as the planting was over, six weeks after that Maria would be home. He couldn't wait.

Because so many kids from the area lived or worked on a farm, school went into a kind of slow motion during the planting season.

Everyone in the community understood and did their part to support each other, even students. There was something about getting your hands dirty, working from well before sunup to well beyond sundown that made a true farmer at one with his or her land. Watching your hard work turn into something that you and nature made together, it was in their blood. Some people compared it to being a sea captain, where being at sea, being a part of something so large and powerful, is what they lived for. There weren't too many farmers that would ever say there was something else they'd rather be doing.

The planting season always wrapped up at the same time every year, and this year even with the additional work from Maria's farm they finished right on time, always four to five days before Thanksgiving. During that last week Maria must have called the house every day. She wanted to hear all about it and how everything was going. Alisha didn't mind taking time out of her day to talk to Maria; she knew it was helping her feel like she was here and a part of it all. The truth was that Thanksgiving was the most honored and celebrated holiday at the Butlers. Preparation was days in the making. A few days before Thanksgiving Marcos would go hunt the biggest turkeys possible - and he never disappointed. Aaron would do some heavy-duty catch-up for school and help out however he could. He was always responsible to make sure there were plenty of fresh fish for the table, and every year it was his job to put out the many tables and chairs for the many guests. Because it was now too cold to eat outside, tables were set all around inside the house: most of the furniture was moved upstairs or out onto the covered front porch to make room. It was always an exciting time. Every day the house smelled amazing, smells you never forgot your whole life, and the buzz around the farm was overwhelming.

Thanksgiving Day had come. Alisha started prepping and cooking some of the food days earlier, but the turkeys didn't go into the ovens or on the barbecue until Thanksgiving Day, usually before the sun was even up. The many guests started to arrive early; no one came without food in their hands. Between the two crews and all the friends, all of whom have been coming to the Butlers for Thanksgiving for years, there had to be well over fifty people. It was not easy, it was crowded, but it was fun. Drinks, food and celebration. It was a successful planting season and everyone involved felt accomplished. You could barely hear it over all the talking but the phone was ringing. Patty heard it and picked it up. She held the phone high over her head calling out to Alisha who was busy with three other ladies getting the two huge turkeys out of the ovens. "Alisha!" she yelled out again.

Alisha turned and saw Patty holding up the phone. "What is it?"

"It's Maria!" she shouted back.

"Oh!" Alisha put down her gloves and worked her way to the other side of the kitchen to Patty. Patty smiled and handed Alisha the phone. "Maria?"

"Hi, Mrs. B! It's me! Can you hear me?"

"Hold on, honey!" Alisha held the phone to her chest, "Everyone!" No response. "Excuse me, everyone!" Only those right in front of her could hear her. She held the phone tighter to her chest and then let out one of her famously loud whistles. That did it. "Sorry! But Maria's on the phone." Everyone quietened down to whispers. "Maria, I'm so happy you called. I wish so bad you were here."

"Boy oh boy, me, too. I can smell your stuffing from here!"

"Happy Thanksgiving, my favorite daughter," Alisha said gleaming.

Everyone knew that Alisha had taken Maria in and they had a special relationship, so no one thought twice when she called her daughter. "Oh thank you, please, please tell everyone that I wish them the best Thanksgiving ever and that I'll be home in two weeks!"

"I know... we can't wait, especially Aaron. I don't know what he's up to but I think he's got some plans for you guys when you get back."

"Really? Oh that sounds fun, I miss him so much." They were only able to talk for a few minutes more: the feast was working its way onto the tables.

"I have to go, Maria. The best to you and wish your family a Happy Thanksgiving from all of us here."

"I will. I'll see you guys soon!"

Alisha loved her job. The job was hard but she lived to make her family, even her extended family, as happy as possible, and her favorite way to do that? Food!

"Okay, everyone, let's make our way to a seat!" Marcos yelled out over the group.

It took a few minutes to get everyone seated but they got it done. Not a spare inch on any of the tables. Marcos pulled his chair back from the table and stood on it. "Everyone! If I could have your attention for just a minute?" he asked as several people started to tap their glasses with a fork or spoon to get everyone to quiet down and pay attention. "Thank you. Before we feast on this amazing meal I have just a few things I'd like to say," he tried to speak loud enough so he could be heard in all the rooms. "Today is a special day. I want everyone here to know what a great job you did and how proud I am of this year's planting season. Because of your hard work we will have a bountiful harvest come fall!" Everyone started to cheer and clap. Marcos held up his hands to get everyone to quiet down again. "It goes without saying, my family, my friends, the Butlers, are the best people in the world, and without Alisha and Aaron none of this would be possible... So I would like to offer a toast. To Alisha and Aaron!" he shouted. "To Alisha and Aaron!" every cheered. "And now for a prayer," Marcos bowed his head and offered a short but powerful prayer. "Amen," everyone replied. That was all it took - food and festivities began.

HOME FOR THE HOLIDAYS

Aaron was pacing back and forth over the same five-foot area like he had to pee. "Aaron, you're going to wear out the floor," his mom told him. He stopped and looked at her.

"What's taking so long?"

"Give her a few minutes to get downstairs: her plane only landed ten minutes ago," Marcos explained.

"Right, okay." Aaron started pacing again. Alisha could only smile.

"He loves her," Marcos whispered to Alisha and Patty.

"Duh! You think?" Patty replied.

Marcos smiled. "Oh. You guys already know that. Well sure, you're women," he laughed.

"There she is!" Alisha shouted out.

They all turned toward the escalator. There was Maria feverishly waving while she was on her way down. Aaron wanted to run over but stayed composed and quickly walked over to meet her at the bottom. Maria practically jumped off the last step and into Aaron's arms. Alisha, Patty and Marcos stood back watching proudly.

Aaron spun Maria around and set her down. "Now that's a serious kiss," Marcos commented.

"Stop that!" Patty slapped him on the shoulder.

Alisha couldn't stand it any longer and pulled them apart. "What about me?"

Maria already had tears building up in her eyes. "It's so great to be back," Maria told her, then gave her a monster hug.

"You might have to go away more often!" Alisha kidded.

"My turn!" Marcos stepped up to get his hug.

"It's so good to see you, Marcos," Maria told him.

Patty stood right next to Marcos. "Hi, Maria, it's good to have you back." Maria didn't hesitate for one second and wrapped herself around Patty. Patty couldn't contain herself and started to cry.

"Holy smoke! What's with you women!" Marcos announced as he wiped away a tear.

"Aaron, let's you and I get Maria's bags."

Aaron kissed Maria again. "I am so glad you're back, I've got so much to tell you," he let go of her hand and followed after Marcos.

The ride home was fun and chatty, Maria wanted to know about everything since she left, and everyone wanted to know as much as possible about how Maria was getting on in California.

"I'm pretty comfortable saying I don't think California is just another state. I'm pretty sure it's a different planet!" Everyone laughed; Patty made Marcos stop at a truck stop so she could go pee. While Patty was out of the truck in the restroom, Maria spoke up. "Marcos, wow, I really like Patty, I mean I have right from the start… but she's really great."

"Yes she is, thank you, Maria. That means a lot coming from you." Alisha punched Marcos on the arm.

"What? Your opinion counts, too."

"So… is she the one?" Maria teased. Aaron and Alisha sat in silence.

"What, no comments?" Marcos joked.

Alisha shook her head no, patiently waiting for a response. "Sorry about that, guys," Patty said as she got back into the truck. "What?" she could see the smirks on everyone's faces. "Okay, what happened? Do I have toilet paper hanging off my foot or something?" she asked nervously. Everyone started cracking up. Even though Patty had no idea what they were laughing about she started to laugh with them, which only made everyone else laugh that much harder.

"Home!" Marcos announced.

"Yeah!" Alisha yelled out as they all got out of the truck.

Maria was anxiously looking around as she headed for the house. "What is it, Maria?" Aaron asked her.

"Where's Elvis?"

Everyone looked around. "Wow that's strange," Alisha said. Aaron called out and whistled for him. Within seconds they heard Elvis's bark, he was running across the field as fast as his legs would take him. He ran right past everyone and leaped into Maria's arms.

"Oh wow!" Everyone laughed.

"I guess he really missed you," Aaron told her.

"And what is this?" Maria asked Elvis.

Everyone looked closer. "It looks like he brought you a present," Marcos laughed. Maria set Elvis down slowly, then he dropped a field mouse from his mouth on the ground right in front of her. "Awe," Alisha said. "How sweet is that?"

Maria knelt down. "Why thank you, Elvis, I missed you, too, but I'm afraid I didn't bring you anything." Elvis barked excitedly. Aaron picked up the mouse while everyone else headed into the house.

It was like Maria had never left: there were no awkward moments, no feelings of missing anymore. Everyone was just glad to have her back, even if it was for only three weeks, which no one dared to mention. They had a great meal, they talked and laughed: lots and lots of stories.

"Mrs. B., the house looks… well, beyond words. It looks like a Christmas dream."

"Thank you, Maria," Alisha smiled proudly.

"Yeah, we all went a little overboard for your homecoming," Aaron admitted.

"No one more so than Marcos… Did you see that tree?" Patty spoke up.

"I did! I can't wait to check it out closer."

"Marcos picked it out, but I helped cut it down," Aaron told her.

"Yes he did, but that was the easy part. Getting that monster in here, that was a challenge," Marcos laughed.

"What? It only took us half a day," Aaron joked.

"Well, I'm proud of you boys, it looks and smells fantastic," Alisha told them. Patty nodded her head in agreement.

"Time for dessert," Alisha announced.

"And tonight in celebration of Maria being home we are having her favorite, apple pie with vanilla ice cream!" They all cheered.

They had dessert and coffee sitting in the family room next to the Christmas tree. After more catching up, and a few fish stories, Marcos and Patty decided it was time to get going. Marcos first walked over to Maria. "It's so good to have you back. Tomorrow we will go check out your place, okay? The crops are really coming in nicely."

"Well, actually," Maria started to say as she looked over to Aaron.

Marcos smiled. "Oh sure, I get it. No problem. We can see the farm anytime, just let me know."

"Thank you, Marcos." Maria hugged him and kissed him on the cheek.

After they left, Alisha announced she was headed off to bed as well. "It's been a long day, I'm wiped out. You guys come over here and give me some love," she demanded.

Maria gave Alisha a long, hard hug. "Thank you," Maria said softly. "Good night, Mom."

"Okay, you guys, not too late. I know you haven't seen each other in a while but it doesn't all have to be in one day," she explained, doing her mom thing. "Oh, and the rules of the house are still in play."

"Okay, Mom, no problem," Aaron laughed. Maria stood quietly and smiled.

Even though Aaron had chores that needed to be done, Marcos insisted he take the day off and spend it with Maria. Aaron kind of knew he'd say that. He, Maria, and Elvis jumped in his truck and headed out to the road.

"Where are we going?" Maria asked, excited to spend the day with Aaron.

"There's a ton of people who want to see you so I thought we'd start with that."

"Sounds like fun to me."

They drove down the road to Mike's house where many of their friends were waiting out front for their arrival. When Maria saw all her friends waiting for her she got very excited. "Oh look! It looks like everyone is here!"

"They are," Aaron smiled.

Aaron set this gathering up a few weeks ago; all of Maria's friends were just as excited to see her. Maria had a great time catching up with old friends and meeting so many new ones. She especially enjoyed spending time with some of Aaron's older friends who shared some inside Aaron information and stories that she never knew. "That was so much fun," Maria told Aaron as they got back into the truck.

"I'm glad you had a good time."

"A good time, no I had a great time! And I learned so much about you that I didn't know," she laughed.

"Well, some of it might be true but most of it... probably not; but I'll never admit any of it."

It was already late afternoon. "What's next?" Maria asked.

"Your choice, but I thought maybe now would be a good time to visit your place."

"Really? Why?" Maria was a little surprised and disappointed.

She thought for sure Aaron would want to go to dinner or head into town or maybe even go to their spot at the river.

"It's up to you really. We can do whatever you want. I'll take you anywhere," he told her. He could tell she wasn't pleased with his idea.

Maria smiled sweetly. "I don't care, I just want to be with you."

Winter was definitely upon them; it was getting pretty cold out. Even though they both had jackets on, the heat in the truck was much needed.

"I forgot how cold it can get," Maria remarked.

"It is cold. Who knows, maybe we'll get lucky and it will snow for us this Christmas," he chuckled.

"Wouldn't that be great!"

Aaron laughed: of course he was kidding. It hadn't snowed in their part of Tennessee in at least twenty years, certainly not since Aaron had been alive. Aaron stopped the truck right in front of Maria's front door. "Welcome home."

She leaned over and kissed him. "Thank you." They both got out of the truck, Elvis, too, and went into the house. It had been some time since Maria has been in her grandmother's house. She handled it very well. You could tell she was a little emotional but she was excited to be there.

"Wow. It feels so good to be here," she told Aaron.

"It should, this is your home."

Truth was Aaron was a little scared to bring her home not knowing how she might react. "So Marcos and I have a little surprise for you."

"Really? What?"

"Come on into the family room." He motioned for her to follow him. Sitting proudly in the middle of the family room, big and noble, was a beautiful Christmas tree.

"Oh my God! Aaron, it's so beautiful! This is for me?"

"Yea. This way every time you're here it will feel and smell like Christmas." She jumped into his arms and kissed him. Aaron held her back and looked into her eyes. "I love you..." he said softly.

"I know, it took you a while, though," she teased. Then she looked at Aaron very seriously. "I've loved you for a long time, and every time I'm with you, I love you more," she admitted.

"Boy, I'm glad to hear you say that," Aaron told her as he let her go.

"Why?"

Aaron smiled, "Oh... well, there might be an early Christmas present under the tree for you," he teased.

"Really? Should I get it now?" she asked, jumping up and down on the tip of her toes, clapping her hands.

"Only if you want to," Aaron teased.

She smiled coyly, then hit him on his chest. "Well now that you told me I have to! So that's why we're here?" Maria skipped over to the tree: there was a small brightly wrapped gift tucked under one of the branches. She picked it up and held it to examine it closer: it was small and very light. "It has no name tag," she smiled.

"I'm pretty sure it's for you."

Maria slowly and carefully unwrapped the paper until she got to a plain brown box. She carefully removed the lid and inside was a black velvet jewelry box. "Oh Aaron. I hope you didn't get me something too expensive," she half-scolded him. She was so excited, her hands were shaking; she had never received jewelry from anyone before. She removed the velvet box from the brown cardboard box and held it in her hand for what seemed to Aaron to be forever. "I'm too excited to open it," she teased Aaron who was already about to burst. She slowly opened the velvet box; instead of a pair of earrings or a bracelet, something that she expected to be inside; there was an elegant, simple, gold ring with a small, beautiful diamond that crowned the top of it. Maria shrieked. "Oh my God... Aaron!" She lifted her eyes to look at him; Aaron bent down on one knee right in front of her; Maria put her hands over her face and started to cry.

Aaron reached up and took one of Maria's hands. "Maria," he started, "I know we are young, I know most people would say we're crazy. But I know I love you and you are the one I want to be with forever," he said as emotionally and sincerely as was possible. "Maria Muccino, will you marry me?" he asked softly. Maria made Aaron a little nervous; she was crying while staring at the ring, but did not answer. "Maria?" Maria was trying to breathe.

Maria put her hands down and smiled at Aaron; Aaron smiled back. Maria pulled Aaron to his feet and looked deep into his eyes. "Of course I will marry you." It was a very passionate kiss. Aaron stepped back to look at her; Maria wiped a tear from his face. "If you tell anyone that I cried that will be the end of this marriage," he joked. They both laughed together. Aaron grabbed her so hard she screeched.

"Oh sorry." Maria started jumping all over the room. She was so excited; Aaron just stood there and laughed. I guess this is a good sign!

After Maria came down off the walls, completely out of breath, she kissed Aaron. "I love you so much, thank you." Aaron took the ring from the box and placed it on her finger. "A perfect fit," Maria yelled. Aaron was beyond excited: his plan worked just as he hoped. Maria was, to say the least, in shock.

"Wow, this isn't exactly what I expected for Christmas," Maria said to him with a big smile on her face, still breathing hard.

"I've been thinking about it for a long time," Aaron admitted. "I know you and I are going to be together... forever; so I decided, why wait? Why not start our lives together now?"

"Wow." Maria was trying to process the whole thing. She loved and had loved Aaron nearly from the moment she first met him. She often thought about if this day might happen, and now that it was here, really here, she couldn't believe it. "This is like a dream... I wish Nana was here." She knew how happy she would be.

"I wish she was, too, but I think she knew one day this was going to happen," Aaron confided.

They sat on the couch for hours in front of the Christmas tree, talking, planning and well, doing things young people do who are in love. Maria was staring at her ring when suddenly she pushed Aaron back. "Does your mom know?" she asked nervously. Aaron laughed a kind of guilty laugh.

"Well, no, not exactly."

"Not exactly! Oh man! She's going to flip out... won't she?" Maria was unsure.

"I thought about telling her, but this is our decision and I think we should tell her together, don't you?" Maria nodded, but looked unsure. "If I know my mom, she's going to be pretty excited for us. Some people might be upset because of our age; I don't know... maybe," he thought out loud. Maria was staring at her ring again, thinking.

"Oh man!" Maria shouted. "She's going to put me on the first plane back to California, that's what she's going to do."

Aaron laughed. "You might be right," he teased. Maria punched him in the arm then jumped in his lap.

Aaron and Maria decided that if they were going to do this, Christmas Eve would be the perfect time. After dinner and during dessert everyone got to open up one present from under the tree: that's when they'll make their announcement. "I think it's perfect," Maria told Aaron. Aaron nervously agreed. They also decided that it would be best to keep the ring out of sight until that night. Maria didn't like it, but agreed.

"As long as I can wear it when we're not at home, okay?" she asked with a Maria smile.

"Sure... of course, but only when we're not around friends, okay?"

"Okay..."

That night at dinner Maria could hardly contain herself. "Maria, are you okay?" Alisha asked. "You seem so frazzled or something."

"Oh no, Mrs. B., I'm fine. Maybe just a little nervous about Christmas. It's only a couple of days away and I'm not done with my shopping," she reacted quickly to the question.

"Well... that's perfect," Alisha said excitedly. "I'm not done either, maybe we can go into town together tomorrow? Wouldn't that be fun?"

"Oh, that would be great, Mrs. B... Perfect, actually."

Anything to get her out of the house and distracted from Aaron. The busier she is, Maria thought, the better. Aaron sat at the table with his arms folded, smiling at the conversation. "And what's up with you?" his mom asked. "You look like a bird dog that just caught a canary," she expressed in the way only Alisha can. Maria burst out laughing. Aaron looked at this mom, "Really, Mom? That's the best you can do? A canary?" Aaron got up and gave his mom a big hug. "I'm going to go see what Marcos is up to," he announced after kissing his mom then Maria.

He walked out of the kitchen and out the front door. Alisha stood there with her mouth hanging open. "What the heck was that?" Alisha asked Maria. Maria smiled and laughed.

"You know, I'm not sure but he's been like that all day," she told Alisha. "I was going to take responsibility for his happiness but I'm not so sure," she laughed again. "Sometimes that kid…" Alisha smiled. "But you gotta love him."

"Yes you do," Maria smiled.

Christmas Eve couldn't come fast enough for either Aaron or Maria. They barely spoke about it: truth is they really didn't have a lot of time together but they did have a plan. All day Aaron felt like he was going to be sick. He got little to no sleep the night before and that day he worked like he had to do a week's worth of chores in one day, anything to help keep him distracted. His mom and Marcos tried to stop him several times with no success.

"What's going on with Aaron?" Marcos asked Alisha when he came in for a drink.

"You got me, he's been like this for the last three days."

"Maybe he's already getting nervous or maybe upset about Maria leaving next week? Maybe this is his way of dealing with it?" Marcos suggested.

"I guess. Maria's been kind of jumpy, too," she started to say, then Alisha had this look on her face.

"What is it?"

"Oh… my… God. Maybe they got in a fight and don't want to tell us because they don't want to screw up Christmas or something like that," she said, upsetting herself. Marcos smiled.

"What?" Alisha asked him sharply, "What if I'm right?"

Marcos laughed. "Relax. Take a look out the window."

Alisha moved to the window, which looked out onto their biggest field and the main barn. A sigh of relief came out of her. Out in front of the barn Maria and Aaron were kissing; Maria had just brought Aaron a glass of water.

"Okay... So that's not it," Alisha said relieved.

"Who knows with young people these days, could be anything," Marcos exclaimed. Alisha nodded her head. "By the way, Alisha, I've been meaning to ask you... Whatever happened with Aaron and the national Elvis impersonation contest? I haven't heard him speak of it in a month."

"Yeah I know. I guess he decided not to do it. To be honest with you, I'm very disappointed."

"Really? I'm surprised. It was all he talked about since the fair, well... that and Maria! I wonder what changed?"

"The last time I asked him about it he got pretty defensive and told me he made up his mind, he wasn't going to do it. He wouldn't say anything else," Alisha explained, shaking her head in disappointment.

"December thirtieth, right?" Marcos asked.

"Yes, that's right."

"Okay, we've got a little time, let me talk to him."

"This is one special Christmas Eve!" Alisha announced proudly to everyone at the table. They were a small group but a close one. Christmas Eve dinner included Alisha, Aaron, Maria, Marcos and now Patty. It was as close as a non-family could be without being blood. Alisha prepared all of her famous holiday foods: there was ham, turkey, three different kinds of potatoes, and four types of vegetables. That doesn't even count the two kinds of salad and dressings and of course Alisha's fair-winning stuffing. There was enough food for forty people, but then that's Alisha. Aaron and Marcos loved it because they ate like kings for two weeks after the holidays.

It was a very festive dinner with lots of laughter. Aaron had calmed down a bit once they started to eat, although he didn't think he'd be able to eat at all. He couldn't resist his mom's food, thankfully, because it helped calm his stomach down almost right away. The guys cleared the plates and food, the dishes were done and the food wrapped up by the ladies. Marcos thought about talking to Aaron about the contest while they waited in the family room for the girls, but he could see Aaron was preoccupied and he didn't want to take a chance of dampening the mood.

It wasn't long till the women emerged from the kitchen with plates of dessert; Maria had the smile a cat has after it just caught a mouse. Aaron could tell she was trying hard not to burst. From the moment dinner started Maria had a smile on her face that never went away. Every time Aaron looked at her he had to quickly look away because he would start to laugh. Maria was in equal parts nervous and excited. Aaron smiled often and made conversation all the way through dinner, but inside he was losing it. This is harder than asking Maria in the first place, he thought. Maria sat down next to him on the couch. She handed him a plate with two different kinds of pie on it.

"Where's yours?" Aaron asked.

"We're sharing," she explained.

"Oh, it's like that, is it?"

Everyone laughed at the young couple.

Alisha sat in the big, overstuffed chair; Marcos and Patty sat in chairs Marcos brought in from the kitchen. "A toast!" Marcos announced. "Hear hear!" everyone responded.

"First I would like to thank our hostess for yet another amazing and memorable holiday dinner… it was fantastic," he said, nodding his head at Alisha and raising his glass.

"Thank you," she responded.

"And I just want to say that it is great to have Maria here. Everything feels right when you're home, and although you'll be leaving us soon… for just a little while longer, before you know it you'll be back to stay!" Everyone cheered a little louder. "Lastly, I want to thank Patty for being here and being such an important part of my life. Thank you, Patty," he said, nodding to her. Patty leaned over and kissed him. "Oh! And Merry Christmas, everyone!"

"Merry Christmas!" everyone laughed and cheered.

Aaron got up from the couch and stepped in front of the Christmas tree. "Well, since we are toasting, I would like to make a toast and pass out the first gifts, if that's alright with you guys?" Aaron looked at his family; they were all nodding their heads in support. Maria thought she was going to pee her pants. He held his glass of apple cider up high. "I, too, would like to thank my mother for an unbelievable dinner. I'm looking forward to eating very well for the next week or so. Thanks, Mom." Alisha smiled and nodded. "Also I would like to take this opportunity to thank Marcos for everything you do for me," he said, looking at him. "I know you might not want to admit this, but it's true. I would not be who I am without your help and guidance, you are a true friend," he told him. Marcos smiled and raised his glass even higher. Patty squeezed his arm tightly. "Last… Sorry this is a long toast," he interrupted himself, everyone laughed but they were all anxious to hear what he was going to say. "I think everyone here knows how important Maria is to me… to all of us really. She makes me a better person, she brings happiness to everyone in her life." Aaron held his glass out in the direction of Maria. "Here's to my Maria."

"To Maria!" everyone happily toasted.

Alisha was smiling from ear to ear; but she had no idea what was coming next. "Maria could you help me?" Aaron asked. Maria got up and stood next to Aaron. "So… Maria and I have a special gift for you, Mom… Marcos… and Patty," he said, looking at each of them. Patty looked completely caught off guard. "We'd like to give them to you now, but don't open them till I tell you, okay?" Everyone nodded. Maria picked up three small differently shaped beautifully wrapped boxes from under the tree; then she passed them out while Aaron looked on. Maria walked back and stood next to Aaron. She kissed him and smiled. She really wanted to go to the bathroom!

"These gifts are so beautiful. I don't know if I want to open it," Patty exclaimed.

"I know," Alisha agreed.

Each of them was surprised and excited at the gesture. They couldn't imagine what all the fuss was about. "Okay, Patty if you would open your gift first please," Maria asked.

"Me! Oh sure," she said excitedly. She very carefully pulled back on one side of a fold, trying her hardest not to damage the beautiful paper. Underneath was a rectangular black velvet jewelry box. "Oh my."

"Open it!" Marcos said excitedly.

Patty smirked at Marcos. She opened the hinged box; inside she found a small, gold key on a thin, beautiful gold chain. "Oh… it's beautiful," she gasped as she held it up for the others to see. "Oh my God, you guys, this is too much, it had to be so expensive," she said.

"Wear it in good health," Maria told her.

Patty jumped up from her seat and ran over to give them both a big hug. "It's really amazing. Thank you."

"Okay, Marcos you're next," Aaron told him.

"Great." He was uncharacteristically excited.

"This is fun, isn't it?" Patty said nervously hitting Marcos on the leg.

Marcos wasn't quite as worried about saving the paper as he ripped it off the gift. Underneath was a small square brown box. Marcos removed the lid and then removed some tissue paper from on top. He reached in and pulled out a very elegant black leather keychain that had a small gold lock attached to it. Patty started to clap excitedly. You could see Marcos was stunned for words. "Wow… I don't know what to say, guys. It's… so great."

"Let me see it!" Patty demanded.

Marcos handed her the keyring; Patty knew what to do… She put her key into the lock and turned it, the lock sprung open. Marcos had a look of shock but in a good way, Patty shrieked, and Alisha started to laugh and clap. Marcos got up and walked over to Maria first and gave her a big hug and a kiss on the cheek. "This had to be you," he told them.

"Oh it was," Aaron laughed.

Marcos hugged Aaron. "This is fantastic… you guys really, but I feel you spent too much money on us."

Patty was shaking her head in agreement as she was putting on her new necklace. Alisha had no idea what to say or how to react: she was blown away. "Marcos, I hope you don't think we overstepped our bounds," Aaron told him as he put his arm around Maria. "Maria and I see you with Patty and it just makes us happy. That's why we gave you the lock that only Patty has the key to." Patty was as gleeful as a teenager. Marcos was literally beaming.

"In all of my life I have never seen someone capture your heart so completely. Aaron and I saw this and knew it was for you guys," Maria added. Alisha started to cry.

"Aaron... Maria," Marcos turned to look at Patty. "It's perfect, thank you."

"Okay, that's it!" Aaron announced abruptly, wiping his hands to indicate he was done. He and Maria sat back down on the couch. They each had a bite of pie. "Mom, this is so good," Aaron told her. Maria smiled in agreement.

"Uh Um!" Alisha grunted. "After all of that... the perfect gifts for Patty and Marcos... You forgot about me and my gift?" she asked, sheepishly holding up her present. Marcos and Patty laughed.

"Oh sorry, Mom. There was just so much excitement, yes, please open your gift," he smiled. The gift was very light, it felt like it was empty. At first Alisha was concerned they were going to play a joke on her, which could be supported by past experiences. She, too, carefully removed the beautiful paper to reveal a thin box about the size of a small photo frame. She removed the lid. Inside was a piece of thick fancy paper, bordered in gold and black trim. It sat perfectly centered in the box with fine black tissue guarding its edges. It had writing on it. Alisha removed it from the box. "What is this?" she asked, looking over at Aaron and Maria. They were both beaming at her. Maria was squeezing Aaron's hand so hard it started to hurt. The card looked like an invitation you might get if you were being invited to a fancy ball or something like that. The writing on it was very fancy, very formal. "It looks like an invitation," she told the group holding it up for them to see. "Should I read it out loud?"

Patty was the first to speak up. "Yes, please!" she said excitedly.

Maria and Aaron nodded in agreement. Alisha reached for her reading glasses and put them on, "Okay… the card says, "Mrs. B., awe, it's from Maria," she smiled, then continued. "I want you to know that I love your son Aaron with all of my heart. I want you to know that there is nothing I wouldn't do for him. I love you, you know I already consider you my mom, but with your permission I would like to call you my mother-in-law, Love Maria."

Patty shrieked and started crying. Marcos sat there with this goofy smile on his face, unsure of what he had just heard. Aaron and Maria stood up; Alisha slowly stood up, she carefully put the card down on the table. She already had one hand covering her mouth and her the other rested on her chest: she looked like she was thinking. No one could tell if she was mad or upset, but she didn't look happy. Marcos and Patty said nothing and didn't move. Alisha stood there staring at the two of them, for what seemed like minutes. Aaron and Maria were both getting concerned, they really believed she would be happy, but now… they were more concerned she would be mad, maybe so mad she would try to stop them or maybe try talk them out of it. Alisha didn't move, didn't react, she just continued to stare. No one said anything, all eyes were on Alisha. Maria was just about to lose it, then the unexpected, tears started to flow from her eyes, her head started to shake and her body started to tremble, and you could hear her whimpering.

"Oh my God, Mrs. B! I'm so sorry!" Maria said as she began to cry and walk toward Alisha.

Alisha dropped her hand from her face to reveal a huge smile. Aaron let out an audible sigh of relief and fell back onto the couch. Patty jumped to her feet and started screaming. Alisha grabbed Maria and started screaming. Marcos looked over at Aaron, Aaron threw his arms up, smiled and started screaming; so Marcos got up quickly and as best he could start screaming. After some time the screams settled down. Alisha was holding Maria and Aaron so tight they couldn't breath.

"Oh my God... Oh my God... sit, sit, sit!" Alisha demanded. Alisha sat on the couch as close as she could next to Maria; Marcos and Patty pulled their chairs over to be closer. "When did this happen? How did this happen? Details! I want details!" she laughingly demanded.

After wiping away some tears Maria started. "Well... the day after I got back, you know Aaron and I went out to see friends and just hang out..."

"Yes, I remember." Alisha was cooing with excitement, crying and smiling.

"Aaron insisted later that day that we go to my nana's house... my house, I guess. I didn't understand why, but I said okay. He had it all arranged." She smiled at Aaron. Everyone, even Aaron was hanging on every word of Maria's story. Every few seconds Alisha would look over at her son: she was beaming with pride, she was so happy.

"Oh man, Aaron! I had no idea you had this in you," his mom exclaimed.

"Yeah, neither did I," he laughed.

Maria went on to tell the story in great detail; Aaron never added a word. When Maria finished the story and brought everyone up to that minute, Alisha sat back and stared at the ceiling.

She abruptly jumped to her feet. "We're having a wedding! My babies are getting married!" she joyfully cried out.

Patty was frantically clapping with excitement. Then almost as quickly, Alisha sat back down. She picked up Maria's hand and held it tight. "Have you guys thought about when you want to get married or where? Are we talking about a year from now or..."

Aaron took this one. "Actually, Mom, as you know Maria will be eighteen in March and I'll turn eighteen in June, so... We were kind of hoping for a June wedding... right here." He barely got the words out of his mouth.

Alisha was back on her feet. "June?! Like this June? Like six months from now... June?!" she kept repeating.

"Well... I guess we could wait some if you think..." Aaron was cut off at the knees.

"NO! June is good, June is perfect!" she exclaimed so loudly people at the next farm could have heard her.

Alisha looked at Marcos. "We can do June?"

Marcos laughed. "We can do June," he said supportively.

Maria and Aaron were laughing so hard Maria had to excuse herself to finally go pee!

"This is so exciting!" Patty said to Alisha.

"I know I'm sort of new to everyone, but I sure would like..." She got cut off as well.

"Patty! I won't be able to do it without you. Can you help me...? Will you help me?" she asked as sincerely as she could, considering how excited she was.

Patty put on this big smile and hugged her. "It would be my honor," she told Alisha.

Well, that just blew me away," Marcos said as he reached out his hand to shake Aaron's. Marcos was proud: you could see it. Aaron imagined his dad would have acted very much the same way.

"Yeah, but this changes nothing," Aaron told him. "I'll be one hundred percent committed to my work and responsibilities," he assured Marcos.

"Trust me, I have no doubts. And you know... anything you guys need, anything I can help with, you just let me know."

"Thank you, Marcos." That was probably the first time Marcos saw Aaron not as a boy anymore but as a man. And he was proud, very proud.

Needless to say, Christmas became second fiddle to the topic of the day. Sure, everyone was over, had a huge breakfast and opened the rest of the gifts, but about every minute or so someone would bring up the night before, or the engagement story or the wedding that Maria, Alisha and Patty were excited to get to work on. Before everyone went to bed the night before they all agreed on the date. The wedding was to be held on Saturday June seventeenth at five in the afternoon, three days after Aaron's eighteenth birthday. While

Alisha, Maria and Patty were in the kitchen cleaning up from breakfast Aaron and Marcos were in the family room picking up trash and straightening things up after the Christmas mayhem.

"Aaron… I am so happy for you."

"Thanks, Marcos, I'm excited. I feel like my life is headed in the right direction… with the right person at my side."

"I couldn't agree more." Marcos paused. "Hey, I've got an out of left field question for you."

"Sure. What?"

"Your mom tells me that you decided not to do the national Elvis event… I was wondering why."

Aaron stopped working and turned to face Marcos. "I was hoping you'd forget about that," Aaron admitted to him.

"I'm just surprised that's all, it doesn't seem like you. I mean, you were so excited."

"Yeah I know, I really was."

"How does Maria feel about it?" Marcos asked.

"Oh, she's not happy about it at all, but you know, she excepted it, sort of," Aaron smiled.

Marcos smiled with him. "And?"

"Hang on a second, I'll be right back." Aaron disappeared up the stairs. A few seconds later Aaron came running back into the room, he handed Marcos a white notecard.

"What's this?"

"Take a look."

Marcos flipped over the card: in big black letters the name 'John from Memphis' was written on it and the name was crossed out in red ink. The name 'Aaron Butler' was written in red ink along the top of the card.

"Okay? Is this from the fair?"

"Yes."

"I don't understand?" Marcos asked.

"The short story is that, after the contest was over, when I went backstage to try to find John I came across this card sitting on the ground." Marcos looked puzzled. "Marcos... I didn't win... John did," he said firmly.

Marcos looked up at him. "Well maybe the judges changed their minds before anyone had a chance to make up a new card," Marcos suggested. "I mean I'm sure it was close."

"No, I know that's not it," Aaron said somberly. "I ran into one of the judges a month or so ago, you know, Abe. I asked him about the card. He told me John went to them and told them to change the winner to me - some excuse about even if he won he wouldn't be able to go to nationals. So plain and simple, I didn't win and I wasn't meant to go."

"Awe, man. That's hogwash and you know it. I don't know why Abe would tell you that, but the truth is you have no idea why this 'John from Memphis' might have really had them cross off his name, if that's even true. It coulda been anything, including the fact that he knew he couldn't go. But you know what, it doesn't matter; if you weren't first you had to be a close second and John wanted you to go, right? He thinks you're good enough to compete, right? As were the judges."

Aaron hadn't thought of it that way. "Maybe. I guess so." Johnny must have known he would win, but he wanted me to go to nationals?

Marcos knew nothing about John being Johnny, but he was making more sense than he might have known. "And do you really want to let down your fiancée or your mom?" he asked sharply.

"You know I don't."

"So quit feeling sorry for yourself and let's do this. I don't know about anyone else, but Patty and I have been looking forward to this for months."

Aaron looked up at Marcos and smiled. "That was a serious pitch," he laughed.

"I thought it was pretty good," Marcos joked. They both laughed.

"What's going on in here, boys?" Patty asked, as she, Alisha and Maria walked in.

"I think Aaron has an announcement he wants to make," Marcos said as he put his hand on Aaron's shoulder. Maria looked puzzled.

"What? Another announcement?" Alisha cried out. "I don't think I can handle another announcement just yet," she said as she collapsed into the big chair.

"What is it, Aaron?" Maria asked.

Aaron looked at Marcos then turned back to the others. "I've decided to do the national Elvis impersonation contest."

"What?! Are you serious?" his mom leaped up from the chair with the last bit of energy she had in her.

"Yes," Aaron smiled.

Everyone, none more so than Maria, was very excited about Aaron's decision. "Man, this will be a blast," Maria said in support.

"Well... it could also be a shellacking," Aaron said humbly. "But if I'm going to do this, I'm going to need you guys' help. I only have a week to be ready," he explained.

"Well, go get your guitar and let's get going," his mom smiled.

Aaron laughed. "I'm talking more about helping me with outfits, song choices and stuff like that," he told them. "This contest is going to be so much more intense. There are three rounds, if you make it to the finals you'll end up doing three different songs, which means three different outfits. If I make it to the finals, that is." He wasn't joking.

"Oh come on," his mom started, "you'll make it to the finals. You're amazing."

Aaron smiled; he was not nearly as confident. "But the cool thing is, you guys, if I do make it to the finals I have a chance to win a prize," he added excitedly.

"Alright, after dinner tonight why don't we sit down, you play your song options and the rest of us will talk about outfits," his mom suggested.

"Great idea, Mrs. B.," Maria threw in her support.

"Sounds like a plan to us," Patty spoke up for her and Marcos. Marcos smiled. "Well okay then. One week's time and we are off to Memphis," Aaron announced nervously.

The next week could not have gone by any faster. Aaron practiced every day for hours: not just his singing and playing, but also working in front of his mom's big mirror trying to get his moves down perfectly. He and Maria even watched some old Elvis movies and acted out some of the scenes together. It was fun because Elvis always got the girl and Maria was always the girl! Before you knew it they were all piled into Marcos's truck headed for Memphis - even Elvis. They decided to go up a day early so they could go out and celebrate the engagement at a more suitable restaurant than anything that was around where they lived, and this way Aaron would get plenty of rest before the big event.

"Man! There are signs everywhere," Patty announced. Patty wasn't kidding: as they got closer to Memphis there were signs announcing the National Elvis Impersonation Contest on just about every corner. 'The Best of the Best!' the signs said.

"No pressure there, big guy," Alisha told Aaron.

"Yeah, no pressure. Can I go home now?" he teased. Everyone laughed.

Not long after, they pulled up in front of the motel they were staying in; of course, Alisha made the sleeping arrangements. Marcos and Aaron were together in one room, and the ladies were in another.

"Makes sense," Marcos said.

After checking in they changed their clothes and headed into town to a restaurant Patty knew of called 'Blue Suede Shoes'.

"Perfect!" Alisha exclaimed as they all got out of the truck. The restaurant had this oversized neon sign out front flashing its name, and hanging off the roof was a giant flashing blue men's shoe: tacky would be an understatement.

"You stay put, Elvis," Aaron told his dog as he tied him up in the bed of the truck.

A couple who were heading into the same restaurant laughed as they walked by. Aaron looked at them. "That's our dog's name, too!" they chuckled. Aaron laughed and ran in to catch up with the others.

The restaurant was packed with Elvis memorabilia, floor-to-ceiling, wall-to-wall.

"You could spend a week in here just looking at all the stuff," Patty said to the group.

A woman dressed in a black tee shirt with 'Elvis' in white rhinestones across the chest and blue suede tennis shoes approached the group. "Y'all have reservations?" she asked.

"Yes we do," Marcos told her. "It's under Aaron Butler."

"Ahh I see. You're in the contest tomorrow?" she asked Marcos.

Patty and Alisha burst out laughing. "No not me, this young man," Marcos explained as he pulled Aaron to the front.

"Oh. Well, that's great," she carefully looked Aaron over.

"Well, well. I think you might be the youngest Elvis we've seen at our national event, at least for some time. Good luck to you, honey."

"Thank you," Aaron bashfully responded.

"Right this way," the hostess directed.

Maria ran up and grabbed Aaron's arm. "Isn't this exciting!"

Aaron looked at her face beaming with excitement. "It is," Aaron told her, without mentioning the fact that he thought he was about to throw up.

"This place is amazing," Alisha was in awe.

They had barely taken a minute to look over the extravagant menu when Aaron spoke up. "I wonder how much of it is real?"

"Oh honey… it's all real," the waitress said in a deep Southern accent as she approached the table.

She looked like she might be ninety but was probably more like seventy. She didn't look quite the same as the other, younger staff in her Elvis tee shirt and blue suede tennis shoes. Everyone paused to listen to her explain. "Yup. I've been here going on nearly forty years… I saw Elvis in here many times - I even waited on him once," she said proudly. "He loved it here so much his guys were constantly bringing in some of this and some of that. After a while the place was full," she explained as if it was just normal.

"That's a cool story," Marcos told her, and everyone agreed. That made the waitress very happy.

"You guys ready? I can take your order now."

It wasn't a big decision, they all got the Elvis burger and the 'All Shook Up' fries. Marcos thought about getting the 'Hound Dog' hot dog, but ended up going with everyone else. After they finished their burgers they were given a surprise dessert, in support of Aaron being in the contest. Marcos felt bad for the waitress: working on her feet all day at her age, it's just wrong, he thought. So he left her a pretty large tip.

"That was really good, don't you guys think?" Marcos asked the group.

"Mine was excellent, thank you very much," Maria said to Marcos and Patty as they walked back to the truck.

"Dinner was great, I thought... but that Elvis impersonator sucked, didn't he?" Alisha laughed. Marcos laughed, and the others agreed.

"Oh man, he was terrible," Patty added.

"You should have gone up there like I asked you to," Alisha said to Aaron. "It would have been good practice for tomorrow."

"I appreciated that, Mom, but unless you wanted to see my burger again, there was no chance of that happening." He wasn't being rude, he was telling the truth, and everyone knew it.

NATIONALS

The next morning Marcos found Aaron in the bathroom on his knees in front of the toilet.

"Oh, man! Are you okay?" he asked, startling Aaron.

"Uhh… well, I've been sitting here for a couple of hours and nothing will come out," he said breathing heavily.

"It's just nerves, you know that, right?"

"Yeah, I know… but can you please tell that to my stomach!" Aaron tried to chuckle.

"Crawl over and jump in the shower, a good hot shower will help you," Marcos told him.

Reluctant to leave the comfort of the toilet, Aaron heeded his advice. A bit later Aaron emerged from the bathroom. "I definitely feel better but not, you know, better," he tried to explain.

"That's because you need some food, otherwise you really will get sick. We don't want you passing out onstage." Marcos laughed.

"Funny!"

"Let me finish getting ready and then you and I will go grab a bite - just us, okay?"

"That would be great: thanks, Marcos."

Aaron was actually able to eat a little and afterwards he surprisingly felt much better; at least he didn't feel like he was going to be sick anymore.

"Man, it's about time you guys got back! Aaron's got to get going," Patty said, scolding Marcos. "Do you know what time it is?" she lashed out.

"Holy crap!" Aaron yelled as he ran into his motel room.

"Sorry, Patty, I guess we lost track of time," Marcos told her.

Like a little army, Alisha, Maria and Patty loaded up the truck with everything they needed and jumped in. Marcos and Aaron sat up front.

"Let's gooooooo!" Patty yelled out the window, holding her hands as high in the air as she could.

Everyone laughed, even Aaron. Thankfully they weren't very far from the fairgrounds. Aaron had to be there two hours before the show started to check in, get his number and get ready. The group dropped off Aaron at the back of the bowl. Hugs, kisses and support all round.

"Okay, guys." Aaron was getting aggravated. "I'll be fine. It's no big deal," he told the group. "I'll see you after." Then he hugged and kissed Maria.

"I believe in you," she whispered.

Aaron kissed her again and walked over to the check-in table. "Aaron Butler", he told one of the ladies checking people in.

"Aaron... You're the kid, sorry, the guy who is a local: you won at the Atoka county fair, right?"

"Yes, well... yes," he answered as he thought about the winning card that had Johnny's named crossed out.

"Great. We're happy you're here. Okay, so here's your number, pin it anywhere it can be seen from the front, and here is your locker assignment. Just see any guy inside with one of these badges and he'll get you settled." She smiled at Aaron and handed him his paperwork.

"Thank you." Then he leaned in close to the woman, and she leaned forward in kind. "There's a lot of guys here," Aaron quietly said to her.

She leaned back and smiled. "Yes there are. After all, this is the best of the best. But you have just as much right to be here as any of them," she told him. Aaron smiled, but wasn't sure he believed her. "The secret is…" She leaned over the table again, Aaron quickly leaned in closer to her. "You have to have fun. This is a contest, you have to deliver but the judges can tell if you are 'performing' or if you are relaxed and just going with it," she advised.

Aaron nodded his head. "Thank you."

Then he went through the door to find his changing area and his locker. He was excited to walk around and check things out before he had to start getting ready. Man! There are so many guys here, he thought to himself. Between the guys outside and the guys inside Aaron figured there had to be forty or fifty contestants. Every age, every size, and an amazing amount of guys who you wouldn't normally think of when you think of Elvis, at least to Aaron. There was an Asian, a Hispanic guy, an Indian and a black guy.

"Wow," Aaron said out loud.

"Crazy, right?" a man's voice said as he approached Aaron from behind. "You look lost, can I help you?"

He was wearing an official-looking contest tee shirt and he had a big badge hanging from his neck that said, 'All Over Pass'.

"Sure. That would be great."

As the man escorted Aaron to his designated changing area and then to his locker he was observing all the different men getting ready for the contest. "There are some impressive-looking Elvises here," Aaron admitted to the man. The man opened up Aaron's locker and handed him the key. He smiled.

"Yes there are." He could see that Aaron was nervous. "I've been doing this for a long time, and I can tell you one thing for sure… Very seldom does the flash meet the results." Aaron looked at him a little puzzled. "Usually the fancier and more outlandish they look, the weaker they are as performers," he said quietly to Aaron.

"Oh," Aaron responded. "Thanks." Aaron wasn't sure if that helped.

Aaron hung up his outfits and put his bags in the locker, then he took off to look around. Judging by what he saw as he walked around the changing areas, it stood out to him that he was definitely the youngest guy there. For some reason Aaron started to relax, maybe it was the advice of the woman who checked him in, or the guy who helped him find his locker, but he was starting to have fun. He was enjoying watching all of these guys getting ready, prepping their clothes and hair, especially the hair! There was a cloud of hairspray covering the entire backstage area. Aaron couldn't help but smile. He kind of wished his mom and Maria could see this. One Elvis was putting on the famous white jumpsuit, but was having difficulties zipping it up.

"Can I help you?" Aaron asked the man who was definitely going to be Elvis the 'fat years'.

"That would be great," the man gasped. Aaron stepped over to him. "If you could just finish zipping me all the way up, please?"

"Sure." In one hard tug, he managed to get the zipper all the way up. "How's that?"

"Perfect!" The man replied. "Are you in this thing, too?"

"Yes, I am," Aaron told him confidently.

"That's cool, I'm Joe, by the way, from Las Vegas."

"Wow, Las Vegas. That's cool. I'm Aaron. I guess you could say I'm a local guy."

"Good to meet you, Aaron, good luck today," then Joe quickly went back to primping.

"Thanks. You, too," Aaron continued venturing around. He spoke to several guys: they were all very nice to him and surprisingly supportive. One group he walked up on were swapping stories about past experiences and how long they'd been trying to make it to nationals. Aaron didn't want to interrupt so he kept on. Eventually he made it to the stage. There were lots of people, mostly staff, buzzing all around doing last-minute preparations, getting ready for the show. Aaron walked out onto center stage and looked out over the seats. Holy! he said to himself. He was totally caught off guard: the venue was much bigger than Aaron expected. He took a deep breath and let it out slowly. That's enough of that, he told himself as his stomach started to dance around again. He quickly walked offstage and went back to his locker. When he got there he sat on a chair and started to go through the paperwork he was given at check-in. Amongst the papers was a list of all the competitors: it had their name, age, where they came from, and what event they won to be there. Aaron's guess was pretty far off: the list had thirty names on it, which was still quite a few to get through in one afternoon. Aaron found his name; he immediately got butterflies in his stomach. He looked to see if by any chance Johnny's name was on the list, but there was only one John and he was from New York. Also with the papers was the contest schedule; everyone would be broken up into groups of ten, your group was determined by your number and the numbers were picked at random. Aaron was in the second group; he would be third to go. Now he was starting to get really nervous.

Suddenly there was a lot of commotion backstage, staff and Elvises alike running around. Music came on in the arena, and Aaron's stomach jumped. He ran to the stage and poked his head out from around the curtain. The seats were already nearly full! He scanned the audience but wasn't able to find his family. As he turned to head back in, out of the corner of his eye he thought he saw Johnny's friend, Red.

"Red!"

He quickly turned back, staring hard into the area where he thought he saw him, but he wasn't there. Why would Red be here? He asked himself. I wonder if Johnny's here? That would be cool, he got excited at the idea. He looked again but saw nothing. He shrugged it off, figuring he must have only seen a guy who looked something like Red. Aaron walked back to his locker; it was pretty crowded around the lockers now. Everyone was fighting for space in front of one of the many mirrors, which were placed all around the changing areas. A man and a woman walked briskly through the backstage area, "Group one, five minutes!", they were both announcing. They walked the entire back area several times, "Group one, five minutes!" You could feel the energy backstage. Aaron finished getting dressed which for his first outfit was no big deal, jeans, a white tee shirt and black hard shoes. His hair was a different story; he messed with it for a while and then just gave up. His mom and Patty had already dyed it nearly black before they left home, but trying to get the Elvis 'wave' just right was giving Aaron a hard time, so he just slicked it straight back. The backstage manager lined up the first group in order of their appearance: some of them stood there waiting, while others moved around trying to shake off nerves. The music abruptly changed to Elvis's entry music that was played at the start of nearly every Elvis concert. Aaron's heart skipped a beat. Then a man's voice very loud over the music...

"Ladies and gentlemen! Welcome to the eighteenth annual National Elvis Impersonation Contest!" he shouted enthusiastically. The crowd clapped and screamed. For a second, Aaron thought he heard his mom's whistle! The announcer went on to make a couple of announcements, introduce the judges and explain the rules of the contest. "There will be three rounds total. For the first round, the performers have been broken into three groups of ten. The contestants from each group will perform one song, then the judges will pick three contestants from each of the groups to move on to the second round. In the second round the nine contestants will go head-to-head. Only three contestants will go on to the final round. In each round a contestant must do a different song." The announcer paused. "So here we go!" he said excitedly. The first Elvis was called onstage; Aaron ran for the bathroom.

From the bathroom Aaron could hear the different performances. They're really good, he thought. But not necessarily better than me, he tried joking to himself. He sat on the toilet trying to decide if he was going to get sick or not. Man, I bet Johnny would be pissed if he saw me right now! he laughed. Someone came into the restroom, Aaron stood up and walked out of the stall: it was Elvis, or one of the contestants anyway.

He looked at Aaron; the man was covered in sweat.

"Are you okay?" Aaron asked the man.

"Yeah, I'll be fine. I just finished."

"Oh, how'd it go?"

"Good... I made it into the second round," he boasted.

"Wow! Congratulations," Aaron told him sincerely.

"Hey, what group are you in?" the man asked.

"Two. Why?"

"You better get going - they called five minutes for group two five minutes ago!"

"Holy cow!" Aaron thanked the man and ran out of the bathroom to the stage area. His group was lined up and the first in his group was already performing. "We thought we'd lost you," the stage manager said as he slapped Aaron on the back. Aaron smiled. The next guy was onstage, Aaron was standing just offstage waiting his turn. The Elvis who went before him was good but not great. That gave Aaron some confidence. He tried to see if he could see his family but still no luck.

"Up next is our youngest performer this year, coming in at only seventeen, help me welcome to the stage Aaron Butler!" Aaron started to walk then trotted to the middle of the stage. This time he heard his mom's whistle loud and clear but still couldn't see her. His music started. Aaron turned his back to the stage. He took a really big deep breath, then let it out slowly. This is for my mom, Maria, Marcos and Patty, he reminded himself. He spun around to face the crowd and let them have it! He held nothing back, the moves, the attitude, the look and especially the voice: he was great. The crowd loved it and was going crazy. Aaron couldn't help but break character a time or two to smile. The cheers and screams were too contagious. Aaron was having a blast. When he was done, the audience jumped to their feet and gave Aaron a standing ovation. Aaron bowed and ran offstage. He could hear his mom's whistle all the way to his changing area. Several of the other contestants came up to him and congratulated him. Aaron was in his element, his stomach was no longer complaining, and he was excited to be there.

Aaron easily made it to the second round. He was drinking some water and changing his outfit for the next performance when a man carrying a couple of garment bags in his hands approached him.

"You were great," the man said.

Aaron looked up at him. "Wow, thank you." Aaron already knew the answer but to be polite he asked anyway.

"How'd it go for you?"

The man held up his bags and shrugged his shoulders.

"Oh. Sorry," Aaron sympathized.

"No don't be, I'm honored just to be here," he said smiling. "I've been trying for years, now that I made it, I know I can make it back."

"That's great, I'm sure you will," Aaron told him.

"I know you have to get going… I just wanted to wish you luck. I'll be watching."

"Thanks," Aaron smiled.

This time Aaron didn't miss the stage call. In the second round he would go third again. The first two guys did slow songs which Aaron had planned to do also, but now he was concerned he might not be able to stand out enough, plus the all the guys who had already gone were good, some really good. Aaron changed his mind. He grabbed the stage manager who was standing right there. "I need to change my song!"

"No way… You're on next," the stage manager reminded him.

"Please!" Aaron begged.

The stage manager was shaking his head no, but couldn't say no. "Fine," he said, then turned away and started talking into his walkie-talkie. He looked back at Aaron just as the second performer was coming offstage to loud applause; he gave Aaron a thumbs-up. Aaron was introduced by the announcer. He paused a second, swallowed, then ran onto the stage. Thankfully, the outfit he was wearing worked for the song: black jeans, white tee shirt, a black leather jacket, and a black beanie. As he got to center stage the audience clapped and cheered; his mom's whistle stood out above them all. He jumped straight into 'Jail House Rock' without missing a beat. Aaron brought it and brought it hard. He was singing, dancing and moving all over the stage, sweating his butt off. Once again, when he was done he received a long standing ovation; Aaron smiled when he heard his mom's whistle. Exhausted, he started to walk offstage: suddenly he heard voices scream out, "We love you, Aaron!" Aaron turned and smiled, then came his mom's whistle again; he smiled and waved then ran off the stage. He was feeling it. The moment gave him chills all over his body. He was smiling ear to ear as he walked down the stairs to the backstage area. Lots of pats on the back and many "Great job!" comments as he worked his way back to his dressing area. Wow, that was fun!

This time, when they announced the performers who were to move onto the third and final round, they called all nine Elvises back onstage. "The finalists will be announced in no particular order..." the announcer started. He called out the first two names; Aaron wasn't one of them. He felt like he gave solid performances, but maybe it wasn't good enough. He and the other seven remaining contestants were sweating with anticipation. Aaron was so excited he didn't have time to think about getting sick. Aaron was making fists so tight his fingernails were digging into his hands. "And the last of this year's finalists is... Aaron Butler!" Aaron's mom and all of his 'family' jumped out of their seats: Maria could barely breathe.

"Oh my God!" Alisha said.

"I knew he'd make it," Marcos said confidently.

Patty couldn't stop screaming Aaron's name. Aaron blew out a huge sigh of relief and then congratulated the other finalists. Now it was down to three.

"We are going to take a fifteen-minute break to let our contestants catch their breath and get ready for the final round!" the announcer said.

Aaron sat on a bench by himself drinking some water, thinking about what song he was going to do: maybe now it's time for Are You Lonesome Tonight? The song he had originally planned for the second round. Yup, that's what I'm going to do. He got up and went to his locker to change. When he came around the corner of the lockers, standing right in front of him was Red.

"Red!" Aaron burst out. "I thought I saw you!" Red smiled.

"Trying to keep a low profile," he joked. He was wearing a baseball cap and sunglasses, but Aaron didn't think anything of it. "Johnny and I came to see you perform."

"Really? Johnny's here, too?"

Red nodded his head.

"Where is he?"

"Oh he's here, but he couldn't come back, so he asked me to come say Hi. He and I have a bet: we wanted to ask you what song you'd be doing for the final round."

Aaron thought it was strange but was still happy to know Johnny was there. "I'm going to do Are You Lonesome Tonight?" Aaron told him.

"Ahh, that's what Johnny said you would do. He thinks that gives you the best shot."

"Really? Johnny thinks I can win?"

"Sure... we both do."

"Man, I don't know... but I'm giving it everything."

"Trust me, you can tell," Red told him. "Everyone can tell. So listen, I have to go back. Good luck in the finals, okay?" Red patted Aaron on the back.

"Sure, Red, thanks. Oh, and please tell Johnny thanks, too," Aaron asked him. Red started to walk away and Aaron started to change. "Hey, Red!" Aaron yelled out. Red turned around. "Will Johnny still be here when it's over? I mean will he stick around so I can say Hi?"

Red looked at Aaron for a second. "Not sure." He walked away.

Aaron was confused about the visit and what it all meant, but he was excited Johnny was there and that he saw his performances. Aaron quickly refocused and finished getting ready. The announcer was back at the microphone announcing the first of the three finalists. This time Aaron was going first!

"Awe, man," he said out loud.

He hated the idea of going first but had no choice. Aaron took the stage with his guitar in hand. He sat on a tall stool in front of the microphone. It was just him and his guitar with no backup music.

He positioned his guitar on his knee and strummed it a few times, then paused. Alisha knew exactly what song he was going to do; everyone in the audience sat quietly. Aaron started to play. His mom and Maria smiled, and then he began to sing "Are You Lonesome Tonight?..." He had the audience mesmerized. Some in the audience started to sing along, which totally pissed off Alisha but it was good: they were responding to Aaron one hundred percent. Through the whole song Aaron only opened his eyes a few times: he was putting his whole heart into it. It was so quiet, it was as if Aaron was all alone; but the second he strummed the last chord the audience erupted into screams, cheers and clapping, and once again Aaron received a standing ovation. Aaron stood, stepped to the side of the stool and took one simple but slow bow. He waved to the audience as he walked off, smiling all the way. The stage manager stopped him when he got to the bottom step.

"Great job, Aaron, but I need you to wait here," he said pointing to an area just behind the stage to wait.

Aaron sat there thinking about his performance, but as he listened to the other two contestants he realized this was not going to be a walk in the park. Wow! This guy is really good, he thought as he listened to the last performer do 'It's Now or Never'. He also got a roaring standing ovation. All three of the finalists were standing just offstage getting instructions from the stage manager; they shook hands and congratulated each other. Standing next to these men made Aaron feel like he might be a little out of his league, especially when it came to the outfits: wow! The announcer was talking with the audience.

"Tell me that wasn't amazing!" he yelled out. "Let's have our finalists please!" he said into the microphone and gestured them to come onto the stage. "Here they are... our three finalists!" They all stood shoulder-to-shoulder to the right of the announcer. The audience was clapping, screaming and whistling. "Just to remind everyone, the third-place winner receives this beautiful trophy and a check for twenty-five hundred dollars!" Everyone clapped. "And our second-place winner receives this amazing trophy, an all-expenses-paid seven-day vacation for two to the Bahamas, and a check for twenty-five hundred dollars!" Aaron could hardly contain himself knowing he was going to win one of these prizes. "And this year's champion will get a two-week all-expenses-paid trip to the Bahamas and a check for ten thousand dollars!" The audience went crazy; the three contestants each had different reactions. Aaron was literally biting his lip trying not to lose it. "Okay! So we will start with the third-place winner!" the announcer explained. Aaron was looking at the Elvis who was standing right next to him: if I wasn't here and somebody asked me, I'd swear this guy was really Elvis, he thought. Aaron was impressed. The next thing Aaron heard was "Brian Houseman, from New York!" Aaron snapped out of it. Holy crap! he instantly realized, that means I'm at least second... He was too excited to think. He was hanging on every word the announcer was saying.

The other Elvis turned to Aaron, "Good luck to you, man," he said in a heavy Elvis voice.

"Oh, thanks. Good luck to you, too." They shook hands.

"And the Champion of this year's National Elvis Impersonation Contest is..." (Yes, there was a drum roll). Alisha was about to come out of her skin. Marcos had already lost his voice and couldn't scream, so he just jumped up and down in one place. Patty was all over the boards, happy, screaming, crying; but Maria was sitting in her chair praying, holding her breath. She couldn't watch.

"Mike Johansen from Las Vegas!" The audience erupted with screams and applause. He was handed the first-place trophy and held it high over his head. Aaron and his family knew immediately Aaron had placed second, but you would have thought he won. Maria leaped from her seat screaming Aaron's name. It was a very exciting moment for all of them.

"And congratulations to Aaron, our second-place winner! You did a fabulous job!" the announcer said, handing him his second-place trophy. Aaron was ecstatic. He was so happy. He couldn't believe it, second place! Funny the first thing he thought of was he wouldn't have even been there if Marcos hadn't convinced him; the second thing he thought of was now he and Maria could go on a real honeymoon!

Aaron couldn't contain himself; he jumped off the front of the stage to find his family. Working his way through the crowd, he was congratulated by everyone he passed. It was a great moment for Aaron. Then he heard someone call his name, a voice he recognized. He turned to look: it was Johnny.

"Johnny!" Aaron hustled over to where he and Red were standing. "It's so good to see you, how are you doing?"

"Hey, kid! It's good to see you, too. That was… well, that was cool, man, very cool," Johnny said with a big smile.

"Thanks, Johnny… and Red, that was really fun," he told them, still trying to catch his breath.

"It looked that way to me," Johnny told him.

"I swear, when I closed my eyes you sounded exactly like the Elvis I knew when we were only young men," Red told him.

Johnny gave Red a funny look. "You knew Elvis, too?" Aaron asked excitedly.

Red nodded his head. "Yeah, I worked for him for a while."

"That is so cool. I bet…" Aaron was interrupted.

"Aaron!" came this loud scream.

"It's my mom… You guys have to meet my family, okay?" Red looked at Johnny. "Sure, kid, but we have to go right after."

"Really?" Aaron thought maybe they could hang out a while and swap some stories, well… hear some stories.

"Aaron!" his mom said, gasping for air. She gave him a huge hug. "I am so proud of you." Just then the rest of the group caught up. Maria walked right up to Aaron and gave him a big kiss and hug.

"I guess we know where we're going for our honeymoon!" she laughed.

"Honeymoon?" Johnny questioned.

Maria turned around. "Johnny!" she yelled, and ran up to him and gave him a big hug. There was a moment or two of awkwardness. Aaron was all smiles.

Johnny looked sternly at Aaron. "Oh sorry," Aaron replied. "Mom, this is my friend Johnny and his friend Red." Red! Alisha thought to herself. "Red and Johnny this is my mom, Alisha, and our friends, Marcos and Patty, oh and you already know Maria," he laughed.

Alisha stepped up to Johnny. "It's a pleasure Johnny."

Johnny reached out to shake her hand. "Aaron never mentioned how beautiful his mom is," Johnny smiled. Alisha smirked; in a very rare moment she didn't know what to say, but before she completely lost her composure she thanked him.

"I guess I should say thank you for saving Elvis's life," she told him. Red started laughing. Johnny was smiling, trying not to laugh. You could see it on everyone's face that they thought it was a strange reaction.

"It was not big deal... really," Johnny told her.

"I wasn't made aware that you and my son became friends. A little strange really, but I have a feeling a story is coming." She smiled as she looked at Aaron.

"This I'm sure is true, ma'am," Johnny said.

Alisha took a step back, and put her hand over her mouth. "Are you okay, Mom?" Aaron asked a little embarrassed. "Do I know you?" she questioned Johnny.

"I don't believe we've ever had the pleasure, ma'am," he said very politely and softly. "I would have remembered, no question," Johnny said smoothly.

Marcos stepped up and shook Johnny and Red's hands. "It's a pleasure," he said excitedly. "What did you think of our Aaron tonight?" he asked, trying to get the conversation back on track.

"Excellent... really excellent," Johnny said proudly.

"He was great," Red added.

"You guys are not going to believe who Johnny and Red used to work with?" Aaron said excitedly.

"Aaron!" Johnny yelled out, cutting him off. "Listen, kid, we really have to go, so why don't you tell that story another time and we'll catch up later. Alright?" he suggested strongly.

"Sure, Johnny." Aaron was caught a little off guard. "Listen, thank you so much for coming," Aaron told him.

"No big deal, kid, really," Johnny chuckled. "So... I have to go, I guess I'll see you guys next summer," Johnny reminded them.

"That's great," Aaron replied, Maria smiled.

The others looked puzzled. "Bye, Johnny, thank you for everything." Maria couldn't resist and hugged him again.

"You take good care of him," he whispered in her ear.

"Don't worry, I will," she whispered back.

"Okay... congratulations, you two. I'm gone."

Red grabbed Johnny's arm, they turned and walked away. Everyone noticed that Johnny was struggling to walk and Red had to support him.

There was another awkward few moments and then all at once everyone broke out in screams, waving their arms and jumping up and down. Alisha was having difficulty putting into words how proud of her son she was, so she just kept hugging him. Aaron was enjoying the attention, but it was starting to get a little uncomfortable. He gently peeled his mom off of him.

"Mom, can Maria come and help me with my stuff? Then we can meet you back at the car. Okay?"

"Of course."

Marcos jumped in. "What do you guys think...? The Blue Suede Shoe for dinner tonight?" Alisha and Patty laughed.

"I wouldn't have it any other way," Aaron told him.

He and Maria headed off in the direction of the stage, and the others to the truck. "This has been one of those nights," Alisha said to Marcos and Patty.

"How do you mean?" Patty asked.

"Oh you know, I'm just so proud. I can't believe what I just experienced, and more than anything I guess I realize my baby isn't my baby anymore," she said tearfully. "Aaron is an exceptional kid, always has been," Marcos said, beaming with pride. Patty walked close to Alisha and put her arm around her.

"You are a great mom and you have a great kid." Alisha smiled.

"So, Marcos… Who is that Johnny guy?" Alisha questioned.

"I have no idea."

"Did he look familiar to you?" she questioned the both of them.

"I've seen that Red guy before, you know, at the store," Patty told them.

"Johnny did look a little familiar but I'm not sure why. Maybe we've seen him around town or something?" Marcos suggested.

"Yeah, maybe you're right. This is going to bug me now for a while," she admitted. "Aaron is convinced he saw a photo with Red in it at Graceland when we were there," Alisha told them.

"Really?" Marcos asked.

"Yeah, I'll tell you the whole thing later. It's a crazy story. By the way, don't you think us not knowing about this friendship with Johnny is a little strange, especially for Aaron?"

When they got to the truck Marcos opened the doors for the ladies. "Why do you think Aaron went back after you told him not to?" Marcos asked.

"Yeah, that surprises me, especially after the whole bobcat thing?" Alisha added.

"What bobcat thing?" Patty asked, feeling a little out of the loop.

"And how would Maria have known him?" Alisha added.

"What bobcat thing?" Patty demanded.

Alisha smiled. "You've got some catching up to do," she laughed.

"We've got a long ride home: good time for some catching up," Marcos suggested.

"Aaron won't be able to hide being stuck in the truck for two and a half hours." Alisha and Patty smiled in agreement.

"Maria, aren't you coming?" Aaron asked. Maria stopped at the top of the backstage stairs.

"Is it okay if I'm back here?" she asked.

"Sure. Most everyone is gone by now, there'll just be some crew around." He took her hand and they worked their way to Aaron's dressing area. They collected Aaron's things and then headed for the truck.

Dinner at the Blue Suede Shoe was almost as much fun as the contest. Alisha made sure to bring in Aaron's trophy for everyone to see, much against Aaron's wishes. He was greeted like a celebrity. Everyone wanted to come say Hi, take a picture with him, and several young ladies asked for his autograph. Alisha was beaming, Maria was not. At one point the manager asked Aaron to perform on their small stage: Aaron was a little easier to convince this time. Marcos ran out to the truck and grabbed Aaron's guitar. After he finished the song, everyone in the restaurant stood up to clap. Aaron was embarrassed but accepted the response.

"Kind of fun to sing in a smaller place," Aaron told the group as he sat down.

"Aaron that was great. Man, you really found your groove this weekend," Marcos told him. As they were wrapping up dinner and Aaron took a few more photos, Marcos asked for the bill.

"We've got a bit of a drive, so we need to get going," he told their waitress.

She smiled really big. "You're all set," she beamed. "The restaurant picked up your bill."

"You're kidding?" Alisha asked.

"No, ma'am… it was our honor to have y'all in here tonight." Marcos didn't know what to say.

"That is very kind," Aaron spoke up.

"Just one thing," the waitress asked. It was painfully obvious that she was a little 'star-struck'. "Would you mind if me and a couple of the other girls took a picture with you? We'd like to hang it on the wall," she explained. Aaron was more than happy to do it, but hang it on the wall? Wow! I'm going to be on the same wall as Elvis!

"Sure thing. Let's do it," Aaron responded. They decided to do it out in front because the photo with Aaron and some of the staff turned into a photo with Aaron and all of the staff. It was a lot of fun for everyone. They said their goodbyes and got into Marcos's truck to start the long trip home.

They didn't get very far down the road when Alisha changed the subject.

"Okay, Aaron, time for some details," she said sternly, but with a smile.

Aaron looked at her funny. "What are you talking about, Mom?"

"Who exactly is this Johnny and how long have you two been 'friends'?" she held up her hands making the quote sign.

The truck got very quiet. Aaron looked at Maria, Maria nodded her head.

"Wow, Mom, you really need this now?" he pleaded.

"Not me... us," she told him. "Marcos, Patty and I want to know the whole story," Marcos nodded his head while Patty quietly clapped her hands.

"Okay..."

Maria reached over the seat and squeezed Aaron's shoulder. For Patty's sake and at the recommendation of his mom, Aaron started his story from the very beginning. Right from the day he first discovered his 'fishing spot'. He left out no details; he told them everything. Maria tried not to interrupt but couldn't help herself when Aaron tried to take the blame for going back to the fishing spot after his mom told him not to. Somehow Alisha wasn't surprised. Together they explained about when they first ran into Johnny and how sick he was; they talked about the house, and the red truck, all of it. Then Aaron told his mom how Johnny had worked for Elvis.

"Actually he and Red both worked for him," he said excitedly.

"Really?" Alisha questioned sarcastically.

"Yes, Mrs. B., we even saw a few pictures around the house," Maria added.

"Pictures with Johnny and Elvis?" Marcos asked.

"No, not exactly," Aaron started. "There were only a few pictures, most of them were of Elvis at a studio or something with what looked like some friends or maybe his security."

"I know I saw one with Red in it," he told them.

"Like you saw Red in that photo at Graceland?" Alisha asked.

"Awe, now I get it." Maria suddenly put the two photos of Red together.

"Aaron, I don't want to burst your bubble. I mean Johnny seems nice enough, but was he in any of the photographs that we saw at Graceland?" Alisha tried to explain.

"To be honest, that's what I was looking for, but I didn't see him in a single photograph."

"How do you know he just doesn't have some strange infatuation with Elvis - a lot of people do, you know," Marcos suggested.

Patty suddenly jumped in. "So, how do you explain his relationship with Red then?" she asked. "That is if Red is the Red?" she added.

Everyone sat there thinking about the question for a minute; then Marcos spoke up. "It could be Red is friends with Johnny, and that's where Johnny gets all his stories from." Marcos was proud of himself for deducing a solid possibility. Things got very quiet; you could almost hear everyone thinking.

Then Maria spoke up. "Well, he didn't have anything else in his house that was obviously from Elvis, no memorabilia or anything like that. And… it wasn't until Aaron mentioned something about his dog that it started the whole conversation about Elvis in the first place," Maria explained.

"Besides, if it's true, what did he do for Elvis? How come no one else has seen him before?" his mother wanted to know.

Maria and Aaron looked at each other. "Actually… I'm not sure," he admitted.

"Huh!" Alisha let out.

Aaron was feeling a little dejected but he moved on; the rest of the story even Maria knew nothing about. It took the entire rest of the ride home to get out the whole story. He had no interruptions, not one. Everyone seemed to move from being suspicious to very interested. Aaron explained the reason he was going back to Johnny's.

"Johnny was helping me get ready for the fair," he told them. "He knew every move, every voice inflection, he even knew Elvis's attitude when it came to understanding a song better. It was really impressive, guys, and very helpful," he explained. Then he told them the reason he was doing the contest in the first place. "I wanted to do it for all of you, but especially for Maria."

"Awe," everyone in the truck reacted, even Marcos.

They were only a few minutes from home. "That's about it," Aaron told them, "Now you know the whole story."

Maria leaned over and kissed Aaron on the cheek. Alisha put her hand on his shoulder. "I don't know what to say, that was a serious story," she admitted to the group. "I still don't get something?" Patty asked.

"What's that?" Aaron responded.

"Well, in your story you never really said why he was hiding out in the middle of nowhere, by himself, mind you, and then only for the summer? That's a little weird, don't you think?"

Everyone was mumbling in agreement. Marcos was pulling the truck up to the front of the house. Elvis was the first one out.

"I know. It is strange. But truthfully I never felt like it was right to ask. I mean if he is hiding out he has his reasons; we became friends and I think we did, you know, at least in part, because I didn't ask those kinds of questions." Everyone nodded their heads like they understood.

FAST FRIENDS

"I can't believe we are here again already," Aaron said to Maria and his mom.

"Sucks!" his mom said loudly.

The airport was bustling with holiday travelers all headed home like Maria. After checking in and getting Maria's boarding pass, the three of them went to get a soda. Maria sat between Alisha and Aaron on a bench near the security area. Maria sat there staring at her ring, spinning it around her finger.

Alisha put her arm around her. "You okay?"

Maria looked over at her. "I couldn't be better," she said gleefully.

Alisha smiled. "These next five months will fly by, you'll see."

Maria smiled; she knew it wasn't true but she appreciated the effort. "How am I going to plan a wedding from two thousand miles away?" she questioned.

"Maria, we went over all of this," Aaron reminded her.

"I know, I know. It's just a little scary," she admitted.

"Don't worry about a thing, Maria. Between Patty and me we will get everything organized just the way you requested," Alisha told her confidently.

"Thank you. But if you have any questions or need anything at all, please call me right away," she pleaded.

"Don't worry," Aaron told her. "My mom and Patty have us covered; look, you already know they won't let me be involved at all, so you can relax about that," he chuckled.

Maria smiled and kissed him. It was time for Maria to go. "This is going to be a rough five months," she said.

Aaron smiled. "You'll be so busy, and we will talk every day… At least if your family lets us," he joked.

"Oh my God!" Maria shouted. She had a look of fear on her face.

"What is it, Maria?" Alisha asked.

"I forgot about my family," she said. "They don't know anything," she added. Aaron started to laugh.

"What's so funny?" Maria asked him sharply.

"Oh, I'm just trying to imagine that conversation," he smiled.

"You can be cruel sometimes, Aaron Butler!" his mom snapped at him. "Look. You have five hours to think about it and what you're going to say," Alisha told her. "I'm sure it will all be fine."

Again Maria didn't believe her, but appreciated the effort. After that, things got considerably somber. The reality of leaving and not seeing her fiancé for five months was starting to hit her. Alisha quickly jumped in. "Okay, Maria, you've got to get going. I love you… Have a safe flight and call the minute you get home, okay?"

"Yes, ma'am," Maria tried to smile.

"Aaron, I'll wait just out on the curb… Don't let Maria miss her flight," she instructed.

"Okay, Mom." Maria and Aaron stood toe-to-toe. "Crazy, right?" Aaron asked.

"Super-crazy." She managed a smile.

"When you get back, one month later we will be married," he reminded her, as if she needed reminding.

She smiled as she let out a sigh of relief. "Please let me know how the plans are coming along for our honeymoon. I'm so excited to go away together."

"Absolutely, no problem." Aaron looked at the clock on the wall. "Maria... you have to go."

She looked at the clock. "Crud!"

She leaned in and gave Aaron a kiss he wouldn't soon forget. "I love you."

"More," he said back. Once again, Maria left Aaron standing at the airport. This completely sucks! he said to himself as he turned to go find his mom.

Alisha was right: at least for her, Patty and maybe even Marcos, the five months were passing very quickly. Patty and Alisha met at least twice a week, planning and organizing. Even though Maria's family didn't like it, Maria and Aaron spoke on the phone almost every night - well, except when his mom or Patty needed to talk to her.

"Oh my gosh, Mrs. B., it all sounds so amazing, I wish I was there to help," she told her.

"You are helping, we are in this together; I think it's working out great," Alisha said. "Don't worry about the day-to-day stuff, right now you need to finish up school and get your behind back here," she joked.

"Trust me, the day I graduate I'm on that plane," Maria said excitedly.

Aaron was working hard and even studying hard. It was important to him that Maria saw how serious he was, and he wanted to get good grades out of respect for her. He and Marcos had no choice: they had to hire a few extra full-time hands to help out, especially now that they were managing two farms. Aaron loved the work: he was so excited when the new crops first emerged from the soil. He was a true farmer. Marcos and Aaron tried their best to stay out of the way of the wedding planning, and only got involved when they were 'commanded' to. They were assigned one job, putting up the decorations, but other than that they just had to show up. Aaron felt kind of guilty, he thought maybe he should be more involved, but his mom made it very clear he was not needed. Truthfully he was okay with that. The house was filling up with stuff: decorations, tables, chairs, vases, fancy glassware, flatware, and a ton more. Even some gifts were coming in from friends and family who were out-of-town. It was getting harder and harder to move around the house: both spare rooms were filled to capacity. But his mom and Patty were making good headway; the things they couldn't make or borrow they bought. Marcos tried to pitch in once and almost got his eyes scratched out. The ladies had this, period.

As a surprise, Marcos took Aaron over to Maria's one morning. "What are we doing here?" Aaron asked as they walked into the house. They were just there the day before and shouldn't have needed to come back for at least another day or two.

"I am the farthest person from being any kind of expert in romance, but you and I need to plan a few things," Marcos told him. Aaron was completely puzzled.

"What are you talking about?" Aaron asked.

"Your wedding night, you dummy," Marcos laughed.

"My wedding night? What the heck… OH… my wedding night," he smiled. "This is where we'll be." It took him a second.

"Right. So we have to make this place look not like Maria's grandmother's and more like your home," he explained. "Get it?"

"Sure, I get it, but I don't think I should be doing any redecorating without Maria," he told him, a little concerned.

"We're not really going to redecorate, we're just going to move some things around, like in the master bedroom, for example, and make it look, you know… different," he explained. "And then the day before the wedding we need to come over here and make everything look, well you know…" Marcos tried to explain.

"I must be slow today because I don't have a clue what you're talking about," Aaron admitted.

"Romantic! You know romantic…" he frustratingly told him.

"Hmm, Patty, right?" Aaron smiled.

"Yes, Patty!"

He looked curiously at Marcos. "But I still think it's a good idea," he confessed. "And she'll kill me if we don't get this right," he joked.

"We need this to look something like a honeymoon suite, get it?" he explained, a little embarrassed himself.

Aaron broke out laughing. "Okay, okay, I get it, Jeez… What did you have in mind?" he asked, trying hard to stop laughing.

"Well, Patty says balloons, flowers and candles."

"Really? Balloons, flowers and candles… Okay, sounds easy enough," Aaron smiled.

Marcos laughed. "I hope so, I've got it all in the truck. We need to hide it somewhere in here so it's ready for us on the sixteenth" - which was the day before the wedding. They grabbed the bags of balloons, candles and even an air compressor to fill the balloons with, and took it all downstairs to the basement. "I'm assuming we'll bring the flowers over that day?" Aaron inquired.

"That's right."

"See, I'm getting this," Aaron laughed.

They spent the next few hours moving some of the furniture around, reorganizing and making it feel less like Maria's grandmother's house. They took all of the furniture out of the bedroom and put it into one of the small storage barns. "Now what? The room is empty." Aaron stated the obvious.

"Don't worry about it, you'll see," Marcos told him with a coy grin on his face.

"Sure… okay. Are we all good then?" he asked.

"All good," Marcos told him, satisfied with himself.

What Aaron didn't know was his mom and Marcos bought all new furniture as a wedding gift for the kids. It was Alisha's idea, but Marcos thought it was a great one and jumped in. Marcos and Aaron left the house and got into the truck. "Marcos… I know I was joking around earlier, but I know you're doing this for Maria and me, I just wanted to say thanks," Aaron told him sincerely. Marcos put his hand on Aaron's head and mussed his hair, something Marcos always loved to do.

"You got it, kiddo. That's how we do it, right?" he smiled.

"Right," Aaron smiled back.

Aaron was out of school one week before Maria was. He was so happy to be done and he accomplished his goal, three A's and two B's. His mom was impressed. "I hate to think what you could have done the previous seventeen years had you applied yourself like you did this time," she said jokingly but meant it.

Six days till Maria got home. The house was ready, every room was packed with wedding stuff, and the kitchen was jammed with food and drinks ready to be prepared. There must have been twenty ice chests strategically placed all over the house, including in Aaron's room. One night, three days before Maria's arrival, the weather started to become pretty nasty. At first a little lightning way off in the distance, then some rain. "This will be good," Aaron told his mom.

"It will help settle down the dust for a while," he told her.

"I don't like the look of those clouds," she told him.

"Awe, it's nothing, Mom, just an early summer storm," he said confidently.

Alisha watched the news for a few minutes to see what they thought; it appeared Aaron was right; it was an early monsoon, but a big one. After their nightly phone call Aaron went to his room. He opened his window to listen to the rain and watch the flashes from the far-off lightning. It started to rain pretty hard after a while. Aaron had already fallen asleep, but the sound of a much closer lightning strike scared him right out of bed. "Holy crap! That was close!" he said out loud. Then another, much closer. "One thousand and One, One Thous…" he counted out loud. 'CRACK!' his counting was interrupted by this tremendous sound and flash of light as the lightning hit somewhere too close. Aaron threw on his pants and ran to his mom's room. "Mom!" he yelled out.

"I'm in here!" she yelled from the kitchen.

When Aaron walked in he was caught off guard. "You're dressed?!" he questioned his mom.

"Yeah, just in case," she explained. She looked at Aaron. "Aaron, please go get dressed… just in case," she requested.

"Sure, Mom." He ran to his room and put on the rest of his clothes.

About halfway down the stairs he headed back to the kitchen: there was another lightning strike, only this time it was so close the house shook, almost knocking Aaron over. "Aaron!" his mom screamed out.

"I'm okay, Mom! I'm right here!" he said as he ran into the kitchen.

"Look!" she pointed out the window.

Aaron stared hard into the blackness. The wind was howling, the rain turned into a downpour. Another flash of light and what sounded like an explosion. In that split second Aaron could see what his mom was pointing at. "Oh my God, Mom, is that a tornado?"

"I'm not sure but we're not waiting around to find out!" she screamed. Just as they got to the door, Marcos came running in soaking wet from head to toe.

"We've gotta go!" he yelled.

Another lightning strike cracked, slightly further away. They ran out the door and headed for the main barn. Inside the barn was a makeshift shelter, something that had been there for generations; the Butlers used it for storage. It was hard to run: between the overpowering rain and the strong wind they had to strain to move forward. The wind was whipping viciously in all directions. Aaron couldn't see a thing; he held his mom's hand tight and just watched Marcos's feet so he wouldn't lose him. The animals were going nuts: the horses were jumping and kicking, the chickens were so loud you could barely hear anything else. It took both Marcos and Aaron working together to get the barn door open, and they held it for Alisha; as soon as she stepped in, the wind ripped the door right out of Marcos's hands and completely off the barn. "Wow!" Aaron yelled but no one could hear him. Marcos and Aaron ran to the center of the barn to where the door to the shelter was. Alisha lay on the floor. One of the tractors was parked right on top of the shelter door. Marcos started to climb up on the tractor but then suddenly stopped.

It got eerily quiet. "What is it, Marcos?" Aaron asked.

They all stared out the open barn doors. Marcos screamed: "Tornado!"

He jumped onto the tractor and started it up. He backed it away from the hatch door and Aaron opened it up; he signaled to his mom to get in. Marcos jumped off the tractor and held the door for Aaron, and then he followed right behind. Together he and Aaron bolted the door tight. Literally within seconds they could hear the barn over their head being torn apart. Alisha put her hands over her ears, dropped to her knees and covered her face; Aaron covered her and Marcos covered him. Aaron could hear his mom praying, she was crying, they were all scared. Marcos held onto them tight. The shelter door above them shook violently. The sound of the wind was unbearable. Alisha began screaming her prayer, Aaron didn't know what to do; he held onto his mom as tight as he could and tried to lock his feet between some boxes. Aaron was the most scared he'd ever been: he was on the verge of tears. He was thinking about Maria, he was so glad she wasn't there... Then came a terrible crashing sound.

"What was that?" Alisha screamed.

"I think it was the tractor!" Marcos yelled back.

The tractor? Aaron thought.

It was the longest ninety seconds of Aaron's life. In an instant the wind was gone, the animals were quiet: a total calm. Marcos sat back. "Are you guys okay?" Aaron got off his mom. She sat up and started to cry; her face was dirty from the dust and tears.

She hugged her son. "Aaron... Everything is gone!"

"Hold on, we don't know that's true," Marcos said, trying to be supportive.

"Let's get out of here, Marcos!" Aaron insisted.

"Right."

He and Marcos unbolted the door and started to push it open. "What the heck!" Aaron yelled out, pushing as hard as he could on the shelter door.

"What's the matter?" Alisha asked, still terrified.

"The door is stuck!" Marcos explained.

"Stuck?" Alisha questioned.

"I think something must have fallen on it," Marcos told her. "Come on, Aaron, let's try again."

Together they pushed with all they had, and the door finally started to open. Aaron could hear something sliding off the door then it easily opened the rest of the way. Total darkness. When they arose out of the shelter they could see almost nothing.

"Stay here for a second!" Marcos yelled at them.

He was afraid if anyone moved they could easily get hurt. They stood there for a minute; finally the full moon poked through the clouds, and for the first time they could see. The barn they were in was completely gone except for the tractor that Marcos had moved and one wall that was somehow strangely still standing. There was debris everywhere.

"Follow me!" Marcos yelled to them as they worked their way out of the barn. It started to rain again, only lightly.

"Be careful!" Alisha yelled out hysterically.

Aaron was holding her hand all the way out until they were clear of the barn. Marcos stood and stared. "What is it, Marcos?" Aaron asked.

"Look!" he pointed in the direction of the house.

"Oh my God! It's still there!" Alisha cried out.

It was a short, bittersweet celebration. Suddenly Aaron started freaking out. "MOM!" he yelled in a panic. "Where's Elvis!" he screamed.

"Oh my God!" Alisha yelled out again.

"Elvis!" they all started yelling at the top of the lungs. "Elvis!" they yelled as they made their way back to the house.

Aaron ran into the house. "Elvis!" he yelled again and again as loud as he could. Marcos and Alisha came in.

"Elvis!" they both screamed.

Then they heard a single bark coming from upstairs.

"Elvis!" Aaron started running up the stairs with Marcos and his mom right behind. "Elvis, where are you, boy?" Aaron called out.

He barked again.

"He's in my room!" Alisha screamed.

They all ran in and looked around, no Elvis. Then he barked again. "The bathroom!" Marcos declared.

Aaron had to push on the door really hard because there was so much debris on the ground blocking it. Marcos stepped up to help. Together they opened it enough to squeeze through, inside Elvis was lying down in the bathtub in a pool of blood and broken glass. Aaron reacted quickly and picked Elvis up. He took him into his mom's bedroom and set him on the floor, Marcos was right behind with a couple of towels. Aaron and Alisha quickly found the sources of the bleeding and held the towels in place to slow it down. Elvis had one large piece of glass in his leg, and several smaller ones in his paws; Marcos carefully but quickly pulled them out. Alisha wrapped the wounds in some gauze from the bathroom and taped them tight.

"He lost a fair amount of blood but I think he's going to be okay," Marcos told them. "He'll need some stitches, though."

The rest of that night they all sat in the kitchen, afraid to move with no light. Aaron held Elvis in his arms. Marcos and Alisha just sat in silence drinking their coffees; Alisha was still visibly shaking. They all needed to sleep but no one wanted to try. As the sun came up they decided it was safe enough to go outside to survey the damage. Aaron set Elvis down on his blanket in the family room. "You stay here," he ordered. Elvis put his head down. When they got outside it was much worse than they thought, certainly worse than they hoped for. The barn was gone, and because the barn was gone you could easily see from the front porch that Marcos's house was gone, too. Alisha walked over and put her arms around Marcos.

"I'm so sorry," she said sobbing with tears streaming down her face. Aaron started down the steps. "Please be careful!" his mom yelled.

"Aaron, there's going to be debris everywhere," Marcos reminded him as he, too, started down the front steps.

Debris was an understatement. Aaron soon came across a dead cow lying just outside one of the pens. "Awe, man."

"What is it?" Marcos asked as he walked up.

"A cow," Aaron pointed.

Marcos looked closely. "Look closer," he said pointing at the cow's brand. "It's not one of ours."

"Whose is it?" Alisha asked.

"Not sure," Marcos answered.

Together they walked the entire farm. It was pretty bad. Marcos was keeping track in his head. "I counted two cows, a horse, and who knows how many chickens. But amazingly all the pigs are okay," he smiled.

Alisha tried to smile. "What do you think happened over at the Muccino place?" she asked. Aaron and Marcos stopped walking.

"I don't know but we need to find out," Aaron said. "I'll go over there," he started to say.

"Oh no, we stay together," Marcos demanded.

"Right. That's good," Alisha agreed.

"Besides we need to check on Patty first," Marcos told them.

"Of course," Alisha said, slapping herself on the forehead. "Aaron, you and Marcos try and clear a path in front of the truck, make sure it will start and I'll get Elvis, maybe we can find a vet, too," she said.

They all got in Aaron's truck. Aaron drove while his mom held Elvis. They normally would have taken Marcos's truck for something like this but they could not find it! The way to Patty's was clear; it looked like any other day. "It doesn't look like the tornado came this way," Marcos said joyfully.

"Oh thank goodness," Alisha was relieved.

They quickly made it to Patty's. "Patty!" Marcos yelled out as he ran to the door. The door was unlocked. He opened it and walked in. "Patty?" he called out gently.

"In here!" Patty responded.

A big smile came over his face. "She's in here!" Marcos called back to Alisha and Aaron.

"Are you okay?" he asked as he knelt down next to her in her bathroom.

"Yes, I'm fine. I'm so happy to see you," she cried.

Marcos wrapped his arms around her and picked her up. Alisha and Aaron came walking in. "Oh Alisha!" Patty cried out as she fell into her arms. "Thank God you guys are okay," she told them in between sniffles.

"I watched the news as long as I could, they said they thought it was headed in my direction and to take cover. The last thing I remember them saying was Atoka took a direct hit! I was so scared I couldn't move."

"Well, thank God you're alright." Marcos hugged her. "Come with us, we need to check on Maria's place."

"Okay, let me just change real quick." She shushed the guys out of her room. "Alisha… how is it?" she asked.

"Not good," she said, shaking her head with tears building up. "But now that I'm getting my mind back from utter terror I'm realizing it could have been so much worse," she said with some confidence in her voice. "Marcos's house and the barn are gone." She started to cry.

"Awe, man. Okay, I'm ready. We can talk on the way."

Alisha and Patty sat in the back with Elvis; Patty was stroking his head. "If nothing else I'm sure Maria's grandmother kept a stitching kit at her house. I can stitch this up no problem," Patty told everyone.

As they drove down the highway toward Maria's, there were virtually no other cars on the road, except for some emergency vehicles that would go flying by every couple of minutes. They listened to the radio intently as it broadcast emergency updates. According to the news, the tornado was labeled a Category two, which in the tornado world is considered medium-strength. However, it was still able to cause major devastation for anything in its path. As they got closer to Maria's the road became more difficult to navigate; there was debris large and small everywhere. "There must be hundreds of downed trees," Marcos observed. Aaron slowed way down. They drove past one farm that was no longer there: the house, the barn and even a large swathe of crops were pulled from the earth. They started to pull over to see if they could help but then they saw the entire family standing about in front of what was their house.

Marcos leaned out the window. "Are you guys okay?" he yelled.

They all turned to look, and the father waved. "Yes, we're okay!" he yelled back. Marcos waved and they started back down the road. Minutes later they pulled onto Maria's property.

"Oh my God," Patty said excitedly.

"Look!" Alisha pointed to the house. "It's untouched!" Aaron let out a huge sigh of relief.

"Amazing," Marcos said quietly.

"Let's go inside to be sure," Alisha suggested.

"I'm going to check on the animals," Aaron told them as he ran off toward the barn.

"Not even a broken cup!" Patty yelled from an upstairs window.

"Perfect!" Marcos said out loud. "Thank God."

It took Aaron over an hour to get to a place where he could find a phone that worked. He had no choice but to call Maria collect.

The operator didn't even finish asking, "Yes, yes! I accept! Aaron, please tell me you and your family are okay? Please tell me!" she started to cry.

"Maria! I promise we are all okay," he said, trying to calm her down.

"You're not just saying that, are you? Everyone's okay, your mom, Marcos, Patty… Elvis!" she asked hysterically.

"Yes. Everyone is okay," he said in a calm voice trying to console her.

"Oh Aaron, please let me speak with your mom, I really need to speak with her," she desperately requested.

"Maria, I had to drive over an hour to find a phone to call you from, my mom's back at the house with Marcos and Patty trying to clean up," he tried to explain.

"Oh my God! Oh my God!" she said hysterically.

"No! Maria! I promise, everyone is okay. The phone company said that we should have service by tomorrow, thankfully the power was only out for a few hours."

"I think I should come home! Don't you think I should come? I can catch a flight tomorrow morning," she strongly suggested.

"Maria," he said calmly, "I need you to take a deep breath. There is no reason for you to come right now; you'll be here in days. Everything is fine and I can call you every day like normal to keep you updated."

Aaron could hear Maria take a deep breath over the phone. "Thank God everyone is okay," she said.

After Maria calmed down a little Aaron filled in some of the blanks. He told her that her farm was one hundred percent intact, and, even though they lost the barn and Marcos's house, his mom was excited to rebuild. Hearing Aaron's voice and how calm he was was helping Maria calm down. "I graduate in five days," she said joyously. "I can't wait to be home."

"No one's more excited about that than me," Aaron confided. After they talked a bit more Aaron stressed he needed to get off the phone so he could get home and help. "I'll call you tomorrow at our normal time," he told her.

"Okay… Aaron… please make sure your mom is around so I can talk with her, too," she requested.

"Of course."

From the day school was out Aaron constantly had the same two things on his mind; getting married, and when Johnny was coming back. A couple of times Aaron went by his place when he and Elvis went fishing, but the house was buttoned up tight. Maria was going to be home soon and a few weeks after that they would be getting married. Aaron was really hoping to ask Johnny to come to his wedding. He even had fantasies about the two of them singing at the wedding as a surprise for Maria. The day before Maria got home Aaron decided to try again. This time he skipped on the fishing and went straight to Johnny's. The red truck! I can't believe it, he's finally back! Aaron ran to the house and up on the porch. He could hear two guys talking inside. He knocked on the door; a few seconds later Red answered it.

"Aaron!" he sounded surprised.

"Hi, Red! How you doing?" he asked politely.

"I'm good, I'm good." You could tell Red was more than surprised to see Aaron.

It was strange: Red never opened the door more than halfway and blocked the other half with his body. Aaron was waiting to be invited inside. "Is Johnny here?" he finally asked. Red stepped out on the porch and closed the door behind him.

"No, I'm afraid not." Aaron knew he heard two voices in the house.

"Is everything okay?" he asked.

Red put his hand on Aaron's shoulder. "Come on, let's sit," he suggested, pointing to the steps.

Aaron was getting really nervous. "What's wrong?" he asked directly.

Red sighed. "Okay… I know you know Johnny is sick, right?"

"Yes."

"Well, he's gotten a lot worse," he struggled to say.

"Really? Awe, man, that sucks. Is he going to be alright?"

Red was shaking his head.

Aaron was feeling sick. Red finally spoke up: "I don't think so." Aaron was surprised and visibly upset at the news. He looked back at the house when he heard a noise that came from inside; he turned back and looked at Red. "That's just a friend helping me out."

"Helping you with what?"

"We came to grab some of Johnny's stuff, some things he wanted," he said.

"Where is Johnny now? Can I go see him?" he really wanted to know.

"No. I'm sorry, Aaron, that's just not possible," Red told him.

Aaron was confused and started to get mad. He felt like he knew Johnny but he also knew he didn't. There were always subjects that they weren't supposed to discuss; like the time Aaron asked about Johnny's family: it was obvious that it was something Johnny wasn't going to talk about. "This is just crazy," Aaron said angrily to Red.

"I know, I do. I wish I could say more... but I can't right now."

Aaron still couldn't understand why Johnny wouldn't want to see him. Now Aaron wished he had asked more questions when he had the chance, even if Johnny wouldn't have answered them. Aaron really didn't want to but he had to ask. "Is he dying?" Aaron asked in a very somber voice.

Red put his hand on Aaron's shoulder and squeezed it, "Yes... he is."

The anger left him in an instant. Aaron was distraught, and felt helpless. "Oh wow... so like... how long?" He knew Johnny was sick; some days when he visited it was pretty obvious, but neither Johnny nor Aaron ever talked about it.

"Not long." Red paused. "You have been a great friend to Johnny, actually a great inspiration to him," Red confided. "Johnny was advised not to go see you in Memphis, but he demanded. He said there was no way he was going to miss it."

"Really? Wow, that's cool," Aaron smiled. "That sounds like Johnny." Aaron smiled.

"Okay, big guy, I've got to get back to it. Did you have a message or something you want me to give to Johnny?"

Aaron shook his head. "I actually came out here to invite Johnny to my wedding," he admitted.

"Oh that's right, the wedding," Red responded enthusiastically. Then his smile changed. "I'm sorry, Aaron, I don't think that's going to be possible; but I'll make sure and tell him, alright?"

"That would be great," Aaron said as he and Red stood up. Aaron reached out to shake Red's hand. "Thank you, Red. Please tell Johnny I'm sorry we couldn't have had more time together, my thoughts are with him. He's been a great friend," Aaron said sincerely.

"For what it's worth, I know Johnny would have come," Red told him.

"Thanks."

"All the best to you and Maria!" he shouted as Aaron began jogging away.

"Thanks, Red!" his voice faded as he got into the trees.

THE BEST LAID PLANS

Maria was coming home. It was a big day for everyone; Aaron did a great deal of pacing trying to keep his heart from exploding. Life was about to change for Aaron. Every day he thought about what was soon to happen and he relished it. He knew from the first time he met Maria that she was special.

"I'm surprised you're not losing your mind right now," his mom said to him.

He smiled. "I am, you're just not seeing it yet."

"Aaron, I am so happy for you."

"Thanks, Mom... really."

"Yeah thanks, but we..." she paused. "Ya know, I just realized we've all been so out of our heads busy, what with the wedding and tornado and everything else; well... you and I really haven't had much time to talk," she confided.

"Talk? Talk about what? We always talk," he laughed. Alisha smiled.

"We do. But you and I haven't spent ten minutes talking about you getting married and what that means to you; how your life is about to change. You know, that kind of stuff."

"Really? Now you want to talk about this?" he smiled.

"I just want to make sure you're happy. You know... you are about to get married. Your happiness is the only thing I live for, you know that." She smiled at him.

"Of course, Mom, I understand." He walked over and sat down in the chair next to her. Alisha smiled. "Mom... I love you and I have so much respect for you, more than I could ever explain. You are an amazing mom." Aaron picked up her hand.

"Uh oh!" Alisha blurted out, and Aaron laughed.

"Please trust me, I know what I'm doing. I love Maria and I know she is the one." Alisha was nervously patting the back of Aaron's hand. "You and Dad are the examples I hope to live by; Maria and I decided together that now's the time; now is when we want to start our life together, with your blessing, of course," Aaron squeezed her hand. Alisha could see it in his eyes.

"I don't know why but from the minute I met Maria I knew you two would be together... Not necessarily at eighteen... but I knew." Aaron smiled.

"She is so good for you, as you are for her. I think the timing doesn't matter as long as that's what you and Maria want, then that's what I want." Aaron sat back looking at his mom; sometimes he saw her not as his mom but as the woman she was. To Aaron she was beautiful, funny and smart. She was strong and lived her life on her terms. In a way she was a kind of a hero to him.

"Don't we need to go, Mom?"

"Yes, let me just change real quick." She jumped up from her chair.

"Is Marcos coming?" Aaron asked.

"Nope, just you and me this time," she said. "Come on! Get going!" She pushed him out of the kitchen.

Aaron hustled up to his room to change. As he walked away, Alisha started to tear. *Not my baby anymore.*

The entire flight Maria could hardly stay in her seat. The people who sat next to her hated her by the end of the flight. She must have gotten up to go to the bathroom ten times. They cut her a little slack after hearing her story about coming home to get married, and that her fiancé was affected by the recent tornado.

"We sure hope everything is alright," the older woman sitting next to her said as they got up to exit the plane.

"Yes, and again congratulations on your marriage. We wish you nothing but the best," the husband added. Maria was barely off the plane and she had to pee again.

What the heck, she said to herself, but she knew it was because she was beyond anxious.

She grabbed her backpack and ran for baggage claim; she got on the escalator to go down when she saw Aaron running up the escalator.

"Maria!"

Maria's heart dropped to her stomach. Aaron ran up to her and picked her up off the step and squeezed her tight. Then he carefully set her back down. He handed her a dozen beautiful red roses and gave her a 'you've been gone too long kiss'. Suddenly there was a whistle so loud you would have thought it was some kind of an alarm. Maria ran down the last couple of steps and into her soon-to-be mother-in-law's arms. It was a long, hard hug; Aaron stood behind watching, enjoying every second.

"Okay! That's all I needed. We can go home now," Alisha announced.

They all laughed. After they picked up Maria's bags they headed for the truck. "I hope this is the last time we have to do this!" Aaron told them. He didn't have to explain, they knew what he meant.

"Elvis!" Maria shouted out as they approached the truck. As soon as she opened the door Elvis nearly jumped into her arms.

"Elvis! Oh... poor guy, how are you feeling?" she asked him, seeing the bandages on his front legs.

Aaron decided to tell Maria about Elvis the day before: he didn't want to have her come home and get upset the first thing. "He's doing great," Alisha said.

"Yeah, he'd probably be completely healed by now if we could get him to stop trying so hard not to heal," Aaron smiled as he petted his dog. He kissed Maria then helped her into the truck. "I'm so glad you're home."

"Me, too!" she reached out with one hand and held Aaron's face. "I love you."

Alisha sat there trying not to cry. The whole way home, every minute of the two and a half-hour drive, to Aaron's total dissatisfaction, Maria and his mom talked about all the details of the wedding. Aaron tried to put the radio on once, but was quickly admonished for it. It was exciting for Alisha to get Maria up to speed and tell her about all the things that she and Patty had already done. Except for a few minor details, the wedding was set.

"Mrs. B..." Maria was starting to say before Alisha cut her off.

"Mom!" Alisha teasingly scolded her.

"Mom," Alisha repeated, looking at Maria as she started to tear. Maria didn't tear, she started to cry and leaned over to give Alisha a hug.

"Mom," Maria said with pride. They both started to cry pretty hard.

"Really?!" Aaron shouted. "You're upsetting Elvis!" he joked.

Actually Elvis looked more confused than anything. They both wiped away their tears and got right back to talking about the wedding.

The wedding was two weeks, six days and seven hours away, but no one was counting. Actually it was so bad Marcos set up a timer he rigged up in the kitchen that was actually counting down to the minute of the big event! At first everyone laughed at him, but as the time quickly ran down everyone started paying more attention to the timer. It was pretty funny around the house. A couple of times a day someone would yell out the time: "One week, three days and two hours!" Patty even made a huge calendar that was also hung in the kitchen for everyone to see and use. It had every possible detail on it; including deliveries, what needed to happen when, who was doing what, and it laid out when out-of-town guests were arriving and when they were leaving. She was proud of her work and would only allow Alisha and herself to make any changes. You'd likely lose a hand if you touched it. Aaron looked at the calendar a couple of times a day, although he did so when no one was around to see him. He was excited for the wedding, but even more so for the honeymoon as a young man should be. This would be the first time for both him and Maria to ever leave the country, and he was really looking forward to some alone time with Maria. With the exception of a few minor mishaps, things were getting done and on time thanks to Patty's calendar.

It was great for everyone to have Maria back; she brought with her a new energy to the process. Marcos and Patty ate at the house almost every night; they wanted to be around Maria... and Aaron as much as possible. Every night the main topic over dinner was the wedding, the honeymoon and coming home as a married couple. Every time it was brought up Maria would beam. It was pretty exciting for everyone, even Aaron. As things got down to the wire Marcos wouldn't even go fishing with him. Aaron's eighteenth birthday ended up being a blip on the radar. Everyone was just too busy, but they did slow down long enough to have a family barbecue and eat some cake. Aaron didn't care: he was glad to be eighteen and not make a big deal out of it. Aaron did go fishing nearly every day. Fishing was the only way he could deal with all the craziness, especially as the wedding got closer. One night at dinner, a couple of days before the wedding, out of the blue Maria asked Marcos if he would walk her down the aisle. You would have thought someone had died. The three women started to ball, Marcos resisted, but he did tear up a little.

"It would be my greatest honor," he told her.

Maria gave him a big hug. Aaron had originally thought he might ask Marcos to be his best man, but thought this was probably more appropriate. He asked his best friend Mike to be his best man, who was also honored to do so. The night before the wedding Alisha insisted that Aaron and Marcos had to sleep at Maria's house, separating the bride and groom. "It's tradition," she explained. That was good for Aaron and Marcos anyway: this way they could get Maria's house ready for the next day. Aaron said good night to Maria for the last time as a single man, then he, Marcos and Elvis left for Maria's. Aaron was surprised at how much fun he was having; he and Marcos were not the decorating type by any stretch of the imagination, but they were totally getting into it. Although, truth be told, Marcos had strict instructions from Patty on exactly what needed to be done - she even drew diagrams! It took hours, but when they were done the house looked fantastic. The master bedroom looked particularly amazing with its new furniture... And now it was full of blue and white helium balloons, hundreds of them floating randomly all over the room. They draped big thick red ribbon from the front door of the house, up the stairs, all the way to the door of the bedroom. They had candles strategically placed everywhere ready to be lit. The only thing left were the flowers which Patty was bringing in the morning.

The guys stepped back to look at their work. "Pretty good," Marcos admitted.

Aaron laughed. "I think we better keep our day jobs."

The day was finally here. Aaron actually slept well that night; Maria not so much. She was a nervous wreck. Alisha and Patty were ready for her, though. Alisha was on breakfast duty while Patty ran to get the flowers for the house and deliver them to the guys. She was impressed with their work and only made minor changes. Together they set up the flowers, then Patty took off to go pick up Maria. It was Patty's shift; she took Maria to get her nails done while Alisha received the onslaught of deliveries and directed the set-up. Then Alisha went to meet up with Patty, Maria and her girl friends who were in the wedding at Maria's favorite restaurant for lunch. Also invited along were some of the women from Maria's family who all had just gotten into town. It was loud and fun! Lots of toasts and speeches. Maria only had a few sips of champagne; just enough to make her a little dizzy and help her relax. After eating, Maria opened some of the gifts that were brought. She was surprised at the thoughtfulness and generosity of her aunt's gifts.

"You guys, thank you so much. Beautiful. I will put these to good use," she smiled.

Patty was excited to give Maria her gift. "Oh Patty... you're just the best," Maria told her.

"I know it's a little unusual, but then that's me," she laughed at herself.

"No, Patty, these are perfect, really," Maria got up and hugged her.

Giving a young woman her first pair of cowboy boots as a bridal gift was unusual, but Maria truly loved them. It was Alisha's gift that got the most reaction. She gave Maria the most beautiful, sensual, sexy nightgown any of these ladies had ever seen. When Maria first pulled it from the box she held it close to her. "It is so beautiful!" she gasped.

It was white silk with black and silver lace everywhere. Maria stood up to see how long it was - it stretched to the floor. Then she held it next to her as if to model it: that's when she and everyone else really got a look at it.

"Oh my," Maria responded.

She looked up at Alisha; Maria was turning bright red. "I thought it only appropriate that I be the one to give you your wedding night nightgown," she smiled.

Even Patty couldn't help but react. "Wow! That'll get his attention!" everyone laughed.

Maria went to Alisha to hug her. "Thank you so much... Mom." Alisha squeezed a little harder. At that point Maria was so flush she had to quickly sit down.

"Okay! Lots left to do. We need to break this thing up and get going!" Patty announced to the group as she pointed to her personal copy of the master schedule. Alisha and Maria laughed but loved it.

"Maria, you're with me, let's go!" Alisha told her.

Maria and Alisha met her bridesmaids at the beauty parlor where they were all getting their hair done. Patty had no interest in this ritual and felt she was needed more at the house for some final preparations. For Aaron, things weren't quite as emotional or as tightly scheduled, just the way he wanted it. However, there were many things that he also needed to get done. His friend Mike showed up at Maria's early to take him out for breakfast and run some errands. At the same time Marcos headed into town to make some last-minute pickups that needed to get to the house right away. He also stopped to pick up his tux. Aaron, Mike and Aaron's groomsmen had a great time at breakfast; for Aaron it was more about catching up. He had been so busy the last many months he hadn't had much time to spend with his friends; all his extra time went on working, school, and of course Maria. Thankfully they were cool about it and they are all truly excited for Aaron and Maria.

"Man! I still can't get over the fact that you're going to be married in like… six or seven hours!" Mike stated loudly. The other friends responded in kind; the ones closest to him started patting him on the back. Aaron didn't look even a little nervous, which surprised most of them.

"Dude! You're so calm!" his friend Dave said.

"Really?" Aaron asked. "Yeah, I guess I am," he told his friends, holding up his hand to show he wasn't shaking. "Can't say why really, I guess because I know this is right," he told them. A couple of them chuckled. "Sappy, right?" Aaron asked smiling.

Mike scolded the friends. "We should all be so lucky!"

"Truth is, I am a little nervous; I'm about to make the biggest change I will ever make in my life," Aaron admitted. "But I have to tell you guys, getting married compared to getting on that stage in Memphis… This is nothing," he laughed.

That started the conversation off in a whole new direction.

Aaron's responsibilities from Patty were clear; after breakfast, go get a haircut with Mike, then meet the guys at the tux shop; then they were all to meet Marcos back at Maria's house to get ready together. Simple and quick. Once they got back to the house they still had a fair amount of time before they needed to start getting ready, so one of the guys suggested some tag football.

"Great idea!" Aaron yelled out.

Between the three guys in Aaron's wedding party and three friends who 'just showed up' and Marcos they had enough guys to play a quick game. In the front of Maria's house there was just enough clear area to play: no grass, just dirt, but that was something every one of these guys was used to. Marcos and Aaron were on the same team; because it was his wedding day, Aaron got to pick the teams; he knew none of his friends would challenge Marcos; they were all scared of him. The guys were having a blast, Elvis was going nuts, trying to get involved any way he could, he was back at full strength. The game was tied at three touchdowns each. Marcos had just given the two-minute warning: they needed to be done and start getting cleaned up. Aaron, because of his speed, was playing a pass receiver. The ball was hiked to Mike, Mike tossed it to Marcos, while Aaron ran as fast as he could for the end zone; Marcos lofted the ball high in the air right into the waiting arms of Aaron. Aaron without missing a step turned to run it the rest of the way in, completely uncontested, but... he didn't see Elvis. Aaron tripped over Elvis running at full speed, launching himself forward. He put out his right hand to catch himself when he heard a loud snap! He screamed out in pain. Elvis came running up, barking and excited; the other guys were right behind.

"Holy crap! Are you okay?" Mike yelled.

"My arm!" Aaron cried out.

It must have really hurt; Aaron was rolling all over in the dirt, holding his right arm close to his chest, screaming in pain.

Marcos took over. "Grab his legs!" he commanded Mike. "Aaron, let me see... you need to let go!" he told him.

Aaron reluctantly loosened his grip. Marcos knew instantly his arm was broken, maybe in two places. Aaron's arm was definitely not going in the direction it should be. "Awe, man!" one of Aaron's friends announced as he saw the arm. "That's disgusting!" another one said. Marcos gave them all the 'step back and shut your mouth' look.

"What are we going to do?" Aaron asked, gritting his teeth.

"Here's what we are going to do," Marcos told the group. "You two guys run in the house and get my and Aaron's tuxes, then come right back here," he commanded. They quickly ran to the house. "Mike, you and the other guys shower up, get ready and go to Aaron's house to start receiving guests - don't be late!" Marcos was handling this with military precision. "And above anything else, tell no one." He looked Mike straight in the eye.

"Yes, sir!" The three of them ran for the house.

"What's your name again?" he asked the last one standing there.

"I'm Tom."

"Do you have a car here, Tom?" Marcos asked.

"Yes, sir, right over there," he pointed to an ugly old Honda Civic.

Marcos would have laughed if he weren't so pissed. "Yea, that's not going to work. Run into the house: my keys are on the kitchen counter, grab them and get my truck from around back; you and I are taking Aaron to the medical clinic."

"Yes, sir!" Tom ran as fast as he could for the house. The other two guys were already back with the tuxes.

"What else?" Dave asked.

"I need to make some sort of splint: run into the barn and see what you can find… any kind of cloth and a couple of small pieces of wood or something else that is stiff," he explained.

"No problem!" Dave took off.

"What can I do?" Chris asked, standing there holding all the clothes.

"When Tom comes around with my truck… oh there he is now," he pointed. "Put everything on the front seat of the truck and then run in the house and get as much ice as you can. Then you can help me get Aaron in the truck after I secure his arm."

"Okay."

Chris ran up to meet Tom and set the clothes on the front seat as instructed; he took off for the house to get the ice. Dave found a couple of things that could work for a splint. Marcos leaned over Aaron and looked him in the eyes. "This is going to hurt," he told him. "Bite on this." Marcos gave him a small towel, and Aaron bit down as hard as he could. Aaron screamed, but with one quick move Marcos was able to straighten out his arm. Marcos wrapped up Aaron's arm tight, with no help from Aaron who was in so much pain he was turning and kicking at even the slightest touch. The guys managed to get Aaron safely in the back seat of the truck.

"Okay. I'll drive, you sit in the back with Aaron and try to keep his arm still," he commanded Tom.

Marcos told the other guys to go home, get cleaned up, and when they got to Aaron's not to say anything to anyone. "The last thing we need is to upset the bride or the groom's mother!" he announced. Everyone agreed.

You would have thought it was the bumpiest road in all of Tennessee. Aaron was tough but this was the most pain he'd ever felt in his life. He never stopped biting down on the towel Marcos had given him, trying to cope with the pain.

"Not long now, Aaron, we're almost there," Tom said, trying to calm Aaron down. Marcos pulled up in front of the clinic and slammed the truck in park; he and Tom jumped out to help Aaron. Tom grabbed him from his left and Marcos his right. Marcos knew he couldn't lift Aaron's arm so he tried to carry him by the waist of his pants. Thankfully the clinic was not busy: there was only one older person there waiting in the front room.

As soon as the nurse at the receptionist's desk saw Aaron she came running around the counter. "What in blazes did you do?" she scoffed at Aaron. "Aren't you supposed to be getting married right about now?" Aaron didn't say anything and he didn't move. Marcos started to say something before he was interrupted. "Come on!" the woman grabbed a wheelchair; Marcos and Tom gently set Aaron in it. She opened the door to the back area and they all went in. "Straight to x-ray for you," she announced. "You two in there!" she commanded as she pointed to one of the treatment rooms. Marcos and Tom followed orders.

Even though they couldn't see Aaron they could hear him - pretty sure everyone within a mile or so could hear him. After the x-rays

Aaron was wheeled into the treatment room with the nurse and doctor in tow. Together they all picked up Aaron and lay him down on the bed. The doctor carefully lowered Aaron's right arm onto an attached tray. Aaron didn't make a sound. Marcos and Tom looked at each other, then at Aaron; he smiled at them. The nurse started laughing. "Oh he's not feeling a thing, except a little happy," she laughed.

"We had to calm him down, we would have never been able to do an x-ray," the doctor explained.

"Okay, guys, you're going to want to wait outside for this part," he told them; Tom was already halfway to the front.

It seemed like ages but it was really only about an hour or so that Marcos and Tom had to wait. Neither could sit, they paced around the front lobby or just outside the entire time. Finally the doctor and the nurse both came out with Aaron.

"Hey, guys!" Aaron called out, slurring his words a little, wearing a newly molded cast on his arm.

Marcos looked at the doctor, "What's the verdict, Doc?"

"Well, actually better than I thought it was going to be when I first saw him. Thankfully it was one break, a clean break. I was able to set it, no problem, and it doesn't look like there is any nerve damage," he explained.

"Oh thank God!" Marcos gasped. Aaron smiled.

"Can I get married now?"

"Yes you can," the nurse told him confidently as she patted him on the back.

"Listen Marcos, I know the wedding is in what... an hour or so, which is about the time the pain medicine I gave him will start to wear off. He won't be loopy anymore but he'll need these to combat the pain," he explained as he handed Marcos a small bottle of pills.

"Okay, Doc, whatever you say. But he's good to go, right?"

The doctor and the nurse both nodded, "Yes he'll be fine," the doctor assured him.

"Great," Marcos said. "Ah, one little favor before we go?" he asked sheepishly.

"Sure," the doctor responded, "What is it?"

"Do you think you guys could help me get him in his tux?"

Everyone, including Aaron, started to laugh.

THE WEDDING

Alisha, Patty and Maria were all starting to freak out. "Where the heck is Aaron?" Alisha said to Patty.

Patty threw up her arms. "You got me, I've called the house, I've asked Mike, I even called the hospital… just to be sure. I don't understand," Patty said frustrated. "You don't think he got cold feet, do you?" Patty asked Alisha, not realizing Maria just came into the room.

"Not Aaron!" Maria scolded. "No way! Something must be wrong."

"I'm sure everything is okay, Maria, they must have gotten held up and aren't able to contact us. I'm sure they'll be here soon… Right, Patty?" Alisha smirked.

"Yes… right," Patty confirmed.

"Maria, let's go for a walk and get you some air," Alisha suggested.

"That would be great."

Maria walked out of the room first, Alisha waited for her to get far enough away. "Patty, keep calling, call everyone who's not here. They are over an hour late, something must be wrong. Call the Sheriff if you have to. Find out what's going on!" she commanded.

"No problem."

Alisha hustled out of the room to catch up with Maria who was in full gown; the only thing that remained was to put on her veil. Walking was actually nice; Alisha and Maria were enjoying some time alone together what with all the craziness going on around them.

"So how do you feel?" Alisha asked Maria.

"What do you mean?"

"You know... as soon as my son finally finds his way home, you and he will be married," she smiled. Maria smiled back, she looked at Alisha; Maria looked radiant, so beautiful.

"It's as if it's a dream, but a dream that you don't want to wake up from," she tried to explain. "I feel like Aaron and I are one of those couples, you know... like you and John were. Silly, I know," she admitted.

Alisha was taking it all in: she was seeing Maria not as the young girl who lost her parents or the young lady who had to step up when her grandmother died, or even as the girlfriend of her son; but as the woman who was going to be her son's wife, his life partner... and she couldn't be happier.

"No, not silly... Not silly at all." Alisha squeezed her hand. "We should probably get back, I'm sure we have some guests getting restless," she suggested. Maria agreed. As they walked into the house, Patty was waiting for them at the door.

"Jeez! How far did you guys go? Never mind! Aaron's here, we need to get you ready!" she said as she grabbed Maria's hand.

"Aaron's here?" Alisha asked. "It's about time! Where is he?"

"He's in his room with Marcos and Mike, getting ready," Patty explained.

Alisha started to head to Aaron's room, "No time for that now," Patty reminded her. "We've got a wedding to put on," she said, all bubbly.

"Right." Alisha jumped to it. "Let's go!"

Aaron walked out the front door and around to the side of the house with Marcos and Mike, trying to avoid the large group of friends and family that were all seated and waiting out back. Aaron was doing pretty well: the light-headedness finally went away and the pain for the moment was manageable. The other two groomsmen were already there waiting with the minister who was all smiles until he saw Aaron's cast.

"Aaron! What happened to you? Are you alright?"

"Yes, sir, I'm fine. Ready to get married."

Marcos excused himself. "I've got a bride I need to collect," he smiled.

The minister and Aaron hustled down the center aisle to the front and stood under the wedding arch. Immediately people started pointing at Aaron and murmuring. The groomsmen stood on the back patio waiting for their bridesmaids so they could be escorted down the aisle. Just inside was Patty, Alisha, Maria's bridesmaids and Maria. Marcos had to pause when he first looked at Maria. "You look so beautiful," he told her. Maria smiled from behind her veil and did a slight curtsy. Marcos reached out and held both of her hands. "This is a blessed day, and you and Aaron are a blessed couple," he told her.

Patty immediately started to cry. Alisha was biting her lip trying to hold back. Maria's eyes welled up but she kept it together. "Thank you, Marcos, that means so much to me."

Patty looked at her watch. "Ah um... don't you think we should get going?" she told them.

"Yes," Maria smiled. "It's time for me to get married!" She raised her fists in the air, everyone laughed.

Patty went out the door first and cued the music. Alisha quickly followed, walking down the center aisle thanking the guests and saying hi to some of them on her way to her seat. Behind her came the three bridesmaids escorted by Aaron's groomsmen. Elvis was supposed to be the flower girl, but that didn't work out so he sat in a seat to the side so he could watch. It wasn't until Alisha sat down in her designated seat in the front row that she saw Aaron's arm. She had shock on her face; Aaron could tell she wanted to come to him so he quickly stepped over to her.

"I promise, Mom, everything is okay, I'm fine. It's a good story that I'll tell you here in a few minutes." Then Aaron kissed his mom. Alisha had no time to react, the music changed; everyone stood up and turned toward the back of the house.

Marcos and Maria slowly stepped down the four steps from the porch to the ground. Marcos was beaming; Maria was elegant and graceful. They slowly walked down the aisle to meet with Aaron. Maria never took her eyes off of Aaron the whole way. Aaron stepped forward to receive Maria from Marcos. Marcos lifted Maria's veil and gave her a kiss, then lowered the veil back down. Aaron started to shake Marcos's hand then realized he couldn't so he grabbed him and hugged him close. "Thank you... thank you for everything," he whispered in his ear. Marcos nodded and went and sat down between Patty and Alisha. Patty was a river of tears. Aaron took Maria's arm and walked the few steps to be under the arch in front of the minister.

"Please turn and face each other," the minister asked.

They reached out to hold hands: Maria gasped loudly when she saw Aaron's arm. She looked at his face; Aaron smiled. Then she turned to Alisha; Alisha could only smile. She shook her head and looked back at the minister. The ceremony was short and sweet. In a matter of minutes Aaron and Maria were husband and wife. "You may now kiss the bride," the minister boasted loudly. Aaron slowly lifted the veil: it was a powerful but respectful kiss. Now Alisha was crying her eyes out. Everyone stood as the bride and groom walked back down the aisle. Aaron was as happy as he had ever been. He was trying to take it all in, he didn't want to forget a thing. As they got to the end of the aisle, Aaron was acknowledging some of the guests on his side of the aisle when he spotted Red standing in the back.

"Red is here," he told Maria.

"Who?"

"You know... Red," he said but Maria couldn't hear him; she was already being mobbed by the many guests.

Aaron looked at Red and waved. Red pointed to a seat in the back row all the way at the end: it was Johnny. Johnny slowly stood; it was obvious he was having difficulties. Even from this distance he didn't look good. He waved and smiled. Aaron tried to indicate he'd be over in a minute as he, too, was overtaken with well-wishers.

After a little while, people started making their way to the reception area, which was feet away but it felt like you were transported to somewhere else. It was nothing short of amazing. Tables with white linen, tall vases with white flowers, chairs covered in blue sheers. From the house to poles that Marcos had set up along the back area streamed blue and white sheers that were five feet wide, almost making it feel like you were indoors. There was a bar, a stage with a band and a wood dance floor with lights and a fountain in the middle of it. Maria was... well, overwhelmed. She couldn't believe her eyes. She cried with joy. She and Aaron walked over to his mom who was pretty much not standing on the ground she was so excited.

"You like it?" she asked the newly married couple.

Maria hugged Alisha with everything she had. "It's a dream!" Maria told her.

"It's fantastic, Mom, I had no idea," Aaron told her.

"I didn't do this by myself!" she admitted just as Marcos and Patty walked up.

Patty went straight to Maria, congratulated her and gave her a hug. Marcos did the same with Aaron, then they switched. They were all excited about the work they did and the outcome.

"You guys are amazing. I never dreamed it would be this perfect," Maria told them. They all had a face of satisfaction, especially Patty.

"You guys need to tend to your guests," Alisha suggested. "The five of us will have plenty of time to catch up later."

Aaron and Maria walked toward the tables to talk to some friends when Aaron saw Red and Johnny sitting in some chairs some distance away from the activity. Aaron excused himself from Maria and walked over to them, "Hi guys."

They both stood up. Aaron was taken aback by just how bad Johnny looked. He was so pale, and he had lost so much weight his face was half of what it was when they first met. What used to be long, thick hair was now thin and stringy, hanging down over his shoulders.

"Nice suit," Aaron said to Johnny.

"Thanks, kid," Johnny laughed. Aaron was just teasing Johnny; he had on a white button-up tux-type shirt with a tall collar, a black leather jacket on over that, even though it was a warm day, and black jeans.

"Hey, Red, can you give us a minute?" Johnny asked.

"Congratulations, Aaron," he said as he walked away. Johnny and Aaron sat down.

They talked for some time, mostly Johnny. Maria kept looking over at them then decided to walk over when Aaron stood up and shook Johnny's hand with his left hand. Aaron walked back to Maria; he gave her a kiss and then said Hi to a couple of people.

"Is everything okay?" Maria asked her husband.

"Yes, everything is great. Where's Mike?"

"I'm not sure, why?"

"I need him… Oh, I see him. I'll be right back," Aaron ran off.

Maria turned back to her friends. "Already!...we only made it fifteen minutes!" she joked, and everyone laughed.

"Mike!" Aaron called out to him.

"What's up, big man?" he replied laughing while he tried to shake Aaron's hand.

"I need your help," Aaron sounded serious.

"Sure… of course. What do you need?"

Aaron pulled Mike away from anyone close by and talked directly into his ear. As he did, Mike started to smile. "You got it. Give me five minutes!" he said excitedly.

Aaron walked back over to Maria. "What's going on?" she asked.

"It's no big deal, I have a little surprise for you." Maria smiled but you could tell she was puzzled.

"My life is going to always be like this, isn't it?"

"Yes, I'm afraid so," he told her, but before Maria could say anything Mike was onstage using one of the band's microphones to get everyone's attention.

"Excuse me, everyone!" he asked loudly.

Alisha and Patty were talking at the time. "What's this?" Alisha asked her.

"I have no idea. It's not on my schedule, that's for sure."

People who were standing sat down at their tables; Alisha and Patty went over to their table and sat with Marcos.

"Thank you, everyone! Hello, my name is Mike... the best man. We have an unscheduled special treat from Aaron to his new bride," he announced.

"See! I told you it wasn't on the schedule," Patty told Marcos.

Marcos and Alisha laughed. They all watched with great anticipation. Tom came from the side of the stage carrying a chair; he placed it just in front of the stage and walked over to Maria.

"Maria, may I have the honor of escorting you?" Mike asked. Maria stood up looked at Aaron, then took Tom's arm and went and sat in the chair. "Aaron, could you come up here, please?" Mike called him to the stage. Tom brought two additional chairs and set them right at the front of the stage: one of the band members helped Tom move two microphones in front of the chairs. Aaron stood next to Mike.

"Hi, Aaron!" he smiled.

"Hi, Mike!"

Everyone laughed.

"What do you think he's up to?" Alisha asked Marcos and Patty.

Marcos smiled. "I would guess a song, right?"

Patty was too focused on the stage to respond. "Aaron has a very special song that he'd like to do for Maria..." Patty hit Marcos on the arm. "And with that, ladies and gentlemen, let me introduce you to our friend and the man of the hour, Aaron Butler!"

Everyone clapped. Alisha couldn't resist and did her whistle. "Thanks, Mom!" he joked as everyone laughed.

"Hi, everyone," he waved. "Today is the biggest day of my life and I want to thank you for sharing it with Maria and me." He looked down at Maria. "Are you okay down there?" he joked. She smiled and nodded yes. "So I planned this some time ago but then I didn't think I'd be able to do it. As you can see, my day started out pretty rough," he joked then held his right arm up slightly. Everyone laughed. "So I want to sing a song for my beautiful bride… my wife. And I've convinced a good friend of mine to help me out. Johnny, can you come up here, please?" Red held Johnny under his arm and helped him to the stage, then to take a seat. "Some of you may know Johnny as 'John from Memphis', the best Elvis impersonator I've ever seen. There is no question in my mind he made the difference in me making it to the nationals," Aaron told the group.

Johnny smiled and nodded. "Are we going to do this thing kid… or what? Not sure how much longer I'm expected to live!"

Everyone but Aaron and Maria laughed. "Right! Sorry, Johnny."

Aaron smiled at the group and then sat down; Red handed Johnny an acoustic guitar. Aaron leaned into the microphone. "Maria this is for you," he spoke softly. Maria held her hands up to her mouth and blew Aaron a kiss.

Johnny strummed the guitar, it sounded awful: Aaron looked at him with fright. Johnny started laughing, "You thought I lost it, didn't ya?!" Aaron smiled and looked relieved; everyone else laughed. Red laughed so hard he had to walk away. Johnny strummed the guitar again. "I hope you enjoy this, kiddo," Johnny said, looking right at Maria; she smiled then blew Johnny a kiss, too. Johnny put his head down, letting his hair fall to the front, then he started to play; the drummer from the band backed him up, and Aaron pulled the microphone a little closer to him. Almost everyone there knew immediately what the song was.

Aaron smiled at Maria, then he started to sing: "Wise men say… only fools rush in," Nearly every female at the wedding either started to swoon or cry. Johnny started laughing but quickly got his composure back. Aaron sang it beautifully, straight from his heart. Alisha and Patty were so gone, quietly crying into their napkins. Marcos was numb. The next chorus came up, Johnny jumped in with Aaron, and together they harmonized perfectly. Aaron had to stop smiling it was making it hard for him to sing. Johnny took the next verse; Aaron leaned back in his chair and watched in utter amazement. Wow! He thought to himself.

He may be sick but he can still bring it. Aaron jumped in at the chorus, then he took the last verse. Johnny watched. He was moved, he knew this was coming from deep inside of Aaron; you could tell Johnny was more than impressed. Johnny looked over at Red, and Red smiled. "And that's why... I... can't help falling in love with you..." Everyone jumped to their feet, clapping and yelling out, Alisha whistling.

"Your mom's good at that," Johnny said, leaning into Aaron. Red came over and retrieved the guitar from Johnny. "Aaron, help me up, would you?" Johnny asked. Aaron stood then helped Johnny get to his feet. Together they took one shallow bow.

Aaron looked at Johnny. "Thanks, man."

"You got it, kid." Red jumped up to the stage to help Johnny down; Johnny stopped him, and he reached for the microphone and held it up to his mouth... "Thank you very much," he told the group just like Elvis would always do at the end of a concert.

Red smiled and helped Johnny down. Everyone continued to clap for some time, then they all sat back down and started chattering and comparing the experience. "That was amazing!" was the comment used by most everyone. Maria, Alisha, Patty and Marcos quickly walked up to Aaron who was standing with Johnny and Red. If a person's face can really glow this was it Maria was filled with so much emotion. She grabbed Aaron's face and gave him a huge kiss.

"Now that's how that song is supposed to work!" Johnny said.

"And you, mister," Maria turned her attention to Johnny, "you were amazing, too! Thank you so much," she told him, then grabbed his face and gave him a huge kiss on his cheek.

Johnny nearly fell over; Red grabbed him. Johnny laughed, looking at Aaron. "Didn't I tell you she was a keeper?"

They all laughed.

"Johnny... that was unbelievably special. Thank you so much for doing this," Alisha spoke up.

"No problem, it was fun," he replied. Johnny put one hand behind Aaron's neck and pulled him close. "Remember what we spoke about, okay?"

"Yes, Johnny."

Johnny let him go and took Red's arm. "Got to go!" he announced and started walking away.

"Elvis has left the building!" Aaron shouted. Johnny kept walking but held his hand up high, giving Aaron a thumbs-up.

"How amazing was that?!" Aaron said excitedly to his family.

"Remarkable," his mom commented.

"Unbelievable really," Marcos added.

"I was completely blown away," Maria told everyone.

"I had no idea he was going to be here, and then he offered to help me when I told him I wanted to do that song for you. Very, very cool." Aaron was still coming down off the rush. He had all but forgotten about his arm.

"Food is being served!" someone ran up and interrupted the group.

"Thank God, I'm starving," Maria admitted.

So they all walked together to their table to sit down to eat. Seconds later the toasts started: Mike went first. His toast reflected growing up with Aaron; some of the things they did, and some of the things they didn't get caught doing. The toast was special and eloquent, funny at times. Then Mike got to a part in his toast where things became very somber, when he spoke about Aaron's dad and some of his memories.

"That was a tough time for everyone," Mike was saying. "But Aaron and his mom were unreal, and because of the love and respect they have for each other and all their friends they managed through it. Aaron, I know your dad is looking down on you, I know how proud he is of you and I know he'll always be in your and Maria's lives." Nearly everyone there was nodding their heads in agreement. Every single woman was crying; Patty was balling. Mike raised his glass (of a non-alcoholic beverage). "So here is to Aaron and Maria, two of the best people I know, two people you know in your heart are meant to be together. May your lives always have love, peace, and happiness. To Aaron and Maria!"

Everyone raised their glasses: "To Aaron and Maria!"

Aaron and Maria sat close together listening to the toasts. Some were very emotional, others funny; some were terrible. But they didn't care; they were so engrossed in each other. Marcos's toast was the hardest for Aaron. It was very powerful and unusually emotional. When he was done with his toast, Marcos came over to Aaron and Maria and hugged them both. Patty cried some more. Alisha knew she'd never make it through a speech so she already warned Aaron and Maria she was only going to say a few words.

"At almost every wedding I've ever been to, in one of the toasts someone inevitably says we aren't losing our son or daughter we are gaining a son or daughter. I don't know, I guess that's true. For me… I am not losing a son, I am gaining a daughter." She smiled at Maria. "But what I'm really getting today is reminder of how much I love my family and our friends." She started to cry. "Ahhh! I told myself I wouldn't cry," she blurted out. Everyone smiled and clapped in support. "My life could not feel more complete…" She took a long pause. "Except now I expect grand babies as soon as possible!" she said, loud enough for it to be heard in the next county. Everyone except Aaron busted up laughing. Maria gave him a little squeeze. "Don't worry, it doesn't have to be this week," she joked. Aaron smiled. The toasts were over; people were eating, dancing and enjoying the evening. Every few minutes Aaron and Maria were able to sneak in a bite of food.

"Did you see the table with all the gifts?" Maria said to Aaron when no one was around.

"Yeah I did. Crazy, huh?" he replied. "Oh. That reminds me…" He pulled a small nicely wrapped gift out of his jacket pocket.

"What's that?" Maria asked.

"Johnny gave it to me, well… us."

"Really? It looks like it might be a ring box or something? Do you know what it is?"

"No idea," he admitted.

"Well let's open it," she said excitedly.

"Johnny gave strict instructions, he said we can't open it till we get back from our honeymoon."

"What? Why's that?" she questioned.

Just then more well-wishers came up to the two of them. Aaron put the gift back in his pocket. "Time for the first dance!" the bandleader announced. "Aaron and Maria on the dance floor, please!" he instructed.

Aaron stood up and took Maria's hand. As is custom, they danced for a minute, and others slowly started to join in with the bride and groom. Or, in Patty's case, both! The evening was full of laughs, food, music and wedding traditions. Except for the constant reminder that his arm was in a cast, it was the perfect night for Aaron and Maria.

BEST KEPT SECRET

The next morning a big breakfast was planned at Alisha's house for all the family, including the out-of-town ones. In total there were twenty-five at Alisha's for a standard Butler Sunday morning breakfast, nothing short of a feast. Aaron and Maria arrived late, as expected. Most everyone was already sitting down to eat. Alisha had two spots saved at her table with Marcos and Patty. When the two of them walked in the door everyone stood up and clapped and cheered. Alisha held her chest. Aaron quickly made his way around the tables shaking hands (with his left hand) with the guys and hugging the women and children. Maria was doing the same only in the other direction. Then they finally sat down. Aaron and Maria were different; both kids gave off a sense of confidence and calm. They had a powerful aura of happiness. Each time they looked at each other they looked as if they were falling in love all over again.

"Mom, this smells so good," Aaron said loudly.

"Here you go! Get started with this," Patty told him as she handed him a platter with a mountain of pancakes on it.

"I love the Butler Sunday morning breakfast," Maria announced. "I hope we can always do this," she added, smiling at Alisha. That's all it took: first Alisha then Patty, then Maria started to cry. Aaron and Marcos sat there eating, smiling at each other.

Marcos spoke up. "So, Maria, how did the house look last night?" he inquired, trying to get them back to the table. Maria wiped the tears from her face and sat back down.

"Oh my God! The house was amazing," she said loud enough for everyone to hear. "It was like living in a fairy tale."

Everyone wanted to know what she was talking about so she explained in absolute detail what it was like for her when she and Aaron got home last night. "I took a ton of pictures so you'll be able to see it later," she explained. After everyone was stuffed most of the guys stepped outside while the food was being put away and the dishes were being done.

"Are you guys all packed up?" Marcos asked Aaron.

"Yes, sir, all set." A couple of hours later the newly married couple with Alisha, Marcos, Patty and Elvis were all on their way to the Memphis airport.

The two-week honeymoon went by fast; Maria and Aaron didn't want to go home. While at home, Alisha was counting down the minutes. She only got to talk to them once while they were gone, and even that was only for a few minutes. Alisha, Marcos and Patty waited patiently in the baggage area, all staring up at the down escalator.

"Finally!" Alisha yelled out and started running.

Marcos and Patty were right behind. Maria started to scream. Alisha was blown away to see how tanned they both were: they looked like two young Greek gods, except for Aaron's cast. It was quite a celebration when they got back to Alisha's. Marcos was manning the barbecue with Aaron standing by; Alisha, Patty and Maria were in the kitchen getting the other food together. Elvis was out chasing rabbits.

"Okay, as your mom I want to know all the details, but as your mother-in-law, I dare not ask, right?" Alisha laughed.

"Well, there's nothing keeping me from asking," Patty joked. Maria smiled and sat down at the kitchen table.

"A lady never tells," she smiled coyly. "But… I will say this… Aaron and I are meant to be together in every way," then she winked.

"Awe… that's not an answer," Patty complained. "Okay fine, your mother is here, you and I will catch up later," Patty joked.

They all had a good laugh. The late dinner was great, and it was good to be home. The evening was filled with the stories of their adventure, and Aaron got an earful from Marcos about how much he was needed. "Hey, guys, what do you say you open up some of your gifts?" Alisha suggested. "They've been sitting here for two weeks staring at me."

"Oh that'd be fun," Maria responded.

"There's a lot of gifts," Aaron said, looking at the pile in the corner of the family room. Really they were both exhausted but they were having so much fun.

"Well, you don't have to open them all," his mom suggested.

"I'll get some paper and a pen," Patty said, knowing they were going to need to record each gift. "You guys sit down on the couch, I'll bring the gifts to you," Marcos offered. "It'll be like Christmas," he added; that made Maria very happy.

Together they opened the gifts - well, Maria opened, Aaron watched, and Patty documented. They managed to get to more than they expected. Aaron was quickly getting bored: "How many toasters do they think we need?" he joked.

"Be nice," his new wife told him. Alisha got a kick out of that.

"Hey, guys, there's a gift here with no card or anything on it?" Marcos told them.

"Let me see," Maria asked for the small gift. "Oh Aaron... I think this is the gift Johnny gave you?"

"I forgot all about that," Aaron admitted. "Go ahead, open it up." Alisha, Marcos and Patty anxiously looked on.

"Johnny gave you guys a gift? That's cool," Alisha said.

As Maria carefully unwrapped the gift, Aaron explained to the others that Johnny had given him the gift in private at the wedding, with strict instructions not to open it until they were back from the honeymoon.

"Well that's just curious," Patty stated. Inside a small box sitting on top of white cotton was a silver key.

"A key?" Aaron asked.

"A key?" Alisha repeated.

"To what?" Marcos asked.

Maria picked up the key and held it up. "Looks like an ordinary house key to me."

"Can I see it?" Marcos reached out.

Maria pulled out the cotton and looked at the box again. "There's nothing else."

Marcos passed the key to Alisha. "You got me?" she said. She handed it to Aaron; he held it in the palm of his left hand looking at it.

"Maria… can we go fishing tomorrow?" he asked. Everyone looked at him strangely, including Maria, but before she answered she got a strange twinge in her mind.

"Sure… I guess so. I mean if you really want to."

"Is that okay with you guys?" Aaron asked the others. They looked at each other and had no objections. "Cool. Let's finish the rest of the gifts tomorrow. We're beyond exhausted and need to go home," Aaron announced. "Marcos, would you mind driving us to our house," he asked.

"With pleasure." Alisha smiled so hard it hurt.

Aaron and Maria didn't speak of the key again, although Maria wanted to about fifty times. Nah, he'll tell me when he's ready, she thought.

The next morning, not that early, they loaded up the truck and headed to Aaron's favorite fishing spot; it was Maria's favorite spot now, too, although not necessarily for the fishing. Elvis was quickly out of the truck and into the river.

"It feels great to be back here!" Maria exclaimed.

"Even though it's this hot?" Aaron questioned.

"We've got the river," she joked as she chased Elvis into the water.

They walked along the bank of the river to 'their' spot. Maria set up a blanket under 'their' tree while Aaron started setting up the fishing poles.

"It's so hot, we're not likely to catch many fish today," he told Maria.

"Well that's not why you brought me out here, is it?" Maria smiled.

Aaron smiled back. "So it's like that, is it, Mrs. Butler?"

"I am your wife, I'm supposed to be able to read your mind now," she laughed.

Aaron set down the gear, walked over and picked Maria up. She screamed: Elvis came running to the rescue, barking and jumping. Aaron carried his wife into the river, and even with Maria's threats, he dropped her into the water. Before Maria could pay him back Aaron jumped into the cold water after her.

"You're going to pay for that, you know that, right?" she toyed.

"I was counting on it," he laughed and then pulled her under the water.

Thankfully Maria anticipated getting wet so before they left the house she wrapped Aaron's cast in plastic. After Aaron fished for a little while with no luck at all, not even a nibble. He put down his fishing pole and went and sat down with Maria to dry off and eat.

"So, Mrs. Butler, you've been married for two weeks and three days, how does it feel to be an old married lady?" he laughed. In a flash she leaped on top of him and started tickling him where she knew it would do the most damage.

"Hey look!" Aaron yelled out.

Maria rolled off of him. "What?"

"Oh nothing..." he laughed as he quickly got up.

Maria only pretended to be mad. "What do you say we leave our stuff here and take a walk up to Johnny's?" Aaron suggested.

"Why, do you think he'll be there?" she asked already knowing the answer.

"No, I don't think so, but who knows? Let's go see anyway."

Even though it had been quite some time since Aaron had been there, from the outside the house looked like nothing had changed. Hmm, maybe he is here? Elvis ran to the door, barking and jumping up and down. Usually by the time Aaron would reach the house Johnny would already be at the door: not today. Maria and Aaron walked up the steps to the front door, and Aaron knocked. No answer. He tried again.

"Remember the first time we were here?" Maria asked. "There was no answer then either. Let's try the back," she suggested as she jumped down off the porch and started running around the side of the house.

Aaron followed closely behind. Maria knocked as hard as she could, calling out Johnny's name. "Johnny! Are you home? Maybe he's asleep."

"With all that yelling? Naw, he's not here."

Elvis already gave up and was chasing after a squirrel. Aaron tried the door, locked. Maria tried to peer into one of the back windows but all the curtains were drawn. They walked back to the front of the house and back up the front steps; Aaron tried the door: locked. "Well I guess that's it," Maria said as she started to turn away.

"Maria... hold on a second, try this," he reached out with his left hand and handed her a key.

"Really?" she smiled. She had a feeling all along but didn't want to ruin it for Aaron. "I know, but just try it."

"Okay," she put the key in the doorknob lock and turned it: click! "It worked!" she cried out.

Aaron smiled. "Try the other lock."

She put the key in the large deadbolt and turned the key: click!

"Wow!" Aaron remarked.

Maria stood there and looked at Aaron. "But why would he give us the key to his house?"

Aaron reached out to hold Maria's hand. "Let's sit down."

They moved to the chairs that were on the porch. "Remember at our wedding when I was talking with Johnny alone?"

"Yeah... sure."

He told me that night that he was dying, he thought he only had days to live, then he handed me the gift," he explained.

"Oh... that's so sad. A little weird, though. What else did he say?"

"Well, he told me we could use this house anytime we wanted, which I still don't understand. But then he told me something kinda strange..."

"Stranger than that? In what way?" Maria was feeling like this was some mystery movie they were caught up in.

"He said... Don't be mad at me," Aaron told her with a puzzled look on his face.

"What? What the heck does that mean?"

"At first I thought he was worried I'd be mad because he didn't tell me he was so sick or maybe because he never told me about where he really lived. But then he asked me to make him a promise," he further explained.

"Okay, this is getting either really creepy or exciting. I can't figure out which yet." Maria was sitting on the edge of her chair. "Well, keep going!" she demanded. "What was the promise?"

"He told me when I find out the truth not to be mad at him and to promise that under no circumstances am I to tell anyone but you."

"What...? Wow. Aaron, you know I like Johnny, but this is a little out there, don't you think?"

"I know - weird, right? I thought maybe being so sick was affecting his mind or something, but then after we did that song together I knew his mind was fine."

"Well, heck, should we go in?" she asked.

"Yes, of course... Let's go in."

Aaron slowly opened the door, yelling hello! every couple of seconds. No one responded. It was hard to see with all the curtains drawn and there was no electricity. "Let's open some blinds," Maria suggested. They opened all the ones at the front of the house as Elvis came running in.

"Wow, nothing's changed," Aaron was surprised.

"It looks like he still lives here," Maria added.

All the furniture was in place; everything looked exactly the same, except the photos that were there were gone. "Let's look around," Aaron suggested.

As they moved around the house they opened the rest of the blinds. "Whew, it's hot in here," Maria commented.

"Yeah, I'll open some windows." Aaron started going from room to room opening the windows.

"Aaron... come here!" Maria suddenly called out.

Aaron came running into the kitchen. "What's wrong?" he asked nervously.

"Look," she pointed at the kitchen table. Sitting on the table was a stack of papers and files; on the top of the stack was an envelope labeled Maria & Aaron. "Fancy handwriting," Maria noted.

They both sat down at the table. "Must be from Johnny, right?" Aaron thought out loud.

Maria picked up the envelope and handed it to Aaron. Aaron opened it and pulled out a single sheet of white paper. "It's a letter to us," he told Maria.

"Read it out loud," she said excitedly. Aaron nodded his head and started to read:

Aaron and Maria, this is Red. Because of Jonny's failing health I'm writing this letter to you as Johnny is dictating it to me.

Dear Aaron and Maria,
First of all congratulations to you both! Thank you for the honor of being a part of your special day, it was special to me as well. A day I will never forget.

"Awe..." Maria cooed.

I know this letter is going to be unusual to say the least, but you guys have become so important to me, I felt I no longer had a choice, I had to tell you the truth, I want to tell you the truth. By the time you read this you'll already know 'My time has come'.

"Oh man," Aaron yelped.

"What? What is it?" Maria asked, but Aaron didn't answer. Maria was getting frustrated. "Aaron, what is it?"

"Oh sorry. It's just funny, he used an Elvis song to describe his passing." Maria shook her head.

"Oh."

Aaron read on.

My wish is that you guys not be disappointed or upset at me after reading this letter. So here goes... I guess the first thing I need to tell you is Johnny is not my name; Johnny was a character in one of my movies, when you showed up at my door it was the only thing I could think of, sorry!

"Movies?!" Maria questioned.

"Oh you remember Johnny, like in Frankie and Johnny. I love that movie," Aaron reminded her.

"Oh yea, I remember that movie!"

Aaron continued reading.

One day quite some time ago, I just cracked. I can't really explain what was happening to me at that time but I could no longer live my life the way it was, it was killing me. Naturally fate soon took over after a few short years and I actually started getting really sick. Ultimately no matter what I did the sickness won out. Since then I've been living my life as a recluse, hiding out for so long I became paranoid of everyone. Until I met you, Aaron. You, both of you, changed me, even at this point in my life. Aaron, you inspired me in a way I can't explain, and let me tell you that's not easy. I believe you can do anything you set your mind to. My only advice to you is if you decide to choose the path of music, be yourself and trust no one. Listen, kid, should you chose this path you <u>will</u> be a star. This I can promise. You have all the right tools.

Maria hit Aaron on the back; Aaron smiled then continued reading.

But understand that if you do chose this path it will not bring you a tenth of the happiness you already have at this very moment.

"Awe," Maria sighed. Aaron smiled. He continued.

You are a special person and you will have a special life. Many great things are coming your way. If you are reading this letter that means you are in my kitchen, hopefully together with Maria.

Maria hit Aaron on the back again.

I have had so much in my life, so many blessings, but knowing you and Maria has been a highlight. I have decided that my wedding present to you two is this simple house that I love.

"Oh my God!" both Maria and Aaron yelled out.

My wish is that you enjoy it as I have and use it as often as you can with as many friends and family as you wish, especially future family.

Aaron was expecting this one and put up his hand blocking Maria from hitting him on the back again. Maria was smiling from one ear to the other. "Is this real?" she asked. Aaron read on.

Nothing in the house means anything to me, except for one thing. If you look in the front room my favorite guitar is leaning up against the fireplace. Aaron, this is my gift to you. It was a gift to me from my mother a long time ago; I want you to have it. It hasn't been played in a long time so I'm sure it will need to be tuned!

They both turned toward the front room but didn't see it.

All the papers and documents you need regarding the house are here, notarized and ready, you don't have to do anything. Please do not sell the house, use it and pass it on. Ultimately I have no say, but I think you'll know what to do.

My last request is the hardest one for me to ask. I'm asking you guys to please burn this letter after you have read it and digested its contents. I know this might be a big request (if not strange), but I trust you to do the right thing. If this letter were to get out it could have a terrible effect on many people, people who I care about. I cannot put into words how much I wish I were there with you telling you these things myself. It has been my honor to know you, I wish for you and Maria only one thing, happiness.

Sincerely your friend,
Elvis Presley
PS. Please say hi to Elvis for me, I'm going to miss him!

Aaron and Maria both sat in silence. Aaron held the letter in his left hand staring at it. Maria stared at Aaron. Finally Maria spoke up. "He doesn't mean... Elvis Presley like in THE Elvis Presley, does he?" she gasped.

"I'm not sure, but it sure sounds like it." They were both a little in shock. "Maybe?" he added as he reflected back about the time he spent with Johnny. "You know, there was always something, I mean beside the whole mystery thing, he always looked a little familiar to me. I don't know," Aaron said a little frustrated.

"Man, he could sing like Elvis," Maria reminded Aaron.

"That's for sure. Do you think any of this is possible?" he asked.

"I don't know. What year did he die... I mean the date they say Elvis died?" she asked.

"1977," Aaron responded.

"Well, let me think... that would make Elvis fifty-one. How old do you think Johnny was?"

Aaron shook his head. "I don't know, maybe about that age," he answered, trying to think. "Did he even look like Elvis to you?" he questioned.

"No, not really... but you remember at the fair, with his hair dyed black, even though his hair was really long, he looked a lot like Elvis then. And that was before I knew it was Johnny," she reminded Aaron.

Maria picked up the other papers that were on the table and started looking through them. A man's ring fell out from the middle of the stack. "What's this?" she asked as she picked it up. It was a large gold ring with a black onyx stone in the center. Engraved on the stone were the initials EAP.

"I remember that ring!" Aaron shouted. "Johnny was wearing it the first day I met him."

Aaron couldn't help himself and put the ring on.

"A little big!" Maria laughed. "Oh man!" she said, looking at the paper she had in her hand.

"What?" Aaron asked as he was admiring the ring.

"Look at this." She unfolded and handed a legal-size piece of paper to Aaron. At the top of the paper it read, 'Legal Deed of Trust'. As Aaron read on he saw that it described the house and the five hundred acres around it as the property of Gladys Enterprises.

"Five hundred acres!" Aaron yelled out.

"Oh wow!" Maria yelped.

At the bottom of the page it was signed and released to Mr. and Mrs. Aaron Butler by the corporate attorney of record.

"Holy crap!" Aaron yelled out again.

"It's true." Maria threw her hands over her mouth in disbelief.

Aaron pushed his chair away from the table. "I'm so confused," Aaron told her. "Why...."

He paused. "I need some water."

"Come on, Aaron, let's sit down in the family room and talk about this," Maria suggested as she got up from the table. Aaron walked in behind her with two glasses of water; he handed one to Maria. Maria sat on the couch. "Come, sit down," she requested, patting the couch cushion.

Aaron put his glass of water down on the hearth of the fireplace and stared at the guitar: is it possible? he asked himself.

"It's a beautiful guitar," Maria told him. "That's not the one that was here before, is it?" she asked.

"No, but you're right, it is beautiful." Aaron picked up the guitar and came over and sat next to Maria. "It looks old."

Elvis lay on the rug in front of them. Aaron strummed the guitar: one string broke the second he touched it.

"Oops."

They both laughed. The guitar was made with an elegant cherry-wood with black albacore trim; it had the letters EAP embossed on it in white mother-of-pearl near the bottom of the guitar.

"Check this out," he told Maria.

"This is crazy, right?" Maria asked but was starting to get excited that it might all be real.

Aaron turned the guitar around to look at the back. At the very bottom in small, white, painted letters was written: To my Elvis, great things come from great people; I think you are the greatest! Love Mom.

"Oh man," Aaron burst out. "Maria… I think I may have been friends with Elvis Presley," he said excitedly.

Maria laughed. "Yeah, and you want to know something crazier… You played with Elvis Presley at our wedding," Maria reminded him, hitting him on his leg as she did. "Wow." Aaron shook his head in disbelief. "I played with Elvis Presley," he looked at Maria. "I guess that was a better wedding present than I realized. What a trip!" Aaron paused. "What do we do now?"

Maria's attitude suddenly changed: she looked at Aaron with a serious face. "Why did he do this? Do we deserve all this?"

"Deserve it? No. But Johnny thought so." He thought for a minute. "Well, if Johnny was really Elvis Presley he might not have wanted anyone to know this place existed. If he had given it to anyone else or sold it, that might have been a problem… maybe."

"Yeah, maybe. But then why didn't he give it to Red?"

Aaron laughed out of frustration. "Who knows? I wouldn't mind getting a hold of him to get some answers, but I have a feeling we'll never see him again either."

"I think Johnny really wanted us to have it," Maria said in an upbeat tone. "Should we tell anyone?"

"No. I don't think we should… at least for now. We should respect his wishes, that's the least we can do. What about the letter? We should burn it like he asked, right?"

"Uh, well, we can… but why right now?" Maria questioned. "Why don't we hold onto it for a while, at least until all of this settles down, let us settle down," she laughed, "and then we can figure out our next step," she suggested. Aaron agreed that was the best idea, just in case somehow it wasn't real. "Besides, we may not be able to tell anyone right now, but if we need to we have proof that we really knew Elvis Presley... Besides, by the time we have grandchildren I'm sure Johnny won't mind if we tell a few stories," she smiled.

Aaron took a deep breath and let it out very slowly. "Wow."

For months Aaron and Maria studied every picture of Elvis they could get their hands on, but the conclusion was always the same: "Maybe." They even went back to Graceland three or four times to scour it for details. Red, they concluded, was definitely Elvis's friend, Red: that was easy to figure out. He was even in a couple of the Elvis movies they watched. There was one fact that was indisputable; the home was owned by Gladys Enterprises (Gladys was Elvis's mom's name), until it was deeded over to the Butlers, dated Friday June 16th, the day before they were married. The title was free and clear; taxes on the property were prepaid for the next twenty years.

"Amazing," Maria said while she was reading one of the documents.

Maria framed the deed and put it and the only photo they had of them with Johnny on the mantle of the massive fireplace at the house. Aaron and Maria agreed they needed to keep the promise for as long as possible, so they decided not to tell anyone about their unusual but amazing wedding present.

"Kind of puts the toasters to shame," Aaron joked.

Aaron was so excited when he found out their five hundred acres went right to the river's edge, right to his favorite fishing spot! Aaron also finally found out where the obscure road went to; it led a fair distance away from the house and the river, had a lot of curves and turns, then came to an abrupt end right up to the highway. Between the end of the road and the highway was a road barrier: Aaron decided to get out and look around: seems silly to make a road and not have it go anywhere, he thought. Aaron walked around; he even went on the other side of the barrier to see what he could see. As he was getting ready to hop back over he noticed a latch on the inside of the metal frame. Aaron smiled. He lifted the latch and pushed on the barrier, it swung wide open toward the forest. It figures, Aaron laughed to himself.

Aaron and Maria spent as much time as they could spare at the house. They still had a sizable farm to manage. Maria decided she wanted to name the house the Presley House; Aaron knew not to argue. Even though it was close to home, when they were at the Presley House they always felt like they were somewhere else. It became easy for them to understand why Johnny - or Elvis - loved it so much. Aaron and Maria knew in their heart of hearts they were friends with Elvis Presley; but because they only knew him as Johnny, plus it would eliminate any chance of a slip up, they only used the name Johnny when they spoke of him.

Every time after that summer when Aaron performed, no matter if he was 'doing Elvis' or not, he always felt like Johnny was around. Aaron never pursued music as a career but he would perform all around Tennessee just for the fun of it. Maria and Alisha never missed a performance.

It was as hard as you could imagine but Aaron and Maria managed to keep this sizable secret to themselves for a number of years. To everyone else, when Aaron and Maria went to the Presley House it was always to go fishing or to visit Johnny. At least until they reached a point that they could support the fact that they bought it.

"Why in the world would you buy this place... way out in the middle of nowhere?" Aaron's mom argued the first time she visited.

Aaron looked at his wife for help. "We thought it would be a great retreat for all of us, especially you and your grandchildren," Maria smiled.

That's all it took. Alisha became an instant fan. Marcos and Patty loved it from the first time they saw it, especially Marcos. After that, the house was used often, many summer and weekend getaways for Aaron and Maria's family and friends. And of course Aaron had to give up the location of his fishing spot. He really didn't mind: the fishing in his spot never let him down. Maria and Aaron even arranged for the kids from the shelter to come out for weekends once a month or so. It was a great experience for everyone involved, and Aaron got to teach the kids to fish, just like Marcos and his dad taught him. Marcos and Patty were married almost exactly one year after Aaron and Maria. They are perfect for each other; they continued to live on the Butler farm in their new house. They were at the Presley House nearly every Sunday. During the summers the Sunday Butler breakfast moved to the Presley House. For Maria it was a dream. The barbecues, with Marcos behind the grill, became legend. When Elvis died from old age he was buried out in the meadow to the side of the house. Two and a half years later, Alisha's dreams were fulfilled: Maria and Aaron had their first child, a boy. They named him John Presley Butler.

"It only seems right," Maria explained.

Aaron could not have agreed more.

END

ABOUT THE AUTHOR

Dutch Jones is a published author of several fiction novels, including Long Trip Home and A Day at the Beach. He has been writing forever but only recently decided to publish his work. "I write to entertain." Born in Southern California he has served in the Armed Forces, served as a police officer and been in business for himself since the age of twenty-four. "I live to write, I love to blog, I am a zealot for business. I have always been a Story Teller, Rocker & Hockey Enthusiast."